PRAISE FOR

'The delicately constructed plot keeps you guessing
until the end'
TLS

'Unputdownable'
Daily Mail

'Dazzlingly evoked'
Sunday Times

'Gripping ... powerful, evocative'
The Lady

'A gripping, bittersweet love story'
Sunday Times

'Impeccably researched and beautifully written'
Daily Mail

'Daisy Waugh delivers her engaging tale with wit
and a real lightness of touch'
Literary Review

'Written in deft, engrossing prose, this story is dizzy
with glamour and heartbreak'
Easy Living

Daisy Waugh's last two novels, *Last Dance With Valentino* and *Melting the Snow on Hester Street*, are set in early 20th Century America. She has also written a non-fiction book about the absurdities and indignities of modern motherhood, called *I Don't Know Why She Bothers (Guilt Free Motherhood For Thoroughly Modern Women)*. She lives in London.

See more at www.daisywaugh.co.uk, follow Daisy on Twitter @dldwaugh or find her on Facebook.com/daisy-waughauthor.

Also by Daisy Waugh

The New You Survival Kit
Ten Steps to Happiness
Bed of Roses
Bordeaux Housewives
The Desperate Diary of a Country Housewife
Last Dance with Valentino
Melting the Snow on Hester Street

HONEYVILLE

DAISY WAUGH

HARPER

Harper
HarperCollins*Publishers*
77–85 Fulham Palace Road,
Hammersmith, London W6 8JB

www.harpercollins.co.uk

This paperback edition 2014
1

Copyright © Daisy Waugh 2014

Daisy Waugh asserts the moral right to
be identified as the author of this work

The Nice People of Trinidad
© Max Eastman published in The Masses July 1914 reprinted
with permission of the Estate of Yvette Eastman.

A catalogue record for this book
is available from the British Library

ISBN: 978-0-00-743177-9

This novel is entirely a work of fiction.
The names, characters and incidents portrayed in it are
the work of the author's imagination. Any resemblance to
actual persons, living or dead, events or localities is
entirely coincidental.

Set in Sabon by FMG using Atomik ePublisher from Easypress

Printed and bound in Great Britain by
Clays Ltd, St Ives plc

All rights reserved. No part of this publication may be
reproduced, stored in a retrieval system, or transmitted,
in any form or by any means, electronic, mechanical,
photocopying, recording or otherwise, without the prior
permission of the publishers.

MIX
Paper from
responsible sources
FSC www.fsc.org **FSC™ C007454**

FSC is a non-profit international organisation established
to promote the responsible management of the world's forests.
Products carrying the FSC label are independently certified
to assure consumers that they come from forests that are managed
to meet the social, economic and ecological needs
of present and future generations.

Find out more about HarperCollins and the environment at
www.harpercollins.co.uk/green

Wilson, Jenny Wilson
This book is for you.

1

April 1933
Hollywood, California

I saw Max Eastman last night. He turned up at dinner very late, apologizing to us all as if the evening had been on hold for his arrival, and it occurred to me how lonesome it must be to shine the way Max does, to feel that you can never simply slide into a room and sit down. I don't think he knows any other way to behave, except as the star of the show.

He arrived with a little writer friend – one of these East Coast novelists, trying to recoup a living from the studios. I don't remember his name. There were twenty-five or so places laid at the table and I had no idea Max was joining us. Our hostess never mentioned it – I imagine because she wasn't aware of it herself, until he walked through the restaurant door. Max Eastman is quite a celebrity, after all. And we do love a celebrity in this town.

When he loped into the room last night, I'll be honest: my heart stopped. And this morning, when I opened my eyes, my face was covered with tears. I've never experienced it before – to wake, from crying. Had I been dreaming? I can't remember. But I woke with a hundred images swimming through my head. Of Trinidad, Colorado, as it was almost twenty years ago. Of Xavier, as he was then. Of myself. Of Max and Inez as they were together; and the blood drying on the old brick pavements.

I still have the letter she wrote to him, its envelope spattered in Trinidad's blood. When he loped into the room I felt many things: shock, delight, anger, affection, regret ... and an image of the damn letter came to mind, yellow with age, brown with blood, nestling at the bottom of my jewel box. I felt ashamed. I should never have read it. I should have sent it on to him twenty years ago.

There was an empty place beside me at the long restaurant table, and Max flopped himself into it with the same long-limbed, bashful elegance that was ever his.

'Is it taken?' he asked, though he'd already pulled back the chair.

'Please!' I said. 'Sit!' But I didn't look at him directly. I was embarrassed. Either he would recognize me or he wouldn't, and I wasn't prepared for either.

Max made himself comfortable. He took the napkin from his empty plate and dropped it still folded onto his lap. He reached for the wine and sloshed it into both our glasses. He had been at the theatre, he explained, having sat through what was 'possibly the lousiest play I've seen all year. And I only went out of loyalty. Which is *always* a mistake, isn't it? Now I shall have to think of something encouraging to say about the damn thing … And I'm terribly fond of the writer, so God knows, I'll have to come up with something …'

He asked if I had seen the play. I told him not, although I had heard good things spoken of it. 'Well *don't*!' he cried. 'If your life depends on it.' And he proceeded to pull the wretched thing apart.

'*Max, old chum*!' the East Coast novelist shouted at him across the table. 'Forget about the darned play, won't you? I've been telling the guys about your adventures in Marmaris. Why don't you tell them yourself?'

'Not Marmaris,' Max said, looking pained. 'I was in Büyükada.' He pronounced it *Buy-u-khad-a* with the soft notes and little hisses, like a man who knew what he was about.

He had just returned from a week in *Buy-u-khad-a*, he explained, visiting with his old friend-in-exile, Leon Trotsky.

'I'm amazed he's still alive,' the novelist said. 'It can only be a matter of time before Stalin sends his people to take a pop.' He made a limp white pistol shape of his hand.

And Max was off. It was his favourite topic: if not the domestic particulars of Trotsky's new life in Turkey (which fascinated us trivial Hollywood folk), then the failure of communism, the evil of Stalin, the tragedy of post-revolution Russia. His trip to Büyükada had obviously been a failure.

'It was quite a trek, after all. To come from Antibes, and I came with one single object in mind: to offer comfort to my old friend. Because he simply *exists* out there, you know? Plotting and brooding – *waiting*. It's rather pathetic. One ear out for the *pop*.'

'*Pop*,' the novelist said. 'Awful.'

'Last time I laid eyes on the fellow we were in Moscow!' Max continued. 'Stalin was a nobody – a booby. A nothing. It was Leon who held the future in his hands ... We believed in a new world ... We were *friends*!' Max paused. He fiddled with his napkin, furrowed his brow and I don't suppose there was a person at the table who didn't want to stretch across and smooth it for him. 'Do you know,' he said at last, 'in all the week he and I spent together in Büyükada, Leon didn't ask me a *single question* about my life.' He looked around at the table. 'Isn't that rather extraordinary?'

The conversation turned back to movies. (You can't keep the conversation from movies for long in this town.) They were discussing the special effects in *King Kong* but I couldn't contribute. After a moment or two, Max turned to me: 'I'm guessing you and I may be the only people in this town who haven't yet watched it, right?'

'I think so,' I smiled.

And then, finally, came the pause I suppose I had been waiting for. He took up his wine glass, and slurped from it in a show of nonchalance – not for me, but for everyone else. He leaned in close.

'We've met before, Dora,' he said.

'Well of course we have, Max,' I said, maybe just a half-second late. I had almost lulled myself into imagining the danger was passed. I smiled into his honest eyes, until he blinked. 'Don't tell me you have only now remembered?'

'Certainly not,' he said. 'I spotted you at once! Why do you think I made such a beeline for the seat?'

'It was the only one that was empty.'

He laughed, and shook his head. 'You know, you don't look a day older,' he said.

And I said – the difference being that, in his case, except for the grey in his hair, it was true: 'Neither do you, Max. Not a day older. You must have a portrait in an attic somewhere.'

'Ha! Yes. I think maybe we both do. Gosh – but it's *terrific* to see you, Dora. I mean … Don't you think so?' He sounded uncertain – as uncertain as I felt. 'It's too incredible! Here we are. *Still standing*. After all these years.'

'Here we are,' I repeated. 'Still standing!'

'Oh, but you *must* know I recognized you, Dora!' He sounded a little petulant. 'How could I possibly not?'

'Well, I recognised you, of course. But you've gotten so famous since. I see your photograph.' I smiled at him. 'I guess I had the advantage.'

'I would have greeted you as soon as I sat down. But then when you didn't acknowledge me ...' He looked so tactful and tortured I had to struggle not to laugh. 'I imagine that your particular situation ... I mean, you look so terribly *well*, Dora. And I didn't want to advertise the circumstances. Not that ...'

'Well, it would be nice if you didn't stand on the table and shout the absolutely exact circumstances. One has to maintain a semblance of respectability. In these autumn years. Don't you think? Even in Hollywood.'

'Ha!' he bellowed. 'We surely do! Even in Hollywood!' We laughed, and the long years since last we met seemed to fade away. 'Well, I apologize,' he said. 'Please accept my apology. I was trying to be chivalrous. In my oafish way. But I'm a fool. I see it now.'

His hand was on the table top between us, long fingers busy rolling small crumbs of bread. So much anxious energy still! I felt a rush of affection for him. 'Dear Max,' I said. 'Ever chivalrous.' He grimaced, as well he might. But I had meant it. At least, I had meant it up to a point.

The novelist was yelling at him again – something emphatic about Charlie Chaplin. This time Max ignored him. He said: 'You remember that crazy evening, Dora? The first night. It was anarchy – the striking miners had taken over the streets, and she was just buzzing with it all. I never saw a woman quite so *alive*. I remember looking at her that night – in the Toltec saloon – with the guns rattling out there on Main Street. She was beautiful. God. The woman of my dreams. I think I fell in love, right there and then.' He laughed, shaking his head. 'Don't you remember? It was so damn exciting.'

Of course I remembered.

'We truly believed the world was going to change. Or maybe not *you*, Dora. You'd seen too much of the world already. But during the siege – those ten crazy days – the rest of us: John Reed, God rest his soul, and me and Upton, and Inez of course – and all the reporters who piled in. We *believed* it! The world was actually going to change. Not just in Colorado ...'

'Ten Days That Shook the World.'

'Ha! That's right. Only imagine. John might have written it about our own, home-grown revolution.'

'And thank God he didn't,' I said.

Max nodded energetically. In the intervening years, since returning from Russia, he had undergone a political *volte-face* that (according to the newspaper articles I read) had made him enemies on both sides. 'It seemed possible, though, didn't it? Colorado might have been just the beginning. It was ...' he paused, seeming to lose himself in thought. 'You remember that Union chap, used to hang around Inez? Handsome as hell – I was rather jealous of him.'

'Lawrence O'Neill.' I laughed. 'You didn't need to be jealous of him, Max. Inez adored you. But yes, I remember him.'

'Well he was another, turned up in Moscow later. Or, not in Moscow, actually. Dear God.' He sighed. 'That is ... Last I heard, he was on his way to Solovki. Poor bastard.'

Solovki Labour Camp. Poor bastard, indeed. Even here in sunny California, the name Solovki resonates with everything that is cruel and broken in the New Russia. Lawrence O'Neill hadn't crossed my mind in many years, but I was shocked – of course I was. Shocked and very sorry. I had been fond of him. 'But didn't he fight on the side of the revolution, just like the rest of you? What did he do so terribly wrong?'

Max looked at me, pityingly. He sighed with enormous weariness, appeared to hesitate, and then to think better of answering: 'Oh God, but Dora,' he said instead, brightening in a breath, 'don't you remember darling Inez – and her terrible, dreadful, awful, *appalling* poem?' Grinning, he pulled back his shoulders, threw back his head: '*For the strikers shall fight and they shall fall ...*'

'*Fight Freedom!*' I cried. The words came to me as if I'd heard them yesterday. Max and I both remembered the poem perfectly and we finished it together with our fists aloft:

And they will rise
And they will call –
Fight Freedom!
'Til all
In America is fair
And the wind in the trees blows freedom to our
streets and all
Good-Americans-take-care-and-pledge-forever-
themselves-to-share ...

She had gone out that morning with Max and a whole bunch of other reporters, to see the carnage for herself. The guards hadn't allowed her into the camp, of course. But she had smelled it, seen it, felt it, and she was wild with righteousness, buzzing with the horror – crazier than I had ever seen her. We were in the Toltec saloon, a great gang of us, and from the hidden pocket of that pantaloon skirt she was so proud of (it celebrated her status as a 'modern woman'), in front of all the cleverest in America (or so it seemed to us then: really it was a motley crew of poets and writers, intellectuals and newspaper columnists who had descended on Trinidad that week), Inez pulled out a sheet of paper. She announced that she had *written a poem.*

I tried to stop her. Max, with all his wit and chivalry, had tried to stop her, too. But Inez had *written the damn thing.* She would not be silenced.

Upton and the others had leapt on the opportunity to mock her, as Max had known they would. And as the evening progressed and more liquor was consumed, they began to chant poor Inez's ridiculous poem aloud – and fall off their chairs with laughter – only to climb back onto them and begin chanting the wretched thing again. Inez took it on the chin. Bless her, I don't think she cared a bit. She simply laughed and chanted along with them. 'Y'all wait and *see*,' she said. 'It'll catch on!' … The smell of young, burning flesh still lingered on the prairie that night, and we knew it. But it was a wild night. I do believe we were never happier.

'Fight Freedom!' muttered Max, lost in his memories. He pushed his plate away and hunched over his long legs, deep in thought. 'The last time I saw her, we had a most idiotic squabble,' he said at last. 'Like a couple of spoiled kids.'

I knew it already, from the letter. But I could hardly admit to that. 'I'm not surprised,' I said.

'Hm?'

'Well. I read the article you wrote.'

He hesitated. 'You mean – the tea party piece?'

'The one she helped you with.'

'Oh. Gosh, no.' Max laughed. 'That wasn't what we fought about.'

'Oh, I think it was! She was mortified.'

'Nonsense!' He laughed again. 'I was reporting a story, Dora! It was why I ever came to Trinidad in the first place. She understood that perfectly. Besides ...' He stopped, seemed once again to think better of whatever he was about to say. 'I'd offered her a job on the magazine! She'd already sent on half her luggage!'

'I know. I helped her to pack it. She was so excited.'

'So don't tell me,' he laughed, 'don't tell me that kid didn't know what she was about.'

'I don't think she had the faintest idea. I don't think there was ever a "kid" more out of her depth.'

But he didn't seem to hear. 'We used it as a perching-place in our editorial meetings for years, you know. "Inez's Packing Case". We used to read submissions aloud and if something was truly, spectacularly bad, one of us would sort of launch something at the packing case, and shout out—'

'Fight Freedom?'

'Fight Freedom.' He sighed again. 'Well. It was funny back then, I guess. I still have that case somewhere. That's right. The darned *packing case* arrived OK. But Inez? Never turned up. I wrote her. A bunch of letters.'

'You wrote to her?'

'After we printed the tea party piece.' He had the grace, at last, to look at least a little shamefaced. 'When she didn't materialize in New York.'

'Where did you send the letters?'

He shrugged. 'I don't remember. A post-office box? It's been a long time, Dora.'

'I never saw any letters. I wonder what became of them?'

'Well – but never mind the *letters*, Dora.' He leaned towards me. 'For God's sakes, never mind the *letters*. What became of *her*? That's what I've been trying to ask you. *What became of Inez?* She simply disappeared.'

Max told me last night that he was here in Hollywood on one of his famous speaking tours. It's why he has come to California. He is on an anti-communist speaking tour. I think. Or maybe an in-favour-of-poetry tour. He is still a poet, after all. Last I heard him speak, twenty years ago, he was stirring up revolution in the bloody coalfields outside Trinidad, Colorado. He was a fine speaker, too. Passionate. Persuasive.

In any case, they must be paying him well. They have put him up at the Ambassador for the entire week. And I am invited to lunch with him again on Friday, which is just five days away. I have told him about her letter. I have told him I will deliver it to him at last.

We have plenty to catch up on, I think.

2

Inez and I were in the drugstore on North Commercial the first time we met. Under normal circumstances, Trinidad being Trinidad and we ladies both knowing our place, we would never have exchanged a word. I would have gazed at her from beneath the rim of my extravagant hat and wondered how she could put up with the limits of her respectable life: and she would have looked at me, from beneath the rim of her more restrained affair and felt – what?

Pity, probably.

And irritation about the hat. I dressed flamboyantly, in silks and lace and satin. It's what made me all but invisible to the good ladies on Main Street, and in the drugstore on North Commercial.

13

There were no other customers in the store that day. It was just the two of us. Behind the counter, Mr Carravalho was coaxing Inez into parting with a few extra dollars for a skin-freshening potion which, had I been inclined, I might have told her didn't work, since I had already tried it myself. I might have told her that she didn't need any such potion in any case. Her skin was quite fresh enough. Everything about her seemed, in my weary state, to sing with a freshness and vim long since lost to me.

I knew who she was. Inez Dubois cut quite a dashing figure in our small town. She worked at the library, though it was generally believed that she had money of her own, and no need to work. She was unmarried, so far as I knew, about 26 or 27 years old. She lived with her aunt and uncle, Mr and Mrs McCulloch, who owned one of the finest houses in Trinidad, and she ran around town in her own little Ford Model T motorcar.

She looked, I used to think, rather like a beautiful doll: with small, pointed nose, and thick golden hair and round grey eyes, and a tiny, slim body that seemed to fizz with energy and life. I had seen her driving up Main Street towards the public library, her scarf flowing behind her, just like Isadora Duncan. And I had seen her at the issue desk in the library. In fact, on several occasions, being an enthusiastic reader, I had presented her with novels to stamp (respectable novels, I should add, nothing like the filthy French novels dear old William used to send me. They didn't stock those at the Carnegie Library of Trinidad). There were occasions when I sensed she might have liked to talk, if only to share her literary opinions of the novels I was borrowing. But she always stamped and returned them without quite looking my way.

So there we were in Carravalho's Drugstore. I was waiting in line to stock up on the usual medications, essential for my trade. Mr Carravalho knew me well and would have a package already prepared for me, and I was in no hurry. Which was fortunate, since Inez Dubois was taking her time. She was fussing and flirting with Mr Carravalho, informing him of her dire need to buy '*something*' to refresh her look, what with the heat of this long summer.

It was a warm August evening – a beautiful evening, after a burning hot day, and it being a Friday, there was much noise and festivity on the street. Beneath the rattle of the tram and the Salvation Army choir, singing its lungs out on the corner of Elm Street, there came laughter and chatter in a score of different languages. It was the busy, noisy, carefree sound you only heard in Trinidad when the hot, dust-filled prairie wind had eased at last, and the sun had cooled, and the long working week was almost over. Miners from the neighbouring camps were piling in off the trolley cars, the brick-factory workers were making their way from the north end of town, and the distillery workers too, and the shop clerks, the farm hands and the cattlemen, the hustlers, the rangers: they were all on the streets that evening. Trinidad was wearing its glad rags. I remember reflecting that it would likely be a busy night at Plum Street.

The door to Mr Carravalho's shop stood open as I waited, and I was content to linger there, catching the evening breeze, listening in on the chatter. But my tranquillity was interrupted suddenly by angry shouts from the street. There, framed by the store's door and only a few yards from where I stood, three men had appeared as if from nowhere and, in the space of a second – the second it took for me to locate them – a violent fight had broken out between them.

I recognized all three men. Two were private detectives, from the notorious Baldwin-Felts detective agency, hired by the coal company to report on revolutionary activity among the workers. They and their like had been throwing their weight around Trinidad these past few months. They roamed the streets with handguns tucked under their shirts, picking fights when and wherever the fancy took them. Nobody seemed to stop them – except Phoebe, my boss and the proprietress of Plum Street. Phoebe didn't ban many men from our parlour house, so long as they could stand the bill. So it was a measure of how brutish they were that she had banned entrance to all the Baldwin-Felts men. They had a reputation for violence, here and across Colorado – all over America in fact. Wherever employers hired them to harass and intimidate their workers.

The third man wasn't much better. Another out-of-towner, come to Trinidad to make mischief. It was Captain Lippiatt, employed by the other side. He was a Union man. And I knew him, because he had visited us at the parlour house.

The three men stood chest to chest, eyeball to eyeball, in the middle of North Commercial, the spit flying in each other's faces: three great bulls of male-hood, of pure and dangerous absurdity, it seemed to me. I had no wish to be anywhere near them. I slipped deeper into the store.

Inez, on the other hand, seemed unaware of the danger. She looked up from her skin-freshening packaging, and exclaimed, 'Oh my!' at such a volume that one of the spitting men – it was Lippiatt – paused momentarily to glance in.

'Mr Carravalho, what are they doing?' she asked, 'What on earth do you suppose they're arguing about?'

'Union men,' he muttered, shrinking a little behind his high wooden counter. 'Hush up now, Miss Dubois. We don't want them coming in here.'

'All *three* are Union men?' she asked, staring brazenly and without dropping her voice. 'Then why are they fighting? You might have thought, after all the trouble they cause, they would at least have the decency to agree with one another.'

17

'There's a bunch of them in town this week,' he replied. 'Causing trouble. Some kind of delegation at the theatre. Talking about a strike—'

'But they're not *all* Union men,' I interrupted. I wasn't supposed to speak to the likes of Miss Inez Dubois. And nor she to the likes of me, except in a soul-saving, charitable capacity. Mr Carravalho looked shocked and embarrassed. They both did. But I persevered. It wasn't that I had any special loyalty to the Union men (far from it), but it struck me as just plain ignorant to pretend that the battle on our streets was being fought by only one army. 'One of them is, but the other two on the right are Baldwin-Felts men. You know that, Mr Carravalho. They're coal company heavies. And it's no good taking sides. Those men are as bad as each other.'

The fight, meanwhile, seemed to have disbanded. Lippiatt was gone. Even so, the two Baldwin-Felts detectives lingered. They crossed over to the far side of the street, looking cautiously about them, dust whipping round their boots. The Friday night crowd gave them plenty of space.

'What are they doing?' Inez asked.

It was hard to tell. They were leaning side by side of each other against a power post directly opposite us, hands resting on guns that poked ostentatiously from under their shirts. They gazed up the street towards the Union offices a few doors down, but nothing happened.

'*Well!*' Inez sighed. 'Thank goodness for that! Is it over? I should be heading back.'

'I'm sure you're right, Miss Dubois,' Mr Carravalho said. 'It's rather late for a lady to be trekking the streets. And on an evening like this. With the Union coming into town.' He shot me a glance. 'You hurry on home. Will you be taking that?' he indicated the package still in her hand.

She looked down, remembering it. 'Why yes!' she cried, as if it was quite the boldest and happiest decision she had ever settled upon. 'Sure, I'll take it! Why not?' And while Mr Carravalho wrapped it, she looked again, past me – through me, I suppose – to the street outside, where the two detectives had still not moved on.

'They really ought to get going,' she muttered, sounding nervous at last. She squinted a little closer, noticed the hands and guns. 'Aunt Philippa says they are quite trigger-happy, these Union men. Do you think it's safe to walk home?'

'Pardon me,' I said again, 'but those aren't Union men.'

She wasn't listening. 'It's getting so rowdy, our little town,' she muttered; I'm not certain which of us she was addressing. 'I really don't know *why* we have to put up with it. I begin to think – *Oh!* Oh Mr Carravalho! *Oh my gosh—*'

Captain Lippiatt had returned. He must have dashed directly into the Union office, snatched up the gun and turned straight back again. It explained, perhaps, why the Baldwin-Felts brutes had lingered. Perhaps they had known he was coming back.

Lippiatt charged towards them through the scattering crowd. 'See *now*,' he shouted, 'see now, cock chafers, see if you'll repeat what you just said to me!' He shook his gun at them. 'Do you dare say it now, sons of bitches?'

In an instant the street emptied. On the corner of Elm Street, the choir stopped its singing and melted into the retreating crowd. But we were trapped. Directly before us, the detectives snatched up their own guns. Lippiatt was already beside them, his handgun poking at them. There was a confusing scramble of limbs, and more cursing, and then a shot. One of the detectives had been hit in the thigh.

Inez screamed. I put a hand on her shoulder to quiet her and she buckled beneath my touch. I let her fall.

This was not the first shooting I'd seen on the streets of Trinidad, nor would it be the last. But it was the closest I had ever been: so close I could swear I heard the soft thump of bullet as it hit his flesh. Afterwards some of the blood got onto my silk shoes, and no matter how well I scrubbed them, it would never shift.

There came another shot, this one from the handgun of the other detective. Lippiatt staggered back. Another shot, and he fell to the ground. And this I can never forget – the first detective stumbled forward and aimed his gun at Lippiatt as he lay helpless at his feet, and he shot him through the neck. Tore a hole through Lippiatt's neck with the bullet. And then he shot him again, through the chest. That's when the blood began to flow.

A couple of Union men appeared within moments, while we stood still, looking on, frozen with fear. They carried his body back into their Union lair, a thick trail of blood following them along the way. Lippiatt was dead. And I knew his name because last time he'd been in town, he paid me a visit at the Plum Street Parlour House. He was an Englishman. Or he had been English, once. Just as I had. It was the only reason I recalled him at all. Perhaps the only reason he chose me before the other girls. We didn't talk about our Englishness in any case. Nor about anything else, come to that. Very taciturn, he was. Unsmiling. Smelled of the tanner – and my disinfectant soap. But they all smell of that. And he left without saying thank you. I can't say I was sorry he was dead. But even so, it was a shock, to have been standing right there and seen it happen ... and to remember (dimly) the feel of the man between my legs. And then there was Inez, collapsed on the floor at my feet. Poor darling.

I was shaken up. We all were. But Inez seemed to take the drama personally, as if it was her own mother who'd been slain before her eyes. She sat on the floor, her long blue skirt in a sober pool around her, and her

21

little hat lopsided. She wouldn't stand, no matter how Mr Carravalho and I, and finally Mrs Carravalho, tried to coax her. She simply sat and swayed, face as white as a ghost.

'That poor man,' she kept saying, with the tears rolling down her cheeks. 'That poor, poor gentleman! One minute he was alive, right there beside me – he looked at me! Didn't you see? Only a second before *he looked at me* … And now he is absolutely dead!'

3

Perhaps, while Inez is down there on the drugstore tiles, grieving the death of my old client, I should pause to explain something about our small town of Trinidad.

Forty years earlier it had been nothing: just a couple of shacks on the open prairie; a pit stop for settlers on the Santa Fe trail. Then came the ranchers and the cowboys, and then the prospectors. Elsewhere, they found iron and oil, silver and gold. Here, in Southern Colorado, buried deep in the rocks under that endless prairie, they found coal. It was the ranchers who settled in Trinidad. It was the coal men who made it rich. And in August 1913, our little town stood proud, a great, bustling place in the vast, flat, open prairie land. Trinidad boasted a beautiful new theatre, seating several thousand; an opera house as grand as its name suggests, a score of different churches and a splendid synagogue; there were numerous schools, two impressive department stores, a large stone library, and a tram that ran to the city from the company-owned mining settlements, or 'company towns' in the hills. There were hotels and saloons and dancing halls, and pawn shops and drugstores and stores selling knick-knacks of every kind, and a large brick factory, and a brewing factory and – because of all that – but mostly because of the coal, there were people in Trinidad from just about every country in the world.

In 1913, Trinidad was the only town in Colorado that tolerated my trade. Consequently, there existed on the west side of Trinidad – from that handsome new theatre, and on and out – a district a quarter the size of the entire town which was dedicated to gentlemen's pleasure: saloons (uncountable) and – according to the city censor – at least fifteen established brothels. Which number, by the way, was the tip of the iceberg. It didn't take into account the vast quantity of independent girls – the 'crib' girls, who operated from small single rooms, and who worked and lived together in shifts; nor the dance-hall girls, nor the pathetic 'sign-posters', who worked not in rooms but wherever they could: in dark corners, shoved up against walls behind the saloons.

For most of us (not perhaps the sign-posters) Trinidad was a good place to be a whore, and a good place to find one. Snatchville, they used to call it. Ha. And the punters came from far and wide. Prostitution wasn't simply legal in ol' Snatchville, it was an integral part of the city. There was a Madams' Association – a hookers' mutual society, if you like – so rich and influential it funded an extension of the trolley line into our red-light district, and the building of a trolley bridge. 'The Madams' Bridge', folk called it: built by the whores, for the whores, although really the whole town benefited. It meant the men travelling down from the camps could be transported directly into our district, without getting lost along the way, or disturbing the peace of the better neighbourhoods. The Madams' Association provided medical care and protection to the girls, too, so long as they were attached to a brothel. And a recuperation house, not a mile out of the city, where we could retire for a week or so, if we needed a break.

Trinidad was wealthy: cosmopolitan in its own provincial fashion, conservative and yet radical. It was new, and crazy, and busting with life. But for all that, it was only a small town.

From its centre, where North Commercial crossed Main (only a few yards from where Lippiatt was shot), the entire city was never more than a ten-minute walk away: the library, where Inez worked, the jail, the city newspaper, the City Hall. Everything was clustered around the same twenty or so blocks. From the red-light district in the west, with its saloons and dancehalls, to the ladies' luncheon clubs, church halls, and elegant tearooms in the east, the distance was hardly more than a few miles.

The ladies of Trinidad spent their dollars in the same stores. We attended the same movie theatres. We washed the same prairie dust from our hands and clothes. And yet, it was as if we lived in quite separate realities; as if we couldn't see one another. Only the men travelled freely between our two worlds.

Inez and I, living side by side in a small, dusty town in the middle of the Colorado prairie might, our entire lives, have brushed past one another on the sidewalk, at the grocery store, the drugstore, the library, the doctor's waiting room, at our famous department store – and never once exchanged a glance or a word. Inez and I were as shocked as each other by the evening that followed Lippiatt's death.

... I suppose, at this point I should also explain something about myself, too? I don't much want to, and that's the truth. But how in the world (the question begs) did an educated English woman, thirty-seven years old and the daughter of two Christian missionaries, find herself divorced, childless and working in an upmarket Colorado brothel? How indeed.

Well, because we all find ourselves somewhere, I guess.

It's all anyone needs to know. There, but for the grace of God ... This isn't a story about me, in any case. It's a story about Inez and Trinidad, and the war that came to Snatchville and tore us all apart.

So there Inez sat, or slumped, on the drugstore tiles. And there were Mr and Mrs Carravalho hovering around her, polite but, I sensed, with a hint of impatience. Outside, there was panic in the voices now, and anger too. The Carravalhos wanted to close up and get home as quickly as possible. But Inez, wrapped in her own horror, was oblivious to their concerns. I might have gone on my way, come back to the shop another day. I had plenty else to do, and I was meant to be working that evening. But Lippiatt's blood was still slick on the street outside, and I didn't much relish the idea of venturing into the angry crowd myself. Not yet.

Mrs Carravalho disappeared into the back of the shop and returned with brandy. A single serving, for Inez – until her husband sent her back for the bottle and three more glasses. I took mine, swallowed it down and felt better at once. Inez took only the daintiest of sips, and continued to whimper.

I told her she'd feel stronger if she drank the thing down in one. She looked at me directly, I think for the first time, and immediately did as I suggested. The alcohol hit the back of her throat and she shuddered. The three of us looked on, intrigued, as the brandy continued its internal journey, until at length she looked up at the three of us, considered us one by one, and grinned.

27

'Thank you all so much. I think, perhaps ...' She belched, and I laughed. Couldn't help it. She glanced at me again, uncertain whether she dared to laugh too, and decided against it. 'I think I should probably head home.'

'Excellent idea,' Mr Carravalho said.

His wife looked at her doubtfully. 'It's set to turn pretty mean out there. You want my husband to escort you?'

'*No, no!*' Inez said, though she plainly did.

'Well if you are certain,' he answered quickly.

I took her empty brandy glass and placed it with my own on the counter. I said, 'We can leave together if you like. Just until we're through the craziness. It'll be much quieter on the other side of Main Street.'

There was an embarrassed pause.

'Well I'm sure I don't think ... Honey?' muttered the wife, looking at me suspiciously. But Mr Carravalho was apparently too busy to notice. 'I really don't think,' she muttered again.

'What's that dear?' He was locking up, counting notes. Protecting the business.

Inez ignored them and turned to me. 'Which way are you headed?' she asked boldly, and immediately blushed. 'That is to say, I am headed east. Perhaps. I mean, for certain, I am heading east. And I don't know – if maybe we are headed in different directions?'

28

'I dare say we are,' I said. 'But we can walk on up to Second or Third Street together. It's sure to be quieter up there.'

Inez glanced through the window. The sheriff had arrived and an angry gaggle had mustered round his motor, making it impossible for him to get out. It looked menacing.

'Well,' she said at last, 'if it's all the same to you, I think that would be just daisy. Thank you.' As she stood up, she seemed to totter a little. Carefully, eyes closed in concentration, she straightened herself. 'Shall we get going?'

'You know I *really don't think* ...' Mrs Carravalho murmured yet again, sending baleful looks at her husband.

'Well, unless you want me to leave you here alone,' her husband snapped at last, 'with all the trouble brewing and the store unguarded, and the week's takings still in the register, and you, no use with a handgun ...'

'Well but even so,' she was saying.

We left them squabbling and stepped out into the teeming street, Lippiatt's blood still damp between the bricks at our feet.

We had hardly walked a half-block before she stopped, grasped hold of my shoulder.

'Hey, what do you say we sit down?' she said. Her face was whiter than ever.

'You want something more to drink?' Truth be told, I didn't feel so hot myself.

She nodded.

We might have stopped at the Columbia Hotel, just across the street. Or at the Horseshoe Club, ten doors down. Or at the Star Saloon at the corner. There was no shortage of choice. But we stopped at the Toltec. At the moment she grasped hold of me, and I was convinced she might faint right away, it happened we were right bang beside its entrance. So we turned in, and plumped ourselves at a table at the end of the room, as far from the hubbub as possible.

The Toltec was plush and newly opened then; a saloon attached to a swanky hotel, both of which, I knew, were popular with visiting Union men. It was a saloon much like any other, maybe a little more comfortable. There was a high mahogany bar running the length of the room, an ornate, pressed-tin roof, still shiny with newness, and a lot of standing room. We sat beneath that shiny ceiling and ordered whiskey. A bottle of it. And for a while the bar was quiet.

'Everyone's out on the streets,' the barman told us as we settled ourselves at the table.

'Making trouble,' Inez said.

'Depends on your way of looking at things,' muttered the barman.

We filled our glasses and turned away from him. 'But you know *everyone* I know agrees,' she told me, sucking back on her whiskey. (She may not have been accustomed to liquor, but I noticed she had taken a liking to it fast enough.) 'These anarchists come into town with their crazy ideas, and then they infiltrate the camps and stir up the miners. The men were perfectly happy before the Unions came in. And now look where we are! Death on every doorstep! Murder at the drugstore!'

'To Captain Lippiatt,' I said, to shut her up. I didn't want to talk politics – not with anyone, and least of all with her. 'May he rest in peace.'

She stared at me, whiskey glass halted. 'Captain Who?' and then, 'You know his name? You mean to say you *knew* him?'

'Hardly very well. But yes, I guess knew him.'

'*How?*' And then, in a rush of embarrassment, and without giving me a chance to answer: 'Oh gosh but never mind *that*! Did I tell you already – I work at the library. Do you ever go in there? You should. I'll bet there are plenty books I could show you that you might enjoy.'

'I love to read,' I told her. 'And I am often in the library. I've seen you in there before.'

'It's quite a thrill you know,' she skipped on (I imagine the library was the very last thing she wanted to talk about). 'I mean, once you get over the shock of it, and all. It's quite a thrill to be here in this saloon. I've been walking past saloons all my life, never even daring to peep in. And now here I am,' she beamed at me, 'in a saloon! With you! It feels like the greatest adventure.'

31

'I suppose it is,' I said. 'For you and me both.'

'Do you suppose your friend Mr Lippiatt—'

'Oh, I wouldn't say he was a friend.'

'No. But do you suppose he had a wife? Or children? Or anything like that? Maybe a mama. I think I should go visit them. Don't you think I should?'

I laughed. 'Whatever for?'

'Whatever for? He and I, we looked at *each other*. Don't you see the significance?'

'Not really.'

'Well, mine was probably the last human face, the last *decent* human face, not in the process of *slaughtering* him, which that poor gentleman ever laid eyes on. And then – *Pop!* He was dead.' She sniffed. Picked up her glass. Glanced at me. 'Y'know this is silly. Here we are, you and me, drinking in a *saloooon* together.' She rolled the word joyfully around her mouth. 'And I don't even know your name. I am Inez Dubois, by the way.'

'How do you do.'

'I live with my aunt and uncle. Mr McCulloch. You've probably heard of him? Have you?'

'No,' I said automatically. Whether I had heard of him or not.

'Mr McCulloch is my uncle.'

'So you said.'

'Well, he's one of the old families. Ranching. Cattle. That's where his money comes from. So he's got no

32

business with the coalmines, *thank blame for that ...*'
She glanced at me. Already, her eyes were growing fuzzy
with liquor. 'Don't you think so?'

'It's all the same to me.'

'Even if the miners *do* get a fair wage. And nice homes
and little yards and free schools and everything they could
possibly ask for. Well, it's all stirred up by the Unions now,
isn't it? And I would hate that. Just wouldn't feel right,
you know? To live off other people's discontent. Whereas
the ranchers aren't like that. They're altogether ...' She
frowned. 'Well, anyway, they're not the same.'

Inez Dubois looked and behaved much younger than
her age. She was twenty-nine years old, she told me that
night (making her eight years my junior), the orphaned
child of Mrs McCulloch's sister, who died alongside
Inez's father in what Inez described as, 'one of these
train-track accidents'. She didn't go into details, and I
didn't ask for them. Her parents died back in 1893, in
Austin, Texas, and after the funeral Inez and her older
brother Xavier were sent to Trinidad to live with their
only living relation. The McCullochs had no children,
and though Richard McCulloch was aloof and unin-
terested, his wife treated her nephew and niece as her
own. Inez never moved out. Her brother Xavier, on
the other hand, had left town some ten years previous,
at the age of twenty-five, and though he wrote to Inez
once a week, often enclosing a variety of books and

magazines he believed might educate or amuse her, he'd not returned to Colorado since.

'He's in Hollywood now. Silly boy,' Inez said, though by my calculation, he was a good six years her senior. 'He's making *movies*,' she said. 'Though I've never actually seen any, so I don't suppose he really is. He says I would love it in Hollywood. It's summertime – only cooler – a cooler summer, all year long. Sounds heavenly doesn't it? Shall we go there together?' She giggled. 'After what happened today, I tell you I'm just about ready to leave this place. I wasn't far off ready before. And now … Truthfully. I'm sick to death of it. Are you?'

'Kind of …' I laughed. It must have sounded more mournful than I intended.

She looked at me with her big, earnest eyes. She said, 'You do realize, don't you, that there are about a million questions I want to ask you. About *everything*. Only I guess I have a pretty good idea what it is you *do*.' She looked so uncomfortable I thought she might burst into tears again. I had to bite my lip not to smile. 'And I don't mean to *pry*. It's probably why I'm yakking on like this. It just makes me nervous, that's all. Because here we are, sitting here, and we've been through this terrible, awful thing together, when normally we wouldn't even *speak*. And I was impolite to you in the drugstore, but you know I didn't mean to be. I guess I just didn't know any better. Because we can't live more than a handful of miles apart and yet ...' She took a breath. 'I don't quite even know where to begin.'

'Well you could begin,' I said, 'by asking my name.'

She opened her mouth—

'And maybe even hushing up long enough to find out the answer.'

4

She discovered my name eventually. Though I'm not convinced she really registered it until some time later. I told her a little about myself – as little as I could – and watched her wide eyes watering, torn between outrage and pity.

'You don't need to feel sorry for me,' I said, when her pitying expression was too much.

'Oh but I don't,' she cried quickly, eyes sliding away.

'After all, I am freer than most women and freer than any wife. I have money of my own. A wife doesn't.'

'Yes of course!'

'A husband can beat and rape his wife and there is nothing she can do to prevent it. If a man beats me or rapes me, it is against the law. And even if it weren't, here in Trinidad, we girls have friends who can make his life a misery. I have freedom. And one day,' I told her, 'when I have saved enough, I can stop this work altogether. And do what I have always planned to do—'

'Yes?' Inez asked, brightening. 'Yes, and what is it?'

In truth the 'plan', if I could even call it such a thing, was no closer to fruition than it had been the first day I'd dreamed it up, seven or so years ago. I regretted mentioning it, and felt aggrieved with myself for having done so. But she wouldn't let it go. She demanded to know what it was, my secret plan: what I might otherwise do that would save my wicked soul. I told her. I was a singer once.

Instant tears sprung. 'A *singer*! Why, and you can be again!' she cried. 'You could sing at our own opera house! I just bet you could! You're so dashing and beautiful and everything ... I'll ask Mr Haussman. He's the manager. He's quite an acquaintance of my uncle. I just bet you—'

'But I don't want to sing at the damn opera house,' I snapped.

'Well, of course you do!'

'I am sick and tired of people *looking* at me—'

'Even so ...'

'However, I admit it – I would love to teach others to sing.'

'Well then!' Inez was irrepressible: 'You could start today! What's stopping you?'

'Plenty of things.'

'Well? Name them!'

But I didn't want to. I didn't want to talk about my dreams. I didn't need to be saved by her. 'I don't want to start today. I enjoy myself,' I said. Or at any rate (I didn't add), I used to. But a girl can have too much of a thing. 'I earn good money. And I never have to cook or clean – or listen to any man bellyaching ... or at any rate not for long. And then,' I leaned in and winked, 'well, they lay down their dollars. And then they *fuck off*. Out of my bed, out of my room. Out of my life.'

She gasped, as I had intended.

'Better a whore than a wife,' I said. 'Any day.'

Inez was neither of course. She was a lady with a rich and indulgent aunt, who volunteered her time at the library. Inez could do whatever and go wherever she liked. It made my head spin to imagine it.

She was 'looking for love', she told me. (I could have told her to save herself the trouble.) Instead we spent much of the evening talking about that. Inez and her search for love. Her search for adventure. Her search for a bigger life. She was restless.

'Aunt Philippa has almost despaired of me,' Inez said with a hint of pride. 'She's utterly convinced I'm going to die an old maid. And I tell her – well *of course I shan't*! But you know, Dora, I do begin to wonder myself sometimes. I know I look younger than I am. People always say I do. But I'm going to be thirty next birthday – it's *old*. For a lady. Don't you think?' She glanced at me. 'I mean to say – you probably ... Maybe you—'

'Oh, I already have a husband,' I muttered. I hadn't intended to confide in her. Certainly not. But there it was: the effect of her warmth, surprising me, inviting me to reciprocate. I had no close confidantes, and didn't want any. But she was difficult to resist.

'*You do?*'

'Somewhere. I haven't laid eyes on him in seven years or so. But I certainly *had* a husband. Until I woke up one morning ... And there – he was gone!' I looked at her astonished face, eyes filling with sorrow yet again, and I burst out laughing. 'Inez,' I declared – and I think by then I had almost come to believe it. 'It was the best morning of my life!'

'But why? Did he? Was he—'

'A louse. He ran off with our savings.'

'*No!* And ... children?' she asked, tentatively. 'What happened to the—'

'No children.'

'Oh. Well. I guess that's something.'

A silence fell.

'Well!' Inez filled it, bless her. 'It looks like I won't be troubled by any little rug rats of my own either. The rate I'm going. And it's not like I've been starved of suitors. Believe me, Dora. Just about every halfway eligible gentleman in Colorado has thrown his hat in the ring.'

'I'll bet.'

'Everyone in town knows I'm wealthy. Rather, they know my Uncle Richard is wealthy. And they know my aunt will be sure to make *Uncle Richard* make *me* wealthy too, the day I become a bride. It's what Aunt Philippa goes around telling everyone.'

'You probably have gentleman queuing round the block.'

'Well – yes. That is, I did. I've lost count of the gentlemen I've refused. And it's not that I'm fussy.'

'Of course not!'

'It's just that the *gentlemen* in this town ... I don't like to be insulting. And I guess – well, maybe you see a different side of them.'

'I guess I probably do.'

'But they're so darned *dull* with me! All they seem to talk about is business. Who made how many dollars buying this or that piece of real estate. And then they talk about hunting. Which is all very well, except I'm not interested. And then they talk about their automobiles. I spend half an hour with them and I'm already thinking to myself, well you're such a dull fish – why, I'd far prefer to spend the rest of my life with my nose buried inside a novel than to have to spend another ten minutes listening to you.'

I laughed.

She looked at me curiously. 'If it's not too silly to ask,' she said, 'do they talk about their automobiles with you?'

Just then the door to the street burst open. Two men, brawny bodies buttoned tight under high woollen waist-coats, necks sweating in collar and tie, strode into the room with such purpose and energy that everyone in the saloon, half full by then, paused in their conversation to inspect them. The two men seemed oblivious to the attention, didn't glance from left to right, but marched directly to the bar. They looked grim, of course. And on the shirtsleeve of the man closest, I could see a smear of blood. Lippiatt's blood. I knew it was Lippiatt's – rather, I suspected it, because I recognized the men as having accompanied Lippiatt on his visit to Plum Street all those weeks ago. We – that is, the three men, a couple of the girls and I – had shared a few drinks, whiled away an hour or so in the ballroom before dispersing to our sepa-rate bedrooms. I wondered if they would recognize me.

I hoped so. I hoped that they would spot me and come across. They were at the centre of it all this evening, and I was curious to know what had happened since we saw Lippiatt's body being dragged away down the street.

'Dora!' Inez whispered so loudly, my name echoed off the wooden floors. 'He has *blood in his sleeve*! Do you suppose—?'

'Hush!' I said.

But he had already turned. They both had. They looked us up and down. We made an incongruous pair. The man without blood on his sleeve looked at me more closely.

He turned to the other, muttered something … *Yes*, the other one nodded. Yes, indeed. It was me. The hooker from Plum Street. Both men raised a hand.

'*What? Do they know you?*' asked Inez, aghast. 'Those terrifying-looking gentlemen?'

I wasn't sure how to answer. It happened I couldn't remember either of their names. And, until they chose to acknowledge me, I was duty bound – honour bound – to deny it anyway.

'Dora!' shouted the dark one.

And so it was decided.

They picked up their glasses and crossed the room towards us. 'A sight for sore eyes,' he said. 'May we join you? Are you working tonight?' They glanced at Inez, uncertain where she quite fitted in.

'*Working*?' Inez cried out. 'Does she *look* like she is working? She most certainly is *not* working. Thank you very much …' She studied them more closely, through whiskey-glazed eyes, and seemed to like what she saw. 'However,' she added, looking pointedly at the blonder one, the man with the blood on his shirt, 'whatever your names may be, if you would like to sit yourselves down here …' She missed the seat, patted the air around it and then seemed to lose her nerve. She glanced at me.

If I had sent the men away, how different things would be today! I didn't do that. The excitement on her face – and the blood on his sleeve, and heck, they were two attractive men, and we were unaccompanied and a little drunk. I nodded, inviting the two of them to join us.

As they pulled up their chairs, Inez muttered something soft and briefly sobering about, 'Aunt Philippa being worried.' I could have called a halt to it then, I suppose. Or she could. She could have said to the men – 'I really ought to be going.' I might have walked with her to her home, since by then she was already canned, and certainly not able to make the journey alone. But I was canned too. I was off duty. I was having a good time. I don't believe the thought even crossed my mind. 'You said yourself you wanted to meet some new men,' I whispered, and winked at her.

She swayed with laughter. 'Oh, you're shocking!' she said gleefully. 'I am in too deep now, for sure!'

Lawrence O'Neill was the taller, blonder, handsomer of the two, and the one with blood on his sleeve. He was an Irishman from Missouri; an activist, employed by the UMWA (United Mine Workers of America) to do his worst in Trinidad. Back then, of course, before the Great War and the revolution in Russia, the battle between labour and capital was mustering strength and fury in every corner of the globe. It happened that, for the time being, the UMWA had designated Trinidad its American centre. It was here, among the mines of Colorado, that the Union was concentrating its funds, its fight – and all its best people. Lawrence O'Neill from

Missouri was among them, he told us. And, yes, it was Captain Lippiatt's blood on his sleeve.

We were all where we shouldn't have been that night. I should have been working, of course. Inez should have been at home with her aunt, playing bezique. And, on the night their friend was murdered, you would have thought those two Union men had better things to do than while away the hours with a small-town librarian and a tired old girl like me.

'Tell me, Inez Dubois,' Lawrence O'Neill leaned his body in towards her, his expression teasing.

'Tell you what, Lawrence O'Neill?' she purred back at him ... A little bit of confidence and polish – the thought flipped through my mind – and she might have made a fine hooker herself. 'What shall I tell you, Lawrence O'Neill? I'll tell you anything you want to hear.'

'Inez, honey,' I interrupted half-heartedly. 'Don't you think we ought to be heading home?'

'What's that, Auntie?' she said.

It made me laugh. 'Just take it easy, won't you?' I muttered. *These men aren't like the ones who talk to you about automobiles.* That's what I should have told her. The blood on their sleeves isn't something they smeared on for after-dinner party games.

Lawrence wanted to talk about the company-owned mining camps, or 'company towns', as we sometimes called them. And they were towns, really: privately owned fiefdoms, fenced off from the rest of America. They had their own stores, doctors' surgeries, chapels and schools; their own set of rules (no hookers, no liquor allowed); even their own currency: miners' wages were paid partially in scrip, only valid in the company town's overpriced stores. Lawrence asked her if she'd ever visited a company town herself.

Of course she'd never visited. For that matter, neither had I.

'I never have,' she said bluntly. 'But my aunt goes out to the little schoolroom at Cokedale every Friday, to help them with religious instruction. Or she used to. Before it all became so troublesome out there.'

'It's going to get worse now,' he said. 'Lippiatt changes things. You watch. It's going to turn, now.' He said it with a grim sort of relish. His friend nodded sagely – and I remember I felt a grim sort of chill. He was right. You could smell it – the turning point. The cold-blooded murder of a Unionist, right there, on North Commercial Street. Lippiatt's death would change everything.

But Inez didn't seem to be listening. She prattled on without missing a beat. 'Aunt Philippa says it was quite the *nicest* little school building she's ever visited, and *far* nicer than St Teresa's here in town, which by the way I attended ... And she says the company provides the sweetest little homes for the workers that are as cosy as can be. And each little family has its own little yard.

45

And plenty of people grow their own vegetables and keep chickens and I don't know what else. And I know what you are going to say. You are going to say that it's perfectly all right for *Aunt Philippa*, who arrives at Cokedale in her motorcar and leaves again in a motorcar and goes home to a lovely house with two great furnaces and servants and honeycake for breakfast and all that – Well, I'm not saying anything about that …'

He laughed – rather gently, I thought, all things considered.

'Aunt Philippa says she simply doesn't know what the workers are complaining of.'

'Well,' he said, 'I'm going to drive you out there, Miss Inez. How about that? I'm going to drive you out there tomorrow and you can see for yourself … The numbers of men who roam about the place with half their limbs missing. Because of just how nice and cosy it is down there in those coalmines. And the women who have to beg and borrow just to feed their own children. You think the company cares for its people? They don't give a damn for the people. They *own* the people. And, by the way – if they cared so much about their damn people, perhaps you can explain to me why they send their Baldwin-Felts thugs to murder them, in cold blood, right here on the sidewalk in front of everyone.'

'You're getting the wind behind you, Lawrence,' I interrupted. 'Watch out now, or you'll blow us all the way home.'

'And excuse me for saying,' Inez said, taken aback by his vehemence but – to her credit – not silenced by it, 'with respect and all: Captain Lippiatt wasn't employed by the company. He wasn't one of their people. That is … He was quite the opposite.'

'He was *for* the miners,' O'Neill replied.

'Oh god,' I sighed. 'I think it's time for my bed.' I'd spent too many hours of my life, listening to men windbagging about the rights and the wrongs of organizing unions, and the rights and wrongs of company towns – and I was sick and tired of the whole subject. If you asked me – but nobody ever did. I wouldn't have told them anyway. It was none of my business.

Inez didn't share my feelings. That much was clear. She was leaning towards Lawrence, preparing to continue the argument, when an elderly gentleman in a worn wool suit approached the table.

'Miss Inez?' he said.

She looked up at him. Her face fell. 'Oh *no*,' she moaned. 'Not now. Please, Mr Browning. Can't you just pretend you didn't see me?' She belched. 'I'm just about getting started.'

'I've been looking for you here, there and everywhere,' he said. 'Your uncle's waiting outside in the automobile. If you don't come out directly, I dare say he'll come in and haul you out by your ears.' The old man glanced around the table: two Union men, one blood spattered – and one old hooker: drunk as lords, every one of us ...'I think you had better come with me.'

With a great, childlike sigh, she set down her glass and stood up.

'What?' cried O'Neill. 'You're running off? Just as it was getting interesting?'

'Well, you can see that I have to.' They looked at each other, and I swear – whatever was going to happen between them was sealed, right there and then. 'But it was fun, wasn't it?' she said. 'Can we do it again?'

'Come to the Union offices. You know where they are?'

'Not exactly.'

'Well – see if you can't find out. Ask for me.' He smiled at her, a liquor-leery smile, and I don't believe he was thinking much about the iniquities of company towns just then. 'I'll be around the next few days, Miss Inez Dubois. Maybe we'll motor out to the Forbes camp together ...'

She was about to leave, but she turned back. 'And I haven't forgotten, Dora,' she said, waggling a single, dainty finger. 'I've not forgotten about the singing lessons, you know.' For a second I couldn't even think what she was talking about. 'Thank you for a beautiful evening.'

'I enjoyed it,' I said.

'It started badly though, didn't it?' she said vaguely. 'Lawrence O'Neill, I am *very sorry* about your friend.'

'Aye,' he said solemnly. 'Thank you.'

'Well. I had better leave. Thank you all. Dora, *thank you* ...' She was swaying, possibly on the verge of tears again. The old man attempted to take her elbow, but she pulled it away. 'It was the best night of my life.'

She weaved her way through the long bar, the old man protective and irritable beside her. She was a fish out of water. A fish that had swallowed far too much sauce ... I see her now, reeling meekly beside the old man. There were snickers and catcalls from either side, and of course she must have heard them. She must have known what a figure she cut. And yet, there was something beyond pride, something grand and oblivious as she made her way through the room. She looked happy and alive – and carefree, and bold and *young*. And she reminded me of what it was like to be someone who still believed – oh, I don't know – that life could ever be more than a thing to be gotten through.

Lawrence O'Neill, I think, watched her leave and was filled with a different sort of regret.

It was a private transaction between the two of us – strictly against Plum Street Parlour House rules. I went upstairs with him, to his rooms at the Toltec, and woke before dawn in a state of shock. I had slept with a client still beside me. I took the cash from his wallet, and left without saying goodbye.

5

I looked out for her, but I didn't see Inez for some time after. I often wondered how her aunt had reacted when she'd rolled home that night, reeking of liquor, and I took great pleasure in trying to imagine the ride back from the Toltec, Inez and her Uncle Richard side by side, Inez belching away, jabbering about politics. That she didn't appear at the Union offices (which fact I learned from Lawrence O'Neill when I met him on the street a week or so later) seemed to illustrate that our evening together was nothing more than an amusing deviation for her.

Inez had melted back into her parallel world of educational talks and pious ladies' tea parties, and I pitied her for it. To my surprise, I also missed her. I considered seeking her out at the library, and once even made it as far as the library steps. But when I glimpsed her at the desk, sober and prim, gossiping with the doctor's wife, I lost my nerve and turned back home again. I suspected that, were we to meet at the stocking counter of Jamieson's Department Store one day (as well we might), she would not even acknowledge me.

Meanwhile, as O'Neill had predicted, Lippiatt's murder was the talk of the town, and the talk of our visitors to Plum Street. Tempers on both sides of the argument were hot and high, and there was no meeting point between them. Only a few months earlier, up in Colorado Springs, so one of my clients informed me, Lippiatt had been found guilty of unspeakable violence against some poor young woman, and there had been moves to excommunicate him from the Union altogether. Now, of course, it was a different story. His death became a focal point. He had died a Union martyr. At the Union conference that weekend, Lawrence O'Neill and his pals wore black crepe bows on their shoulders in remembrance of his heroism. But they hadn't watched him, as I had, returning to the fray with his handgun. They hadn't heard the blood-lust in his shout as he waved his weapon at the two detectives ... Any more than they had watched the two detectives, standing side by side over his dying body, and shooting him again – tearing a hole through his throat and then his chest.

But I had been living at Plum Street seven years by then, and I'd learned when to share my opinion and when to keep it to myself. So I kept my mouth shut. They were all fools to me.

The Plum Street Parlour House was situated in an imposing, four-storey red-brick house, which stood apart from the lesser buildings on either side of it. It was handsome: there were steps leading to the front door, and before it was a porch with ornate wrought-iron banisters. There was an electric light, set in a three-foot-high candle carved in stone by the side of the door and, on the door, a vast and shiny brass knocker. Everything about the place offered up the same message: the smell of perfume and burning opium that seemed to leak from the bricks, the shine and splendour of our brass knocker, those flamboyant railings, the rich red and gold drapes at the windows, the sparkling chandeliers within – not even a child could have been in any doubt as to the building's function. There were other brothels, even on our street, and in handsome houses too. But ours stood out. It glowed with lubricious promise. We were the most exclusive whorehouse in town, and those of us who lived and worked in it took a certain amount of pride in the fact.

There were eight of us working girls living at Plum Street back then. In addition we had Simple Kitty greeting at the front of house, two more housemaids, two kitchen maids, a cook and a barman, a musical director, who played piano in the main parlour and organized musicians for the ballroom each night. There was also Carlos, the man-of-all-work. And overlooking us all with her beady eye and the tightest pocketbook in Colorado, there was Phoebe: once a working girl herself, now Madam to the most popular parlour house in Trinidad. Unlike me, she had learned early on how to keep hold of her money and get the hell out of the game.

Phoebe must have been among the wealthiest individuals in town, but there was never a time when she wasn't on the lookout to be making more for herself. Any chance for another buck, Phoebe would be onto it. She'd developed a hundred sly ways to cheat the johns so that they wouldn't feel it, or didn't care. She used to cheat us girls too, charging interest on debts we'd run up here and there. In the early years, I hadn't used to mind so much. I was grateful for such a comfortable place to live. But more recently my attitude had changed. After so many years on my back, splitting my earnings with Phoebe and having nothing whatsoever to show for them, I had been trying, at last, to get myself in hand. I had eased up on the laudanum. Eased up on the liquor too. And I was beginning to keep some of my money back.

One of the girls must have told Phoebe I was trying to get myself together, and she didn't like it one bit. At thirty-seven years old, I wasn't the youngest girl in the house, and maybe I wasn't the prettiest either, but I knew what I was doing. I pulled in more than my fair share of business and Phoebe wasn't ready to lose me.

The morning they shot Lippiatt she had presented me with an unpaid receipt from a dressmaker who'd been dead for two years. Maybe it was genuine – I had been drinking a lot two years before then, and the laudanum would have been playing its part. In any case, I had no way to check up on it. Even if I had, there wasn't much I could have done about it. Phoebe held the town in her pocket. If she decided I owed her – well then, I owed her. For all its comforts and luxuries, Plum Street was a jail of sorts. Leaving it was never going to be a simple business ...

As I sit here twenty years on, at my little desk overlooking the warm Pacific Ocean, it seems the greatest of miracles to me that I ever did.

But life at Plum Street had its compensations. For a few years I used to think that William Paxton was one of them. He owned a gun store in town, and a few others upstate, and from the frequency of his visits to see me, I assumed they made him a good living. He'd been my regular client since his wife was sick and dying, and he was a decent man: quiet, gentle and generous.

He used to talk to me about his wife when she was dying and, after that, when his grief had eased, about all sorts of things. Sex and music and ... well, sex and music, mostly, which were our interests in common. Maybe a little bit about real estate and automobiles, too. In any case, we became friends. I told him something about my life before I came to Trinidad – not all of it true, of course. But I told him how I came from England, the child of two Christian missionaries, one long dead, the other long since returned to England – which was true. And I told him how, before circumstances changed, I used to travel the Western circuit with a group of popular musicians and stand before a full hall and sing and dance, and that once, long ago, I was quite a music hall sensation. Which was also true, so far as I recall.

He bought me a little, old-fashioned harpsichord – heaven knows how he found it – which I kept in my rooms (Phoebe said a piano would have made too much noise), and we used to sing together; or, more often, I would sing for him. I told him, as I told Inez, about how one fine day, when I was too old for this game, I wanted to open a little singing school, perhaps in Denver. He pinched me and laughed.

'Don't be absurd, Dora,' he said, and I know he meant it kindly. 'You'll never be too old for this game. You'll be adorable until the day you die.'

He used to tell me how much he cared for me. And I believe he did. Occasionally, when we were alone together, he used to mutter tender things; and I am convinced that in the last few weeks and months, before Lippiatt's death seemed to change everything in our little town, his feelings for me were stronger than ever. He said to me, a month or so before Lippiatt died, that he was 'missing the comfort of a wife', and on another occasion, around the same time, I remember he said: 'I want to behave to you as a gentleman should.'

Inevitably, perhaps, I played the words over until they meant what I wanted them to mean: something vast and precious. And I began to believe that he loved me and that I loved him.

Well, he came to see me in the week after Lippiatt's death. The streets were still cluttered with angry delegates, and the sheriff's men roamed among them, waving their guns. William sought me out at Plum Street in the midst of it, earlier in the day than was usual. If he had been anyone else, I might have kept him waiting. But William was different, and when I came down to the ballroom I greeted him warmly – too warmly. Beady Phoebe swept across the room and shot me a warning look. It was against house rules to form strong attachments. 'For your own protection,' she used to tell us. 'I don't want my girls getting their hearts all smashed up. Bad for business.'

'No heart left to smash,' I used to say.

But afterwards, I knew I should have listened. Our heads were side by side on the pillow ... and I wince to remember the affection I felt as I looked across at him. He glanced at me, sheepish as hell, gave a tug on his moustache, which he never did before and, for the maddest moment, because he looked so terribly ill at ease, I was certain he would speak the words. He said:

'Dora, I've been meaning to mention ...'

'Mention what, William?'

'Only the fact is ...'

'Yes, William?'

'Because I want to do right by you, Dora. Never doubt it.'

'I never would doubt it, William.'

'I probably would have been sunk without you, after Matty died.' He laughed. 'I tell myself you kept me sane. I believe you did.'

'Nonsense. You kept yourself sane. I just ...' I couldn't think how to finish the sentence, so I left it there.

'Fact is, Dora ...'

I stroked his face and kissed his shoulder. His shyness melted my heart! 'The fact is, *what*, darling man?' I said.

'Fact is, I've met a girl in Denver.'

My heart gave a double beat of misery.

'She's the sweetest girl.'

'A sweet girl?' I repeated. 'You have met a sweet girl in Denver?'

'I'm sure you'd take to her.'

'Oh. I am sure ...'

'I mean to say, if you ever met her.' Idly, awkwardly, he stretched an arm across the bed to caress me. 'She is the most lovely girl I ever met,' he said, and as he spoke he continued to tweak and squeeze and massage. 'And the beauty of it is, she's young enough for a whole brood of children!' He laughed. 'Unlike you, Dora! You and I are as old as the hills.'

I smiled. And smiled again. I wasn't so damn old.

'And the point of it is, Dora. Well, she has very kindly – crazily – but yes, Dora. She has agreed to be my wife.'

'Oh!'

'Yes. I'm kind of reeling from it myself, truth be told.'

'It's wonderful news.'

'Yes. Yes indeed it is. Only the reason I mention it,' he said.

'The reason you mention it …' I kept smiling, but my hand brushed his away. And I can picture his face now: an expression of slight hurt, mild surprise. He rested his arm by his side. 'Since this nonsense with Lippiatt …' he continued. 'Well, it was the last straw. And I want you to believe, Dora, that my only regret in all of it will be leaving you. But I have decided to settle in Denver. It's a better city. Don't you think?'

He seemed to expect a reply. 'I hardly know,' I said.

'There is so much vice here in Trinidad,' he said, without a trace of irony. 'I don't want my wife and children living in such a place. Trinidad's not the place it used to be.'

'But I'm sure it won't always be like this,' I said, as if anything I said might have altered anything. 'It's only

these past few weeks that things have gotten so bad.
I'm sure as soon as the two sides can find agreement ...'

He shook his head. 'They found a company man
on the rail tracks outside Forbes camp last night. Shot
dead.' Somehow his hand had worked its way back to
my breast. 'Retaliation killing,' he muttered. 'It won't
be the last, either.'

'Well, but—'

'But ... but – nothing,' he said. 'I just want you to be
happy for me. Can you manage that? *Please?*'

'Of course I'm happy for you, William,' I said. He
looked relieved and grateful. As if he believed me! And
then he climbed on top of me again, and he mumbled
to the pillow above my head: 'I bought a nice house in
Denver. I wish you could see it ... But I'll see you right,
baby. It's a promise.'

6

Since Lippiatt's death the mood in town had soured, there was no doubt. Each evening, miners travelled in from the outlying camps to listen to Union men preaching, to be harried and beaten by the Baldwin-Felts detectives, and to harry and beat them back. Both sides stomped the streets, drinking and fighting, their heavy boots kicking up the dust, as if the town belonged only to them. The Union had an anthem, and intermittently the gathering miners would break into song, filling the streets with their bellowing voices. It was a song we would all, in Trinidad, become more than familiar with in the months to come. I wake with it sometimes, even now, playing in my head.

We are fighting for our rights, boys,
We are fighting for our homes ...

It was early afternoon, a day or two after William Paxton had told me he was moving to Denver, and I was still recovering – if not from the heartbreak of it, then from mortification at my self-delusion. In all the drama of the last attempt, I still hadn't fetched my package from Carravalho's Drugstore, and I was making my way there, ignoring the miners, the police and the Unionists, the baking heat and the wretched, constant thrum of promised, longed-for violence. It was the first time I had been along North Commercial since the murder, and I couldn't help pausing at the spot where Lippiatt had fallen. In the dry summer, I noticed, faint stains of his blood still lingered. I was studying them, somewhat ghoulishly, when I heard Inez's voice:

'Oh! It's *you*!' she cried. 'I can't tell you how pleased I am to see you!'

I don't think it occurred to her I would be anything but equally delighted to see her. And of course she was right. She looked young and fresh and full of hope, and so unlike the girls at Plum Street that I felt my heart lift. She said: 'I wanted to come and find you days ago, but I didn't know quite *how* ... And now I'm on my way to the Union offices! What do you think about *that*?' She sounded triumphant. 'For heck's sake, don't tell Aunt Philippa though. She'll murder me ...' She looked down at her feet, at the stain of blood. 'Not literally, of course,' she added. 'I should think Lawrence O'Neill will be quite shocked to see me. Don't you think so?'

I laughed. 'He'll have given up on you by now. I should think he'll be astonished.'

'I was lying low.' She rolled her eyes. 'Had to, Dora. But it's only been a week. Ten days. He can't have forgotten me already. And if he says he has, I'll know he is lying. He said he'd take me out to the camps. I'm fairly certain he promised me. So. Here I am. What do you think?'

Again, I found myself laughing. 'You're a braver woman than I am,' I said. 'I wouldn't get into an automobile with a Union man if my life depended on it. And certainly not if he was threatening to take me out to the towns ... It's dangerous,' I felt compelled to add. 'You realize, don't you?' Despite all she had witnessed, and on the very spot we were standing, I don't believe she ever really understood it. 'The company guards are no less trigger-happy than your Union friends.'

'I *know that*! Actually, I was going to ask Lawrence if you might come with us,' she said. 'For the sake of ...' She stopped, frowned – and melted into that merry laugh of hers. 'Well, I was going to say, "for respectability", but it's not quite what I mean, is it? It can't be.'

'Nothing respectable about me,' I smiled. 'Why don't you visit Cokedale with your aunt instead?' I said. 'Leave Lawrence O'Neill and his Union well out of it. And me,' I added. 'It would be far safer. Didn't you say she helped at the school?'

She shook her head. 'Uncle Richard won't allow it any more. Not now it's finally gotten interesting.'

I wanted to tell her, *it's not a game*. But she kept talking.

'Anyhow, it would be more educational with Mr O'Neill. Don't you think so? Plus, he's absolutely right. I can't be living here all this time, with bullets flying and people marching and everyone absolutely itching for a fight and still have not the slightest idea what they're complaining about.'

'Well I can *tell* you what they're complaining about,' I said. 'If that's what you want. You don't have to go all the way out to the company towns to find out.'

'But I *want* to go out there.'

It sounded plaintive. Standing on the spot where Lippiatt died, and almost – very nearly – stamping her little foot, her innocence and sweetness seemed less delightful suddenly; her open-minded curiosity not admirable, but heartless and effete. 'So you can look at the miners and their families like they're zoo animals, I suppose,' I said. 'And risk getting shot. What would your aunt and uncle think?'

'Why, I certainly don't think they're zoo animals,' she replied. 'And really what my aunt and uncle might think about it is hardly any concern ...'

'There's plenty for the miners to complain about, I assure you.'

'Oh, I'm sure there is,' she said. She began to retreat. 'Well ... Dora ... Miss ...' It occurred to me I had never told her my second name – my married name. I didn't offer it then. 'Miss ... whatever your name is. Have a good day.'

She turned away from me, clumsy with hurt and surprise, and I felt ashamed. Ten minutes earlier, I'd have expected her to walk right past me with her nose in the air. Now here she was, greeting me like an old friend. She wanted to drive out to the towns and see for herself what the fight was about. It was more than I had done.

'Inez!' I moved to catch up with her again. 'Wait!' She didn't hesitate. She reeled around at once, her face absolutely beaming. '*Oh, and thank goodness for that!*' she said. She put an arm on my shoulder. 'I was dreading going in that place on my own. Shall we go in together?'

'Didn't your aunt and uncle have something to say,' I asked, as we fell into step, 'about the company you were keeping the other night? You could hardly stand up when last I saw you. What did they make of it?'

'*Oh, them!*' she shrugged. 'They're out of town in any case. Thank goodness. So don't let's worry about them! Anyway, it wasn't you they were worried about. In fact I don't think Mr Browning quite registered you. It was the saloon that upset them, and the gentlemen company, and the fact that I was unable to walk in a straight line.' She giggled. 'They worry about me constantly. Either I haven't found a husband or it's something else. Poor darlings,' she added. 'I can't do anything to please them. So I might as well please myself. Besides. If I'm clever about it, *which I am, Dora*, they really needn't have the faintest idea – I mean, not about anything I ever get up to.'

We stepped into the Union office – two rooms on the ground floor with nothing much inside them: a handful of untidy desks, some metal chairs scattered about and, on the front counter, quantities of printed leaflets, several of them in languages I couldn't recognize. In one corner, propped up for all to see, there were a couple of hunting guns.

Leaning over the counter in front of us was a tall young boy. Dressed in black felt hat and fresh, unsullied working clothes, he looked as if his thin bones were growing longer even as he slouched there. We waited in the empty room as he leafed slowly through his magazine, ignoring us. Finally, I said:

'Excuse me. This is the office for the Union, isn't it?'

The boy turned another page, pointed at the sign behind him, which confirmed the fact, and continued to read.

I glanced at Inez, torn between laughter and a strong urge to leave. She winked at me, gently shunted me out of the way. 'It must be awfully interesting, whatever it is you're reading,' she said, leaning over the counter towards him, 'if you can't even look up from it to speak to us.'

He glanced at her without interest, and then back at his magazine. 'Surely is,' he replied, turning yet another page. 'What can I do for you, ladies?'

'Why!' Inez cried. 'But you're reading *The Masses*, aren't you?' He glanced at her again. 'You are!' she said. 'I recognize the picture. It's all the way from New York. Young man, I find it hard to believe there's more than one copy of that magazine in this little town. May I ask you where you came by it?' She smiled at him, coquette that she was, and already he was melting. 'I hope you didn't take it from my home. Because the last I knew, the only copy of that magazine that ever made it this far west was lying in a little heap at my own bedside.'

I had never heard of *The Masses* – not then at least. It seemed extraordinary that Inez and this sullen Union boy should share the same reading material.

He said: 'You read *The Masses*?'

'Gosh, no,' she waved it aside. 'I look at the pictures. It's all about the pictures, if you didn't know. The pictures really are something, don't you think? I look at the pictures, and then heck, I usually throw the darn thing away.'

He stared at her.

'Can you help us please?' she smiled at him again. 'We're looking for Mr Lawrence O'Neill. Do you know him?'

'Sure I know him,' he said. He tapped his magazine. 'I bought this with me from Denver. In case you're thinking. And there's quite a line of people wanting to read it. So if you ain't reading yours, maybe you could drop it by the office, would you? When you're done looking at the pictures.'

'Certainly not!' she said. God knows quite why the idea so outraged her, but it did. 'I'm going to pass it to my friend here, once I'm done with it. And then I shall make it available to everyone in the town by putting it on display over at the library ... If they let me,' she added doubtfully. 'There's not many in this town will appreciate the gesture ... But if you Union men want to come over and read it at the library, you'll be more than welcome ... At least on Thursdays and Fridays. That's when I'm working there. Maybe don't bother otherwise. I don't suppose Mrs Svensson's going to be that happy to see you. She's the one runs the place ... Won't you tell me kindly, have you happened to see Mr Lawrence O'Neill at all lately? Do you have any idea where I might find him?'

'He's out at Cokedale today,' he said.

'Do you know when he might be back?'

'Nope.'

'Today? Tomorrow?'

'Maybe today.'

'All right,' she said slowly. 'Well maybe ... do you think you could tell him we came looking for him? It's

Miss Dubois and Miss ...' She stopped again. Looked at me and laughed. 'For crying out loud, Dora, won't you please tell me the rest of your name?'

'Whitworth. Dora Whitworth.'

'Whitworth!' she gasped, clapping her hands together, rolling her eyes to emphasize her relief at being permitted to know it at last – and making me laugh aloud, once again. It was a miracle, I thought. I had left Plum Street feeling as gloomy as could be.

We left the Union offices with assurances from the boy – Cody – that he would pass our message to Lawrence O'Neill. Inez said: 'Tell him we'll be back at the same time tomorrow would you, Cody? With our travel suits on, ready to drive out to whichever town he chooses. You be sure to tell him, won't you? I think Forbes. The camp at Forbes is closest, isn't it?'

'Cokedale.'

'Well, Cokedale then.'

'He's out at Cokedale today. I told you. He'll prob'ly go out to Forbes tomorrow.'

'All right,' she said again. 'Well – you be sure to tell him. And tell your friends, if they want to read a copy of *The Masses* which hasn't had your greasy thumbs all over it, there'll be one waiting for them at the library from Thursday.'

He looked at his thumbs. 'Awww,' he said, close as damn to smiling. 'They ain't *so* greasy.'

*

It was mid-afternoon still, hot and sultry. I wasn't in the mind to return to Plum Street – ever again, the way I was feeling. Inez and I were both at a loose end.

With anyone else, I might have suggested the saloon and a cooling glass of malt liquor. But with Inez I wasn't certain. We could go to a tearoom, perhaps, or for a walk by the river. But whatever we did would involve our being seen out together, and that, I assumed, was an impossibility.

'I know what we can do!' she said, as if she had read my thoughts. 'Let's go to Jamieson's Department Store and look at the hats! Shall we? We'll need hats, for the Forbes visit. *Serious* hats. Black felt hats. Do you suppose they'll sell any?'

'I doubt it,' I laughed. 'And if they do, you're welcome to them.'

We fell into step together, although a casual observer might not have realized it. We were careful to leave a space between us on the sidewalk and, as we chatted, we tended to look at our feet.

'I never thought my darling brother's silly magazines might come in handy one day,' she said. 'You've no idea the magazines he sends me. Because he's convinced I don't put enough fresh ideas into my head. He says I have a small-town mind and he wants to expand it. He may be right about that. I can't wait to write him about

Cokedale or wherever we go tomorrow.' She laughed. 'He won't believe it!'

'I'm not sure I believe it yet,' I said. 'It's about the last place on earth I want to go.'

'He sends me the most ridiculous literature through the post. I haven't the heart to tell him but half of it – I mean *most* of it – goes straight into the garbage. Only I must admit to liking *The Masses* very much. Because of the pictures. I have to hide it from my aunt, but it impressed the boy, didn't it? Why, I think it even impressed you!' She froze. 'Oh God,' she said, gazing up the busy sidewalk. 'Oh dear – oh Dora – here comes Aunt Philippa. I thought she was in Walsenburg today. She said she was going to Walsenburg to see the doctor! She has a weak heart ... Do you think she's seen us?'

'Which one is she?' I asked.

Inez shook her head. It hardly mattered. 'Hurry – why don't you cross the road? I'll get shot of her fast as I can and I'll meet you at hats in ten minutes. All right?'

At the hats, a half-hour later, and full of apologies for keeping me waiting, she bought herself a most fetching capeline in pale grey silk, with two silk flowers at the brim. The clerk told Inez they had ordered it especially with her in mind.

'Well, it's perfect,' she declared. 'How do you do it? You seem to know what I like even before I know it for myself.' The shop clerk glowed. We left the store,

Inez several dollars lighter, with a new silk hat. 'It's not nearly serious enough ... But no bother,' she whispered. 'I shall remove the flowers on the brim before tomorrow and it'll be just right.'

She said she wanted to come back with me to my rooms. 'Because then I shall know exactly where to find you when I need you.'

'Or maybe I could come back with you,' I teased her. 'We could have tea *à trois*. You, me and your Aunt Philippa.'

She seemed to consider me. 'You know,' she said, without a flicker of humour, 'when I saw you earlier, outside the drugstore where your friend was shot—'

'I already told you, Inez, he was hardly a friend.'

'Well, I saw your face before you saw me. And I'll tell you what I thought. You'll have to forgive me ... I thought I had never seen anyone sadder-looking in all my life.'

'Pardon me?' I said, hoping I hadn't heard her quite right.

'It hurt my heart, just looking at you.'

'Well – I'm sorry to hear that ... Fact is,' I added defensively, 'I just had some bad news.'

She wasn't listening. 'There's me, fussing about never finding a sweetheart or a husband or whatnot – and there were you with a face more tragic than Helen of Troy.'

'I told you. I just had some bad news.'

'And I don't even care *what* you say about a fallen woman is better than a wife. I thought about it over and over after you said it. And heck, how do I know? I'm not even either. And maybe it *is* better and maybe it *isn't* better. But I know from your face you're not happy. And I have an idea. About the singing school. Remember? That's what I wanted to talk to you about. So that's why I decided we should go back to your rooms – you have a sitting room or something, don't you? Where we can talk, without others listening in?'

'Of course I do.'

'Well then. Let's go there – I have a perfect plan for you. A perfect plan – and it's going to save you.'

'I don't need saving, Inez.'

'Yes, you do.'

'No. I don't.'

'Oh! Don't be absurd,' she said, taking my arm. 'We *all* need saving!' and she spun me towards Plum Street. 'Especially you.'

7

The tall thin boy at the counter looked even taller and bonier when we returned the following day. He was leaning on the same counter, reading – I'm fairly sure of it – the exact same article. Lawrence O'Neill was at a desk behind him, stretched out on a metal chair, large and brawny, dwarfing the furniture around him. He had a rifle cocked between his thighs, which he was in the process of attending to.

'Here they are, Mr O'Neill!' the boy – Cody – declared. 'The ladies I told you about. I told you they'd come.'

Lawrence O'Neill glanced up, looked the two of us up and down. He nodded politely at me – an acknowledgement of what had passed between us – before letting his bright blue eyes rest more warmly upon Inez. Slowly, he laid the gun on the table and stood up. There were sweat stains around the armpits of his shirt and waistcoat, and his chin was unshaven.

'Well, well,' he said, lifting the counter flap and stepping through. Inez, hardly five feet tall, looked like a child beside him. Or he looked like a giant. Either way, I thought they looked faintly ridiculous together. But it seemed not to bother them. On the contrary, the attraction between them was intense and obvious. I glanced at the boy, Cody. He was staring at them, with his mouth hanging open. 'Just look here what the cat brought in,' O'Neill said softly. 'Tell me. How's your head today, missie? It was fairly swimming the last time I saw you.'

'Oh, it's fine,' Inez said. And then nothing. Silence. I'd never before heard her make such a short statement. It was a struggle not to giggle.

There was no window in the front office and no one had troubled to switch on the counter lamp, so the only light in the room came from the open door behind us. O'Neill's face was bathed in afternoon sunlight, and the pleasure in his brilliant blue eyes burned bright for all to see. Inez's facial expression, her back to the door, was impossible to read. Not that anyone needed to. Good God – she was squirming with it! She could hardly stand straight.

'I didn't think you'd be back,' he said after a pause. 'Thought you'd be chicken ... But you've come to see how the other half lives, have you?'

'I certainly have,' she said.

He exhaled – something close to a laugh. His lively eyes fixed on her as she wriggled and swayed. 'I'll make a revolutionary of you yet, my friend.'

'Oh! I doubt it very much, Mr O'Neill.' It sounded pert. 'I only long for the day my little town is peaceful again.'

'Peace first, fairness some other time, huh? Isn't that how it should be?'

She bridled, uncertain if he was teasing. 'No! *Yes*. Perhaps ... What I mean to say ...' I might have told her, except I thought it was obvious: politics wasn't a teasing matter, not for the likes of Lawrence O'Neill. Not for the likes of anyone in Trinidad, that summer. 'What I mean to say is, that Trinidad used to be a nice place to be ...'

'I'll just bet,' he said. 'A woman like you has a lot to lose. Why in the world would you want to change things?'

'Well, I didn't say things shouldn't change. Maybe they should ... I only remarked that anarchy, socialism ... all these sort of things we read about ... and then you Union men coming in from out of town, stirring up the workers for your own political ends ... it doesn't strike me as a fair way of going about things either. So. Please. If you wouldn't mind. Don't insult me and I won't insult you.'

He blinked but said nothing.

'I have come here because you offered to show me round one of the company towns,' she continued. 'To educate me. Well, here I am. Very interested to see what you have to show me. Will you drive us? Or shall I?' She indicated the beanpole boy. He was leaning his sharp elbows on the counter, still gawking at her. 'Your young friend here said you were headed to Forbes today. So will you take us there or won't you?'

He took a moment to think about it, and shook his head. 'It's dangerous,' he said abruptly. 'I was drunk. You should probably go home.'

'Of course it's dangerous!' I think she stamped her foot. 'If it weren't dangerous I would have driven out there on my own. You said you'd take me, Lawrence O'Neill. Are you going back on your promise?'

Another pause. This one seemed endless. The three of us watched and waited.

'Well, missie,' he said at last, 'if you're certain. But I'm not taking you any place in that hat.'

Her hands sprung to defend it – the very hat she had bought for the occasion, and from which she had, last night, already removed the garland of silk flowers. 'But I have to wear a hat!' she cried. 'I don't have another. Not with me. What's wrong with this hat in any case?'

'It's a very fetching hat, I dare say, if you're drinking tea with the King of England. Why don't you wear Dora's hat?' he said. 'It's simpler. Better. You won't look like the laughing stock.' He returned to the other side of the counter, picked up the gun he'd been cleaning, slipped a couple of shots inside and snapped it shut. 'Well?' he said, looking back at her, the loaded gun hanging by his side. 'Are you coming or aren't you?'

'But I can't take Dora's hat!'

'Sure you can.'

'What about Dora?'

'Sorry. But I ain't taking Dora.'

'What?' She looked at me, aghast. 'Dora?'

I shrugged. I wasn't going to put up a fight. Everything I needed from the camps (and more) came to me at Plum Street. I was happy to leave the rest to my imagination.

'Of course you're taking Dora!' Inez said. 'Why wouldn't you take Dora?'

'Hookers ain't allowed in. They're strictly forbidden.' His blue eyes glanced at me with a smile, not unfriendly. 'The company guards'll spot her in a jiffy.'

'Well. I am not going without Dora. Certainly not!'

'*Well*, I ain't going with her.'

'Dora?' she turned to me, rather pitifully. 'Darling? Don't you want to come with us?'

'Heck. It's all the same to me,' I said.

'No but really,' she said again. 'I'm not going without Dora.' It sounded less adamant this time.

'What's that, missie?' he teased her. 'Are you afraid?'

'You bet I am,' she said.

He laughed. 'Don't be chicken. I'll make it interesting …'

I felt a stirring of responsibility. She was a grown woman, yes, but a terribly naive one and I had introduced the two of them. 'I don't think you shall go, Inez,' I told her. 'It's dangerous out in the towns. Feelings are running so high.'

'If anyone tells me again that it's dangerous!' she said. 'I *know* it's dangerous. And please won't you come, Dora?' She turned to Lawrence. 'Won't you please let her come?' But by then I think we all knew the answer. Inez had already begun to unpin her hat.

We exchanged hats, and they set off together. 'You look after yourself,' I said to Inez as she climbed into the back of the Union auto and tucked herself out of view. 'Come and see me tomorrow if you can – and bring me back my hat!'

'I'll come and tell you all about it! My new life as a Union organizer ...' She giggled, waiting for O'Neill to start the engine. 'Don't you dare tell Aunt Philippa!'

I smiled and waved, and wondered when she imagined I was likely to do that.

8

There was a back door to the house that the girls were supposed to use when we were off duty, opening onto a narrow servants' stairway (the contrast between it and the plush richness of the front of house was almost comical). The stairway led directly up to the second floor, where I had my private rooms: a parlour, in which to entertain my clients after we had departed the ballroom, with bedroom, dressing room and bathroom leading off it. They formed, by necessity (as all the girls' rooms did), an oasis of apparent privacy. As Inez knew from her vist the other day, it would have been a simple business for her to slip in and out of the building without meeting anyone. Even so, she didn't come. I waited for almost a week, until finally I was concerned enough for her welfare that I called in at the Union offices to ask after her.

Lawrence wasn't there. He'd been summoned to Denver that morning. I asked Cody (the bony lad) if he'd seen Inez recently, and he laughed.

'She's in here most the time,' he said.

I was rather hurt to hear it, which surprised me. I left him with a sullen message for her, asking for the return of my hat, and trudged back home through the hot streets, feeling glum and slightly foolish.

She was sitting on a wall on the corner of Plum Street, tucked into the side of our imposing parlour-house porch, waiting for me, swinging her feet in the sunshine.

'*There* you are!' she cried, leaping off the wall and coming towards me. 'I thought you would never come home! Where have you *been*? I have so much to tell you. *So much!* First about the camp. And then about Lawrence. You realize, don't you, that I'm *in love*. At last, Dora! And I have you to thank for it.'

'In love?' I repeated, a touch sourly. 'Well, goodness me!'

'*Absolutely* in love. Of course I am in love. And by the way, if that's you "acting surprised", then you need to work on your acting skills, darling. You look just the same as if I had said to you: after night comes day. Was it really so predictable?'

In the face of such excellent cheer it was, of course, impossible to remain chilly for long. I said: 'Well. You look very happy, Inez.'

'Because I am!'

'He seems like a good man,' I said pleasantly, though in truth I'd not given it much thought.

'Oh he's *awfully* good,' she replied. And she smirked and blushed and giggled. And wriggled and writhed.

'Oh ...' I said slowly, examining her. 'Oh *my* ...'

'What?' she said. '*What*, Dora? Why are you looking at me like that?' Her face and neck had turned quite purple.

'You fucked, didn't you?'

She emitted a feeble, miniature gasp, something between outrage and delight.

'You're a fallen woman!' I laughed. 'Well well ... And welcome to the club!'

'What? Shh! Silence! For heck's sake, Dora!' She peered frantically up and down the empty street.

'Hey – no one's likely to be terribly scandalized round here,' I said.

'Oh God. There is so much I need to tell you,' she said. 'Can't we please just go inside?'

As we climbed up the back stairs to my rooms, I put a finger to my lips. I didn't want to have to introduce her to Phoebe, who would doubtless have invented a rule on the spot to prevent Inez from staying. Inez nodded her understanding, and made a show of dropping her voice to a whisper, but whispering wasn't a skill she had mastered. 'You must teach me all the precautions, Dora,' she announced as we paused on the landing outside my door. 'And then we have our project to set in motion. Have you forgotten?'

Inez's project: to rescue me from my life of sin. I had not forgotten it, though I was unwilling to admit that too easily. She and I had discussed our 'project' when she first visited Plum Street after our hat shopping trip, and though in my heart perhaps I always knew it was preposterous, it gave me hope because I was lonely; it gave Inez hope, because she was a woman who needed a project. It gave us something to do together. And I had been quietly stewing on its possibilities all week.

(It was in fact a very simple plan, requiring above all that the nice ladies of Trinidad conformed to expectation, and etiquette, and failed to recognize my face. If I dressed demurely and spoke – this had been Inez's brainwave – with an Italian accent, 'the ladies won't have the faintest idea who you really are. No one in Trinidad knows anything about Italy,' she had said. 'Or about anything else, come to think of it. You only need to throw out a few names. Michelangelo, Botticelli – oh gosh. That'll do. And they'll fall at your feet. Trust me.')

I asked Kitty to send up lemonade and we stretched out in my small, overstuffed sitting room, taking one sweaty, silk-swaddled couch each, on either side of my empty hearth. I opened the window, to catch what small breeze there was. First, we talked about Lawrence.

She was smitten. 'But you mustn't tell Aunt Philippa,' she kept repeating.

'For heaven's sake,' I said at last, 'I don't know Aunt Philippa. And even if I did ... But she must have guessed something's up, hasn't she?'

'Aunt Philippa? Oh, gosh no,' she said, waving the suggestion aside – and it struck me what a strange mix she was. Her childlike openness was so fresh and natural and disarming, and yet she possessed an equally fresh and natural – *artless* – talent and willingness to deceive, if not Aunt Philippa, then (should our project go ahead) all the gentlewomen of Trinidad. It was so instinctive, so pragmatic – I don't believe any judgement of it even crossed her mind. I rather envied her the freedom.

She continued, forgetting Aunt Philippa: 'Lawrence took me to a *fleapit*,' she said. 'Well, no, it wasn't a *fleapit*. It was a perfectly pleasant hotel. Out in Walsenburg, because we couldn't do it in Trinidad. And he signed us in as a married couple. I thought I would die of shame. But then. Gosh, *darn it* Dora, I can hardly believe you've kept it to yourself all this time!'

I felt a prickle of unease. Had he told her of the night we spent together? But it was nothing – a mere transaction. Surely not. 'Kept *what* to myself?' I asked.

'What? Why, sex of course!'

I laughed. 'Believe me. You can get tired of it.'

'Impossible!'

'Trust me.'

She uttered a sound, a sort of gurgle, a mix of mirth, smugness, wonder, lust ...'Well perhaps. In your line of business, maybe you can. And I guess not everyone can be as pleasing as Lawrence. But anyway you must tell me all your tricks – will you? You must have hundreds of clever tricks.'

'I'll tell you plenty of tricks so you don't conceive his child,' I said. 'And I'll tell you what and how and where to go if my tricks let you down.'

'No – I mean *yes*. Of course, you must. And thank heavens to have a friend like you. But I meant the other tricks – you know ...' She looked coy. 'The *filthy* ones. So he doesn't wander. So that I please him absolutely and completely and he never looks at any other woman ever again.'

I managed not to smile. 'I shouldn't fuss on that count,' I replied. 'If he's going to wander, he's going to wander. The only trick I've got for you is to darn well please yourself, Inez. Please yourself, and the rest will likely follow. Probably. Sometimes. Or at least for a while. Enjoy yourself.'

Inez nodded very solemnly, as if I were divulging to her the one and only true secret of the universe, and it occurred to me that, of all women, Inez hardly needed the advice. She pleased herself instinctively and, by way of pleasing herself, instinctively pleased others. And by way of pleasing others, pleased herself. She was warm and bold and open-hearted enough that the two were generally one and the same.

Not for the first time, I reflected what an excellent hooker she might have made, if she had been born in different circumstances. I wondered if it would amuse her for me to tell her so – and decided against it.

'But you haven't even asked me about the company towns, Dora,' she said suddenly. 'And the dreadful plight of those poor miners. You really should have come to Forbes with me! You can't imagine ... Did you even *know* ...'

Of course I knew. Coal company managers and Union agitators – they all passed through my rooms. Miners too, sometimes, when they got lucky in the gambling halls. If what you wanted was a balanced view of the hatred and distrust that consumed our corner of the prairie, I was surely best placed to provide it. There wasn't much I didn't know about the misery of the company towns, where miners lived and worked and raised their families, cut off from the rest of the world. It was why (aside of course from the fact that hookers were forbidden) I never had much inclination to go visit them for myself.

Of course *I* knew – but I was surprised by how much she knew now and what a turnaround had occurred in her thinking since last I saw her: the transformative effect, I reflected, of a few hours at Forbes, and a few hours in bed with Lawrence O'Neill. She proceeded to lecture me, with the convert's passion and certainty, about the collapsing, exploding tunnels, and the miners killed and maimed ... and the long hours, the late pay, the poverty, the danger and the darkness. 'The companies don't employ the workers,' she said. 'They *own* them: their homes, their schools, their doctors, even their currency – and then they keep the prices so high in the company stores, the poor miners can afford to buy only half of what they could afford to buy in town ...'

When she seemed to have finished, I assured her that I agreed. 'They treat the men like animals,' I said. 'It's a disgrace.'

'On the contrary!' cried Inez. 'They treat the animals *better*. It matters to them if a mule is lame. It still has to be fed. If a mule is blown up in one of their careless explosions, that is so many dollars wasted.' I could hear Lawrence's voice and turn of phrase in everything she uttered. He had recited the same speech to me too. 'But if a *man* is maimed. If a tunnel collapses on him, and he is maimed and blinded or killed ...'

Yes, yes.

'Well – never mind he has five children to feed and a wife with another on the way – he is worthless to them! If he can't dig coal out of the rock at the same rate as the other man – he might just as well be dead. And *then*, Dora, tell me, what is to become of him and his wife and children then? It's all very well for the company to boast of its schools and its pleasant houses, and the little back yards with chickens and so on – but what becomes of a man the moment he is of no use to the company? What then?'

I sighed. Couldn't help myself. And wished that Lawrence were back in town so the two could rant at one another. 'It is a wicked and unfair world, Inez.'

'Yes it is, Dora.'

'I'm sorry you have had to wake up to it.'

She had opened her mouth to speak but she closed it again at once. She smiled, shamefaced. 'It's true. I am rather late ...'

'Better late than never.'

A graceful pause. But Inez couldn't stay subdued – or shamefaced – for long. 'By the way, darling, I was thinking about your wardrobe,' she said. 'For our project I mean, of course.' She nodded at the door that opened into my dressing room. 'I thought it might be fun to look through your clothes and decide what you should wear, so as to look suitable. Something sober and not at all ... you know. If you look too flashy they won't take to you and our entire project will be lost.'

Inez had taken to heart my wish to set up a singing school. I dare say that even after her nights of sin and sexual awakening with Lawrence, she could never quite accept what it was I did for a living. Ladies of leisure,

I note, seem to be born with reforming zeal deep in their blood and bones. No matter what, they encounter a woman like me – a woman who isn't like them – and they feel the need to change her. Added to which, with Lawrence away, Inez was bored. I think it amused her to conjure such a mischievous plan – especially one that might simultaneously bring her new friend so much happiness. In any case, Inez was determined to rescue me.

And I was touched – more than touched. And even if, in the cold light of day, I thought her project was a little preposterous; even if she and I had only half thought it through; the mere fact of there being one – of my having a friend who cared enough to want to conjure it for me – was a wonderful thing. Inez was determined to rescue me and – whether I needed it or not; whether she could rescue me or not – I felt blessed.

9

The Project? Inez was going to use her connections to help me start up a singing school in town so that I could leave my life at Plum Street behind and become a respectable woman again.

The plan? Was this:

I was to be introduced to the Trinidad elite as an Italian from Verona whom Inez had found, searching for books about Italian opera in the Carnegie library.

'Brilliant, no?' Inez giggled (the opera idea having been hers). 'An excellent touch for added *veracity*. There you were, not looking for ten-cent romantic novels like every other lady in Trinidad, but seeking out improving books about Italian opera! In fact, Dora, why don't we say you have written one? In *Italian*? You could offer to send for it – pretend to have one sent all the way from Verona.

And then, once you're properly established, we can say it was lost, and pretend we are sending for another ... and then another. Wouldn't that be too funny? They'd be so impressed.'

The idea had been that I should give a recital at the Ladies' Music Club, which convened at 4 p.m., according to Inez, on the third Tuesday of every month. Each month, just like the Ladies' Plant Appreciation Club, the Ladies' Historical Club, the Ladies' Travel Club and numerous other clubs, it took place at the home of a different lady, whose task it was to provide both refreshment and entertainment. Inez said it was her Aunt Philippa's turn to be hostess:

'Or at any rate, if it isn't, then it ought to be. I shall make it happen. She has the only decent piano in Trinidad, so they really oughtn't to complain. Assuming,' she added as an afterthought, 'you know how to play it?'

'Of course,' I said, indicating my beloved harpsichord, sweltering beneath a velvet throw and sundry decorative knick-knacks in the corner of the room.

'Good.' She glanced at it. 'Oh, is *that* what it is? How adorable! The ladies love to go to Aunt Philippa's anyway,' she added. 'Because of the honeycake. We have *the best* honeycake, and Aunt Philippa swears she will take the cook's recipe with her to her grave. Which is horribly mean of her, I always think. Never mind. We need to decide what you will sing – something God-ish, *definitely*. And then something romantic.'

'I don't have an operatic voice, Inez. It's more of a dance-hall, vaudeville type of singing.'

'They won't know the difference. Believe me, they won't have the slightest idea. We need to choose you some clothes. And then we can tell all the ladies how lucky they are that you're setting up in town as their singing instructress. And I shall make a great performance about how much you have helped me with my singing – and sure as night follows day, the ladies will follow me. And it'll be perfect! We can put on a show at the theatre in the New Year, and *le tout* Trinidad will turn out. *Et voilà!* Goodbye Rotten Plum Street. Hello ... Well. Hello, somewhere else! The best plans are always the simplest ones.'

'You honestly don't suppose that they will recognize me?' I asked her. 'Because I'm certain I shall recognize most of them. If not their names, then their faces.'

'Absolutely not!' she said, leaping up from my small couch. 'We can make your hair as dowdy as can be – and we can make sure you only wear the plainest clothes – and if you don't have anything suitably drab in your wardrobe, we'll go to Jamieson's together and pick something out! So. Are you going to show me your dressing room or aren't you? For heaven's sake, we only have a week or so to prepare. Do let's get on with it!'

10

Lawrence was out of town for several days afterwards, and Inez dedicated herself to our project. On the morning of the event, she arrived at Rotten Plum Street (as she now referred to it) unannounced. She rushed up the back stairs and burst into my small sitting room without knocking. 'I have thought of everything!' she said, dropping herself onto the nearest couch.

I was alone at my harpsichord, playing to calm my nerves. Her entrance made me jump. 'Inez!' I said. 'You can't simply burst in like this. God knows – what if I had been with someone?'

She looked around the small room. 'But you're not,' she said. 'Besides, it's ten in the morning – and didn't you tell me you never allowed them to stay the night?'

'Even so ...'

'It's horribly airless in here, Dora. Why don't you

open a window?' She stood up again, and went to open it herself, impatiently pushing aside the knick-knacks and ornaments on the sill. 'You should throw out half this junk. What do you keep it for?'

'They're gifts,' I told her. 'Believe me, I long to get rid of them. But I can't. Otherwise ...'

'*Pour encourager les autres*,' she said.

'Something like that.' I smiled. 'Most of it's junk, but not all.'

'Well. You'll be out of this dreadful place soon. As soon as we've set you up. And, by the way, when you tell them you've written a book, you'll be able to charge a fortune. You can't *imagine* how much money there is flushing round in this town.'

I laughed at that. 'Oh, I believe I can ...'

'By the way, it occurred to me in the middle of last night that you're going to need an address! Quite why we hadn't considered it before, I cannot say.'

'I thought a post-office box,' I said. 'See what interest I can muster and then—'

'You can't give singing lessons in a post-office box. And the ladies have to know where to find you. That is, until you can find a little place of your own. And by the way, I have seen the sweetest little cottage on South Elm Street, which you might easily be able to take once your students start to roll in. And in the meantime, Dora, I have come via the Columbia. I've taken a room for you there in your new name. It's only for the week, mind. But I thought – if we are to do this, we must do it properly. And nobody could doubt the credentials of an Italian opera singer if she is residing at the Columbia!'

The Columbia was the oldest and by far the most luxurious hotel in town. It stood elegant and proud at the heart of Trinidad, on the corner of Commercial and Main Streets. 'I can't afford that!' I said.

'It's my gift to you, Dora, to thank you.'

'Whatever for?'

'For being my friend,' she said simply. 'You can't imagine what a thrill it is. And for introducing me to Lawrence; and for showing me that even in this Hicksville-*Snatchville* of a town ...' She giggled delightedly. Ladies didn't call it Snatchville. They just about called it *Honeyville*, if they were being especially daring – if they called it anything at all. 'No matter what my brother Xavier thinks, life *can* be absolutely ... exciting.'

'But it must have cost you a fortune. I can't accept—'

'Oh don't be silly, darling!' She waved it aside. 'I have already paid for it in cash. The room is sitting empty. It's under your new name. It's a suite. And I have told them to put a piano in there – you can play the piano, can't you?'

'You know I can,' I said. 'I already told you. And I was just playing when you came in.'

'Oh yes, of course you were. Well then, *Maria di Leopaldi*,' she pronounced it badly, but with relish. 'You can leave the ladies a card with your name and details on it – and for a week you can hold court at the Columbia. Offer them trial lessons or something. It's perfect. And after that, we had better find you a place.'

For authenticity we decided she would come to fetch me from the hotel, where I would be waiting in the room she had hired, in the Italian opera singer disguise she had helped to pick out, and that we would walk the five minutes or so east along Main Street to Aunt Philippa's house together.

It was, I think, the longest walk of my life. God knows – in the exhilaration of cooking up the plan with Inez, I hadn't allowed myself to fully acknowledge the risks. Shuffling along Main Street with my head down, stomach churning with fear, the risks hit me like a bucket of ice-cold water. If Phoebe discovered I was trying to make my escape, and she surely would, she would not only put a stop to it, she would exact a vicious kind of revenge. I dreaded to imagine quite what; although I knew, whatever it was, it would cause her no loss of income. It gave me some comfort. She wouldn't murder me then, or have me beaten to a repellent and uncommercial pulp of flesh ... My mind skittered from one vengeful alternative to another, and I might have turned back, but Inez marched us forward, and I hardly had a chance.

She made a point of waving and smiling at just about everyone we encountered.

'You haven't met Trinidad's new celebrity,' she shouted proudly to anyone who stopped – and to several who didn't. 'She's performing for the Ladies' Music Club this afternoon, but if you or your wife are interested in singing instruction ...'

By the time we reached Aunt Philippa's house two blocks north of City Hall, Inez had already collected three eager lady students. 'Between you and me, they're not quite *wealthy* enough to be part of the Ladies' Music Club,' Inez explained to me in her noisy whisper, as soon as they passed, 'which makes them all the keener to hang onto our coat-tails, Mrs di Leopaldi. I tell you what, you're going to make a fortune, Dora! And no one to take any commission off you, either.'

Mention of Phoebe and her commission – or rather Phoebe and her imminent lack of it – made my stomach lurch so violently that we had to pause. What was I even thinking? Phoebe would kill me if she discovered what I was attempting. She would send her stooges round and have me beaten until I begged for mercy. Was I mad?

Even now, I feel a prickle of fear, remembering. But I wasn't mad. In retrospect, I know the word is 'desperate'. Remote as it was, Inez seemed to be offering me a way out: a new life that didn't depend on the whims of a single, vicious woman whom, over the years, I had learned to hate.

'Oh we can deal with Phoebe!' Inez said blithely. 'For crying out loud! Let's just concentrate on getting ourselves through this!'

As we turned into the McCullochs' street – three times the width of Main Street, and each handsome house as large as any mansion, I felt my knees buckle, and Inez had to push me up the steps to the great front door.

'Inez!' I whispered, as we waited for the maid to answer. 'I can't speak Italian! Not a word!'

'For heaven's sake,' she said, stamping her foot. 'Nor can they! They've just about heard of Michelangelo. And Rome. Relax! You're going to be *just fine* ...'

Aunt Philippa looked nothing like her niece; twice her girth (though the same small height), her hair and eyes were as dull and pale as Inez's were alight with colour and life.

'No, no, she surely didn't inherit all that prettiness from me!' Aunt Philippa remarked cheerfully, putting a plate and doily into my hand, and an array of small, unwanted sandwiches. 'Why, she looks more of an Italian. Like you, Mrs di Leopardaldi.' She looked at me again: at my light brown hair and hazel eyes. There was nothing Italian about any of us. 'Even more so,' she muttered vaguely.

'Inez tells me you're a wonderful opera singer! Well, have
you glimpsed our little opera house? Of course you have
– it's right opposite you at the Columbia. Built by Jews,
by the way. But we don't mind that. Here in Trinidad,
we are terribly open-hearted, you will discover. Italians
too – just about *anyone* is just fine with us. And the opera
house – I call it little, but it's not *really* little, now is it?
It's our most handsome building – after the Columbia,
some people say. I disagree. I think it's handsomer than
the Columbia. But what do *you* think? You're an Italian.
You know about these things. Do you think it's more or
less handsome? As a building? I should love to know ...'

Philippa McCulloch might not have resembled her
niece in any physical way, but I wondered who got the
first word in edgeways at dinner. She didn't wait to hear
my answer: not that I would have given it to her, anyway.
I hated the opera house. The opera house was what had
brought me to Trinidad in the first place, and seven years
on, I couldn't walk past it without a shudder.

We had been the Martin Whitworth Troupe (not opera,
but vaudeville) and doing the 'Western Tour', spending
a week or so at every town with a decent-sized theatre
through the Middle West, and on to California. Except
the week we were in Trinidad, the troupe went on without
me and I was left behind. My husband was the epony-
mous Martin Whitworth. He founded the troupe; he was
its star performer. When he left, he took everything but

the clothes I was sleeping in. One morning in Trinidad I woke up – and he had gone. The whole troupe had moved on. He had fallen in love with our co-star – my best friend. They ran off and left me behind.

Was I familiar with the opera house? Seven years on, I could never walk past without remembering that final night. The three of us, on stage together as usual. We were singing to a packed house. It was one of our best nights since we left Chicago, and as we took our bows the applause was almost deafening. The people of Trinidad adored us! The cheers were ringing in our ears, and the three of us caught one another's eye. My husband winked at us both. We were happy! No. No, *they* were happy. I was the fool.

Was I familiar with the opera house? I surely was. And now Philippa McCulloch was pushing a plate of cheese pastries into my chest. Did I want to begin with a small introduction from herself, she was asking me? Or would I prefer a few words from Inez, who would do it so much better? Aside from which, she reminded me, public speaking was not terribly recommended, not with her heart condition. But of course I should eat something first. A small cheese pastry or some honeycake? I felt a wave of nausea. Also, quite suddenly, a tremendous urge to weep.

I looked around the room. There were twenty or more ladies scattered about, sipping tea and trilling pleasantly,

awaiting their turn either to fuss over Inez, or to be introduced to me. This was Trinidad's richest and smartest,
Inez had assured me. I knew it anyway. I knew plenty
of their husbands, too.

Mrs McCulloch's parlour looked as plush and as
fashionable as any I had seen in any magazine. It was a
large room with high ceilings, furnished in the heaviest
mahogany. There were drapes at the windows, too thick
in the heat of the late summer, but a welcome comfort,
no doubt, when the long winter came and the snow
lay thick. This afternoon the drapes were pulled back,
the windows were thrown open to the hot, dry street,
and thick shafts of dust-dappled sunlight poured into
the room.

Aunt Philippa saw me glancing up at the glass chandelier above our heads. It was the largest I had ever
laid eyes on outside of a theatre. She clapped her hands
with glee: 'It's from Italy!' she cried. 'I'm so glad you
have spotted it! I simply *knew* you would spot it. Being
an Italian. I bought it in Denver but it was put together
all the way back in Italy! Can you believe it? I gaze at
that chandelier every single day, Mrs di Lelpeodi ... And
I say to myself: how in the heck – if you'll excuse my
language – how in ding's name did they get that great
big thing all the way across the ocean and all the way
across to this great land of ours – and not a break or a
chip in it anywhere to be found?' She shook her head at

the wonder of it. 'Anyhow,' she continued, 'I just knew you'd appreciate it. Being from Italy and all. I only hope it won't make you too homesick.'

Aunt Philippa dragged me around the room, introducing me carefully, slowly, and differently to each one of the ladies. This then, was the cream of Trinidad. If not quite Mrs Astor's Four Hundred, then Mrs McCulloch's Twenty-Five: old and young, tall and short, fat and thin, and yet somehow uncannily similar. One or two of them, I was certain, looked at me strangely, as if they felt they had seen my face before. But I stuck to the plan. Talked in my Italian accent, looked them full in the eye and silently dared them to voice their doubts.

They didn't. They had other matters on their minds. The perfection of the McCullough honeycake, the evil of the Unions: above all, the naughtiness of Inez for failing to find a husband and settle down.

'She needs a man with a strong will,' they said between mouthfuls of pastry, as if it was something that had been said so often, and for so long, there was no need to wait until she was out of earshot to say it again. 'Someone who can take her in hand,' they agreed. 'Mrs McCulloch has spoiled her. That's the problem. And now it's hardly a surprise poor Mrs McCulloch has a weak heart – who knows how long she'll be here to look out for her headstrong niece. And naughty Inez, almost an old maid.'

'Mrs Butterworth!' Inez smiled affectionately. 'You are too old fashioned! I am a long way from being an old maid, and in any case I don't need a man to look after me. I am perfectly capable of looking after myself!'

'Every woman needs a man, dear. And every man needs a good wife.'

But Inez, glowing from her secret affair, only shook her head and smiled.

The conversation moved on. From the unseemliness of Inez to the lawlessness on the streets. Somebody said, 'Anyone remotely associated to those horrible Unions should be shot. Pure and simple.' And somebody else said: 'Starve them to death, I say. Save yourself the cost of bullets.'

Inez said: 'I think the miners have a great deal to complain about. Somebody has to fight for them.'

But beyond Aunt Philippa's playful swat – an affectionate, '*Oh Inez you silly-billy-goat. You know you haven't the foggiest what you're talking about!*', nobody seemed to hear her. They certainly paid no attention. At length, Mrs McCulloch cleared her throat, and tinged teaspoon onto teacup until the ladies fell silent.

I took my place by the finest piano in Trinidad. Chairs had been arranged in a semi-circle around it. I waited for the ladies to be seated.

'Ladies,' began Inez, standing before them, her back to me. 'Until two weeks ago I had never met Signora Maria di Leopaldi. I was lucky enough to encounter her leafing through our outstanding music section at the library. When I asked her if there was anything I might be able to help her locate, she told me she was in search of a transcript of *La Traviata*, that memorable opera written by the great Italian composer, Giuseppe Verdi ...'

At this point, encouraged by extreme nervousness, I began to feel bubbles of laughter rising from the pit of my stomach. From the sound of her voice, I wondered if Inez was similarly struggling.

'Ladies, not only was Mrs di Leopaldi *looking* at opera books, I have to tell you that, although she was quite unaware of it at the time, she was actually *singing* opera too! Quietly: *oh so quietly*. Under her *oh-so-Italian* breath.'

I bit the inside of my cheeks.

'And I declare, *that voice*! Never before have I been so privileged to hear such a sound!'

I coughed.

In front of me, I could hear her for certain now, swallowing back her own laughter.

'An angel's voice!' she declared confidently. (She had never heard me sing.) 'Well – knowing how well our own little music club would appreciate such a wonder, I accosted her *at once*! And here she is! It is with real pride that I present to you: Mrs Leopaldi of Verona!'

Daintily, they began to applaud me. But then Inez held up her hand for silence.

'Before I leave my friend to transport you all to Italy with her fine music – and trust me, she will! – I must warn you *now* that this extraordinarily talented lady is currently only intending to spend a single week in Trinidad before climbing back onto that train and heading on West to Hollywood, where – *listen to this!* – it is her intention to set up a small singing school for ladies … *Ladies!* Do you hear me? It is up to us to prevent her! She has taken rooms for a single week at the Columbia Hotel, where she has a piano at her disposal. I urge you to approach her, before it's too late. Take your first lesson with her there at the Columbia and, if she satisfies, well then, book her until Christmas! She has taken a great shine to our small town and she has assured me that if, between us all, we can provide her with enough work to remain here in Trinidad, then remain here in Trinidad she certainly will! I'm convinced there's not a soul among us who wouldn't benefit from some outstanding singing tuition … And then, ladies, who knows? Perhaps, with Mrs Leopaldi's help, we can bring some much-needed music to these troubled streets of ours!'

'Here, here!' the ladies chirruped. 'Bravo!'

'We need you Mrs Lepodarri! Don't you dare to abandon us!'

I sang to the johns from time to time, but it had been seven years since I'd sung before an audience of more than one. I had forgotten how alarming it was. I fumbled the first chord, and then the next. But then, somehow – just as they always used to – my fears washed away and everything fell into place.

It wasn't Inez and her storytelling which was my undoing. It was me, who kept singing for far too long. I was only meant to sing three songs, and then our plan had been for me to break for further tea and pastries, so that Inez and I could canvas for students. But the ladies kept asking for more songs and I was so flattered, and was having such a wonderful time, I couldn't bring myself to stop.

Midway through the sixth or seventh ditty, the drawing-room door opened softly and somebody joined us, a fact I was only dimly aware of until I finished singing and the applause had started to fade.

'Cedric Hitchens!' cried Mrs McCulloch, fluttering up to greet him. 'What in heaven's name are you doing here? Don't you know this is a *ladies'* event!' She tapped him playfully – or perhaps, to get his attention, since his eyes were fixed on me: 'It's a *Ladies'* Music Club, Mr Hitchens!'

'I heard the music from the street,' he said. 'I could hardly believe my ears – such a beautiful, individual singing voice, right here in the middle of Trinidad. I just couldn't resist coming in.'

'Well, honey, now that you're here, you had better meet the wonderful Mrs di Lepodi of Ronoma, Italy. She's an opera singer, and she's written a book, if you please, and she's come all the way from *Italy*! Inez found her in the library and positively dragged her here to see us! And now she's going to teach us all to sing, if only we can persuade her to stay right here in Trinidad, and bring some music to our troubled streets, and absolutely agree not to climb back on that train to California.'

'Bravo!' cried the ladies. 'Hoorah for Mrs Lappolli!'

He said: 'Well, and ain't *that* something? ... All the way from Italy, you say?'

He smelled of tobacco and uncooked offal. It's just about all I could ever remember about him. And my borrowed soap (but they all smell of that). And he asked me to sing for him whenever he visited and his prick was as thin and bent as a half-snapped pencil.

11

He leaned against the doorframe to watch as I took my leave. He didn't say anything to expose me. Why would he? I might have been tempted to repay the favour.

'Don't forget,' Inez called out over the hubbub, 'you will find Mrs di Leopaldi at the Columbia for one week only! Hurry now! Or we may miss the chance ...'

She followed me to the front door.

'Oh God Dora. Is it ...?' she whispered, her face crestfallen, 'Is it what I think?'

I nodded, too disappointed to look at her. 'It was crazy of me ever to think it might work.'

I stepped out into the bright sunlight, onto the high stone McCulloch porch. Inez tugged my sleeve. 'Do you suppose he'll say something?' she asked. 'Are we ... Am I ... to be exposed?'

'Not you,' I said. 'Just stick to your story. They will

assume I lied to you.'

'All right, but—'

But I couldn't bear to linger a moment longer. I thanked her for trying to help me, detached her hand from my clothing and turned away. I heard her calling my name but in my haste to return to the part of town where I belonged, I had already broken into a run.

I nursed my disappointment quietly, with well-practised skill. Nobody could have guessed at my wretchedness, and of course I'd not mentioned my plans – or their failure – to anyone in Plum Street. They were my secret.

Nevertheless, when Phoebe sidled up to me a few evenings later and invited me for tea in her private rooms, I feared the worst.

'Are you unhappy, Dora?' she asked, her beady eyes on my face.

'What? Not in the least!' I replied.

'It's what I thought. We are a *happy* family, aren't we, Dora? Here in Plum Street.' She gave a heartless tinkle of laughter, and offered me cake. 'Only I've been hearing the oddest stories!'

'What kind of stories?'

She bit into her cake. 'Try some!' she said. 'It's delicious.' There were crumbs at the sides of her mouth and I stared at her, unable to look away. The sight of them there made me queasy.

'What kind of stories?' I said again.

I denied everything as convincingly as I needed to. Not all her details were correct, in any case, but she had grasped the nub of the thing: namely that I was trying to leave the house, and to set up a separate existence right under her nose here in Trinidad, and in between the heartless tinkles and my denials, and the mouthfuls of cake, she succeeded in putting the fear of God into me. She made it quite clear: as long as I lived in Trinidad, I would be at Plum Street; and I would be at Plum Street until such a time as she decided I should leave.

'I look after my girls,' she said, brushing the crumbs from her lilac silk lap. 'And my girls look after me.'

I didn't go near the Columbia Hotel after that, but Inez did. She told me she dropped in several times to find out if there were any enquiries. There were not. The rooms – and the piano – remained silent the entire week. I saw Cedric Hitchens, motoring up Sante Fe Avenue with his smiling wife beside him, and a picnic hamper in the trunk. I had no wish to be Mrs Cedric Hitchens. None whatsoever. And yet, just for that moment, her bovine complacency, her dumb comfort, left me breathless with lonesomeness.

Inez took the precaution of avoiding me for a week or so, and for a while I wondered if her aunt had somehow winkled the truth from her and forbidden Inez from seeing me again. Inez might have disobeyed her, of course. But she would need to be careful about it. Without her aunt and uncle's love and money, she was as vulnerable as the rest of us.

And then, finally, she came to visit me. She let herself in through the back door early one morning, unannounced, and I emerged from my bedroom, in pale green silk kimono, to find her sitting right there on my couch.

'I think it's the safest place for us to meet each other for the moment,' she said, by way of greeting. She glanced at my kimono. 'Are you all right? You look dreadful.'

'Well. I have only just woken up. Hello there ... Good to see you. How long have you been sitting here?'

'About a minute,' she said. 'I've been reading your filthy novel.' She dumped it on the table at her elbow. 'Where do you find that stuff?'

I smiled. 'I have plenty more if you like it. A client sends me a new one every couple of weeks. It's a devil to keep up with them.'

'No, thank you.' She sighed. 'Unless you have any in English? Your French must be a lot better than mine ... Darling, I am so sorry.'

'Sorry? Whatever for?'

'We had them eating out of our hands, didn't we? I swear, if that wretched man hadn't walked in when he did.'

'Did anyone say anything after I left?' I nursed a childish hope that perhaps all was not absolutely lost.

But Inez's gaze slid away. 'Oh, nobody said anything much,' she said. 'Mr Hitchens couldn't exactly say much, could he? Not without giving himself away. But he hinted enough to ruin everything for everyone. By the way,' she added, 'I have been relieved of my duties at the library.'

'No! Because of me? But that's ... Why? Did you not stick to our story?'

I opened the door to the landing and shouted down for Simple Kitty to bring me my morning coffee. 'You want some?' I asked Inez.

She shook her head. 'I took mine hours ago. You're up late this morning,' she glanced again at my kimono, haphazardly fastened. 'You're not even dressed.'

'I work late, Inez.'

'Of course you do ...' She fidgeted, embarrassed. 'Maybe I will have that coffee after all.'

So I shouted out onto the landing a second time.

It stirred the girl in the next room, who yelled at me from her bed to hush up, which (since she happened to be the noisiest of all of us, day and night) encouraged me to slam the door with enough force that the floor shook. As I plumped myself, silk kimono billowing, into the little couch opposite Inez, the girl was still bellyaching at me through the wall.

'Apologies for the neighbour,' I said.

Inez shrugged. 'She sounds a little crazy.'

'You've been fired from the library? But why?'

'Well no, I haven't been fired,' she amended. 'Not exactly ...'

'I don't understand.'

'I only meant to say ... Oh! That I know how disappointing it must be for you – but that there were some sharp words directed at me afterwards too ... Aunt Philippa was mad as a March hare.'

'You didn't tell her we were friends?'

'Of course not. Dora, I'm not stupid. I told her we met in the library and I stuck with the story.'

'Well then?'

'Well then ... So she said ...' Inez laughed self-consciously. 'Well, she said she might have to have a word with Mrs Svensson.'

'Mrs who?'

'The lady who runs the library. I don't need to tell you, Aunt Philippa's still pretty puckered about that evening when – oh gosh, Lippian? Lippians?'

'Captain Lippiatt.'

'The night he was killed, and I rolled home half-corned.' She giggled. 'Poor Aunt Philippa. She doesn't know the half of it, does she?'

Simple Kitty arrived with the coffee. She placed it on the small table between us, staring in open-mouthed wonder at my respectable-looking female guest, and spilling sugar on my best silk tablecloth in the process.

We waited until she had left.

'So she had a word with Mrs Svensson?'

'Well. No.' Inez looked uncomfortable. 'No. She said ... she might. Because of the immoral people I might meet as a consequence of being at the library.'

I laughed, but she didn't.

'In any case, I'm not so sure I really like working at the library any more. It's sort of ... restricting. It doesn't feel right.' Inez gave a great sigh and, spreading her arms, threw herself back onto the green silk cushions behind her. 'So here we are, Dora. All day ahead of us ... *What shall we do?* I tell you, nothing ever damn well *happens* in this town. And I wish ... oh gosh ... I just wish ...'

Lawrence O'Neill had been away on Union business for over a week by then. Inez had dropped by the offices to find out when he was due back, and been told by Cody that it wouldn't be for another fortnight at least. His tour of undercover meetings in the mining camps upstate (mustering support among the men) had been extended.

Cody reminded Inez that Lawrence had banned her from hanging around the Union offices while he was away.

'"Mr O'Neill told you to keep away." Those are the very words that impertinent young boy said to me, Dora! He said, "So you'd better git. Or you'll have me in trouble." He was terribly rude,' she added, 'especially considering I thought we were friends.'

Inez had nothing to distract her. In the days that followed she would come to my rooms in the early mornings, and sit on my couch and sigh – until my work began and I would kick her out, and she would meander back across town to her other life of card evenings with Aunt Philippa and church fundraisers, and educational teas, only to return to me the next morning. She never seemed to go to the library. When I asked why, she just sighed and said, 'Because there's no *fun* in it any more.' She was bored.

'You need to find a husband,' I told her. 'Have some children before it's too late. Don't make the mistake I did.'

She gave a lovesick groan. 'But you have *no idea* how I long to have his children! Oh God where *is* he, Dora? Why doesn't he return? Do you suppose something has happened to him? Those company guards have no respect for life. You saw it for yourself ... God knows, he might be lying in a ditch somewhere with a bullet through his chest. And I am just sitting here, killing time on your couch, wasting my life away, waiting for him.'

She was accidentally 'passing by' when she saw his car pull up outside the Union office a week or so later. He must have been gone about three weeks altogether. Inez said she rushed across to him and then, as she was about to call out, abruptly lost her nerve.

'But I think he saw me,' she said. 'I'm certain he did. He was with two other men, and they all looked *so serious*! And then they all disappeared into that dreadful office and

114

Dora – can you believe it? After all these *weeks* and *days* only longing for his return, there he was, hardly yards away from me and I lacked the nerve to follow him!'

'It's probably a good thing,' I replied.

'I think so too,' she said. 'Since he's banned me from the office. But Dora, *you* could go, couldn't you?'

'I suppose so.'

'After all, he's a friend of yours. Couldn't you go and see him for me? Find out what he is thinking of me, find out if he is absolutely longing to see me, as I am him? Couldn't you go to him and tell him how much I have missed him?'

'I'll go for you, Inez, all right? At the end of the day.'

'I just have to know if he ever wants to see me again.'

'I can't go right now, Inez. I have a bunch of things to do.'

'Thank you, darling. You're so kind … It's just the *not knowing* that's sending me so crazy …'

But she wouldn't let it rest. Within a half-hour her determination had worn me down, and I was on my way to North Commercial Street to find him for her.

He was in the same leather chair, long legs stretched across the sawdust floor, at the same messy desk as the last time I visited. Once again, he was staring into the barrel of an open shotgun.

There was no one else in the office. I leaned on the counter and waited quietly. He must have sensed it; the

115

rustle of skirt, the smell of perfume – uncommon enough in that room, I assume. But several moments passed before he spoke. He said, with his eye still stuck down the gun barrel. 'It's you is it, Dora? Come to speak up for your little friend?'

I said, 'She's wondering where you are. I told her not to bother with you, but she won't listen.'

He gave a small snort.

'It's a good thing she didn't come herself,' he said, snapping the gun shut, and looking across at me at last. Sandy hair, those startling blue eyes, and a mouth that seemed to be constantly battling not to chortle at an unspoken, private joke. He was tall and well built and handsome, by anyone's standards. He didn't do much for me, but to a young woman who had spent her life in church groups and libraries, in the company of gentlemen who could only talk about automobiles, he must have seemed irresistible.

'She did come and see you herself. As I dare say you know perfectly well. She said you saw her. And that you looked so sternly at her, she lost her nerve. And then you didn't come after her.'

He glanced around the room, checking we were still alone. 'Yes. Well … Tell her sorry, will you? Of course I saw her. Only she mustn't come by here any more. I told her that. It's not helpful. If she wants to help—'

'She wants to see you,' I said. 'That's what she wants.'

'And I want to see her,' he said. 'Very much.'

'Good. She'll be happy to hear it.'

He looked at me frankly, surprising himself, I think, by what he was about to say. 'I missed her, Dora.'

'She'll be happy to hear that, too. Why don't you tell yourself?'

'She mustn't come round here any more,' he said again.

'So you keep saying.'

'Tell her ...' He stopped. 'Tell her I miss her. That I want to see her. And that I may have a job for her, if she wants one.'

'What kind of a job?'

'None of your business, my friend,' he said.

'All right,' I said. 'Maybe it isn't. But you can tell me this at least. How's she going to meet with you or do any kind of job for you if she can't come round here to find you? She's got to meet up with you someplace, and I don't think you'll be terribly welcome at her aunt's place.'

He didn't respond.

'Lawrence?'

'Hush up a second, won't you?' he said. 'I'm thinking ... What's the name of that old dram shop – the queer one, up by the Avenue?'

'Crazy Annie's.' I laughed. 'Is it the best you can do? I've never even been inside, have you?'

'Tell her I'll meet her there.'

She was waiting for me at a tearoom a couple of blocks away. When I turned into the street, she was standing at the door, peering out, in search of me.

'He has a task for me?' she cried. 'What can it possibly be? I'll do anything – *for the cause*,' she added quickly, and giggled. 'No, but I mean it. Honestly. I care so much about the miners now. You know that, don't you?' She kissed me on the cheek and dashed away.

12

I spotted her a day or so later, speeding through the streets behind the wheel of her automobile, bright silk scarf flowing behind her. She waved, almost running down a trio of miners in the process, but she didn't stop, which was just as well. They were singing something angry, and if she'd stopped they might well have lynched her.

Once Lawrence returned to town, I saw much less of her, and felt rather bereft. I had grown accustomed to her lovelorn presence on my couch each day. But he kept her busy (and happy) at her secret Union task.

I guessed the nature of it long before I winkled it out of her. It was too obvious. She would, of course, have made a perfect spy: dazzling in her prettiness and charm, and to anyone unaware of her link with Lawrence (which was everyone, if you didn't count Cody and me), she would seem about as far removed from being a Union sympathizer as it was possible to be. Lawrence sent her into the camps, alone, in her own automobile, with a supply of Bibles and improving stories for the young, which had been brought in from Denver for the purpose. Her instructions were to ingratiate herself with the miners' women and children. She was then to report back on families who confided a lack of sympathy with the Union, so that the Union plants employed within the company could feed back false information to their company managers, get the poor saps falsely labelled as pro-Union troublemakers and revolutionaries, and thrown off the camp. Off the camp, that is, and out of home, and job, and school, and future ... out onto the wide prairie to fend for themselves.

I didn't agree with what she was doing. It seemed to me she was meddling in something that didn't concern her, something that, with so much money and security behind her, she could never understand.

'I am ashamed, Dora,' she said to me once, lying back in her limpid pool of newborn sensuality, only killing time in my rooms until she was summoned by her lover again. 'I am ashamed,' she said, 'that I have lived beside these fine, brave, working people all my life – and until now I never once paused to see things from their side.' It was the weekend of the Miners' Conference, the streets were spattered with men shouting from soapboxes, there was a sense of sullen expectation in the air, and I was sick of the whole subject: the bitterness and self-righteousness on both sides. I was sick to death of everyone's inflexible opinions.

'But you aren't seeing it from their side,' I snapped at her. 'You're seeing it from Lawrence's side.'

She wasn't listening. 'The workers must be *forced* to unionize, Dora. Don't you see?'

'Not really, no.'

'And of course the company wants to stop them. And of the course the workers are afraid. They are terrified of the company discovering they are Union sympathizers and throwing them out onto the road—'

'Which is what the Union is doing when you report on them as non-sympathizers to Lawrence. Why can't you see it?'

'Exactly!' she said. 'Why can't *you* see? If the workers are made to understand that their livelihood isn't safe unless they agree to unionize – well then. They will unionize! And the workers will win! The trouble with you, Dora,' she added carelessly, 'is you see so many company men in your work that you're biased ...'

'I see plenty of others,' I said. 'They all come to me, Inez ... Your Union men, too. Your Union men, most of all.'

She blinked, and coloured up. I might have set her mind at rest with a harmless lie, but I was angry. I didn't feel inclined.

'Well,' she said. 'You may see "plenty of others". I'm sure you do. And don't bother to blame *me* for that. I tried my best for you ...'

'I'm not blaming you,' I laughed. 'Why would I blame you?'

'Oh, but never mind that,' she hurried on. 'Only I *know* you entertain more of management than of workers here. Of course you do. Don't tell me those pathetic little Greek miners—'

'Not so pathetic, really. When you get to know them. Far from it, actually. But you are terribly patronizing, Inez.'

'Don't tell me they get their toes inside that ballroom very often. Not on their wages, and with children and wives and parents back in Europe and goodness knows what else to support. Don't tell me they can afford you. Because they can't.'

'You'll be amazed what a man can afford, Inez, if he wants it badly enough. Even though his wife and children go hungry.'

'No! They are not like that!' she cried. 'And in any case, even if they were, which they are *not*, you should turn them away. Send them back to their families. You shouldn't take their money.'

'Thank you,' I said. And I stood up. 'I'll bear your advice in mind. But now, Inez, I have things to do.'

'What, this very minute?' she was affronted. 'But it's

not even noon! You never start work before noon – I know it. You're angry with me!'

'Well, yes I am. A little,' I replied. (A 'little' being a lie.) 'I also have things to do.'

But she stayed where she was. 'Please, darling Dora. Don't be angry. I am telling you what I think ... because I have woken up at last! Don't you see? Isn't that something to celebrate? I have lived side by side with this terrible injustice all these years. And all I saw was the grime on their skin, and their dirty boots and their grisly, angry little faces – the women, too – cluttering up my beautiful town ... And now,' she said triumphantly, 'I see them as people! Does it sound too absurd?'

I didn't bother to answer.

'And Dora, I am trying to see what their lives must be like. And I am determined to help them.'

'You're seeing it from Lawrence's point of view. Because he turns you into a quivering idiot, Inez. Who can think of nothing but the fire that's burning in her twat.'

'Oh! You're revolting! Why won't you listen to me?'

'I have listened enough for today. And now I have an appointment at the surgery. If you would like to know, if you would like to see life from *my* point of view, I need to renew my certificate of clean health. It costs me a fortune each month. And of course I must pay the doctor well over the odds because without his certificate,

I cannot work. So please. Enough. For today. No more lectures from you. I think what you're doing for Lawrence is about as wrong as wrong can be.'

'As wrong as taking money from a man who should be spending it on his wife and children?'

I hesitated. Smiled. 'About the same, my friend. But needs must. It's not something you would understand.'

She left my little parlour then. She yanked her childlike body from the sea of green silk cushions, and swept out of the door, muttering something inaudible, uncertain, and I think – I know, because I saw the damp on her cheeks – that she was crying.

I never did leave the house that afternoon, after all. Instead I hung around inside feeling overheated and miserable. It was an airless, burning hot day – one of the last of summer. All the windows in Plum Street were open and the house was filled with the noise from town: the stomping of boots, the banging of drums, the playing of pipes, and the sound of male voices singing. It grew louder as the day progressed, and by evening the prairie seemed to throb to one single chorus: *We are fighting for our Rights boys, We are fighting for our Homes, Cry the battle cry of Union! Cry the battle cry of Union! We are fighting for our Homes ...*

Rumour had it that Mother Jones herself was in town: the notorious Mother Jones who could no doubt rouse a roomful of stock traders to fight for a worker revolution, if she found herself in a room with them long enough. She was an eighty-three-year-old widow, scourge of the capitalists, who toured the country rallying workers everywhere to fight. Love her or loathe her, in 1913 I don't suppose there was an adult in America without an opinion on her. And by all accounts she was staying at the Toltec this evening, and she was addressing the miners' rally tonight.

There would be fighting in town tonight. At any rate, we all thought so in Plum Street. The stuffy air seemed thick with trouble. And I, for one, had no enthusiasm for joining the fray. Instead of dragging myself through town to the surgery, I went to the ballroom, to while away the afternoon with some of the girls. Their gossip, I knew, would be a welcome distraction.

We huddled in the usual corner, on the red velvet cushions and couches beneath the empty stage, as far from Phoebe's vision and earshot as possible. The ballroom's thick curtains were drawn, to keep the hot sun out, and we lolled on our cushions, beneath the darkened chandeliers, almost hidden, we liked to think, in the half-light: smoking and drinking, talking in half-whispers. There was an unspoken understanding that the more softly we spoke, the smaller the chance of Phoebe descending, and adding to our misery by reminding us of her existence.

I had been aloof from the other girls for too long. There was, I discovered, plenty of good gossip to catch up on.

Councillor Titchfield had a secret wife in Houston, Texas. And a whole bunch of full grown kids ...

Deputy Sheriff Westbroke had been so drunk two nights previously, he'd been unable to get his cock up, which was unlike him ...

Pastor Norton had insisted on Nicola bringing her fourteen-year-old daughter Maude upstairs with her on Wednesday.

('He's a randy fucker, Pastor Norton is,' Luella said. We none of us argued with that.)

Jasmine thought Nicola had set Maude to work too young, but Chloe said Phoebe had insisted ... now that she ate like a woman, she could fuck like one too. We all agreed it was a wonder the pastor had funds enough for one girl, the number of visits he paid, but two at a turn, and one of them untouched! We wondered what price had been set.

And so the afternoon spun pleasantly by. It was a lull before the storm. Whether the men called to strike tonight, or they didn't, once Mother Jones had said her piece, their blood would be up. There would be plenty of business tonight.

But at six o'clock that same day, Inez returned to Plum Street. She didn't burst in, as she usually did. She tapped politely on the door. I had returned to my rooms to prepare for the evening's work by then, and I assumed the knock was Kitty's, telling me I was needed downstairs already. I pretended not to hear.

'Dora, it's me!' she said. 'It's Inez. I hate fighting with you. And I am sorry we disagreed.' She pushed open the door. 'Only, darling, I desperately need you this evening. Lawrence won't take me. He is too busy with all his organizing. But Mother Jones is speaking at the theatre! It's such a great event – and I daren't go on my own ...'

Somewhere in the back of my mind, I had feared that she might never talk to me again; might never come to cheer me and divert me, in these airless rooms. For a moment, my relief at hearing her voice seemed to stop everything. I could hardly speak.

'Please, Dora,' she said, seeing me hesitate, misreading my silence for hostility. 'I swear I'll never ask anything of you again. Only Lawrence doesn't want me to attend. He thinks I should stay home and spend the evening playing Bridge. That's what he said to me! Because he's so darned *protective*. But I'm determined to be there. I want to watch and listen and learn and I'm begging you, Dora. Please. We can disguise ourselves and sneak in at the back. Whatever you like. But we cannot miss it! *Mother Jones is speaking*! And history, Dora. *This is our history in the making.*'

I laughed happily. 'Never mind history,' I said. 'I couldn't give a fig about the history. But I guess it'll be quite a show. I'll come with you. Only afterwards I shall

127

have to return here directly. Do you understand? And of course there may well not be space in the theatre—'

'Oh, I'm convinced there'll be space!' she said. 'And if there isn't I can ask Mr Rossiter. He's the manager – and he is quite a friend of my brother Xavier's. Or he used to be, before Xavier left … They were friends at school, I'm sure of it. In any case, I am certain there will be room for us. Have you been in there? It's *vast*, Dora! It's the grandest theatre in the West. Will you really come? Thank goodness. Thank you, darling. I *hate* it when we argue. This morning when I left I was so sorry. I was quite certain you would never speak to me again.'

'So was I,' I said. 'And I am sorry too. And, by the way, I am coming with you tonight because …' I stopped, uncertain why, exactly. It was because she was impossible to refuse. 'Because I am curious,' I said. 'Because I should like to hear what the legendary Mother Jones has to say.'

Inez gurgled with delight. 'I should think you'll be out striking with the rest of us by the time she's finished.'

I didn't bother to say it, but Inez would not be striking. If they called for a strike tonight, the company would not be throwing her out of her comfortable bed. And there would still be honeycake for tea.

She tracked down her brother Xavier's old friend, Mr Rossiter, who, even in the flurry of urgency surrounding him, appeared flattered beyond sense that pretty, warm

Inez should remember him. He dislodged the wives of
two Union delegates from Pueblo so that we didn't have
to stand and, thanks to him, and the great charm of
Inez and, no doubt, of her mysterious brother Xavier,
we ended up with two of the best seats in the house, in
the front row of the middle tier. I felt the usual flutter
of nostalgia and regret as we settled into them. Theatre
halls always did that to me then. In fact they still do.
And sitting there, among that angry, unlikely, unperfumed
audience, I admit I felt a longing for my old life as strong
as any I had felt before.

The auditorium hummed with barely tethered energy
and expectation that night. Inez had vastly underestim-
ated the numbers who would turn out to hear the old
woman speak. The theatre was packed, not just with
Union delegates and miners, but with miners' wives and
miners' children. The company had peppered the place
with their spies and informers, and there were reporters
from across America come to witness the event. Every
seat in the house was filled, and in every space between
them stood another pair of feet. The crowd spilled out
beyond the theatre into the lobby beyond, and beyond
that, through double doors, thrown open onto the hot
and dusty street.

Mother Jones came onto the stage at last. She'd
arrived fresh from a tour of the minefields of Northern
Colorado – and, before that, from the picket lines of

West Virginia. Along the way she had clearly learned a trick or two in public speaking. Eighty-three years old, tiny, upright, white haired and dressed head-to-toe in black, she instantly cast a spell on us. In fact, before even opening her mouth to speak, she played a small trick to win us over. She unpinned her hat and simply threw it to the crowd. And how the audience roared!

Within moments of her beginning, my seat was shaking with their whistles and cheers; they grew louder and wilder as time drew on and she whipped the crowd to ever-increasing anger and frenzy. And it was impossible not to be moved. The tales of suffering, the low pay, the violence, the danger; I was familiar with all the stories. Nevertheless, as she spoke, I raged against the company exploiters as never before, and when she bellowed out to the packed room:

'It is Slavery or Strike! And I say *Strike*, until the last one of you drops into your graves ...'

Inez was on her feet – and so was I. We were shaking our fists in the air and chanting with the workers: *Strike! Strike! Strike!*

The people did indeed vote to strike that night. Afterwards there was a moment of absolute silence; as if at last we realized – no, *they* realized what *they* had done. The strike was set to begin in one week's time.

13

It was on our way home from the theatre, as we weaved between the crowds, that Inez announced she had persuaded her aunt to allow her to rent herself the cottage in town.

'For you to live in?' I asked her, astonished. 'You and Lawrence?'

'Certainly not!' she replied.

I laughed. 'Well what else would it be for?'

But she wasn't amused. 'It really surprises me, Dora,' she said, 'and so soon after you have heard that incredible little woman, that your mind should descend to such levels. As it happens, I want a place of my own because, as I said to my aunt, I am a grown woman. And the way things are looking, I shall almost certainly never marry.'

'Oh for God's sake!'

'And I can't live at home for ever.'

'Why not? It's what ladies of your class generally do, isn't it?'

'In any case,' she continued. 'It's especially infuriating because Xavier is allowed to keep his inheritance, whereas mine is under trust, so I'm forbidden from spending it without my aunt and uncle's say-so.'

'Unjust,' I agreed.

'On top of which, I hardly need to point out, there is important work to be done here in Southern Colorado. Especially now. And I am doing it, Dora. And as I said to Aunt Philippa, I need a place where I can work undisturbed.'

I asked her (it was something I had been wondering for some time) how she accounted for her busy days when her aunt asked her at dinner what she had been doing with herself since breakfast. Inez gave a little skip of pleasure at the reminder of her own, simple duplicity, a gurgle of laughter. Her self-importance evaporated.

'I've explained to her,' Inez said, 'that I am *writing a novel*! How about that? And she is such a darling. It's the last thing she wants me to be doing. She doesn't even *like* novels! She wants me to be marrying the likes of Bill Paxton. Except now it's too late, thank goodness – which funnily enough is just exactly what brought the whole thing to a head.'

'Marrying William Paxton?' I repeated stupidly.

She stopped. 'Don't tell me you *know* him?'

'Know Bill Paxton? Why, no,' I said quickly. 'Only you never mentioned him before. Is he a suitor of yours?'

'Absolutely *not*!' Inez declared. 'Though not for want of Aunt Philippa's trying. He's a widower. He owns a number of gun stores: one in Trinidad, and a few others further north. He's dull as ditch-water, Dora. But he's one of the wealthiest gentlemen in Trinidad.'

'Is he?' I muttered.

'Aunt Philippa's all tuckered up because last night she learned – what I've known for simply *ages* – that he has become engaged to marry a girl from Denver. Aunt Philippa took it terribly badly.'

'Did she? Why?'

'I don't know why it hit her *quite* so hard,' Inez replied. 'It was as if he suddenly seemed to represent –' she shrugged – 'the very last man on earth who was ever likely to marry me. Which is ridiculous. I told Lawrence about her reaction. I thought it might make him laugh, but he went quite peculiar.'

'Perhaps he thought you were proposing marriage to him?'

Inez shook her head. 'It was nothing like that. No, Lawrence *knew* him, Dora. He knew William! And I received the distinct impression ...' She stopped. 'You know, the older I get, the more I realise ... Nobody's ever quite what they seem, don't you think so?'

'Lawrence knew him? Did he say how?'

She shook her head.

'How very strange ... And do you *dislike* this Mr Paxton?' I couldn't resist asking.

She gave me a funny look. 'Not especially. I didn't especially like or dislike him, to be truthful. Even if ...'

'Even if what?'

'I'm just saying you never can be sure, in these troubled times, who is really on what side. *Pro*-Union, *Anti*-Union ... And it may be that William and I would have agreed over much more than I realized. In any case, he's found himself another wife at last,' she added. 'And in the meantime, Aunt Philippa tells me she's *longing* to read my brilliant novel! I shall have to give her something to look at some time! I shall have to *write* something ...' She glanced at me slyly. 'Perhaps I could just copy out one of your filthy French books? What do you think?'

'In French?'

Inez shrugged with utmost merriment. And once again it struck me how easily and lightly she was willing to deceive the people she loved. Could she lie to me like that, I wondered? But why would she ever need to? Could she lie to Lawrence? Without a doubt. 'French, English, Japanese. Honestly, I don't suppose Aunt Philippa would notice the difference. She doesn't read novels.'

I was meant to be back at Plum Street, ready for work, but she insisted we walk by the new cottage first.

Trinidad being a small town, it was only a handful of blocks out of my way and, in any case, I was curious.

She led me to a wood-frame little ranch bungalow on the corner of Convent and Third Street, about halfway between her aunt's house and mine; in the heart of the city. It was a pretty little place, painted rusty pink, with a wide porch out front, and gingerbread latticing running along the eves. I had walked past it often – there had been a 'For Rent' sign outside for several weeks now. And because of that, it so happened that when I had envisaged my life as a singing instructress, it was of myself living in this very house that I had allowed myself to dream.

'What do you think?' she asked, as we drew up beside it. And then, without waiting for my answer: 'Can you believe it? This is where I am going to live, Dora! Isn't it perfect? There is a parlour and a kitchen and a pantry, and a bedroom to the side and a little room for the maid – only I shan't have a maid. Not to live in. They are only delivering the keys to me tomorrow, so we can't go in, but we can peep through the windows, if you like. There is a window around the back with the shutter half ajar ...'

She must have seen something in my face. She touched my arm. 'But you can stay here with me whenever you like – you know that, don't you?' she said. 'You will always be welcome. Always, Dora.'

14

That week, Trinidad was buzzing with strangers. Union delegates, miners and company men were all in town, preparing for the great battle ahead. It meant Plum Street was buzzing too. There was a sense of excitement and self-importance in Trinidad, at least among the people involved in the strike: they talked in louder voices and made their busy presence felt in the streets. It was especially grating, set against the weariness of other townsfolk, who knew only that a winter-long miners' strike – during which angry, able-bodied men would roam the city day and night with not enough to do, and not enough to eat – spelled nothing but trouble. I disliked the mood of the town; and there was plenty of work to be had at home, so I spent more time than usual tucked away at Plum Street. Inez, meanwhile, had possession of the keys to her new little house. And so we saw little of each other. We were both occupied.

I glimpsed her a couple of times around town, however, ducking in and out of shops. I saw her through the window of Cassell's Furnishings, standing beside her aunt. She was pointing at things, frowning and laughing. She looked exorbitantly happy. I saw her again, lingering outside the Union offices on Commercial Street, her face lighting up as the Union car spun on by.

The sky was still a clear blue the day before the strike was set to begin, but there was a bitter wind, a reminder that summer was turning. In the mid-afternoon, I headed out to Jamieson's Department Store to purchase a gift for Inez's new house and as I walked I started thinking, not of the gift I might find for her, but of the year that had passed, and the winter to come. I was thinking (my mind often turned to it) about my concert at Mrs McCulloch's, and of all the ladies who had been on the point of employing me that afternoon; and of the little bungalow I might have rented. I was thinking, as we are wont, I suppose, when the year begins to turn – about the future and the past – and of where I might have stood in the world on that particular afternoon, if only things had been different.

It was a melancholy walk. Here was winter, approaching again. I felt old and tired and – increasingly nowadays – fearful for the future. Images of myself, ten or fifteen years hence, presented themselves before me: not for the first time, but more vividly than before. I saw myself walking these same streets, offering my services as only the old and hideous must: hidden in the alleyways, my own hands holding up my skirt ...

A cold breeze blew down the street, through to my bones. Might it really come that? More to the point – why wouldn't it? And then I thought of William Paxton, and the hopes I had allowed myself to pin on him, and what a fool I had been.

I was pushing through the turning doors into the central emporium of Jamieson's, my head down, trying to banish the memory of his voice muttering in the pillow above my head: 'I have bought a nice house in Denver,' ... and I walked slap into the woman. She was young, dainty and expensive, and she was standing before me, looking entirely dismayed, with a small arsenal of prettily wrapped parcels scattered at her feet. Fussing around her, bending to retrieve the shopping, was a large gentleman whose dark hair and cologne were instantly familiar to me.

'I am so sorry,' I muttered. 'I wasn't watching where I was going. Do you have everything there? I hope nothing is broken ...'

The young lady glanced at me, nodded, but said nothing. She simply stood and waited, dumb as a doorknob, until William Paxton, struggling under the shopping bags, straightened to stand beside her.

William said, 'Nothing is broken, thank you.' He gave a small bow, his eyes on a space to one side of my head. 'Good day to you,' he said and, unable to take his beloved's arm under the bulk of so much shopping, he motioned to her with his head. 'Dearest,' he said, 'come along. Your poor mother is waiting for us in the auto.' They walked away.

I wandered on through the bustling, sweet-smelling hall, past a million knick-knacks and glittering distractions. Ordinarily, the grandeur of Jamieson's – its sweeping stairs, and curving, looping mezzanines – never failed to raise my spirits. But not today. I had come to buy a present for Inez – of course – but for several moments I simply walked, not looking left or right, imagining the bride from Denver and her little face, too fearful to look at mine; her pretty shopping bags, her simple belief that William would see to everything for her; the fallen packages at her feet, the fallen woman who blocked her path to the turning door. I felt something I rarely felt for virtuous women – something, more accurately, which I forbade myself: jealousy. I hated her. Fleetingly. It was easier to hate her than to give room to my own despair, my dreadful loneliness ...

Coffee cups!

No, too dull.

A little ivory elephant? Inez would love that. Or would she? It cost more than I could afford. Perhaps

the gilt-framed looking glass would be better in any case
... I felt a tap on my shoulder, and heard a voice from
behind me, whispering my name.

'Dora?'

It was William. He glanced around him. 'I had to come
back.' A look of anguish had settled on his face, and
something else, much warmer. He missed me. 'I wanted
to say – *hello*. And to apologize. And ...'

'Don't apologize! I sent the poor girl flying!' I smiled.
He smiled. A pause.

It seemed we had nothing more to say to each other.

'Well!' I said brightly. 'The strike begins tomorrow.'

'I'm afraid so.'

'The Union has a million dollars behind it, I'm told.
It might last right through the winter.'

'A million, huh?' he said stupidly. He wasn't listening.

'So I heard ... They have tents coming in from the
strikers in West Virginia.'

'Uh-huh.'

'So I guess you made the right call. Getting out to
Denver.'

'It'll be more peaceful there.'

'It surely will,' I said.

Another pause.

He said, 'I shall miss you, Dora.'

I would miss him, too. But what was the point in
saying it? 'Well!' I said instead. 'It's an exciting new life

you'll have in Denver. Look me up, won't you? If you ever come to town. When are you leaving?'

'Next week.'

'Oh!'

'Don't want to get caught up in the mayhem. The roads are going to be hell for a few days. With the miners moving. They're setting up a big camp out at Ludlow.'

'So I heard. The tents …'

'I have to go,' he said desperately.

'Your future wife will be getting cold.' I smiled. 'Her mother, too.'

He said, 'Dora, I heard about the music club incident. At Philippa McCulloch's place.'

'I'm sorry,' I said.

'Cedric Hitchens was chortling about it. But you know Cedric—'

'I wish I could say I didn't.'

'I told him it wasn't funny … y'know?'

'Thank you.'

'I meant to say it's the talk of all the best drawing rooms in Trinidad – once the ladies retire.'

'I'm pleased to have amused you.'

He shook his head. 'It's not what I meant. I know how much you … At least – I know you told me about the singing … And hell, I don't know what I'm trying to say, Dora. But I just wanted to tell you that I haven't forgotten you. I'm a man who keeps his promises. And

I'm going to see you right, Dora. Believe me. I'll drop by Plum Street before I leave town. I swear to it ...'

I reached forward and, hidden beneath my coat, I put a hand on his arm. 'I'll look forward to seeing you, William. I thought you'd already left town without saying goodbye.'

'Oh, I'll say goodbye all right. Rest assured! I'll drop by and ... I'll leave you with something decent. Good enough to get you started in that singing school you wanted.'

He watched my response with frank, most precious tenderness, and after a moment, tipped his hat and slipped away. He left me standing, smiling like a fool in the midst of the busy crowd, the small ivory elephant grown warm and damp in my hand.

'See you soon, William,' I muttered. I'm not sure I expected him to hear, but he turned back.

'Oh, you bet you will!' he grinned.

But I never saw him again.

15

The following day the strike began. In company-owned towns across Southern Colorado, four thousand men and their families were thrown out of their homes. And on the same day, the first of the winter snow fell. It was the earliest beginning to the longest, hardest, most bitter winter anyone could remember. Added to that, the tents that were supposed to have arrived from the strike just ended in West Virginia failed to materialize, and the strikers faced a night without even canvas to protect them against the bitter prairie cold.

Inez dragged me up to the Ludlow Road in her uncle's dogcart (the automobile couldn't make it through the snow) and insisted that I witness it for myself: the workers' trek from company-owned home to Union-run campsite. Snaking up beyond the horizon, the ousted men formed a long, dark line. They walked silently between leaden sky and prairie snow, their wagons piled high with children, wives, whatever belongings – pots and pans and blankets – they had been allowed to bring along. There was no jubilation that day – no Mother Jones to goad them forwards. No voices breaking into song. They looked cold and terrified.

'Right *there*,' Inez said, her words softened from beneath her thick fur muff and coat. 'Right *there*, Dora! You see those children's faces? You see the hunger and want? It's why we have to win, Dora ...' She turned to me, and there were tears in her eyes. 'Doesn't it make your blood boil? To see the way the company treats its people? It makes me half crazy to see it. We have to win, Dora. You understand that, don't you?'

Afterwards, we travelled back the ten miles or so to Trinidad and she invited me into her new cottage for the first time. She had spent the week arranging it but had only moved in a day and a night before, and I could hardly wait to see it.

'It's just me! No maid!' she said, sliding a dainty house key into the lock. 'My second night in my very own little place ... Aunt Philippa says she will send me her girl, Rachel, during the day, until I can find a girl of my own. But Rachel leaves me the place to myself in the evenings. I can't begin to describe to you the feeling, Dora, of having a place absolutely to yourself ... *Welcome*, darling,' she cried, pushing back the door and throwing open her arms, 'to my beautiful new home!'

And I never saw a home so beautiful, either. To the right of the parlour lay Inez's bedroom, and beyond it her bathroom. A door at the back of the parlour opened onto a kitchen, onto a second, smaller room for a maid to sleep in, and a pantry.

But the front door opened directly into the parlour, which was large and yet snug simultaneously, and bathed in soft, warm light. Two identical couches of soft, pale leather (I had seen and admired them in the window of Cassell's Furnishings) stood on either side of the hearth, and between them a small ottoman and a patterned rug, soft and warm and pale. There was a wooden rocker with a large velvet cushion resting on it, and a small bookcase already half filled with Inez's books, and two identical standing lamps with matching pale green, velvet shades. There were thick green and gold brocade drapes pulled closed at the windows, and in the grate, mysteriously – since we'd been out these past five hours – a warm fire was already burning. The suffering on the Ludlow Road was a world away. On that cold night, it would have been hard to conjure a more welcoming place.

'You've made it lovely,' I sighed, closing my mind to the scenes of wretchedness only just left behind. 'And so quickly, Inez! How do you do it?'

'Isn't it sweet?' Inez laughed. 'I couldn't have managed without Aunt Philippa. She has such a talent. Oh gosh, and just look at that!' She dropped her muff on the nearest couch and held out her hands to the flames, shuffling along to make space for me beside her. 'Rachel has lit the fire! Isn't that too thoughtful? Mind, I have to be careful,' she said, dropping her voice, wrinkling her nose, 'I'm certain Rachel intends to report on me to Aunt Philippa. I shall just have to make absolutely sure I leave no clues for her to report on, that's all. You can't imagine how peaceful it is here! I can sit quietly on the couch in the evenings and read, when Lawrence isn't visiting. Which by the way he *hasn't*. Not yet. Of course he can't, with so much to do out at Ludlow. You know he is spending the night out there tonight, trying his best to make things comfortable for everyone … He is quite dedicated, Dora.'

'I should hope he is,' I said. But she wasn't really listening.

'Or if I don't like the couch, I can sit at my desk over there and do my work …' She giggled. 'My "novel". Actually, Dora, I *am* writing something. But you mustn't tell Lawrence. It's inspired from something I read in *The Masses* … *The Masses*,' she repeated, impatiently, seeing my blank expression. 'You remember? The magazine the boy Cody was reading in the Union office, yes?'

'Oh yes, of course.'

'Lawrence reads it, by the way. He says it's almost *the only thing to read*. For anyone who considers themselves in favour of change in this country of ours. So you can imagine how impressed he was when he discovered *I* read it too. And, by the way, I read an article which you absolutely must read, Dora. It's about the coal strike at Paint Creek and how wicked the other papers are, not to be reporting on it. And about how the man who wrote the article is about to be prosecuted for writing it, because the authorities simply won't put up with that sort of thing. He's terribly handsome. Not that it's important. But he is. He's the editor of *The Masses*.'

'I'll look out for it,' I said. 'Have you any liquor in the house? Or must we make do with tea?'

'Lawrence says it's the best magazine there is. So you absolutely must read it.'

'Well then I will. Shall we have a drink?'

'The magazine is terribly in favour of the strikers and the Unions, and terribly *out* of favour with the powers that rule this blessed country. My brother still sends it me. Sweetly. Well – and I'm very grateful to him for it. Bless him. You would adore him, Dora. But I swear he is the most impossible fellow. Worse than I am, Aunt Philippa says, because he *simply won't* get a wife. He's impossibly artistic. That's the difficulty.' She paused. 'Never mind Xavier. They put on a series of tableaux and absolutely filled Madison Square Garden.'

'Who did?'

'Oh, the intellectuals and the poets and these sorts. In New York. And the frightfully handsome magazine editor I was just telling you about. Max Eastman. They put on a series of tableaux.'

'A series of what?' I said.

'Little dramas. To illustrate the plight of the workers.'

I must have rolled my eyes because she stamped her foot. 'I know what you're thinking!' she said.

'Do you?' My irritation, I noted, was rising in line with my thirst. 'What am I thinking?'

'But Dora, at least *I* have been out into the company towns! *You haven't!* You think the company takes care of the men—'

'On the contrary. As you know, I think the company exploits them mercilessly.'

Once again, she wasn't listening. 'But those company towns are more like *jails* than real towns.'

'Why are you telling me this, Inez?' I asked her. 'I have lived in this town long enough. You think I don't know it?'

'No,' she said, and there were tears in her eyes. 'But I think you think *I* don't know it. You think it's all about Lawrence for me. Well it's not. Do you even know how many men have been killed in the Colorado mining camps just this last couple of years? Do you? I'll tell you!'

'How about a drink?'

'Seventy-five at the Primero mine; seventy-nine at Las Aminas; ten at the Leyden mine; seventeen at Cokedale; twelve at Hastings ... All of them blown sky-high. And you tell me there's no need of a Union?'

'I don't tell you that.' I was impressed by her new knowledge; and moved, too, by her passion. 'But you know that the company men are as convinced it's the Union men, blowing up the mines—'

'Wicked nonsense!'

'To persuade the workers of the need to unionize ...'

'And you believe them?'

I shrugged. 'I don't believe them, no. On the other hand, I don't quite *not* believe them either. Passions run so high. I think men are capable of any amount of evil when they believe themselves to be in the right, and if they are determined to win the argument ... And both sides are convinced they have God behind them.'

'But the Union *is* right! How could it not be right? You cannot disagree!'

'I don't disagree that the workers are treated abominably. Or that the miners' wives are treated even worse; or that the miners' mules—'

'Well then!' She looked uncertain. 'We can agree.'

'If you like. In any case, I don't see much point in arguing. Let's for goodness' sake open some gin – do you have any?'

'I have bourbon ...' A rueful smile. 'Lawrence brought it here as a welcome. But he's not coming tonight. Of course he isn't. He's out at Ludlow tonight.'

'So you said. Bourbon will do perfectly, Inez. Why don't you fetch us some glasses and I'll build up the fire?'

She did as I suggested; seemed to calm herself as she bustled about her American *Petit Trianon*, fetching and humming and carrying.

'Only you have to understand, Dora,' she said, returning with bottle and glasses, 'even if you think I'm just a silly rich girl – at least I'm *trying*. I may be rich – but I still have eyes! This town – this strike – it's as if, right now, Trinidad were at the centre of the world. Do you see? Here in Trinidad we are living through the very battle that could decide *everything*. That's what Lawrence says. This is the future! What happens here, matters *everywhere*. It's a war, Dora. For justice. *And we have to win!*'

'Enough, Inez!' I said. 'Everything matters. Nothing matters. What's the difference? What matters to me right now is that we sit down in front of that fire and open that bottle of bourbon.'

'So it's not about *him*. You do understand that?'

'Yes!' I cried. 'I understand that.'

'It's about justice!' she said.

We drank the bottle that night – and I slept on her couch, and ten miles up the road, Lawrence and his colleagues struggled their hardest to deal with a situation already half unravelled, as four thousand cold and angry miners, their terrified wives and hungry children, lay cowering against the bitter wind on the icy, open prairie.

It would be a week before the tents arrived from West Virginia.

16

Inez was right, it was a war. And as the weeks of the strike rolled on, it became increasingly a war played out on our once peaceful, elegant streets. Fist fights were commonplace – and, in the saloons, gun fights, too. The streets, at least, were reasonably safe during the day – and in truth we ordinary townfolk were generally left alone. The guns were rarely pointed at us. Nevertheless the sense of threat and violence was always present.

Each week came news of another death; another murdered body left in a ditch for its enemies to find ... Both sides accused the other of the same atrocities: kidnap, murder, torture. Strikers, Unionists, company spies – outsiders, almost all of them: they roamed our little streets as if they owned them. The county sheriff applied to the state governor for military help to restore a little of the old order, but nothing happened and nobody came; and the violence increased, and the snow fell, and the miners and their families shivered through the icy winter. And still, the two sides, Union and management, would not sit down to talk.

In November, within just a couple of weeks, a strike-breaker was attacked and murdered in Main Street, on his way back from visiting the dentist; the wife of another scab set off another riot when she visited town to see the midwife, ending in her death; and yet another strikebreaker, a sickly fourteen-year-old Mexican boy, was attacked as he limped along Commercial Street, on his way back from the doctor. Two strikers defied their own side to protect him, a shoot-out followed and all three died on the spot.

On both sides, the death toll and the ill temper rose. The sheriff's people pretended to be neutral but they were as violent and unruly as the worst of them. They threw anyone into jail they suspected of sympathizing with the Unions. The strikers, meanwhile, were frightened and frozen and angry, and the Union men made it their business to keep them angry. And the strikebreakers dared not show their face outside their guarded encampments for fear of murder. It was madness. The streets of Trinidad were crowded – but not with us. We townspeople might have sympathized more with one side than the other, but we kept our heads down. We learned to carry guns, and to stay home unless it was completely necessary to venture out. All except for Inez.

So it was: another day, another shoot-out. Three miles north of town, the sheriff's department arrested forty or so picketing miners. Inez was walking back from Jamieson's, on her way to see me at Plum Street to discuss a new item of clothing which she believed appropriate to her new revolutionary calling (a red felt hat – red being the Union colour of solidarity), and so happened to be on Main Street when the arrested men were frog-marched by, en route to the county jail. It was the second day in succession that arrested miners had been paraded through the streets at gunpoint.

'Even you, Dora,' she said to me afterwards, 'even *you* would have found it intolerable. For once, we all did! For once, the town stood up for itself. I wish you had been there.'

She said the whole town – all of Main Street – had paused to voice its anger. But since the strike began, the streets were mostly full of striking miners themselves. The streets were so full of the strike – the Union men, the agitators and the company guards – that often there was no space on the sidewalks for the rest of us. In any case, somebody threw a rock, and then shots were fired, and somehow Inez got herself caught up in the rout.

She burst into my room at Plum Street as I was changing into evening clothes, still wearing the dress she had torn in the ruckus. 'They arrested me!' she cried. She looked exhilarated. 'Dora! What do you think about that! I am so angry I could explode. And at the same time –' in her exhilaration she took my shoulders in her hands – 'I feel at last as if I were one of them!'

'One of whom?'

'I threw a stick at the guards as they passed by. And I swear it hit Deputy Sheriff Belcher on the hat. He turned around and he looked directly at me, Dora. And I swear he lifted his gun as if he was about to shoot me ...'

'What stopped him?' I asked.

'God knows!' she cried carelessly. 'Dora, I have just come from the police cells.'

'*What?* This afternoon?'

'Well – yes!'

'Where is Lawrence? What does he say about it?'

'Oh you *mustn't* tell him, Dora. *Promise* me you won't. He would be so mad with me he'd be fuming!'

I considered her a moment. 'Most of the folk who get dragged into that place don't see the light of day for months, Inez,' I said. 'How come you made it out so fast? Did you tell them who you were?'

'Hm?' She shook her head but didn't quite answer my question. Afterwards, I wondered (I still do) if she'd really been thrown in the cells that day, or if she was simply exaggerating the extent of her adventure. 'What's important,' she said irritably, 'is that I *threw the stick*. Look! You see how my dress is torn?' I nodded. 'And then in a few moments, there were sticks and stones flying, and the deputies were firing shots in the air ... And I suppose there were some shots from our side too. I swear I felt a bullet whistling right by my ear. And then from nowhere – that is to say, it came sweeping down from County Hall, Dora – the *Death Tank*! In our own streets, Dora! Eight Baldwin-Felts men riding the back of the vehicle, and all we could see of them were their hats, and the nozzles of their terrible machine guns, swaying at us through the crowd. I never in all my life saw anything so menacing. And to think it's happening right here, in our beloved Trinidad. How can we have come to such a dreadful pitch?'

17

And so it dragged on, the bitter winter and the bitter fight. In December, three months after the strike began (and a full four months since Captain Lippiatt was shot in the throat outside Carravalho's Drugstore) Governor Ammons of Colorado finally came to town to witness our troubles for himself – though not for long. He was so overwhelmed by angry crowds that he locked himself into his hotel bedroom and would not come out.

He returned to Denver the following morning and sent in the State Guard. That same day, hardly a yard from the spot where Inez and I watched Detectives Belcher and Belk shoot Captain Lippiatt to death, Belcher himself received a bullet to the back of his brain. He dropped dead, right there, outside the Toltec; lay in a pool of his own blood, I heard, until the sheriff's department arrived to clear up the mess ... And *still* Mr Rockerfeller and his coal company stooges would not negotiate with the Union, and still the Union forbade them from negotiating with anyone else. A stalemate. A bloodbath. A small, fat general installed at the Columbia to take charge of us all. A small, unhappy town held under martial law, brimming with self-righteousness and hate.

In the midst of this, Inez blossomed. She walked proudly through the streets, in clothing which altered subtly over the weeks, and then not subtly at all. She began to dress like the bohemian 'new women' of Greenwich Village, whose pictures she saw in the magazines, and whose Madison Square Garden tableaux she wanted to imitate. She abandoned her corsets and petticoats and encouraged me to do the same. (And perhaps I would have done if my livelihood hadn't rather depended on the wretched things.) Via catalogues, she ordered in the new-style clothes: loose-fitting skirts that flapped several inches above her ankles, and pantaloon skirts, and skirts with secret pockets, ('for carrying the sorts of things that modern ladies aren't supposed to carry,' she explained to me,) and ridiculous black felt hats that flopped over her face.

'And I am learning to smoke!' she said, some time in December. 'Lawrence thinks it's charming to see a lady who smokes. I'm finding it perfectly disgusting – but I think it *fits*. Don't you Dora? As a modern woman ...' She giggled.

'Our little fat general will have you chucked in jail. What with the smoking and that ridiculous hat of yours, he'll have you for an anarchist.'

'Oh, Dora! And he wouldn't be far wrong!' she said. I warned her to be careful.

Inez and I spent all our free days and free evenings at her small cottage, drinking Lawrence's bourbon. We talked about anything and everything. Politics, of course, was much on Inez's mind, since she had only just discovered it; and sex too – also on her mind a great deal, and on the matter of which, she was convinced, I had much wisdom to share. We discussed clothes fashions (appertaining to the modern woman) although neither of us was certain what they were. And above all, we discussed Lawrence, and *Lawrence*, and *Lawrence and his intentions*; and what would happen to *Inez and Lawrence* after the strike was over.

'It feels,' I said, 'as if this strike will never end.'

'It has to end, Dora. The Union is running out of funds. And then ...' She was stretched out on the small couch before the fire in her little cottage and opposite her, as usual, I was stretched out on the other. We had both been drinking enough bourbon to feel it coursing nicely through our veins – and the end of Inez's nose was shining. She leaned forward rather unsteadily, resting her weight on one elbow. '*And then ...*' She frowned, forgetting where the sentence had been taking her. 'In any case, it's why there has to be action, Dora. Our pockets aren't as deep as the company's. We don't stand a chance. Not unless we ...' And she stopped. Fell back on her cushion and fell silent.

'Unless we?'

'Nothing.'

It was unlike her. 'Unless we what, Inez?' I persevered. 'It sounds lousy. Whatever it is. What are you planning?'

'I said, nothing!'

'*Be careful*. I keep saying it and I know you think I'm tiresome. But Lawrence O'Neill is filling your head—'

'I fill *my own* head. Thank you, Dora. I am not simply a receptacle, for thoughts to be poured into.'

'Well I know that,' I said, unconvinced.

'As if I had no filtering system of my own.'

'I think your filtering system is contaminated. That's all. Contaminated with your desire. And I think it's dangerous. Lawrence is a good man, I dare say. On a good day. But he is dangerous. He cares too much about his cause and not enough about your welfare.'

'Meanwhile, of course, while you are dispensing all this advice, I suppose *you* have everything in your life so well worked out.'

'I didn't say that. That's not what I meant.'

But she wouldn't let it go. I had annoyed her. 'You're not happy, Dora. Anyone can see it!'

'I'm happy enough, thank you.'

'You simply let the days slip by, one after the next, and you do nothing to help yourself. You're so busy offering me advice. But what are *you* going to do ... when Phoebe throws you on the street? Which she will, you know. Eventually.'

'I'll think of something,' I said. 'I have a few years left in me yet.'

'I dare say you do. But time is slipping by. And since you have given up entirely on our previous plan – which might have worked, you know.'

'You saw what happened, Inez. It was impossible.'

'But you might at least have *tried*. You might have stuck around and not simply run away at the first, smallest hurdle. You can think I'm a fool – and by the way, I know perfectly well you do,' she said, watching me. 'I know Lawrence does too. And I am determined to prove him wrong. Both of you. But Dora, at least I am willing to fight for something. And at least I know what I shall do, if – when – Lawrence attempts to leave town after the strike ends, and if – *when* – he doesn't offer to take me with him. I'll follow him! That's what *I* shall do. But what are *you* going to do?' It was the single question I most hated, and she knew it. She looked at me and sighed. Waved her glass, splashing liquor onto her new, revolutionary skirt. 'Oh, forget it!' she said. 'I'm only being so vile because I am afraid. And I suppose we all are, really. Aren't we?'

161

We were silent, lost in our own worries.

'Sometimes this war,' she said after a while, 'and the things that Lawrence expects from me – and from himself, too, of course … I get frightened, that's all.'

'Then you should say No to him,' I said. 'It's not your battle, Inez—'

'Oh!' she cried, cutting me off, bursting back to life. 'You'll *never guess what*! Darling, silly Xavier has sent me a catalogue! He's such a naughty boy! And it has the most wonderful things in it, Dora. It's a spy catalogue. Or a police catalogue. Or heaven knows. A catalogue for detectives! Did you ever hear of such a thing?'

I asked to see it but she was already standing up, rummaging through the papers on her desk to show it to me.

'How could he ever have guessed?' she continued. 'It's the most magical little catalogue I ever set eyes on. I can't imagine where he laid hands on it, but there is invisible ink disguised as hair lotion, and little pistols and little swords disguised inside walking sticks, and hair combs with absorbent tips for poison, or something along those lines. I've gone quite mad with it! *Do Not Tell Lawrence!* It's only for fun, really. But he won't find it amusing … I have a whole box of stuff arriving soon; I have no idea what I shall do with it. And I ordered them to send the walking stick to Xavier. He'll die laughing when he sees it. Shall we open another bottle?' she sighed. 'I don't suppose Lawrence will be coming round tonight.'

18

In January, four months after her last, fateful visit, Mother Jones returned to Trinidad. The small fat general had her arrested within the hour and locked her up in a makeshift jail a mile or so out of town. The miners' wives, we were told, organized a protest march through town a day or two later. The townsfolk stayed away.

'You watch,' we girls said to one another. 'There'll be a riot. No mistake.'

A riot ensued. From my rooms at Plum Street I heard the sound of the women singing – so full of defiance; I heard the sounds of their shouts and jeers and, at one point, a most wonderful explosion of raucous laughter, and then, almost immediately after, the sound of the general, commanding his men to open fire.

I did not venture out to witness it. I wanted nothing to do with it. The thought, the sound – everything about it sickened me. I despised them all, and that's the truth. So I buried myself in a filthy French novel and waited ... for nothing. For the noise to stop.

An hour or so later I was summoned from my room by Kitty, with instructions to come downstairs at once. It was barely teatime. I was not prepared for work and found myself (as was increasingly the case) intensely irritated by the summons. I dressed quickly and carelessly. No doubt if Phoebe had seen me first she would have sent me back upstairs.

It didn't matter. When I glimpsed Lawrence standing by the fireside, it was clear that he was sober, in a state of agitation – and very much on business.

He watched me crossing the long salon, which always smelled stale and wretched to me in the daylight hours. 'Looking gorgeous as ever, Dora,' he said politely. 'Even if I got you out of bed.'

'You didn't get me out of bed,' I snapped, although he had. 'How can I help you this afternoon? I'm not working today, so—'

'You heard there's been trouble?'

'There's always trouble,' I said.

'In town. This afternoon.' His expression lifted a moment, and suddenly a smile spread across his face. He said: 'The general took a topple. He fell off his horse, Dora. Right there, in front of the women! Landed in a puddle of snow in front of everyone: his own men, in front of all the wives ...'

164

I could feel, in spite of myself, a broad grin stretching across my face. It was impossible not to be delighted by the image. General Chase – small, pompous, aggressive – was loathed by everyone, even his own side. 'I wondered what it was,' I said. 'I heard great gales of laughter from my room.'

'Good, huh?'

I nodded. 'I hope he hurt himself.'

'The women were laughing so hard,' he said, 'they couldn't see the guns pointing at them. Either that, or they didn't care. You heard the gunshot? Maybe not. It's the other side of town.'

'I heard it, yes. You too?'

'Did I hear it?' He was surprised by the question. 'Of course I heard it. Anyhow. No one was killed. So that's something. And there'll be photographs in the papers tomorrow. Men on horseback shooting into a crowd of women. Mrs Drayton – you know her?'

But I didn't tend to know many of the miners' wives. Why would I?

'She lost her ear. Sliced off with a bayonet. Someone picked it up and gave it her and I don't know what she's supposed to do with it now. Send it to the newspapers maybe? Defenceless woman ... all that ... losing her ear ...' He was muttering, more to himself than to me.

'Are you looking for Inez?' I interrupted. 'Because if you are, she's not here.'

'Hm? No, I'm not looking for Inez. No. Matter of fact, the opposite. I know just where she is. Young Cody watched her getting thrown in the back of a goddamn paddy wagon along with a bunch of others. I wanted you to go fetch her out. She's in the city jail. Stupid kid—'

'In the jail!' I cried. 'Why didn't you say?'

'I just said, didn't I?'

'But you didn't say she was marching ...'

'I told her not to.'

'Is she all right?'

'I told her to spend the day at home. But she wouldn't listen.'

'Has she been hurt?'

He didn't seem to hear. 'She's a liability to us, Dora. I wish I'd never got her involved.'

'Lawrence – she was trying to help!'

'Help *who*?' he asked. He sounded suddenly very angry. 'Not us, I assure you. She's not helping us any more. When she insists on making such a show of herself. How can I help her when she is so darned wilful? How? She won't listen to me.'

'Is she all right? Has she been hurt?'

He shrugged, too annoyed to give the question much thought. 'She's all right, or she'd be in the hospital. There's plenty of girls up there. Anyhow,' he added, 'she can't be left in the cells. It's too dangerous. I came to ask if you might fetch her out.'

'Me?' I said. 'But why? She was fighting your fight, Lawrence. And you're the one she cares for. Why can't you do it?'

'Why can't *I do it*?' he repeated. 'Well, Dora – I think that's about the dumbest question I've heard yet. Right now, she's just a silly little girl, out of her depth. We want to keep it that way. It's important we keep it that way.' He handed me a folder of dollars. 'Get her out of there – can't you? Pay them whatever it takes. Only for heck's sake, do it before she starts squealing. If they get a sniff she's with us, they'll never let her out of that place again.'

19

With his mix of surliness and familiarity, the police sergeant made it clear that he knew my line of business. As if I cared. When I gave him Inez's name, he looked down the list of the women in his charge, and couldn't find it. He twisted the paper across the counter so I could see for myself. And there it was: among the long list of foreign names, Greek and Welsh and German and Swedish, 'Miss Dora Leopaldi'. I suppressed a smile. Inez wasn't such a fool then, after all.

'I do apologize,' I said. 'She's new to our house. I confused her name with someone else entirely. That's the one. Miss Leo-whatnot. That one. God knows. It's hardly worth remembering. She won't last long with us after this.'

He took Lawrence's dollars in his meaty chop, pocketed half, slid the rest into a locked drawer by the counter, and led me through to the back of the building.

I followed him down narrow stairs and along a cold, dark corridor, to the single basement cell where the women prisoners were kept. The sound of their chatter rose up the stairway to greet us. It grew half deafening as we drew closer.

Inez sat silently among the women, bolt upright, wide eyes shining, hat and hair and clothes awry. There were fifteen or twenty women squeezed into the cell along with her, most of them deep in conversation. They paused when they heard their jailor's keys clank, looked briefly from the sergeant to me, and turned back to one another. Inez rose quickly to her feet.

'Dora!' she cried. There was a thick gash on her cheek and a smear of blood running from the gash to the collar of her shirtwaist. Her hair had been wrenched from its knot, her hat was crumpled, and her face was alive. Perhaps in the light of what happened afterwards, my memory exaggerates. But I know that when she stood and called my name (beneath the bitter blow that it was I, not Lawrence, who had come to fetch her), she shone with a wildness, an excitement at her surroundings that I might have envied, if her surroundings had been more conducive. As it was, I felt a jolt of horror. She looked half crazy with life.

'Are you all right?' I asked stupidly. 'I have come to fetch you out.'

'Have you paid my bail?' she asked. 'Or did—'

'I paid it,' I interrupted, to shut her up. (I would explain later.)

'You?' She seemed to shrink. And then, like a flower reaching out for sunlight wherever she might find it, she asked: 'But does he know I am here? Perhaps he doesn't realize—'

'I have come to fetch you out. That's all I know. I'm sorry to find you here. That's a deep cut,' I added. 'You need to clean it.'

She touched it, vaguely, and looked about her at the other women, some of whom had paused again and were watching us. 'But what about the others? What about my sisters here? I can't simply abandon them.'

Those who were nearest to her, and whose grasp of English was strong enough to understand, patted Inez on the back, not much concerned. Inez might look on them as sisters, but there was no doubt that they looked upon her as a stranger; a woman from another planet, where women didn't live out the winter under canvas tents, but slept in warm beds and woke to breakfasts served to them by maids, of hot tea and griddled toast and fresh eggs and honeycake.

'Aw now, don't you vorry about us,' one of them said, in an accent I couldn't place. 'Git going, now. Git yerself out of har vhile you can.'

Inez looked to the other women, most of whom were already half turned away. 'I want you all to know,' she said, her voice shaking, 'that when I leave this place, I am not leaving *you*, whose bravery humbles me. *You* are always in my heart. And I will fight for you. For your rights as women, and wives, and mothers ...'

The women looked at her with dead-eyed bemusement. She had forgotten, perhaps, that the majority of them didn't speak English.

'And I want you to know,' she continued, a little louder, 'what an *honour* it is—'

'Inez,' I snapped. 'Come along. Come with me.'

A couple of the women pushed her, not quite so gently. 'We shall keep up the fight!' she cried as she half tripped through the cell door. 'As Mother Jones tells us we must, so we shall. We shall fight until there is no life left in our bodies! Until Mr Rockefeller himself comes before our great Union on his knees and he surely begs us to negotiate with him!'

'Fer heck's sake,' came a weary voice from the back of that dank cell, 'git her outta here.'

We turned to the police sergeant. His gaze flicked between us, resting briefly on Inez with lazy dislike, before leading the way back up the dark corridor. Behind us, the cacophony of mother tongues returned to its earlier volume, our intrusion forgotten. Beside me, Inez limped a little. She took my arm and pulled at me to slow down. And over the noise, she whispered:

'Where is Lawrence, Dora? Why didn't he come?'

'I have come,' I said. 'Isn't that enough?'

'No!'

'Let's discuss it when you're home.'

But she only clutched my elbow, so hard that I yelped in pain and snatched my arm away. 'What in hell's the *matter* with you?' I snapped, rubbing my arm. She shook her head. 'Let's just get you home,' I said impatiently. 'You need some rest. And I have work this evening.'

'But I can't go to the cottage,' she whispered frantically. '*I can't!*'

As we waited, and the sergeant completed his paperwork, he remarked several times on his disbelief that a young woman, 'and a hooker to boot', would want to be involving herself in such matters. I waited for Inez to launch into one of her tirades but she said nothing. Her hands were shaking as she sat, waiting for permission to leave, and I wondered if the experience in the cells might, after all, have frightened her to silence at last.

But her fear seemed to intensify as we reached the street. She didn't thank me for fetching her. We scurried silently through the cold streets and, as we were passing the spot where, only hours before, anarchy had reigned, the fat general had lost his seat and poor Mrs Drayton had lost her ear, Inez stood still. There were puddles of muddied, bloodied snow at her feet, and tears were rolling down her cheeks. 'Stop!' she said, but I was cold, and frightened to be out in the town so close to dusk. Any men not at home by now would soon be drunk, if they weren't already, and feeling trigger-happy. I wanted to get back to Plum Street. I kept walking and ignored her.

'You have to *listen*,' she said. She tugged me back towards her, forcing me to halt. Her eyes darted left and right, she leaned into my ear and whispered:

'*There are guns, Dora.*'

'What? *Guns*? Where?'

'Shhh! For heaven's sake.' She sounded frantic.

I sighed. 'Honey, let's not stand here in the street. Let me take you home. Better still, let me take you to your aunt and uncle. You're in a state. I don't want to leave you alone.'

'*But you have to help me*,' she whispered vehemently. 'You have to tell Lawrence … it wasn't my fault.' She shook her head, correcting herself. 'I should never have joined the march. Is he very angry with me?'

'He's not happy.'

'Oh God!' she cried. And then, like a tragedy queen: 'It's all so *pointless*, isn't it?'

'*What* is pointless?'

'I can't go back to the cottage. Not until he's cleared it.'

'Cleared what? What are you talking about Inez?'

But she wouldn't say. She just shook her head and began to weep. 'He will be so angry with me. I know it.'

She refused to return to the cottage, refused to go to her aunt, and I could hardly leave her standing alone in the cold night. I had no choice but to take her back with me to Plum Street. She would have to hide in my little dressing room, I told her. On no account was anyone to know she was there.

And somehow, in spite of everything – her terror, her sadness, the seeping, swelling gash on her cheek, she began to giggle. 'Shall I hear you at work then?' she asked. 'I can make noises if it helps. Perhaps I can hide under your bed?' she continued to laugh, but she was half hysterical. I wanted to shake her. Knock some sense into her. She stopped laughing as abruptly as she began. 'Anyway, I can't go home,' she said, 'because I have allowed the Union to use my cellar as a storeroom.' Another stupid laugh, 'I should think there are more guns in my cellar than in the rest of Southern Colorado altogether.'

I had known she was in love. I had known she was reckless, too – and unimaginably foolish. But *this* seemed to me to be stupid beyond all comprehension. She saw the look on my face.

'But they had to use it, Dora. You know as well I do – the general's men confiscate our guns wherever they find them, and then they hand them over to the other side. How could I refuse? Well, I couldn't. That's all. And the police are bound to come now, aren't they? And Lawrence – I shan't see him for the dust. Will I …?' A feeble note of hope lingered. 'I just wanted to help him,' she said.

'*Help* him?' I laughed. 'You wanted to *fuck* him.'

She sighed. Didn't argue. 'Well, what does it matter now, anyway?'

20

We continued our journey in silence. When we arrived at Plum Street, I gave her something to clean the wound and told her to hide in my dressing room until she heard from me again. I sent a message to Phoebe that I was sick and would not be working that night, and set out in search of Lawrence.

They'd not seen him at the Union office. Nor was he at the Toltec, nor at any of the Union's preferred saloons. It seemed obvious to me that I should return via the cottage, if not to venture inside (I had no wish to be implicated in her trouble), then at least to inspect the place from afar, and take note of any activity within.

I approached it with trepidation, intending only to glance at the house as I strolled on by, preferably without even turning my head. But as drew up beside it, I noticed the front door hanging open and, in the hall, the electric lights were on. I stopped and waited, fiddled with my coat and then my hat, and then made a show of looking for something I had dropped on the sidewalk – but no one came or went. There was no sign of life inside. I couldn't bring myself to walk on by, simply leave the place with the door wide open for all to see, so – with heart in my throat and legs trembling – I walked through the front gate and up the few steps to the porch.

I could see that the door lock had been forced. The latch was hanging from a single nail. Other than that, however, the house appeared to be in order. There was ash in the hearth, and a couple of empty glasses balanced on the ottoman, but (I reasoned) they had no doubt been left there by Inez, since the house-girl only visited in the mornings.

I called out. No answer came. There had been men passing through, though, I felt certain of it – and not many moments before. I could smell them in the cold air: sweat, tobacco and a mix of colognes. It was not an unpleasant smell. I checked the bedroom, the bathroom – and finally, though I dreaded what might be lurking, I ventured, along the short dark corridor at the back of the parlour, into the scullery and kitchen.

I had never seen the cellar – was unaware, until Inez informed me there were munitions stored inside it, that the property even possessed such a thing. It didn't take me long to find it. There was a hatch on the scullery floor, with steps leading down and in their haste, whoever had been there had not paused to close it. A single electric lightbulb still burned from the ceiling. The cellar was empty. There was no sign of Lawrence. No sign of any living thing.

I switched off the light. I reattached the screw on the front lock as best I could so that the door would at least stay closed behind me, and headed home to Plum Street again.

21

Inez had removed herself from her hiding place in my dressing room and was lying limp as a doll on my bed. She looked sick: there was a waxy film about her – her cheeks and neck had taken a whitish glow against the angry red gash – and there was an oily gleam behind the eyes, detached and yet frantic. It alarmed me.

'Your cut is worse. It's swelling up.' I said. 'We should call a doctor.'

She pulled herself up, or halfway up, before the effort sent her tumbling back on the pillows again. 'Did you find him?' she asked. She had wrapped my green silk kimono around her torn clothes, and though there was a fire burning in the grate and the room was warm, her body was shaking. 'What did he say? Is he terribly angry? Oh God – you didn't tell him I told you? Please Dora, tell me you didn't tell him you knew about the cellar.'

'Honey. You need a doctor,' I said.

'*Dora, Did you tell him?*'

I shook my head. 'I didn't find him. But I went to the cottage and, whatever it is you were keeping down there, it's gone. The trap door was left open and I think someone had only just that moment left. So you're safe. It's safe. The guns are gone. You can go home whenever you're ready.'

She hardly seemed to hear me. 'But Lawrence?'

'Forget Lawrence,' I snapped. 'A man who asks to store illegal weapons in your house – in this town, at this time in our history – is no friend for you, Inez. No friend for anyone.'

'But he said ...' Her thin shoulders seemed to fold in on themselves, and she began to sob. 'Now the guns are gone, do you suppose he will ever come back?'

She cut a pitiful figure among the silks and satins of my ludicrous, opulent bed. I longed to hoist her out of it. Send her home. I needed to get back to work. But she was sick – too sick to move, and too crazy to be left on her own.

From my small parlour behind me, there came a tap on the outer, far door. I gritted my teeth. 'Give me a half-hour,' I shouted through. 'Tell Phoebe I'll be down in a half-hour.'

But it was Phoebe who was knocking. She didn't wait to be given permission to come in. The door between my bedroom and my parlour was wide open and, in my bed,

Inez languished, centre stage, perfectly framed. Phoebe – short, round, trussed and perfumed, and as beady as any woman anyone ever met – stepped through the threshold, from parlour to bedroom. Her busy eyes flicked from Inez to me and then back to Inez again and I could hear her mind rattling: *a body in the bed. Clothed. A body unknown to Phoebe. Was I cheating her of commission? Yes? No? Who was this clothed woman? Not a pro. A sick woman. With a gash on her face. Why was she lying in one of Phoebe's beds without Phoebe's permission? Was Phoebe being cheated in some way, not immediately obvious? WERE THERE DOLLARS OWED?*

I said: 'Phoebe, this is Inez. Inez, Phoebe. My friend Inez is unwell. I was just arranging—'

'She needs a doctor,' Phoebe said. 'I can see that. But you'll need to get her out of here. There's a gentleman downstairs, wants to see you ...' She eyed Inez, taking in the sickness, the torn hat, the delicate features. 'Get her out of here,' Phoebe said. 'For all I know her husband is sitting downstairs.' She turned to Inez. 'What's your name, missie? What are you doing here? What in the hell's the matter with you, Dora, inviting trouble in?'

'I was in the protest,' Inez muttered.

'What protest?' asked Phoebe, though she must have known.

'And please don't blame Dora. It's not Dora's fault I'm here. Only I wouldn't go home.'

'Well you gotta go home,' she said.

'I was looking for – tell me: do you happen to know Lawrence O'Neill?'

Phoebe blinked. The smallest of pauses. It told me that Lawrence was downstairs right now. She looked at Inez, said: 'Can't say I do.' And then, to my surprise: 'There's a maid's room lying empty up a floor. Why don't you get yourself up there, so Dora can get on with some work.' She looked at me. I felt her cold eyes, calculating her commissions, lost and gained, and I felt a chill crawling slowly along my spine. I was getting old. Worse, I was getting lazy. One day – inevitably, but perhaps sooner than I realized – my time would be called. Just then, with her eyes on me, I felt that day lurching closer. 'You can go home tomorrow,' she said to Inez. 'When you're feeling stronger.' She turned and left the room.

Inez put her head in her hands. I thought she might have apologized for the trouble she'd caused. Instead, she let out a pathetic whimper, and once again began to weep. 'She knows him, doesn't she? She probably knows where he is right now—'

'Oh, for heaven's sake!'

'What am I to do?'

I told her to do as Phoebe said. I rang for Kitty and asked her to make Inez comfortable in the unused maid's room, and finally I prepared myself for my work – with more effort than usual. Phoebe was watching. I knew it. And the strike would end eventually, and the years were rolling by.

The ballroom beyond the long salon was exceedingly busy, as it had been every night of the strike; always full of life, and light, and music, and laughter – no matter what ears had been severed from what heads just a few hours before, or what pathetic colonies of the dispossessed sat shivering under snow-covered canvas a few miles up the road. The ballroom at Plum Street floated separate, in a magical, carefree world of its own.

Phoebe, ahead of all of Trinidad's madams, had a talent for keeping the two warring factions apart. Gentlemen guests, depending on their affiliations, were guided towards one side of the room or the other, and it was our task, when we danced on the floor in the middle, to keep them so happily amused that they would forget each other altogether; and they generally did. If not, at the first sign of a disagreement, Phoebe would descend on them, a cloud of smiles and lace and perfume. She would disarm them with playful chatter. And if *that* failed, everyone knew she had no qualms about throwing them out on the street. Since the troubles began there had been only two brawls at Plum Street, both initiated by Baldwin-Felts men. It was after the second that Phoebe banned Baldwin-Felts from the house altogether.

When I came to find Lawrence, he sat at a table on the side of the room furthest from the general's men. He was alone, tapping his foot to our ragtime music and slurping his bourbon from crystal.

Lawrence O'Neill had asked to see me in private and so, with Phoebe's beady eye following, I brought him upstairs to my rooms. He was drunk, unhappy, agitated.

He lay fully clothed on the bed that poor Inez had just warmed and vacated – rather, he tumbled back onto it, bleary eyed, and asked me to lie beside him.

He pawed at me half-heartedly.

'What in hell's the matter with you?' I asked, slapping him off.

He rolled onto his back, stared at the ceiling. 'I don't know.' He sighed. 'Forgive me … I thought it was expected.'

'Are you crazy?'

'Didn't want to offend … Thought it was expected,' he said again.

'Dear *God*,' I laughed. 'You *are* crazy!'

A pause. 'Just a little oiled.' He smiled at me. 'That cockchafer friend of yours, Phoebe, wouldn't fetch you down until I ponied up some.'

'Well of course she wouldn't. What did you expect?'

'I said I only wanted to talk.'

'I'm guessing she told you she wasn't running a charity?'

He smiled faintly. 'Her exact words. Fifty bucks she took off me. My, but you're expensive.'

'Worth every cent,' I said. 'As you no doubt remember. I assume you've come to ask about Inez?'

A long pause. He looked wretched.

'She was all right, was she?' he asked at length. 'They hadn't beaten her too badly?'

I didn't want to tell him she was here in the house. After the danger he had placed her in, I didn't want to offer him any information at all. As best I could, I wanted to keep the two apart – at least until Inez was back in her senses. 'She was OK,' I answered. 'She was fine.'

He sat up, delved into a pocket for his pipe. Another silence. I watched as he lit it. He seemed to make an effort to pull himself together, but he sounded no less maudlin when he spoke again – the same question: 'So she was all right?'

'I told you.'

'You took her to her aunt's, did you?'

'I did.'

'And they were good to her? Were they? They took her in?'

'Of course they did.'

'And did she ask about me?'

'What do you think? Of course she asked about you. She couldn't understand why you hadn't come to fetch her yourself.'

'And did you explain to her –' his tone changed abruptly; he was drunker than I had ever seen him – 'how it was impossible? Did you tell her what a damn coot she's been? How she's wrecked it for us now? She's going to get herself killed. She's going to get us all killed. Did you tell her she's a damn coot, and a dangerous one, and I can't see her any more? And did you tell her she had better stay out of sight, hide out at her aunt's place for a while, if she wants to stay alive?'

'She knows you're angry.'

He leaned across to me, loomed over me, and every part of him reeked of liquor: 'Does she understand the kind of danger she is in?'

'Maybe she does,' I said, pushing him away. 'She didn't use her own name at the station. I had to look through the list to find her.'

'Is that right?' He sounded pleased; and as surprised as I was, I think.

'I don't know why you ever involved her, Lawrence.'

'I never should have,' he said, and then, clumsily, he stood up. 'I have to leave. I only wanted to be sure she was safe.'

I watched him straightening his shirt, adjusting his hat, running his fingers over his moustache; looking at me, not quite looking at me. 'I'm gonna miss her,' he said abruptly. 'Too bad, huh?' His face looked bleary with the drink and sadness. 'It's too bad.'

I imagined Inez, upstairs, pining. He was about to leave. 'Can I give her a message maybe?' I asked him. 'Anything? Just a word from you.'

'You tell her to take care of herself,' he said. He kissed his fingertips, and brushed them against the end of my nose – a strangely affectionate gesture, not intended for me, I sensed – and he closed the door gently behind him.

I didn't go to visit Inez that night. I left her to sleep. In the late morning, after I had eaten breakfast and still heard nothing from her, I ventured up the rickety back stairs to the maids' quarters, and tapped on her door. When she didn't answer, I crept in all the same. She lay still on her back, her eyes half open and her pale skin glowing with the fever. She looked terrible. It seemed unlikely she would be able to sit up in bed, let alone have the strength to leave Plum Street that day.

... Nor even the next day. Phoebe sent for a doctor ('don't imagine for one second I'm paying for it'), who administered various medicines, and was adamant that Inez should remain in the house until the fever lifted.

Two more days passed and still the fever didn't lift. Phoebe didn't want Inez in the house any more. So, finally, I did the only thing I felt I could do. I called on Philippa McCulloch.

22

She didn't recognize me, or at least she pretended not to. I suppose neither of us saw much point in rehashing past events. I told the housekeeper – who looked about ready to slam the door in my face – that I had come regarding Inez, and the old woman raced off to fetch her mistress. Within moments Mrs McCulloch had come to the front door herself.

She was sweet: worried and embarrassed in about equal measure. She showed me into the parlour, where I avoided looking at the piano, and so perhaps did she. She invited me to sit down but I declined. She asked if I would like tea. I shook my head. Finally, her manners gave way. 'Sakes alive – Miss ... Mrs—?'

'Whitworth,' I said. 'My name is Miss Whitworth.'

'What has happened to her, Miss Whitworth? I left a note for her three days ago, and another at the library

– but there's no sign of her! And my girl Rachel goes to clean there each afternoon and she says she's not laid eyes on Inez all this time – and none of her old friends has seen her – not for weeks. These past few months she's been so strange with all of us ... But you ...' She looked at me, and there was panic in her eyes: fear, suspicion, confusion and the threat of imminent tears. 'But I understood you had left town?'

'I have not left town.'

'You haven't left town,' she repeated vaguely. 'Dag-*blame* it – excuse my language, but what has become of her, Miss Whitworth? Is she in trouble? I know she has got in with a terrible crowd. And I don't mean to insult you, ma'am. Miss. Of course I don't mean to insult you but ...'

As she spoke, the door to the parlour opened and a man I had not met before slipped quietly into the room. He was in his late thirties – my age, perhaps a little younger – and the resemblance was unmissable. The same slim build, the same straw-blond hair and heavy-lidded, clear grey eyes. And yet, where Inez seemed to burn with hope and life, this man emanated sadness: an elegant, exhausted melancholy. He was rather beautiful. Just like his sister. Effeminate. He wore a pink silk pleated shirt, collarless and unbuttoned at the top; no jacket, no tie, a large beret of dark brown felt, a pair of chocolate brown silk pants, snugly tailored, and beneath them some flashy white and tan pumps.

The effect was – above all – of a man who didn't come from around here. He looked eccentric, dandy. He looked wonderful, and I took an instant shine to him. He also looked like what he was: like the sort of gentleman – how might I have worded it to Mrs McCulloch? – who would be unlikely to be paying a visit to the fallen ladies of Plum Street any time soon. Xavier was a nancy boy: as clear as the nose on my face. Or so it was to me.

Mrs McCulloch glanced at her nephew with a mixture of exasperation and relief. 'Oh Xavier – thank goodness ... This is my nephew, Mr Dubois. Xavier, this is ...She stopped, too bashful to continue. 'Well, this is ... she said again.

'I am Dora Whitworth. I am a friend of your sister. She's talked about you a great deal.'

'Has she?' He sounded pleased. He crossed the room to take my hand. 'Have you seen her? She's all right, is she? My aunt is horribly worried, and I admit I am—'

'She's quite safe,' I interrupted him, though – after three days' fever, an afternoon in jail, and who-knew-how-long harbouring munitions for the Unionists in her cellar – that might not have been the most accurate description. At once their faces relaxed, and the thought flitted through my mind: *what must it be like to be so well loved?* 'However,' I continued, 'I have come here to tell you that she is sick. And she needs you to come and fetch her. One of you – perhaps, Mr Dubois? It might be better ... She doesn't even know you are in town, so far as I am aware. She will be so happy to see you!'

'Where is she?' they asked at once.

'Where is she?' Of course they would ask, and of course I would have to tell them. Until that moment I had not quite envisaged how. 'Well, she is at my home,' I said at last. 'I have been looking after her. She has seen a doctor.'

Mrs McCulloch rested a pudgy hand on my forearm: 'We heard she had been in the cells. But there were no records. Nothing. Do you know about that? Is it possible?'

'The cells? I certainly don't see how,' I said quickly, with a little laugh. 'I have been with her all this time. I think you are mistaken.'

Mrs McCulloch looked flustered. 'Somebody said something ... It's too silly.'

'She is sick in bed, Mrs McCulloch.'

'They must have been confused,' she agreed at once. 'And thank goodness for that. So ... where has she been? Tell me, dear.' She dropped her voice to a tactful whisper. 'Is there a ... man?'

'No!' I said. 'No, no, no. There isn't a man. But you must ask her, in any case. When she is well again. For the moment she is quite sick. It's what I came here to tell you. And she can't stay where she is. My landlady has said she has to leave today.' I turned to Xavier.

He was holding a glass of whiskey, watching me with thoughtful eyes. It seemed to me that he understood. I smiled at him. 'Mr Dubois, why don't you come with me? Your aunt might prefer to wait here and prepare for her arrival?'

'Nonsense,' said Mrs McCulloch. 'Of course I want to come.' But she glanced at Xavier as if hoping to be overruled. She was nervous. As was I. The prospect of leading her through my home – past the fish-eyed stares of the other girls, through the reek of perfumes and perhaps of burning opium – made me feel quite queasy. I sent a meaningful look to Xavier.

'Perhaps it would be simpler if you stayed home, Aunt,' he said. He had a soft voice with a promise of laughter in it. 'Call the doctor. Get him to come visit her here at once. Have her room made ready. Have cook make her some honeycake. Is it still her favourite?'

'Well – you bet it is!' Mrs McCulloch grinned, on safe ground again.

'Good then. It's settled. Don't you think so, Aunt? It doesn't need a great crowd of us. And you must take care of your heart. Don't put it under unnecessary strain – didn't the doctor say so? Miss Whitworth and I will only be gone a short while. It's not far, is it?'

'Not at all.'

So we set off, he and I, armed with broth and syrup cookies from the McCullochs' kitchen, and a thousand messages and instructions. 'You can tell her from her aunt,' Mrs McCulloch said, as she followed us out through the hall, 'that she's not going back to that silly cottage again – not until I know she is well. And not until I can trust her to keep out of mischief. And Xavier, honey, I expect you to find out *exactly* what it is she's been getting herself into these past few weeks and months. Because really, if there's anyone to blame for all this, then it's surely you ...'

'How's that?' he laughed. 'Aunt Philippa, I've not been home in ten years. How can I be to blame?'

'All these dreadful periodicals you insist on sending her. They've been putting the silliest notions in her head.'

'What kind of notions?'

'Never mind, "what kind of notions"?' she said, shooing us towards the door. 'You know perfectly well, darling. And while you're quite safe, all the way out there in Hollywood, entertaining your modern notions, *we* are living with the consequences, don't you see? It's all very well, teaching your sister about "socialism". But she doesn't have the mental resources you do, Xavie darling. And if you ever bothered to put your nose out the window here in your old home town, you would understand the sort of damage that gets done in the name of Notions ... Not to mention socialism. And now here's your sister, getting herself into all sorts of trouble ...'

At the front door, Xavier took his aunt's fat little shoulders in his hands, as if to stop the flow of words. 'I promise, Aunt. I won't send her any more periodicals.'

'Well. Good,' she said, not quite mollified.

'We'll get her back here in no time,' he said. 'Just you stay here and hold onto your horses.'

23

I didn't return to the McCulloch house with Inez that day. It seemed unnecessary. Instead I waved her off from Plum Street, leaving her in Xavier's care. We had come in Inez's Model T, assuming Inez would be much too weak to walk. Xavier had parked by our back door and, after a touchingly warm reunion between them, he carried her in his arms down the stairs from the maid's bedroom and drove her home to her childhood bedroom.

He kept me abreast of her health with little notes, delivered by the errand boy, and it soon became clear that the danger was passed. After three or four days of McCulloch comfort, eating her favourite McCulloch honeycake (lighter, fluffier, sweeter than anything I ever tasted – and rather sickly for it, I always thought), and after being generally indulged and fussed over, she was strong enough to sit up in bed and hold court. I received a letter from her, this one hand-delivered by Xavier, inviting me to come and call.

'Will your aunt allow me into the house?' I asked Xavier doubtfully.

He shrugged – that beautiful, loose-limbed shrug of his. Xavier moved like a dancer, with minimal effort and maximum expression. There were times, I thought, the way he moved, when he hardly needed to speak at all. Not that it stopped him.

'Better not come when Uncle Richard is about,' he said. 'But Inez explains that in the letter, doesn't she? Come right now, if you can. I'll be standing beside you. Aunt Philippa won't dare to turn you away. Especially,' he added, 'after everything you've done for Inez.'

'Depends what you count as "everything",' I said. 'She might well hold me responsible for the lot. How much does she know, by the way? I presume – almost nothing?'

Xavier laughed. 'Well now,' he said, 'she knows you're a hooker. But everything else you told me, and whatever Inez tells me (though I never believe a word she says, and – by the way, Dora – nor should you), I have kept to myself. Have you heard from the man? Mr O'Neill? She talks about him obsessively whenever we are alone.'

'I've not heard from him since the evening it all happened. No. He may have gone to Denver or somewhere. He is often out of town. But he has told me he won't see her again. And I think he means it. Does Inez understand that?'

'I'm not terribly convinced that she does. You must tell her yourself, Dora. Will you come? I mean, will you come right now? What are you doing this minute? Please come with me if you can. Inez is so longing to see you.' It was mid-morning and I was still in my kimono breakfast gown. Xavier had snuck into my rooms, as Inez did, via the back door. I left him perched on my couch, lifting trinkets, examining and replacing them without comment, and went to get dressed.

Mrs McCulloch knew I was expected and had clearly decided that the best way to deal with such a situation was to pretend to be unaware of it. She tolerated my presence remotely – I assume because she felt she had no choice. But she did not come to greet me. I was grateful to her on both counts.

I followed Xavier to Inez's first-floor bedroom – as light and fragrant and sun-filled as expected, and I sat beside her silk-canopied bed, beneath a golden-framed looking glass and adorable oil portraits of the McCulloch spaniels, and the maid brought us lemonade and cheese sandwiches, neither of which Inez touched.

She looked thinner and even younger than usual, but the waxy-yellow complexion was gone, and she seemed calmer. She didn't ask me whether Mother Jones was still incarcerated in the San Rafael jail, or whether Mr Rockefeller and the Union had found a way to negotiate. She didn't ask if any more donations had been made to Union funds (how would I know?), or if I thought the strike would ever end. Actually she seemed quite tired of the whole subject. She only asked about Lawrence. Had I seen him? Had he left messages for her? Had he called at the cottage?

'He left me a message for you,' I told her. 'But you know that, because I told you before you left Plum Street. After all the fuss of being in jail, he said it was too dangerous for you to see each other any more. He was quite angry, if you remember.'

'What? He said that? Nonsense! When did he say it? I don't believe you, Dora.'

'Yes, you do,' I said patiently. 'You knew that was what he was going to say. The moment you were dumb enough to get yourself arrested. It's why you were in such a state when I fetched you. Well. And that's exactly what he said. He came to Plum Street while you were still very sick. He doesn't want you to see each other any more. He says it's dangerous. For you especially. And Inez,' I tapped her, 'he's right. You know it.'

She plaited the tassels on her coverlet, her fingers working faster the longer I spoke, but she said nothing, and I didn't press her for a response. We talked about the weather. Xavier had spent so many years in

California, he had forgotten, he said, about the long, harsh Colorado winters.

Once her aunt had Inez back in the house, she was – understandably, perhaps – unwilling to let her go again, and as she and her husband controlled the purse strings, Inez had no choice but to do as she was told and stay put. Her aunt decreed that she should return to living at home, at least for the time being, and that Xavier, if he wanted it, could take over the lease of the cottage. She also insisted that Inez, as soon as she was strong enough, should return to her work at the library, at least three days a week. 'The devil makes work for idle hands,' she told Inez (who reported it to me). 'And since you refuse to marry anyone, we must keep you busy, at least.'

I think, with Lawrence gone from the scene, Inez was relieved and grateful to be back in her old bedroom in any case, with maids and loving aunts and honeycake on tap. If she hadn't been, I feel sure she would have put up a better fight. But she took her aunt's ruling like a lamb, and Xavier took over the cottage.

He was uncertain how long he would be staying in Trinidad and, when I asked, he would only ever say something evasive and infuriating, like 'as long as it takes'. He claimed he needed to be out of California to catch up on his work, but I got the sense there was a lot more to his unexpected presence in Trinidad than work.

When I asked him what prevented him from writing his photo-plays in Hollywood, as he usually did (as well as producing them), he was evasive. He shrugged, in his eloquent way, made a self-deprecating comment about lack of self-discipline. But there were often times when he fell silent and was lost in his own thoughts; when his usual expression of melancholy was replaced with something much fiercer. Something seemed to fill him with dread. I thought perhaps he'd come home to recover from something: an illness or a failed romance, and I asked Inez if she knew. She said, 'Oh *Xavier*! That boy is always unhappy about something. I should think some silly girl has broken his heart again. Or they won't make one of his photo-plays into a movie. Or – I don't know! It's his artistic nature, Dora. Artistic people are always miserable. I thought I spotted Lawrence this morning, did I tell you? In the back of the Union auto. But it was travelling so fast, I couldn't make it out. Have you seen him, Dora? You would tell me, wouldn't you, if you had seen him?'

Whatever it was that was eating at Xavier, he kept it to himself.

Inez and I used to spend a lot of time in the cottage with him. He didn't seem so terribly desperate to be getting on with his writing whenever we went calling, and the three of us whiled away hours in front of that warm hearth, drinking his whiskey. God knows what we talked about – Inez, mostly, I suppose. What she was to do with the rest of her life, since 'clearly nobody wants to marry me. And now Aunt Philippa won't pay me my allowance without checking on every single movement I ever make …'

'Oh, come on,' Xavier chuckled. 'You can run rings round Aunt Philippa, and you know it.'

'It's not really the point though, is it, Xavier?' she said. 'Heaven knows what trouble you get yourself into out there in Hollywood, and yet here you are, with the freedom to rent this cottage – *my* cottage – and dispense with your inheritance exactly as you fancy.'

'Not much left to dispense with,' he said. 'I've already dispensed with most.'

'Whereas *I* must have *everything* decided for me. I am *not* permitted to spend my inheritance as I would like. For example, on this beautiful cottage. Because I am a woman. And therefore not deemed to be responsible.'

'Oh baby,' said Xavier. 'It's not fair. I know it. But look at it this way. At least you've got some money left, even if you can't get your mitts onto it yet. And I'll bet you wouldn't have a bean, if you'd been given my freedom. You'd be as poor as I am … Maybe,' he added, considering her, '*even poorer* than I am. I still have a bit left.'

'Well, it's not fair,' she said.

'It's certainly not fair,' I agreed.

Xavier glanced at me and smiled, embarrassed. 'What

about you, Dora?' he said. 'You think, if you happened to come into an inheritance, you'd be able to keep a hold of it? Or do you think you'd blow it, same as I have. More or less. Same as Inez would, if she had half a chance.'

'Oh, I'd blow it!' I laughed. 'Without a doubt.'

A silence. We watched the fire, and I thought of the money I had blown; the hopes and dreams ... He said: 'Forgive me for prying. Only I've been longing to ask so long ... how did an Englishwoman like you come to be living in a place like this? In the middle of Colorado, of all places? It seems such a strange place to wind up.'

'In a brothel, in the middle of Colorado?' I said. It was what he meant.

He smiled. 'It doesn't seem the obvious choice.'

'Oh Xavier,' Inez said. 'I told you already! How can you forget already? It's the most tragic story! She was doing a show at the opera house, and her husband did a moonlight flit with the other singer. I mean – with the whole travelling show. And the other singer was Dora's best friend *and* his secret lover. Can you imagine? And they all left her behind. I *told* you—'

'No, I know about that,' he said. 'But before that?'

He asked me about how I came from England, and why and when – and I told him. I was a missionary's daughter. I came to New York with my mother and father, when I was fourteen years old. My mother died when I was twenty-one, by which time I was married

201

to the man Whitworth, who would later abandon me in Trinidad. I loved him. I loved our life together. My father wanted to return to England and I didn't, and so he left me behind and we never saw each other again.

It was all true. But I don't think they believed me.

Of course now I wonder – what might have happened if I had returned to England with my father? My husband would never have followed, and so I would have been leaving him behind. It was always out of the question. Everything that happened afterwards – his abandonment, my slow drift from musical entertainment to less musical entertainment, to Phoebe's irresistible invitation – looking back it feels as if it was all inevitable: a sour chapter or two in the story that has brought me here, to this sunny desk, this new life. I am happy. For the moment at least. And honestly, that is more than I ever expected. It is enough.

24

Inez was not happy. She talked incessantly of Lawrence, and I think – though she never admitted it to us – that she used to linger outside the Union offices on North Commercial, and sometimes even venture inside. But so far as I could tell, her dealings with Lawrence and the Union were over. She made no more trips out to the company towns (occupied now only by those non-Union scabs who refused to strike, in any case) and nor, without Lawrence, could she gain access to the strikers' makeshift encampment out at Ludlow – even if she had wanted to. She stayed in town, and dedicated her energies to the library. It needed more desks, she said. Or better lights, or more French classical literature. It always needed something, in any case. She rarely mentioned the strike, if at all. It was as if she had forgotten everything about it.

And then one day she bumped into Cody.

'You remember Cody?' she said, bursting into my room, euphoric again – like her old self. 'That sweet boy at the Union who was reading the magazine. He looked like he needed feeding. You remember him?'

Of course I did.

'Well, his mother is sick. He's working in the hardware store on Maple Street now, since the Union can't pay him full pay any longer. And he was full of news, Dora! Lawrence has been in Walsenburg these past six weeks! It's why I've not seen even the tail of his coat all this time. You see? ... Cody said – well, he said a lot of things. He's unhappy about a few things. The way the Union does things. I said to him – you have to remember what we're up against. As long as the other side is fighting dirty, *we* have to fight dirty, and he agreed with me. And I know *you* don't agree, Dora. But it's the way of the world. That's what I said to him.'

'You said that to Cody?'

'Yes, Dora. I did.

'Did he laugh at you?'

'Laugh at me? He certainly did not. What's the matter with you? He brewed me up some coffee in the back room there, and we are firm friends. I intend to call on him often, Dora. And there's nothing you or Aunt Philippa or Lawrence or anyone else can do about it. So. Anyway, I have to be careful. That's what he said ...'

'Why?'

'He says you can never be sure who to trust in this town. So much spying and double spying and God knows what – and it's true, isn't it? It's as if the whole world is gone topsy-turvy.'

'Did Cody,' I couldn't help asking, 'did he know about what went on in your cellar?'

'Gosh – no! *No!*' She looked alarmed.

'But he knows about you and Lawrence?'

'Well – yes. I guess so. He knows we were friends. Of course. But it's difficult to know ... who knows what about anything sometimes, isn't it? I get the sense Cody's a little in awe of Lawrence. He was constantly asking me things.'

'What things?'

'Nothing, really ... Or nothing *I* know anything about ... Anyway, he says I can drop in at the store whenever I like. How about that? He says he can tell me all the gossip. So we're quite friendly now. There's a new issue of *The Masses* out. He says he's going to lend it me, now that Xavier can't – or *won't*. I'm going to drop by at the store tomorrow. And *maybe* – he said *maybe* he might have a message for me from Lawrence.' She looked, for just a half-second, as if she might be about to cry. But then she stopped herself. Pasted on that sparkling smile again. 'I have to go,' she said. 'I'm late for the library. I just wanted to drop by and tell you the news ... And

Xavier wanted to know if you were free for dinner this evening. By the way, I *get a feeling*,' she added with a merry little giggle, 'that my silly brother is developing quite an unsuitable crush on you.'

I laughed. 'Unlikely,' I said.

'Yes, it's too funny,' she giggled. 'Only imagine what poor Aunt Philippa would say! I should think Uncle Richard might actually send someone out to shoot you! Promise me you won't, darling,' she said. '*Promise me* you won't encourage him. Or I shall feel absolutely terrible about having ever introduced you.'

And with that she left, still laughing.

A week or so later, at the cottage again, with Inez and me stretched out on our opposite couches, as usual, and Xavier on the rocker, and complaining about it, as usual, Inez suddenly interrupted an account of something that happened to her at the library – 'Oh! And it's too *awful*. I meant to tell you, Xavier. You'll never guess what Cody told me this afternoon ... You remember that fellow from the old days?'

'Which fellow?' Xavier said.

'Oh, you know! He was in your class, Xavie. D'you recollect? Big, tall man. Everybody adored him. Oh bother, how can I have forgotten his name, when I was only talking about him with Cody? Dora, we were discussing him just the other day because of Aunt Philippa being so upset, and I remarked that he might not have been quite the dreary old dub we thought he was and, listen here, I tell you what, he most certainly wasn't—'

'William Paxton,' I said.

'He had the gun shop – a couple in Walsenburg, and the big one in Trinidad. And—'

'William Paxton,' I said again.

'That's right! Oh Gosh. Poor, darling Bill Paxton ... Well I'm glad I didn't marry him, poor man. It's an awful thing that's happened. Dreadful!' She leaned in towards us and half whispered the words: 'Someone found out he was helping the Union.'

'Helping the Union?' said Xavier.

'He was double-dealing, Cody said. I suspected as much – didn't I say so, Dora? On account of Lawrence knowing so much about him. I mean, I think they were friends ... Well, Bill Paxton was selling arms to the general's men and then informing the Union where and when, so then they could sneak up and snatch the stuff right back again ... without paying for it. Understand? It doesn't matter anyway. He was shot. Last week, driving out of Pueblo. Ambushed in broad daylight, and shot dead in front of his little wife ... Poor man.' She shuddered. 'Who would've known it, Xavie? Dear old Bill Paxton died a hero ...'

I said nothing. Of course not. I stared at my hands until my vision blurred. I don't think the moment lasted long – but there was a silence. I spent it trying to keep my breathing even. Because: it was Bill who had been shot, and I thought of his lifeless body in a bleeding heap, with his silly wife bent over it; and I imagined him beside me in my bed; the smell of him, the feel of his warm presence; and I imagined his profile, as he lay back on my pillows, his eyes creased from thinking – from trying to say what he thought I might like to hear; and I remembered his tenderness. I thought of all those things and felt grief, pure and pure. And I remembered his promise to me when I saw him at Jamieson's Department Store, a promise now never to be fulfilled, and I felt my dreams crashing round my feet. The tears, which blurred my vision and which I would not let flow, were of grief, sorrow, self-pity, and fear for my own future. I said nothing.

'Old Bob Paxton?' muttered Xavier. I felt him looking at me. 'That's terrible.' Later he admitted he couldn't picture the man. Couldn't remember the name at all.

It must have been around that time that Lawrence paid me another visit at Plum Street. On this occasion, to save himself $50, he waited outside the door until somebody other than Phoebe passed into the building, and he gave them a message asking me to come out.

I sent a message back, telling him I wasn't available (though I was), and suggesting we meet at a tearoom on South Animas Street a couple of hours hence. It was the last place on earth a man like Lawrence O'Neill would want to spend his time, and I suppose that's why I sent him there. Sure enough, when I arrived, a good half-hour late, there he was, waiting for me, sipping tea, his felt hat resting on the table beside him. He was the only man in the room and, though he had lost weight and his thick woollen waistcoat and the collar of his shirt hung loose on him, he still looked much too large on his spindly-legged tearoom chair, as if the slightest movement might crush all the dainty furniture around him, and send cups and saucers flying.

I resented being asked to meet him. I assumed he wanted to see me for news on Inez, or so that I could pass on a message to her, and I disliked the role that seemed to have befallen me, to act as their go-between. In my opinion, it was a doomed relationship. He should never have involved Inez in his business. When he asked to use her cottage as a storehouse, he had put her life at risk to a degree that I felt, as her true friend, was unforgivable. From the hangdog expression with which he greeted me, it was obvious he knew what I thought; and perhaps even thought it himself, too.

He half stood up as I came in, made the table rock, and spilled tea into his saucer.

'For goodness' sake,' I said, 'sit down.'

We sat. I ordered tea and waited. But he seemed to have nothing to say. He looked haggard. Finally he said: 'You look tired.'

'It's been a long winter. What do you want, Lawrence?'

He shrugged his great big shoulders: like a miserable bear, I thought, and I tried not to smile. 'I just wanted to ... A friend of Inez's was killed last week. Paxton. William Paxton. You know him?'

I didn't reply. He didn't seem bothered either way.

'Cody told me she was cut up ... That's all. I just wanted to check she was all right.' He looked at me. Not a grizzly bear, perhaps, but a great big miserable puppy. 'She's all right? Safe and sound?'

'Safe and sound,' I said. 'Staying at her aunt's. I'll tell her you asked after her.'

'No. Don't. Just ... I just wanted to tell her to be careful. That's all.'

'You might have thought of that before.'

'I just want to be sure she's keeping safe.' He tapped the lacy tablecloth with an oversized hand. The table quivered. 'I miss her. That's all.' And with that, he stood up. 'Thanks for coming to see me, Dora. You're a good girl ... Take care of her, will you? Drum it in, about Paxton, won't you? Shot in the back of the head. In front of his girl, too. She needs to understand this isn't a game. Maybe – I think she should think about leaving town.'

Afterwards, I dropped by Xavier's cottage to tell him about the meeting. I found him, stretched out on the floor of the parlour, ever-present glass of whiskey at his side, and around him a grand confusion of paperwork.

'Come on in,' he said. 'Ignore the papers. They don't make any sense anyway. They'd probably be improved by a few dirty footprints.'

'What is it all?' I asked, looking down at the chaos. There were papers with columns of figures, and others, which looked like official letters, and among them all the scattered pages of what looked like a script, or a play.

He sighed. 'God only knows. I wish I did. I was trying to work out how I might ever get back to California. The climate here is getting me down, Dora. Not to mention the brutality. I finally remembered who that poor man, William Paxton, was.'

'Oh, you did?'

'I liked him, Dora. We all did. I remembered we snuck out of school a couple of times – there was quite a gang of us; we used to play stink-base down by the brewery. You know stink-base?'

I shrugged. 'Maybe it's an American game.'

'Oh, it's a great game. You all have to hide in the first place and then one of you has to chase after the ...' He sighed. 'He was a good sport in any case ... Are you busy, Dora? Shall we have a drink?'

I had come to talk to him about Lawrence, and though Xavier had never met him, he agreed at once that it would be kinder to Inez to make no mention of my tearoom encounter.

'The sooner she forgets about him, the better,' Xavier said. 'And if she's the same darling girl she always used to be, which I believe she is, then she has the memory and the soul of a gadfly, and she'll have probably forgotten him by the end of the month. And by the way, I say that with nothing but love, and a whole heap of envy. I wish I could step so lightly through this infernal life. Don't you?'

To my surprise, I blushed. 'How do you know I don't?'

He didn't reply. He took a slurp of his bourbon and lay back on his couch, the better to examine the ceiling. 'Give it a week or two. All right, maybe a month or two ... I don't suppose she'll even remember the poor fellow's name.'

'He'll remember hers,' I said. 'He looked wretched. I think he feels terrible.'

'Serves him right.'

We were talking about California when Inez joined us. He was telling me about the orange groves, and the sunshine, and the golden beaches of Santa Monica, and the big blue ocean.

'We should move out there,' Inez said. 'Don't you think? Get away from this horrible strike, which never seems to end – and start afresh. I could write my tableaux ... If there really is sun all year round, it would be impossible not to feel the inspiration. Don't you think, Xavier? Why don't I come back to California with you? We could live in Santa Monica. And I could catch fish ...'

He looked over at me. It was my turn on the rocker. 'What do you think, Dora?' he said. 'Want to come to California and catch fish?'

I smiled, because he was smiling. But I wanted to weep. What did he think? That I *wouldn't* want to go to California and catch fish in the sunshine? I said, 'Nothing I'd like to do more ... But I have to save a little money first.'

'You sure do,' said Inez.

As time passed, our late afternoons and early evenings took on a pattern. They were precious hours, before my work at Plum Street began, and before Inez was expected home at her aunt's house for dinner. I would usually arrive first, rescuing Xavier from his fruitless paper-shuffling at about 5 p.m., and Inez would appear soon afterwards; sometimes having spent the day at the library, often having stopped at Cody's hardware store for tea along the way. She kept up with news from the strike through Cody, but – just as Xavier predicted – she mentioned Lawrence less and less, and finally, not at all.

For an hour or so each day, there we would sit, the three of us, chewing the cud at Xavier's fireside, discussing nothing much at all, but discussing it happily, until the moment when the McCulloch car arrived to transport Inez to her home, and I would walk the ten minutes to mine.

Slowly the snows melted and the days lengthened, and the weather softened, and by the start of April, eight months into the strike, that long, cruel winter was just a memory. The wind blew gentle and warm off the long prairie wheatgrass, and in the grey scrubland, wildflowers burst into beautiful colour, and in the trees green leaves sprouted ... And still the strike dragged on. And the killing continued. And the little general tightened his iron grip on our little town, and filled our jails to bursting. There was not even the faintest pretence any longer that General Chase and his 'peacekeeping force' were anything more than an added security arm for the rich coal company. Picket lines were beaten back by the general's forces so that fresh workers could be brought in by train from the East; and while, just a few miles out of town, the striking miners grew hungrier, angrier, more desperate, and the Union coffers ran dry, the company's mine operators continued to pump out coal regardless.

It seems extraordinary to me, looking back, that so much could have changed in my life in so little time. But, by the start of that April, Inez and I had only known each other nine months, and yet the world without our friendship seemed unimaginable to me: ancient history. It is contradictory, and perhaps I shouldn't admit it, when there was so much violence in the air, and with poor William's murdered body still fresh in its grave, but this short period – spent by the fireside with my new friends – was the closest I had come to happiness in many years. In as long as I could remember, in fact.

And then three things happened.

1) Somebody shot young Cody as he stood behind his cashier's desk at the hardware store on Maple Street. The store's owner arrived to find Cody slumped over the counter, his thin body in a lake of blood, and the top half of his head blown off. The cash till was unopened, and full of dollars.

2) Two days later, on 20 April 1914, up at Ludlow, where the tent colony had been living out that long winter together, a day of gunfighting between striking miners, Union activists and the general's men escalated into something so appalling and so deadly it would make newspaper headlines across the world.

The camp had been evacuated in a day-long battle, and by evening the general's forces were running amok, setting fire to the abandoned tents.

They set fire to the encampment's maternity tent, where two women and eleven children were still hiding, trapped by flying bullets and apparently too sick or too frightened to leave at the same time as everyone else. The following morning, cowering in a dugout cellar beneath the tent, their bodies were discovered, burned alive.

3) Oh yes. And Inez fell in love again.

April 1933
Hollywood, California

The Ludlow Massacre, 20 April 1914. In school text-books, the event has a name: it is a piece of American history. I suppose as I sit here in the Californian sunshine almost twenty years on, it seems unimaginable that I was there, so close to the midst of such tragedy, and yet am unable to describe the horror: the sound of the screams, and the hammer of the bullets, the rising smoke and the general's men cheering as they set their torches to the empty campsite; the smell of burnt flesh as the dead children were pulled from the dugout the following morning; the weeping of the women standing by – all of it the culmination of a winter of violence and hatred.

I can't do it. I wasn't there. We townsfolk had spent a winter – a lifetime – staying away from the miners' troubles. And in truth, the tales from people who were present are so thick with hatred and so immutably partisan, it is impossible to know who to believe – or whether to believe any at all. Except, of course, for what we know. We saw with our own eyes the line of white coffins make their way down Main Street to the cemetery. At the end of it all, eleven small children were murdered.

The campsite was ten miles out of town, and in Trinidad we had become inured to its distant, brutal rattle. When the violence strayed into town, as of course it had from time to time, we kept our heads down until it strayed right back out of town again. It was not our war. We did our best to live alongside it as if it wasn't there. But when the news came of the children's deaths, there was no avoiding it any longer, no matter whose side we were on. Our streets became the warzone.
And so for ten days, anarchy ruled in Southern Colorado.

25

1914
Trinidad, Colorado

That was when Max Eastman descended. Inez's letter to him, which I will deliver at our lunch on Friday, lies in front of me as I write this. It is painful to picture the two together: the jauntiness of Max as he was on that first day, and then this ancient, bloodstained letter, written for him only a week or so later, and which I never allowed him to see.

Max arrived in town with a reporter friend named Frank Bohn, and a loud voice, and a suitcase full of pens and papers, and a lot of well-worded outrage. The rail track ran along one edge of the tent colony, or what was left of it, and Max Eastman's train passed by the carnage at Ludlow before it drew into town. The campsite was still smoking, and the dugouts beneath many of the tents were still being excavated. He told Inez afterwards that the smell of burning flesh had made his stomach heave, and I dare say it did. He looked as white as a ghost that first morning, the first I set eyes on him. He was lugging his New York luggage up North Commercial Street in search of a hotel, just as twenty or more strikers were marching by, and he seemed to cower at the sight of them. I did too, actually. Though such was their rage and grief, I am certain we were invisible to them.

Strikers were marching in haphazard units up and down throughout the town that day, shouting and firing their guns in the air. They dominated the streets and I dare say Max Eastman and his chum were terrified. I know I was. I hadn't wanted to come out, but none of the other girls was willing, and one of us had to.

Until that point, I had stayed aloof from the politics – taken great care about it, too – and I intended to return to being aloof as soon as possible. But the burning of those women and children was beyond politics. The tent colony had been set aflame, and now several thousand people were without any place to go. Nobody could live alongside that kind of suffering and remain unmoved – and still consider themselves human.

Phoebe wasn't human. But there were plenty of us at Plum Street who were. We had made a collection of food and blankets and dollar bills, and a couple of us were transporting them to the Union offices, only because (in spite of everything, it didn't matter who started shooting at whom first, or even why) the Union had systems in place to get help to the newly homeless.

It was Jasmine and me who took Phoebe's auto the short drive from Plum Street to the Union offices on North Commercial. Jasmine didn't want to come into the building, and nor would Carlos, Phoebe's man-of-all-work, so I hauled our booty to the front desk on my own.

In Cody's place at the counter that morning there stood no one at all. I felt a pang of sorrow for his missing figure and wondered, briefly, what and whose misdeeds had led to the bullet in his head – before the poor boy had even finished growing. The office was deserted. I wasn't sure what to do. I could leave the blankets and the food on the front desk, where there was already a large pile of donations, but I hesitated to do the same with our dollars. So I stood for a moment, dithering.

A shadow crossed the door behind me. I turned to see Lawrence looming.

'What's up?' he said. 'Has something happened?'

'No!' I said. 'Nothing.'

'Why are you here?'

It sounded hostile. 'Same reason anyone else is.' I indicated the mountain of donations. 'The girls got a collection of stuff together ...'

'Oh,' he said, his voice relaxing. 'I thought maybe Inez … Well, thank you. Leave it on the counter there, will you? I'll get one of the boys to sort through it.'

'Well, that's what I was going to do, but what about the cash? I didn't want to leave a bunch of loose dollars without knowing someone has them safe.'

'Cash? How much have you got there?' He held out a hand.

'Just more than three hundred bucks,' I replied, passing it over. 'Not a single cent from Phoebe …'

'Hm. What do you know?' He gave me a thin smile. 'Well, thank you, Dora,' he said, moving past me to lift the counter hatch. 'Thank you kindly. Much appreciated.' He stopped. 'Inez all right then?' he asked. 'She heard about young Cody?'

'She heard about him.'

'Bad news. She took it all right, did she?'

'She seemed to,' I said. 'It all came in together – what happened up at Ludlow yesterday, and then Cody just the day or so before … God knows.' I shrugged. I didn't know what else to say to him, because when she told us yesterday, it was almost as if she had been reporting on the weather.

'I went to Cody's hardware store this afternoon,' she'd informed us. 'Because I knew he could tell me what was going on up at Ludlow. But he wasn't there. Mr Paulin said he got killed. Shot dead right there in the store yesterday afternoon. Can you believe it? Little Cody ... I don't know, Dora. Everyone just keeps *dying*.' And she'd sighed. 'It's getting so horrid, isn't it? I'm not sure I can stand it much longer.'

After that, we'd talked about the shooting at Ludlow. We'd argued about which side had fired what shot first, and whether it even mattered ... And we didn't mention Cody again.

Lawrence watched me, as if he might learn some added secret from my face. But I had no secrets and, after a moment, he seemed to accept the fact. 'Well,' he said. 'Thank the girls, will you? For their generosity. And you tell Inez to take care.'

He disappeared into the depths of the office and I turned back to the street. I must have taken longer inside than I'd realized. Either that, or Jasmine and the driver had been too afraid to wait for more than a second. I was searching the street for a sight of the car, when I spotted Inez and Xavier striding purposefully towards me, waving.

There weren't many on the streets – that is, not many who weren't in from Ludlow, here to muster for the fight. Amid the angry male faces, hobnail boots and rugged working clothes, my two dainty friends stood out absurdly. As if to illustrate the point, there came a volley of gunshots from behind them as they drew up beside me.

'What in hell are you doing out here?' I asked over the noise. 'Are you crazy?'

'*There* you are, Dora!' Inez shouted, ignoring my question. 'Isn't it *awful*? Gosh, I was so hoping to bump into you. I knew you'd be out!'

'I only came to drop off some stuff from the girls. But I don't want to be here. I want to get home. What are you two doing, roaming the streets? You'll get yourselves killed.'

'By the way,' said Inez, ignoring my question again, 'we can't get back up to Main Street from here.' She pointed in the direction I would have headed. 'It's too dangerous, darling. Men everywhere. Do you want to come with us?'

I shook my head. 'No. Not at all. And you should go home, Inez. I don't like it out here one bit.'

'None of us likes it,' said Inez, with shining eyes. 'Xavier's been trying to drag me back home this past half-hour. But this is our city, Dora! Why should we hide away?'

'Because we don't want to get killed?' suggested Xavier. I glanced at him. Beneath the laconic manner he was livid. He couldn't abandon her, and yet he knew as well as I did what madness it was to be roaming the streets. Though the rabble ignored us now, who knew for how long, or when it might turn? The air was nil with violence and hatred. Here and there came the sound of objects thrown, raised voices, and then – from somewhere or nowhere – gunshots; there were men brazenly carrying guns. Nobody was stopping them. There was nobody *to* stop them. General Chase and his men – where were they now?

'We should go home,' I said again.

'I keep telling her,' Xavier said. 'I can't just leave her here, can I?'

I glanced at Inez, but her attention had already skittered on down the street. She was gazing through a gap in the crowd, at a handsome man I would soon discover was Max Eastman. Tall and lean – and terrified, as I have mentioned; dressed in linen suit and cravat, he and his suitcase looked even more out of place than we did.

'Oh my giddy aunt!' gasped Inez. 'Oh the blessed saints … You know who *that* is, don't you, Xavie darling?' Her eyes were round as saucers and her voice came out in a gust of wonder.

He turned to look.

'Nope,' he said. 'No idea.'

'*Yes you do!* He wrote the article, Xavier! The one about the … For heck's sake, the editor of *The Masses*! That's who has come to Trinidad to write about our troubles! Max Eastman! And if Max Eastman is here, I should think the whole world will be here next. I should think we are finally going to get the attention we deserve … He looks rather lost, don't you think?'

'Not really,' Xavier said.

'Yes, he does.'

There came a roar from the direction of Main Street – what sounded like the battle cry of at least thirty miners. It was followed by the smashing of glass and then another volley of shots – from not one but several rifles. Max Eastman and his companion stopped still, looked about them: a couple of New York intellectuals in linen suits scared out of their wits, in our frontier town. If I hadn't been so afraid myself, I might have laughed at the sight of them.

'I'm going to help him,' Inez said. '*Them*,' she corrected herself. And in a flash she was gone, marching towards them in her pantaloon skirt and red felt hat. From where I stood, thirty yards or so behind her, I could see Max Eastman spotting her approach, and the delightful transformation that came over his stance, his face – his everything – as she drew up before him.

She held onto her hat and tipped her head. He lifted his own hat and half bowed and smiled; and put a hand on a hip, and nodded encouragingly, as she pointed this way and pointed that – and in a moment, with the odd, stray, distant bullet still firing somewhere on Main Street, they were deep in conversation.

'Good God!' I said to Xavier, laughing.

'Can you believe it? In the middle of this, they are *flirting*! ... She is irrepressible,' he said. His voice was full of affection. We stood quietly, looking on in wonder, until there came yet another gunshot from the direction of Main Street, perhaps slightly closer than the last, and Xavier said, 'Can we leave her alone out here? I don't think we can.'

'If she won't come back with us, then I think we must,' I said. 'She's an adult. If she wants to get caught in the fight, that's her choice. But I'm heading home. And I think you should too ... Inez can look after herself.'

As I said it, and tried to believe it, Inez's voice rang out, shouting our names and beckoning us over. When we didn't move immediately, she tugged at Max Eastman's linen sleeve and brought him over to meet us.

'Dora, Xavier,' she babbled, 'I told you it was him and it is! This is the genius, Max Eastman. And this is ... This is Frank ...'

'Frank Bohn ...' Frank gave a half-bow as he introduced himself.

'He's another writer. And Max says there's a whole bunch of reporters and writers making their way here. What do you say about *that*? They're looking for a hotel. But *The Masses* being *The Masses*,' she said, rolling her beautiful eyes, 'sadly they don't have much cash. I suggested the Toltec but I think it's pretty much packed out with Union men. The Corinado is better, for a budget. Don't you think so? Not that I have the faintest idea *really*,' she added. And blushed.

26

That evening, Phoebe closed the Plum Street Parlour House for the first time since she'd opened it fifteen years before. She gathered us all in the ballroom at about three in the afternoon to announce her decision. Jake Trueman, our house musician, had lost two of his brothers at Ludlow (company men, both) and therefore wasn't working tonight, she explained. Added to which the small fat general, in a forlorn attempt to restore order, had imposed a curfew on the town. The saloons had been ordered closed and the strikers had taken possession of City Hall. Nobody in their right mind would be coming into Snatchville tonight.

'Besides,' Phoebe said primly, 'it's not a night for dancing. I don't believe it would be appreciated.'

She was right, of course.

Even so, the curfew was a joke. After the Ludlow burning, General Chase lost what control he'd ever had in

Trinidad. He might have ordered saloon closures until the geese flew south again. The saloons stayed open anyway.

That was the first night we all gathered at the Toltec. Inez was at the heart of it all, with Max Eastman beside her, laughing elegantly at all her sweet jokes. But it was Max Eastman who was the star of the show, as ever. And so, by association, was Inez, as she basked in his approval. Aside from Max and Inez there was Frank Bohn, the travelling companion, an activist and poet and a leading light, I learned, among the thinkers of Greenwich Village. Beside him there was Xavier and there was me, two fish out of water, gazing in. There were two lady reporters, one from a paper in New York. (I forget her name now. She managed to be simultaneously drab and dreadfully brash. I didn't take to her much.) And there was another lady named Gertrude Singer, much more lively, from a publication in Denver. There was a young Jack Reed, charming, funny – preaching revolution (dead now, of course, his famous bones buried in the Kremlin). The writer Upton Sinclair was there too, a shrivelled, sanctimonious little figure in the corner. And there were several others.

The group grew larger as the week wore on, but that first evening at the Toltec Saloon, with the shutters pulled, and only the back room open for business, there were no more than ten of us. It was the night Inez read her poem.

I caught Xavier's eye as she and Max were gazing at one another, deep in earnest discussion. The room was shrill with the noise of our visitors, each one straining louder to express their horror at the tragedy over at Ludlow – what it meant for America, and for the working man, and for the future of capitalism, and for revolution and for a new world ... Inez had a hand on Max's forearm, and they were leaning towards one another as if, any moment, they might kiss. I muttered to Xavier:

'I think her heart is mended, don't you?'

He laughed. 'Hers is,' he said quietly, beneath the hubbub. 'How about yours?'

'Mine?' I laughed. Xavier had a habit of saying things that startled me. 'Honestly, I'm not certain there's anything much of it left to mend. How about yours?' I asked.

'Ah!' he smiled. 'Mine brings me nothing but trouble.'

'Amen to that.' I wondered if I dared to ask something further, but he beat me to it.

'Was William Paxton a friend of yours, Dora?' he asked. But he didn't wait for me to reply. 'Perhaps you're not allowed to say. Even though I wouldn't tell it to a soul ... Only I saw your expression when Inez told me he had been killed. You've been kind of subdued ever since.'

'Absolutely not,' I shook my head. 'I didn't know him.'

'Right you are,' he nodded. 'I hope I didn't offend you?'

'Not at all.'

We looked away for a moment or two, pretending to attend to the opinions filling the air around us, and then we both apologized at once. We glanced back at one another and laughed.

'Well, the truth of it is yes, I did know him,' I whispered. 'I was very fond him. But you mustn't, you really mustn't ...'

'Gosh, no, Dora, of course not. Although, I can't honestly imagine who I'd tell it to, in any case. It may have escaped your notice, but I don't talk to many folk in this town. Or maybe they don't talk to me. Anyway, you and Inez are really my only friends. At least ...' He looked bashful. 'If that's not impertinent. May I count on you as a friend?'

'I should certainly say so!' I said. And I dare say it was a combination of everything – William dying, and then the shock of that poor lad, Cody, and then the tragedy that had taken place at Ludlow, and the fury on our streets, and the anarchy, and the cruelty and injustice of it all; and the sense that nothing, anywhere, was safe ... And then all these smart, clever people descending on Trinidad, telling each other, in their shrill, opinionated voices that this small town in the middle of the prairie – *our* small town in the middle of *our* prairie – was the shame of Colorado, of America, of the civilized world ... All of this played its part. But I had to leave the table, just for a moment. Because when Xavier said he counted me as a friend, it seemed that his words were the kindest ever spoken. And I did not want to weep, not in front of that crowd.

When I returned, Inez was telling everyone about her 'spying kit', which had finally been delivered to the cottage last week. 'Only look at this!' she was saying, and from the secret pocket of her pantaloon skirt, she produced a tiny, kid-leather purse. It had a silver catch, which opened onto a silk-lined pouch with space enough for a looking glass and rouge pot inside; and hidden beneath the silk-lined pouch she revealed another tiny catch.

'Look, look, *look* at this!' she cried. 'Only *please*, you must all look at this! You need this sort of thing, if you're a single girl in Trinidad. Isn't that right, Dora?'

I nodded, waiting to see what sort of thing it was we single girls might need. Tucked neatly behind the mirror, she revealed a pistol small enough to fit into the palm of a lady's hand. Inez pulled it out by its mother-of-pearl handle, and we gasped. Or most of us did. It was, after all, the smallest, prettiest, most well-disguised little gun any of us had ever laid eyes upon.

'For heck's sake, Inez,' said her brother. 'We have enough guns in this town already. Put that thing away!'

'Oh Xavier, don't be so dull.'

'Put it away!' he snapped.

'I will,' she said. 'I *will* … Only please do look! I haven't finished … I'll just bet you all think this is a tiny pot of rouge, don't you?' Beaming like a child, she held it up to the table.

'Surely not!' Max laughed. 'I'm sure a girl like you wouldn't dream of wearing any such thing! Rather, I would have said it was a tin of peppermint sweets.'

'Well,' she said. 'It isn't either of those things. It isn't even *meant* to be peppermint sweets anyway. But never mind. If you hadn't already seen my little gun, you would never have imagined, would you, that it contained ...' She opened the little tin, and there were the little gun's little bullets.

And standing right behind her, his face expressionless, was Lawrence O'Neill.

He nodded at me. Didn't look at Xavier. Ignored Inez completely. He addressed himself to Max Eastman. 'Excuse me, sir, for butting in,' he said. 'I heard you were in town ... You too, Mr Reed.' He nodded at Jack Reed, whose work was often published in *The Masses*. Lawrence looked quite shy – an expression I'd never seen in him before. He explained his connection to the Union. 'I wasn't in the office when you dropped by. I was sorry to miss you. But I understood you made it out to Ludlow ...'

'About four of us went out there,' Max Eastman nodded. 'The camp guards let us in without a fight.'

'I'll bet you didn't get much information out of them.'

'Nothing but lies,' agreed Max. 'We need to find some characters not so well primed in talking to the press. Don't we Jack?'

Jack Reed nodded sagely. 'Some honest people,' he said.

'Well, the general's men, who you will have found up there guarding the burned-up site today: they've been lying so long they can't distinguish what's truth any longer.'

'That was clear enough,' Jack said. 'They were smooth as – whatever's supposed to be smooth ... Very, very smooth. It was creepy. Are you drinking? If you're joining us, you have some catching up to do.'

Lawrence shook his head. 'Don't want to interrupt your evening. I just wanted to say – here I am. Lawrence O'Neill, at your service. I've been with the Union these past five years and if there's anything you need while you're here in Trinidad, any information, introductions – just let me know. Leave a message for me here at the Toltec. Or at the Corinado. I'm staying at the Corinado.'

'You moved?' I said.

He smiled. 'Too crowded here. Otherwise you can get me at the Union. Where are y'all staying?' And then, while they collected themselves to answer, he glanced down at Inez, whose shoulder must have felt the warmth of his body, standing so close behind her. He said: 'Miss. You should put that away. Like the gentleman says – we have enough guns in this town already.'

'Oh, you bet there are enough guns,' Inez said. 'You bet there are.' She sounded angry, but only for a second,

233

and then her lips curved into a smile and the moment was gone. Slowly, she put the little gun away. She didn't look at Lawrence. She waited until her new friends had answered his question: most were staying here at the Toltec or at the Corinado, same as him. It was only thirty or so yards further down the hill. They invited him again to sit down but again he refused. He said it had been a bad day, and they discussed that for a while, and that he was turning in, and that he hoped to see them all again in the morning. And all the while his hand rested on the back of Inez's chair, and it seemed to me that she leaned back, and it seemed as if his fingers were tangling softly with her hair. But I asked Xavier afterwards if he had noticed and he had not. He said I was probably drunker than I realized – which of course I was – and that my protective instinct, when it came to Inez, had led me to imagine things.

There was a pause while the men (and the lady reporters) chewed on whatever solemn words they had most recently agreed upon. Inez broke the silence. She leaned forward, away from Lawrence, and announced to them all: 'By the way, I have written a poem … It's about today. And yesterday. And all the terrible things that are happening. And seeing as there are some terrific poets here this evening,' she looked at Max, 'I wondered if anyone would object to my reading it? Would anyone like to hear my poem?'

At which point Lawrence smiled for the first time, and said: 'I think I will head for bed.'

And Max and Xavier and I groaned simultaneously.

But she read it anyway. With a great show of literary passion; and I watched Max Eastman bite his lip and lower his head, and try his hardest not to snicker, or wince, or howl. And when it was over, Upton Sinclair said:

'*That*, my dear, was quite possibly the worst poem I ever heard. I insist that you read it again!'

And they all cheered, and chanted, 'Again, again, again!' And Inez giggled. She honestly didn't care! As long as it was fun and everyone was smiling at her, and Max kept his hand on her elbow.

Max said: 'Inez, sweetheart, they're being odious. But it's only because they're jealous.' And then his face cracked into an almighty grin. 'Upton, you're an idiot. It's the finest poem I've read this century!'

And we ordered more liquor. And then we ordered more. And the more liquor we drank, the more remote the world outside appeared to us, and the more ludicrous and joyful Inez's poem.

For the strikers shall fight and they shall fall ...
Fight Freedom!
And they will rise
And they will call –
Fight Freedom!
'Til all
In America is fair

235

And the wind in the trees blows freedom to our streets and all
Good-Americans-take-care-and-pledge-forever-themselves-to-share ...

'Y'all wait and *see*,' she said. 'It'll catch on!'

It was growing light by the time we parted company, and for a little while the streets were quiet. Inez had sent a message home hours earlier, and informed her helpless aunt that she was staying the night with Xavier, and so the two of them set out to walk back to the cottage together. There were plans to meet up at the Toltec again the following evening.

'Will you be able to join us tomorrow?' Xavier asked.

'You better had,' said Inez. 'I've been cooking up some important plans to aid Max in his work here, and I'm certain we'll need your help.' She stopped, just for a moment. 'You look tired, darling,' she said. 'Will you be all right, walking home alone? Perhaps Xavie and I should walk you home together?'

'Of course not!' I said.

But she insisted. They both insisted.

So we walked together to Plum Street. For once, Inez stopped chattering, and it was wonderful. Peaceful. We walked together through the silent streets, lost in our own thoughts. My two good friends and I.

27

Inez was back at my door just four hours later. This time she didn't wait in my parlour for me to appear. I opened my eyes, in my own bedroom, and there she was, staring down at me, and already talking. Her clothes were changed, but she obviously hadn't slept.

'Dora, *wake up*. For crying out loud! This isn't a time to sleep. Our entire world is falling apart – right outside your window. There are entire *battalions* of revolutionaries marching up down the streets, with guns and everything. And here you are, slumbering in bed. Shall I order Kitty to bring you coffee? Drinking chocolate? Which?'

'No. Go away.'

She opened the door onto the landing and shouted down. 'Kitty! Dora needs chocolate at once! Make it two cups. And some pastries.' She returned to my bedside.

I smiled, without opening my eyes. 'Phoebe will have something to say about that,' I said. 'She told me you were never to come back here.'

'Oh. Well. Too bad. Dora, I thought I would pay a visit to poor dear Cody's mother. What do you think?'

'I think you should be staying inside your house,' I muttered. 'And lying low.'

'Nonsense, Dora. You're such a fusser! They're not interested in us. I just walked right past a bunch of them, and I might as well have been invisible ... Their fight isn't with us, darling. It's with the entire capitalist world ... Do you suppose Kitty will be long with that chocolate? I am almost *dying* of thirst.'

'I think you should leave Cody's mother well alone. If you're asking me. Which I don't suppose you are, really ... I think you should keep to your own business.'

She wasn't listening. 'Yes. I think it would be nice to go see her. She might rather like to think that Cody and I were friends. Perhaps I could make a donation of some sort. I know they're not rich. Cody's pa was a miner. Did you know that?'

'Probably could've guessed.'

'He lost both legs in a mine explosion in ... I think it was the mine at Engleville. Fifteen years ago. And not long after he went out and shot himself.'

'Inez!' I groaned. 'Please. I haven't even woken up.'

She pulled back the coverlet. 'Get *up*!' she said.

'Lazybones! I am going to see Cody's ma. He told me she lives down by the river, and I reckon if I ask a few people, someone will surely know where to find her … And I'm taking Max Eastman with me! If he's willing. Otherwise I'll probably meet up with him later. He says I can help him, gathering information and so on. Due to my local knowledge. Don't you think he's the most delightful man who ever breathed? So educated and handsome and – I adore him!' When I didn't reply immediately, she sighed, went to the window, pulled back the drapes and opened the window wide. Sunshine poured in. '*Wake up!*' she said again. 'It's a beautiful day!'

'But why,' I asked, reaching for a pillow to put over my head. 'Why must I wake up? Why have you come here to tell me all this? Can't it wait?'

'I wanted you to know how much I completely adore Max. And how completely and utterly recovered I am from … the other fellow. Ha! Can you believe? For a moment I actually forgot Lawrence's name. Well. And that just about proves it, doesn't it? I, Inez Dubois, do adore Max Eastman.'

'All right …' I said. 'I think I know it. Will you go away now?'

'He's magical though, isn't he? Imagine – to be so full of ideas and wisdom and passion, *and* to be such an elegant, handsome, charming man. *And then* to be such a fine writer and poet.'

'Have you read his poetry?'

'Of course I have.'

I laughed. The sun and fresh morning air were beginning to bring me round. 'Liar,' I said.

She ignored it. 'And he's funny and charming. And he makes me feel ... as if I were the only woman in the world he cared for! Do you think he does it to all the women? I wonder ...'

'He has a lot of charm.'

'He believes in Free Love,' she said, half bursting with pride. I think she was hoping I would ask her to tell me what it meant.

'Bad news for us hookers,' I said.

'He's married. To a sort of ... *very serious woman indeed*. But he doesn't love her and she doesn't love him. Or that is, they *do* love each other. But it's a free love ... So they can love ... freely. If it pleases.'

'Whatever works for folks. Has my breakfast arrived?'

She bustled back into my parlour and opened the door onto the landing again. '*Kitty!*' she yelled, just as Kitty appeared at the door, bearing a tray laden with steaming cups of chocolate, fruit compote, iced water and sweet pastries ... I lived in luxury at Plum Street. It was hard, sometimes, to remember quite how good I had it, living under Phoebe's roof.

Kitty laid the tray onto the table in the parlour, and finally I submitted to the irrepressible will of my uninvited

guest, and climbed out of bed. She passed me my silk
kimono and, as she did so, she said: 'You know, Dora.
There are sides to your life – that breakfast, this kimono
– which make me quite envious, and that's the truth.'

'I can't complain,' I said. But I was touched. It was a
generous thing for her to say.

'Well then?' I said, picking up my chocolate and flop-
ping onto the couch. My head ached. 'I am up. I am
awake. Now tell me why.'

She'd fought with Xavier after dropping me at Plum
Street last night. On the way back to the cottage, she'd
told him about a plan she had cooked up with Max,
and Xavier had been 'thoroughly loathsome' about it,
she said. 'Because he doesn't care, Dora. Because he is
so wrapped up in whatever it is that keeps that miserable look on his face when he thinks nobody's looking,
he can't even *see* the wickedness and the suffering that
is all around him. Innocent children were killed, Dora.'

'Yes, I heard about it.'

'Xavier doesn't seem to *realize*.'

'Of course he realizes. Just because you insist on
making a bigger noise about it, doesn't mean you feel it
any more than he does.'

She sent me a queer, irritable look and continued:
'What happened at Ludlow the day before yesterday has
tainted our city for ever,' she declared. 'Trinidad will never
be the same. And I don't even care if he disapproves. He

doesn't know anything. He doesn't even know how to make a movie as far as I can make out. Or whatever it is he's been trying to do over there in Hollywood all this time. And he can disapprove of me as much as he likes. But Dora – I have to do it. My conscience is telling me. And I need you to help me. Will you help?'

'It rather depends on what you are trying to do,' I said.

'Well, I am going to be their researcher,' she said grandly. 'Their person-on-the-ground, so to speak. The Union can provide our reporters with plenty of grieving victims, and that's essential, for a balanced argument. But what *I* can do, Dora, from my socially privileged position in Trinidad, is to provide the reporters with people on the *other side* ... Do you see?'

In a nutshell: what Max and his writer friends required – what the press always required – was villains. And if the company-hired guards and the company-funded general's army (as good as the same thing) were too worldly to fulfil that role, reporters would have to look further afield.

So Max had decided to arrange a tea party, to be made up of the gentlewomen of Trinidad most likely to provide him with the self-incriminating quotes he needed. Inez knew all the gentlewomen of Trinidad, and if she didn't already know their addresses, she could easily unearth them from library records.

'I can give him the best names, and I swear my head is *bursting* with all the dreadful ladies I could send to him – I mean only the *worst* ones, of course. Not my darling Aunt Philippa. Certainly not. In any case, she has to take care of her heart – and goodness knows ... But I can think of plenty of other ladies, and I'm sure you could too, after our music club fiasco. Weren't they ghastly? I love them dearly, of course ... In any case, Xavier's livid about it because he's a dreadful old blue-nose, isn't he? Underneath it all. But never mind him. We *desperately* need *you* Dora – to be present at the tea party with Max, and to help him, you know? Because I can't be there, of course, and you understand this town like nobody else, and you can help Max to winkle out the most dreadful remarks—'

'Was this your idea, or his?'

'What?

'That I should be present at this horrible event. Was it your idea? Or his?'

'Well it was ...' She paused to think about it. 'Why do you ask?'

'I don't know,' I said. I had finished my chocolate, and between us we had polished off the pastries. Over our empty plates I felt a sudden and violent dislike for her. I stood up. 'It's about the stupidest, nastiest idea I've heard yet, Inez, and no, I'm certainly not helping you. And, by the way, if you're inviting the women from the Ladies' Music Club, as you say you are, I would be no use at all. You forget that they have already met me. What disguise would you have suggested I use this time? Or did you envisage I simply turn up as the hooker I really am?'

She gazed at me uncomprehendingly. 'Oh, but you're not just a hooker Dora!' she said. 'You're ... better than that!'

I sighed. 'The tea party,' I said. 'Have you sent out invitations already? Is it too late for you to back out?'

'But I don't *want* to back out of it!' she snapped. 'Why would I? Those ladies deserve whatever they get! They prance about our city, thinking they are better, simply because they are fortunate enough to have been born with wealth. Max met a miner's wife yesterday who overheard two ladies – and they were actually *delighting* in what had happened at Ludlow.'

'I heard him tell us so.'

'Well?'

'Well? Honestly, I think either Max, or the miner's wife – or both – were wickedly exaggerating. And I've watched your beloved Max. He's handsome and charming as anyone I ever met. I should think he could persuade just about any woman in the world to say just about anything he wants them to. That's what I think.'

'He *is* charming,' she said, looking pleased.

'Inez, have *you* ever heard any ladies celebrating what happened at Ludlow? Can you even imagine it would be possible?'

She wouldn't look at me. 'But I bet they *would*,' she said, 'if they thought they could get away with it. I mean – you heard them at the music club. They're hardly sympathetic to the working man's cause.'

'It's not the same as celebrating mothers and children being burned alive. And you know that.'

'You'll see,' she said. But I thought there was a moment when she wavered.

'Oh, Inez, can't you stop it?' I asked her again. 'Can't you see how he is taking advantage of you?'

She stood up. 'First it's Lawrence you think is taking advantage, then it's Max. You're like my mother, Dora. And it's a bit rich. Frankly. Considering all the men who take advantage of you. Every single night.'

'They don't take advantage,' I said.

'Yes they do. On a nightly basis.'

'For which I charge.'

'I have to go.' She glanced at me, uncertain and unhappy. 'I *hate* it when we fight. And you are wrong, you know. You and Xavier are wrong. You just can't see how important it is that the world understands—'

'Understands *what*? That your neighbour, Mrs Ingleby on Third Street, whom you have known all your life, turns out to be a dreadful bigot? And that Max Eastman, because he is a charming, ambitious reporter, who will make her feel important for a minute, is going to take her idiotic chatter and twist it round and turn her into a fiend for all of right-thinking America to feed on?'

Inez seemed to watch the words flow from my mouth as if they were some strange and unpleasing curiosity: a cloud of tiny mosquitoes. It was hopeless. She couldn't hear me. She gave a sad, defensive shrug. 'You don't seem to like Max very much,' she said finally. 'Whereas he likes you *awfully* ...'

'Of course I like him. How could anyone not like him? He is funny and charming and clever. I only think we should remember why he is here in Trinidad. He is a reporter. We should never forget that.'

'All right,' she said, waving me away. 'I wish you would stop going on. I have to leave now, in any case. I have to find Cody's mama.'

'Well, good luck,' I smiled, not wanting to fight, but relieved she was leaving. 'I hope you find her.'

'She'll probably be a lot happier to see me than either you or Xavie seem to be. Is Phoebe closing up again tonight?'

'I think so, yes.'

'Well, if she does, you had better come and join us.' She looked on the edge of tears again. 'Please will you? Maybe Max can persuade you, even if I can't. And even if neither of us can make you understand, at least we can still be friends. Can't we?'

'Of course we can!' I said. We embraced each other

across the tray of pastry crumbs. But I didn't feel warm towards her, nor she to me. 'I'll see you later, no doubt.'

She had dragged me out of bed at an ungodly hour and left me high and dry, with a vile headache, and feeling slightly sick from the pastries and hot chocolate. I returned to my bed, taking a novel with me, and I must have fallen back to sleep.

When I awoke a couple of hours later, it was still too early for any sign of life at Plum Street, but I was too restless to stay in my room. I wanted company, so I decided to repay the Dubois compliment, take myself over to the cottage and – since I strongly suspected he kept the same hours as a call girl – haul the slumbering Xavier out of his bed and invite myself in for a second breakfast.

The town was subdued that early morning, and empty of women. I scurried past one group of armed miners, struggling under the bulk of looted groceries. Behind them, a store window had been smashed, and the men were making their way – quite casually – uptown, towards the City Hall. I was careful not to catch their eye. And Inez was right. In their midst I was indeed safe enough. Though our streets had become a warzone and our stores a free-for-all, I was all but invisible to them. They were fighting a war all right, but it wasn't with me.

At the door to the cottage I wavered. Perhaps he would think it odd that I had come to call on him so early – before he was even out of bed? Perhaps he would think it rather shaming that a whore should come to see him while he was still in his pyjamas? He had said he was a friend – but it didn't give me licence to barge in on him any time I fancied.

I had a hand already raised to beat on the door, but I pulled it back and was instead beating a rather shamefaced retreat when I heard the door swing open behind me.

'Where are you *going*?' he cried. 'Dora, I saw you through the window and I couldn't think of anyone in the world I wanted to see more, so I rushed to let you in. And now here you are, rushing away again. Where are you going? *Please come back!*'

He was dressed in a paisley silk wrapper, in an abominable shade of lilac, and a pair of royal blue, velvet Aladdin slippers with shiny silver bells at the toes. I laughed aloud at the sight of him, because he looked wonderful. I had been worrying about maintaining respectable appearances on his behalf, and yet here was I in grey silk skirt and shirtwaist, scuttling homeward, and there was he, shouting to the world from his doorstep in lilac silk and silver bells.

He invited me in, cleared a space on the nearest couch and disappeared into the kitchen to make coffee.

'It's a mess,' he said, reappearing with the coffee soon afterwards, his words slightly obscured by the cigarette between his lips. 'Aunt Philippa sends a girl around once a week. Or she did. But I think the poor darling has become rather horrified –' he dropped onto the couch opposite mine – 'by my Californian ways. I'm not quite certain *what it was* she found. Or didn't find. But she hasn't come back. Not for ages, now that I think about it.' He looked at me, his expression serious. 'Do you think I should do something ... Perhaps try to find a replacement? Or tidy things up? Is it unpleasant? Inez thinks it's becoming unpleasant. She may have a point.'

I looked at the pandemonium surrounding me: the ash-filled hearth, the array of empty whiskey glasses on the mantelpiece (no food remnants, thankfully; Xavier never seemed to eat), the books and papers and clothing on every surface. The entire room now resided, it seemed, under a thick film of dust ... I remember how it had looked the first time I'd seen it; so elegant and warm and snug: a little corner of heaven. 'She may indeed have a point,' I said.

A silence fell. It was absurd: I had sat in this parlour, in its different states, more times than I could count – and often, since I tended to arrive before she did in the afternoons, without Inez. But during those visits it was always understood that she was on her way, and so the comforting assumption that I visited primarily as a friend of hers could always be sustained. Now, here we were, together. He had counted me as a friend. And I had crossed town to call on him. I felt self-conscious and so, I sensed, did he.

We gazed at one another silently, he with his slim legs crossed at the knee, sleek and limber, smoking his cigarette, considering me; and me, wondering if perhaps now was the time to take up the habit myself. He made smoking look elegant, like everything he did. I fiddled with my skirt, and tried to remember why I had come.

'Oh hell,' he burst out. 'Shall we forget about coffee? Drink something a bit wetter? I know it's early, but I feel like bourbon.'

'You don't have things to attend to?' I asked. 'I mean, business matters that require ... sobriety?'

'Hardly!' he said, looking glum. 'At any rate, I'd much prefer to spend the morning getting stewed with you.'

On a normal day, there was plenty I might have been doing myself. But this week, in Trinidad, everything was in suspension. In any case, on a normal day, it being only ten in the morning, I would still be asleep in bed. I said: 'Well then. For heaven's sake, let's get stewed!'

And still, we couldn't seem to find much to say to one another. It was the one and only time, and it lasted no longer than it took to reach the bottom of our first drink. The next couple of hours slid by, bourbon on top of hot chocolate and fruit compote and sweet pastry – it seemed to settle very nicely. There was no need for a fire

– which was fortunate, since I don't suppose either of us would have spared the effort to build one. We sprawled opposite one another, just as Inez and I used to do during the long winter, when the cottage was hers; and through Xavier's tobacco-stained windows, the spring sun shone and warmed us.

We talked about Inez, mostly. After that, somehow, after we had exhausted the subject of Inez (her new love, her old love, her ability to leap from one to the next, her mistaken decisions regarding munitions stores and tea parties), I found myself telling him about William Paxton, and then, though I never intended it, describing the moment when I believed he was about to propose to me.

'A nice girl in Denver?' he laughed. Whenever Xavier laughed, his eyes watered, and by the time I had finished my story, there were tears rolling down his cheeks. 'Oh, you poor girl! He had the nerve to say that to you? *This town is too full of vice!* ... I don't know whether to laugh or cry, Dora. Do you suppose he sensed your disappointment?'

'Not for a moment,' I said, smiling. 'What do you take me for? Actually, he asked me if I didn't agree with him, about Trinidad being too full of vice these days,' I giggled, 'as he lay right there on top of me.'

'Ha!'

'But he was a good man, you know. And I was very fond of him, though I must admit, I had no idea – all that time he was helping the Union, and I had no idea.'

'I'm sorry, Dora,' he said, wiping his eyes. 'I shouldn't have laughed.'

'Yes you should,' I said. 'It was funny. I would have been offended if you hadn't.'

I told him about William's promise to settle money on me. 'And no, it wasn't the first thing that crossed my mind when Inez said he was killed. But I admit it came a damn close second.'

'I'll bet it did,' he said. He wasn't laughing then.

I shrugged. 'That's life, huh? And so here I am. Still working. What about you? What brought you home to Trinidad after all these years? What are you running away from?'

'Nothing.'

I laughed. 'Of course you are. So what is it? Money troubles? Maybe you owe somebody a ton of money? Or maybe you're in trouble with the law? Or maybe your heart is broken? Or maybe it's all three? It's got to be something, Xavier. I watch your face sometimes, when you think no one's looking. So does Inez. I swear you've got some battle raging inside your head worse than any we have going here in Trinidad.'

'You're drunk.'

'I certainly am.' I must have been too, because I persevered. I received the sense that, whatever it was that troubled him, it was on the tip of his tongue, only waiting to be expressed, as if he longed to tell someone about it.

'Why don't you tell me?' I coaxed him. 'What's eating you, Xavier? Are you going to hide out in this town forever, shuffling little sheets of paper around, drinking bourbon for breakfast? I'd be happy for the company. But ...'

He sat up a little. 'I need,' he said abruptly, 'to get back to California. That's what I need.' I waited but he didn't say any more.

'So what's stopping you?' I asked.

'Oh.' It was a low groan. 'We were on the point of shooting our first series. We raised the money. We had a beautiful Swedish girl playing Agatha. *The Adventures of Agatha*, it was called. We had outlines for the first twenty-five instalments. Twenty-five little two-reelers. We were ready to roll, Dora. It was going to be ...' He fell silent.

'So what happened?'

There followed a painful pause, so long I wasn't sure if he would ever speak.

He said: 'I'm ashamed to tell you.'

'*Me?*' I laughed. 'And after what I just told you?'

'It's far worse ...'

'In heaven's name. What is it? Did you kill someone?'

'No! *No!*'

'Did you steal from someone?'

'No! On the contrary – my business partner has stolen from me. After the wretched thing made the *Times* – it was such a scandal, and I didn't have a leg to stand on.

They named a few of us, Dora. Not all of us. My friend John Lamb. He couldn't stand the disgrace of it. He poisoned himself. Whereas I ... well, I simply ran away here back to Trinidad.'

'What kind of scandal?' I asked him. But by then, I had almost guessed. The name John Lamb stirred faint memories. I had read about him. A scandal. That's all it was. A handful of California fairies, caught up in some kind of honeytrap ... I probably wouldn't have read about it, all the way in Colorado, except for the self-poisoning. John Lamb had been an upstanding church member, businessman, family man, arrested for taking part in sex orgies. 'You were arrested?' I asked him. 'Along with John Lamb?'

He blushed a deep, deep red. '*You heard about it?*' he whispered.

'But I didn't read any mention of your name,' I said quickly. 'I'm certain of it. Or I would have remembered.'

'No. Well, the other names probably didn't go any further than the Los Angeles papers. But – you know ... that was far enough.'

'Were you sent to jail?'

'For a month. And our investors – all our investors, one by one, they heard about it, and pulled out.' He smiled and reached for another cigarette. 'No more *Adventures of Agatha*. The world will have to struggle along without. For the time being at least. I still have the photo-plays of course.' He nodded at the jumble of papers on the floor between us. 'But my Swedish Agatha is long gone. Back to Ohio, I think. The stories in the papers horrified her that much. And while I was licking my wounds in Long Beach County Jail, my partner took the business off me ...'

'I don't suppose there's *much* of that I can laugh at really, is there?' I muttered.

'Ha! You can laugh at the whole damn lot of it, so far as I can see. Except for poor John ... It was a sting, Dora. We were set up. It was a private party. Not a party for all tastes, I grant you ... And the police came bursting in and threw us in their loathsome paddy wagon. So. Maybe that was funny, actually. A paddy wagon full of screaming Marys, half undressed and completely hysterical ... terrified out of our tiny wits.' He smiled. 'And now here I am. Trying to make sense of it. I miss my life back in California. I guess I'm just waiting to feel bold enough to go back. Start all over again.'

'I'll miss you when you leave.'

'Well come with me then,' he said. He threw it out there, in just the same tone of voice he might have said, 'Want another drink?' But he looked across at me, eyebrows raised. 'What's stopping you, Dora? You could find a job – doing something ... I don't know ... Until you found something else.' He chuckled. 'Inez told me about the singing classes. But that was never going to work in a small town like this. What were you girls thinking? You would have been exposed in a week!'

'Rather faster, it turned out. And, by the way, there aren't any bits that are funny in that.'

'Oh *come on*! How can you say that? *Mrs di Leopaldi*. Sure, it's funny. It's hilarious! You could work for me. If you liked. How about it? Once I got myself back together.'

He looked as if he meant it. He did. And I felt a rush of something wonderful – hope – and I was about to say so, but there came a loud knock on the door, making both of us jump. And the moment passed.

It was Inez. Xavier let her in. She brushed past him into the room, muttering about the time it had taken him to answer. 'I just want to fetch my—'

She spotted me loafing on what had once been her couch. 'Oh!' she said. '*You're* here.'

I felt as if I'd been caught doing something I shouldn't. I sat up. 'You woke me so early, Inez,' I said. 'I didn't know what to do with myself. How was Cody's mama? Did you find her?'

'Cody's mother?' Inez looked from one to the other of us. 'I didn't speak to her,' she said. 'I didn't see her. I didn't lay eyes on her. She has left town. Apparently. Or she is in hiding somewhere, with her grief.'

'OK,' said Xavier slowly. 'So what's up?'

'Nothing is "up",' she snapped at him. 'Nothing at all. I just came by to fetch that little purse I showed you all yesterday. With the little hidden pistol. I brought it back here. I wanted to take it.' She looked around her, under seats, behind the drapes. 'I'm going with Max ... He needs someone to show him round Cokedale. I said I would and I thought ... Ah!' she said, pulling the purse from behind the cushion Xavier had been resting against all morning. 'Here it is.'

'What do you need that for?' Xavier asked her. 'You're not intending to shoot anyone, I sincerely hope.'

'If you bothered to put your nose outside your window any once in a while,' she snapped (just as her aunt had), 'you might realize it's gotten kind of dangerous out there ...'

'Thank you sweetie,' he muttered. 'I wasn't aware—'

'Anyhow, it's just a precaution. That's all it is. And, by the way, I can't hang around. Unlike you two, apparently, I have a lot to do today, and besides, Max is waiting for me. I have given him a list of ladies to come to the tea you both despise so much,' she added defiantly. 'And that slightly dreadful girl – Eunace? Iris? The reporter girl from last night ... She's delivering the invitations this afternoon.' There was a brief silence.

Suddenly Inez jumped. '*What was that?*'

We stared at her. She looked terrified.

'What was what?' I asked.

'You didn't hear it? Is someone else here? Is someone in the back?'

'No!' said Xavier. 'Of course there isn't. What in hell is eating you?'

'Nothing,' she said. 'Anyway, I have to go.' She stepped back towards the front door and then stopped, turned back to us again. 'By the way, I don't think you two should be spending so much time together,' she said.

'What Inez?' I laughed. 'Why on earth not?'

'Inez, darling,' Xavier said. 'I think you should sit down, baby. Why don't you sit down just for a bit? I'll make you a cup of coffee. Or warm milk or something maybe? Something to calm you down. I don't know what's up with you today, but you're acting even crazier than usual.'

'It's not healthy,' she said to me, as if Xavier hadn't spoken. 'That's why not. And you know it. Anyway. I'll see you both later ... I'm going to tell Max and everyone to meet up here. Xavier, would you mind? I think it's a lot more fun. I'm sick and tired of the Toltec.'

'Why? What's wrong with the Toltec suddenly?' I asked her.

'Nothing. People interrupting. I don't like it. That's all.'

'It's because you're avoiding Lawrence,' I said. 'Isn't it? Honestly – I begin to feel quite sorry for him.'

'I'm not avoiding him,' she said. 'Why would I do that? Of course I'm not avoiding Lawrence. I don't care a fig about Lawrence, I told you that. I *told* you. Why won't you listen to me? Lawrence *Who*?'

I laughed. 'Poor man.'

'I don't see why you say that,' she replied. 'He obviously doesn't give a fig for me either. After all, *he* was the one who wouldn't see me. He was the one who broke my heart.'

'Mended now though,' Xavier chipped in. 'Thank heavens.'

She rolled her eyes. 'It has absolutely nothing to do with Lawrence O'Neill. I just think it's nice, when strangers come to town, if folks show them inside their homes every once in a while. But if you won't have them here, then you won't. Seeing as this is now your house, Xavier, there's not a great deal I can do about it. Well. Then I guess it's the Toltec tonight all over again. Well.'

'*Well*, I don't think that little whirlwind of a visit did much to improve our spirits,' Xavier sighed, settling back onto the couch as his sister swept out onto the street again. 'On the subject of which, I've run out of whiskey, Dora. And if that band of East Coast degenerates is really going to be descending on the cottage this evening, perhaps I should venture out and find some … somewhere. That is, assuming all the liquor stores haven't been looted. Or shut down.'

I chuckled. 'Degenerates indeed! Distinguished band of activists, poets, editors and … so on.'

'Degenerates, every one.'

I didn't stay very long after that. The spell between us had been broken, and though I think it was on our minds, we were too bashful – both of us – now that we were on our own again, to pick up where Inez had interrupted. Had his invitation been sincere? I lacked the nerve to ask him. What would it be like, I wondered, to leave all this behind? To move to Hollywood. To take a low-paid, humble job, in the movies perhaps. And to make my own breakfast? I knew as much about movie-making as I did about anything else, for that matter. What did I know? Nothing, about anything. Except I knew how to sing. In any case, it hardly mattered. The moment was gone.

I stood up. 'Shall we venture out together? I don't hear any guns just yet. It's still quiet out there.'

'Likely it'll heat up this afternoon.'

'Seems to be the pattern,' I agreed. 'So I'll be back here about seven o'clock. Unless it's too dangerous ... Or unless Phoebe decides to open up tonight. In which case, I can only wish you the best of luck with your degenerates ...'

'I got the impression yesterday that there might be a whole lot more of them in town by today. Inez may well change her mind about bringing them back here. Or there may be simply too many, and I might just shoo them all away. Stop by the Toltec on your way over, why don't you? Fingers crossed, you might yet find us all there.'

28

That evening, and the evening after, I decided it was too dangerous to go out. Plum Street stayed closed to business. Phoebe said it was 'out of continued respect to the dead up at Ludlow'. Those were the actual words that came out of her mouth, and we girls sat, straight faced, as she uttered them. What she meant of course was: 'the lousy cocksuckers won't come out tonight. It'll cost me less to stay closed.' And I think those words were also uttered by her before our meeting was finished. Either way, it came to the same thing.

Along with most of Trinidad, we girls stayed quiet at home.

Beyond the city limit, there was unrelenting anarchy. Bands of men continued to stalk the landscape, shooting indiscriminately at passing cars. Up in the hills, the company towns had been surrounded, and the guards barricaded in: Unionists and miners, hiding out in caves and gulleys, were launching murderous attacks on the towns at night, blowing up the mines, killing mules and men and setting fire to buildings.

But in Trinidad, by that third evening, the streets seemed to be quieter. In fact, apart from the occasional sound of gunshots around City Hall, situated at the furthest end of town, it seemed – almost, with half-shut eyes and ears closed – as if we had reverted to a version of normal. Yes, guerrilla troops continued to muster on the streets (and, when necessary, to loot whatever was left in the gun and grocery stores), but the real bloodletting was out on the prairie now.

In any case, by that third night I couldn't stand to stay in any longer. Plum Street was still closed, and my cabin fever had reached such a pitch that I longed to be on the move.

It was dusk as I stepped out for the Toltec. I walked quickly, with my head down, but the damage wrought to the heart of our town since last I had ventured out was nonetheless visible here and there – broken windows and buildings pocked with bullet holes. And on closer examination, the people were altered too. Those fool-hardy few (aside from myself) who had dared to come out were a breed apart from our usual crowd. These folk talked in bossy voices and bustled about with notebooks and pens as opposed to shopping baskets. They weren't cowboys and miners, or shop girls and factory workers, slip-slopping to the nearest bar, or Christian gentlewomen (and hookers) en route to the library – but newspaper reporters. Plenty of them. The eyes of the world were assuredly on Trinidad that week.

And by eight o'clock that evening, it seemed as if the eyes of the world had gathered around one large table in a back room at the Toltec. I found them there, exchanging noisy opinions over bottles of Scotch. I don't know where they had gathered the previous two evenings, but tonight, for sure, not an eighth of them would have fitted into Xavier's parlour.

Max Eastman sat at the centre of it all, as ever; with Inez his queen beside him, her eyes shining a little too brightly, her hands on her lap fiddling with the loaded purse, clicking it shut, clicking it open, never leaving it alone. Everyone spoke at the same time, shouting and arguing, and bellowing with manic laughter. Inez gabbled as noisily as any of them, but only Max seemed to pay her much attention. Max paid everyone attention. He distributed his warm approval, his wit, his mighty observations and his gentle teasing through the room with a lightness of touch that was quite spellbinding. I never saw a man or woman so socially adept.

At some point, he said to me from across the table (we were several places away and yet, in spite of the noise, he didn't need to raise his voice): 'Inez tells me you're quite an opponent of our little tea party. I'm very sorry to hear it. Are the ladies in question especial friends of yours?'

'Hardly!' I said, smiling – because one couldn't *not* smile back at smiling Max. 'But they are friends of Inez's. Or, if not friends, they are certainly the people she grew up with.'

'She came with us to Ludlow,' said the man called Frank Bohn, sitting somewhere between us. 'Perhaps it's why she feels she is doing the right thing. Perhaps if you had gone out to Ludlow you would understand too. *Did* you? In fact? Go out to Ludlow?'

'I didn't,' I told him. 'I thought it was ghoulish.'

'Ah,' he said.

Ah, indeed. *Ah*. I ignored it.

But, bless him, Max laughed. 'Good God, Frank!' he said, 'How dare you "*ah*" this lady? Who in heck do you think you are? You arrived in this town less than twenty-four hours ago. Don't "ah" my friend here, who has endured a long winter through this bloody awful strike, and who probably understands the situation a hundred times better than you or I ever will ... *Ah* indeed! Apologize this instant!'

'I didn't "ah" her,' Frank said.

'Yes you did!'

'I didn't.'

'Frank, you're a fool. Dora, may I apologize on his behalf? Since he won't do it himself, though he knows perfectly well he should.'

I laughed. Of course I laughed. Who wouldn't? '*Ah*-pology accepted,' I said. Ha ha.

Max thought it was a terrific joke. He laughed so willingly that I began to laugh myself. Inez asked what we were laughing about, and I said, '*Ah* can't explain.' And so it continued. Max's light was shining on me, and it felt wonderful.

'It makes perfect sense that you should have reservations,' he said later. 'You see a crowd of reporters descending on your town. We drink the place dry – at least, I should think we will have done before this night is through. We sweep in, we sweep out – we draw our grand conclusions, publish them for all to see – and then we move on to the next outrage. Onwards and upwards.'

I shrugged. 'You said it.' I looked across at Inez. She was watching me speak with a glazed look in her eye. 'In the meantime, Inez has given you a list of her neighbours and friends for you to pick apart and sneer at.'

'*But don't you see, Dora?*' He leaned forward and I could smell his cologne, his passion, his exquisite integrity: 'What happened at Ludlow wasn't simply *yet one more* assault on the rights of our fellow man,' he said. 'What happened at Ludlow was *different*. You have a … It was a massacre, Dora. Capital against Labour – yes. And armed men against unarmed women and children, trapped beneath the ground, too frightened to attempt to escape. *Burned alive, Dora …*'

'She knows it,' came Xavier's voice, softly spoken from the other side of the table.

Max held up a hand in apology. 'I apologize. Of course she knows it. And you too. We all know it. I only keep repeating it because it's … I don't know why I keep repeating it.'

'Because you must,' said Upton Sinclair, patting the table with a small writerly fist. 'Because it is our duty to say it. Again and again. And to seek new ways of saying it, so that each time we say it, it continues to shake us to the core. Don't apologize, Max. You repeat it because you must. Two women and eleven children were burned this week. For greed. For American greed. I don't recall your name, sir,' he said to Xavier. 'But I think it's a fact we should take care to carry with us …'

'Put a sock in it, Upton,' said lively Gertrude Singer.

'My name,' observed Xavier with utmost pleasantness, but more for his own amusement than for the sake of informing anyone, since by then they had returned to squabbling among themselves, 'is in fact Xavier. Xavier Dubois. At your service.' He was drunk.

Max allowed the conversation to meander, and when he picked it up again, he took care to include both of us: Xavier and me. 'I believe, if you travelled out to the camp as Inez has, you would agree with her that if it might help to prevent such a tragedy from occurring again, then any means at all would justify the end. And frankly,' he smiled at us, 'holding a small tea party for ladies who are more than happy – hungry, even – to present their side of the story, is hardly on the same scale, when it comes to assaults on the rights of individuals.'

'Nobody ever suggested the two were comparable,' said Xavier. 'Only that you have asked Inez to betray people she has known all her life. And when you are gone, she will still be here to deal with the damage that you and your article leave behind.'

'But Xavier, that's just what I've been wanting to tell you!' Inez burst out. 'It's quite decided, isn't it Max? I can tell them, can't I? Only we decided it together this afternoon.' She leaned across the table top and placed a hand on each of us. 'Darlings, when all this is over, I'm going back to New York with him! He has offered me a job. Haven't you Max?'

Xavier and I turned to Max.

'I certainly have!' Max confirmed, swiping his floppy hair from his handsome forehead in a self-deprecating flurry. He grinned at her. 'The way you helped us these past couple of days, Inez, we'd be lucky to have you! We don't pay anything at the magazine, mind. But you know that. It's a labour of love ...'

'A labour of *love*!' she said, smiling right back at him.

'You see?' she looked from Xavier to me. 'So it's perfect! I just have to persuade Aunt Philippa and Uncle Richard to release some of my money ... and it *is* my money, after all. And Xavier, I absolutely expect your support on that. You will help me, won't you darling? You have to come with me tomorrow or the next day, when I introduce them to Max. He promises not to mention politics *at all*. You promise, don't you Max, darling?' She took his hand. 'We're going to say he is editor of a magazine called *Home Topics*. Which is true. In a way. Because politics *is* a home topic. Or certainly it ought to be. I think Aunt Philippa will like that ...'

She had leaned away from us and taken hold of Max. Their hands were entwined on the table top. It looked odd. Everything about them, about Inez that night, seemed wrong and peculiar. Her eyes shone but there was no life behind them. She seemed to be only half present in her own skin: not my friend, nor Xavier's sister, but an exaggerated, distorted version. On her lap, her free hand snapped open the catch of her spy-girl purse, and snapped it shut, *open and shut, open and shut* ... Xavier's eyes flicked unhappily from one of her hands to the other, to her face. He was thinking the same thing.

'Did I dream it,' I said to Max, 'or did Inez mention that you already had a wife?'

'Oh for absolutely heaven's *sake*, Dora,' snapped Inez. 'How can you be so *drab*! Trust you to be so completely bourgeois! We're not talking about Trinidad, Colorado. We are talking about *Greenwich Village*!'

The comment seemed to strike a chord with Xavier. He burst out laughing. 'Oh, what a dub you are, Inez darling. This time last week, you'd barely heard of Greenwich Village! If you want me to lie to Aunt Philippa and Uncle Richard for you, then so I shall. It won't be the first time, let's face it … But the way you're behaving lately, sweetheart, I begin to think you deserve absolutely whatever's coming to you.'

29

A couple of days later Phoebe reopened for business. Not, I imagine, because she expected there to be any, but because she couldn't stand the sight of her girls eating her food, living under her roof, and not at least being available to the possibility of making money for her, should the opportunity arise.

Inez came to find me, sounding sweet and conciliatory, and saying she missed our afternoons together. She seemed a little calmer – or perhaps I imagined it. But in any case, I was touched that she had come. It was shortly after lunch and the parlour house was like a graveyard, just as it had been all week, so when she asked me to while away a few hours with her, I didn't hesitate. I slipped out of Plum Street by the back door without telling anyone I was going, safe in the knowledge that my absence would not be noticed. We scurried through the town back to Xavier's cottage where many of her belongings still remained, and I kept her company while she packed.

She had made a start on the packing before she came to find me. There was a trunk already opened in the middle of the room when we arrived, but Xavier was nowhere to be seen.

'Oh, he went to Colorado Springs, I think,' she said. 'To find a lawyer, or something. Although I dare say there are plenty of perfectly good lawyers in Trinidad. So I don't really see why he couldn't manage to find one here.'

It seemed an odd time to go to Colorado Springs. I thought perhaps, more likely, he had buried himself in a den of indecency somewhere right here in Trinidad, and had only mentioned Colorado Springs to put his family off the scent. There were a couple of dives I could think of in town that would have suited him. 'Perhaps he was feeling lonely,' I said. Mostly, I think, to gauge her response. 'And I suppose there is a greater assortment of people to choose from in Colorado Springs. I dare say he wanted a break from us all.'

She looked at me curiously. 'Lonely? ... Do you mean *lonely*, lonely. As in: *amorous*? Is that what you mean?'

'I suppose so.'

'Well that's completely ridiculous,' she said. 'This is Trinidad, for heaven's sake. There are more women available right here in old Snatchville than in the entire

American West. You do talk a lot of rot, Dora! Anyway, I wish he *hadn't* gone. Max says three men were shot dead on that road yesterday.' She sighed. 'Of all the times to feel "*lonely*". In any case, he is due back this evening, he has promised me, and in good time to see Aunt Philippa and Uncle Richard. He better *had* be back in time, or I swear I shall never forgive him.'

I sat on her soft leather sofa, drinking tea, while she buzzed around me, throwing knick-knacks into the trunk: bits and pieces from her spy shop order, and novels, and private journals and my ivory elephant (I was touched to note). It seemed haphazard, to say the least.

'I suppose you will leave anyway,' I said, 'whether or not your aunt and uncle release the trust money? I can see you're dead set.'

'Certainly am.'

'So – what will you do for money? You'll need to have some, at least. Will Max take care of you?'

'Max says you can live very cheap in Greenwich Village. He says everyone worth talking to there is as poor as a church mouse. And then there's a woman called Mabel Dodge. She's very wealthy. And if she takes a shine – which Max says she will if he asks her to – then she feeds us all. We all feed each other. That's how it works. You see? We look out for each other.'

'Gosh ...' I said. It sounded rather wonderful. 'And who is this Mabel Dodge?'

'Oh, she is a widow and she is frightfully rich. And she likes to surround herself with poets and intellectuals. Max says that Jack Reed – you know? The small fellow with the pug nose? He was sitting next to Frank – who arrived on the train with Max? Apparently Jack is her current – what did he call it? *Squeeze*. Well, in any case, they're sleeping with each other. Which is funny when you think of her being so rich, and him being such a crazy little socialist. Max says she gives these wonderful parties, and all the cleverest people in New York come to eat her food and drink her wine and do you know, Dora ... I just feel so fortunate. To be leaving Trinidad right now. It's terrible, isn't it? That the tragedy out at Ludlow should have led to so much happiness for me. But I can't help it. Max Eastman has·changed everything for me and I am just so terribly grateful and so excited. Why don't you come with me to New York? You and Xavier? Oh, gosh, perhaps not. I don't suppose you would really enjoy it.'

Across town, in a room at the Corinado, Max's dreaded tea party was already taking place. Inez had asked to be present, but Max didn't want her there. 'Typical Max,' she said. 'Being his extra-thoughtful self. He thought as long as I was present, the ladies would always associate me with the occasion and, knowing that, he said he would be inhibited by his protectiveness towards me when writing the article. Isn't that sweet? ... That little *me* could actually impinge on Max Eastman's integrity as a reporter and editor. You see? He's not *such* a monster, is he?' She giggled. 'I had to remind him that by the time the article was published, I would be with him in Greenwich Village … It's quite a motley collection I put together for him, Dora. The worst of the worst. Mrs Chandler and Mrs Stratton … And Mrs McCloughlin and Mrs Howell. You don't know them, of course,' she said. 'Count yourself lucky. They're the horridest and silliest women in all Trinidad. I should think he's having quite a time of it.'

She couldn't pack her clothes, most of which were at her aunt and uncle's place, until she had informed them of her plans. But in her frantic state of mind, she needed to stay busy. She was determined to get the wretched trunk full, ready to transport to the train station first thing in the morning, when the streets were calmer and safer. 'Because once I've sent the trunk, Dora,' she said, 'I shall feel like I am already half on my way.'

I asked her how soon she intended to leave town. Very soon, she said. 'But you know, now that I've made the decision, every moment here is purgatory.' She must have read my expression. 'Oh, Dora I don't mean that exactly. I shall miss you awfully. It's only thanks to you that any of this is even happening. Yes, it is! When I think back to how boring my life was before we met, I almost want to *cry* with gratitude. It's true! You changed everything. You, Dora, are my greatest friend. Even if that is quite the oddest, most unlikely thing – which it is, when you stop to consider it. And even though Aunt Philippa must *never know*. You're my greatest friend, Dora. My only friend ...'

'Xavier is your friend too,' I said.

'Oh yes. And Xavier too. Of course. Perhaps he will come and see me in New York. He might like it there. Max says there are plenty of gentlemen who dress like him in Greenwich Village.' She laughed. 'Imagine that!' She surveyed her trunk. It was bursting with her arbitrary belongings. She closed the lid and sat on it.

Max, she said, would be leaving tomorrow or the next day, depending on developments. (Anarchy in Colorado could only hold the front pages for so long.) Inez hoped to leave town on the same train.

'He has a wedding to go to next Tuesday. And he needs to be back in town by then,' she said. 'Although of course he doesn't really think of "marriage" in the way you or I do. For him it's a lot more sort of ... oh, *nuanced*. He believes—' There was a noise outside. Someone was at the door, fiddling with the lock. She froze, a look of terror on her face.

'Who is it?' she whispered. 'Do you hear that?'

'There is someone at the door,' I said. 'Perhaps Xavier has returned.' I was about to call out to him, but she grasped hold of my arm.

'*Shhhh!*'

'Why?' But her fear was infectious. God knows, I felt it pounding in my chest too. We stayed still, waiting.

She released my arm. Put a finger to her lips and bent down. On the floor between our feet lay her little spy-purse (never far out of her reach, I noticed). Silently, delicately, she slid out the revolver.

More scratching at the door. The turn of a lock, and a creak ...

She stood up and, with steady hand (surprisingly steady), she pointed her gun at the door and pulled back the hammer.

The door pushed open, and there stood Xavier. 'What in hell?' he said, indignantly.

With an exclamation, half irritation, half relief, her arm dropped to her side. '*Xavier*!' she said, as if it were all his fault. 'What are you doing, standing there? You scared the life out of me. For heaven's sake!' She slid the gun back into its case. 'You shouldn't sneak up on people like that ... It could end so badly.'

'I wasn't sneaking up!' he said. 'I didn't know anyone was here.'

'Well you should've known.' And then, realizing how absurd she sounded, she burst into laughter, put her arms around him, and kissed him on his cheek. 'Where have you been anyway?' she said. 'Oh my gosh, darling ...' She pulled back a little, waving a hand under her nostrils. 'You reek. What is that smell?'

It was opium. I knew it at once, of course. The smell tends to cling for hours after.

'Well, I must say that's quite some particular welcome,' he said, exchanging quick glances with me and ignoring the question. He extricated himself from his sister's hold – rather irritably – and headed towards the kitchen. 'Coffee. Is what I'm offering today. Either of you girls want some coffee?'

'Actually, no,' Inez said. 'I have to leave.'

'What?' he said. 'Again? Already? Why are you constantly having to *go* places? You seem to be permanently in some kind of a mad rush.' He sounded plaintive. 'It's ridiculous, Inez. I wish you would calm down, just a teeny bit. Honestly. You worry me ...'

'Well, it's because I have so much to do, Xavier. You haven't the faintest idea. I'm leaving town in a couple of days, and I haven't even told Aunt Philippa or Uncle Richard yet. And I want to get this trunk to the train station for tomorrow morning. And then I said to Cody's mamma that I would deliver something for her ...'

'What sort of thing?' asked Xavier. 'Deliver what? Where? Can't she deliver the ruddy thing herself?'

'Oh, it's nothing,' Inez replied, fiddling with her coat buttons.

'Nothing?' he repeated, more alert now.

'Nothing much. Something for her brother. And no, she can't do it herself, poor darling.'

277

'Deliver it where?' he asked again. 'This "nothing much"?'

'*Nowhere*. Out at Forbes camp. Nothing. She can't get out there herself, poor thing. And Cody used to do that sort of thing for her ...'

'Forbes?' he looked aghast. 'You can't go out to Forbes, Inez sweetheart. Not this week. You do realize that, don't you?'

'Don't be silly, Xavier,' she said. 'Of course I must. I have promised. Anyway, you're one to talk, fresh back from your crazy jaunt. How was Colorado Springs?'

'I didn't go to Colorado Springs,' he said.

'But you told me—'

He shook his head. 'You misunderstood. Of course I didn't go to Colorado Springs – I'm not crazy ... But I've just been speaking with a gentleman who came in on the road yesterday morning, and he said there were men up in the hills taking pot shots at his motor as he drove by. Twice. *Twice*, Inez, his car was shot at. There are snipers out there. Bands of men hiding out in the hills, planning their next attacks ... It's terrifying. It's not a joke. He is lucky to be alive.'

But once again Inez wasn't listening. 'Don't fuss, darling. Please. Really. Max says it's quite safe, as long as you ride with a white flag out of the window, and I just bet your friend forgot to do that ... Anyhow, Cody's ma doesn't have a car of her own, Xavie. Of course she

278

doesn't. And she has a great gaggle of children. I couldn't even count them. And no Cody to help her any longer. So how is she to get out there? You tell me that. And if you saw how heartbroken she was ...'

'But Inez,' I said. 'I thought you said you didn't see her?'

'What?' She looked confused for a moment, and then irritable. 'Well, I did see her. That's all ... And if I don't make it out to Forbes today, I shall have to go tomorrow or the next day, and I don't want it hanging over me. On top of which, if you don't mind me saying it, you two aren't the *only* people in Trinidad I need to see before I leave. There are other people in town I want to say goodbye to. Friends.'

I asked her if she would say goodbye to Lawrence. I couldn't resist.

'I wouldn't even know where to find him,' she snapped. 'Oh gosh, I wonder how we're ever going to lift that great trunk into the car. It's awfully heavy ...'

Poor man, I thought. Poor Lawrence. Poor Xavier. Poor Aunt Philippa and Uncle Richard. Pity any one of us who loves her. Pity Max Eastman. She takes us up and tosses us aside, but she doesn't mean it badly. I pictured Lawrence the last few occasions we had met: thin and brusque – missing Inez.

'Maybe you'd like to send him a message?' I said. 'I could pass it on to him, if you like. He might appreciate it.' I remembered suggesting the same thing to him all those weeks ago.

She blushed. 'I don't think so,' she said. 'But thank you.'

'Inez,' Xavier burst out. 'I don't care a hoot about your spurned lovers. But you *must not* go to Forbes. Is that clear?' I had never heard him so emphatic. 'Do you have the faintest idea of the danger?'

'Of course I do,' she said. 'Probably rather better than you.'

'Of all places, Forbes camp especially. They've got the company guards barricaded in with the scabs. They're all trapped in there. And if anyone tries to get out, the strikers shoot them dead. Night before last, every mule in the camp was slaughtered. Every damn one. They came in the night and slashed the beasts' throats. *And they didn't make a sound*, Inez. Nobody heard a thing. These men are lethal … And don't please imagine they intend to leave it at that. They'll be back for the scabs and the guards and the women and children tonight or tomorrow. For crying out loud, it's all anyone was talking about in town last night!'

A beat.

'Did I say Forbes?' she said with a little frown. 'Well, I didn't mean *Forbes*, did I? Aren't I silly? I actually meant Cokedale. Cody's papa is out at Cokedale.'

'I thought you said Cody's uncle—'

'I really have to go. Won't you please help me get this trunk into the auto?'

Xavier crossed the room, took hold of her thin arms and shook her, gently. 'Inez, honey, I'll take the trunk anywhere you want me to take it. I'll take *you* anywhere you want me to take you. I'll do anything you ask. Only promise me, whatever it is you want to deliver to Cody's uncle – father – whatever in hell it is you are up to: stay away from Forbes. Will you?'

She looked into his eyes. I saw her. 'I am not going to Forbes, Xavie,' she said softly. 'I promise.'

He considered her a moment. 'I don't believe you,' he said at last. 'Why must you always insist on lying?'

But she stuck to her story and left soon afterwards, reminding him one last time about his date with the McCullochs that night. 'Max and I will be at the door at six o'clock prompt. Don't you dare to be late, darling. Please. Please, please.' She kissed him goodbye, leaving him with the trunk, and the task of transporting it to the train station in the morning.

Two long days followed. Plum Street remained open for no business at all, and the state of emergency in Southern Colorado grew worse – quickly and considerably. The snipers and strikers brought their battle in from the hills and onto the streets. Nobody sane would be spending their evenings reciting lousy poetry and drinking bourbon in the Toltec now. The city was too dangerous.

I didn't hear from Inez. I wondered whether she ever made it out to Forbes. I wondered whether she and Max had already left town. I wondered how the meeting had gone with Mr and Mrs McCulloch. Plum Street had a telephone, as did the McCullochs'. I might have called, but I didn't, and nor did Inez call me.

Time crawled by. We grew tetchy and irritable in the house, Phoebe especially. And, in the background, the gunfire continued. I lay on my couch, with the fear always gnawing, reading the last French novel William Paxton ever sent to me.

And then Simple Kitty knocked on the door to tell me Lawrence was downstairs, crying.

30

I saw Max Eastman last night. He turned up at dinner, very late, apologizing to us all as if the entire evening had been on hold for his arrival. When he loped into the room, I'll be honest: my heart stopped. And this morning, when I opened my eyes, my face was covered with tears. I've never experienced it before – to wake, from crying. Had I been dreaming? I can't remember. But I woke with a hundred images swimming through my head. Of Trinidad as it was almost twenty years ago. Of Xavier, as he was then. Of myself. Of Max and Inez as they were together; and the blood drying on the old brick pavements.

*

But the blood in my dream can't have belonged to Inez, because they killed her on the prairie, ten or so miles out of town. When Lawrence found her, twisted in her little heap, she was still warm, he said. The earth around her was damp and red. He carried her back to the auto and drove her home through the prairie. He drove directly to the town morgue.

He parked up in the side street by the entrance. The morgue was on Main Street, in the basement of the blessed Jamieson's. For reasons of commercial sensitivity, its entrance was purposely hard to find, even for those who knew where to look. Lawrence carried Inez in his arms and banged on the basement door until Mr Adamsson the mortician let him in.

Faraway in Washington, the president was, at last, ordering in the National Guard. In New York, John D. Rockefeller was releasing press statements to explain why the bloodbaths in his frontier mining towns were not his responsibility, and all the while we lived in anarchy ... When Lawrence came to the morgue door, Inez growing cold in his arms, the normal rules did not apply. Certificates of death and other such formalities were not a priority. It was more a question of getting the bodies off the streets, restoring some semblance of order.

So Mr Adamsson took Inez without the usual questions. When he returned to the front stall, paperwork in hand, Lawrence was already vanished. Lawrence couldn't linger. It was too dangerous. But he loved her, poor man, and so nor could he leave her quite abandoned. He was on his way to Plum Street, to fetch me.

He arrived at the parlour house – our first visitor for days – and sent Simple Kitty up to fetch me. I was upstairs, lounging on the couch in my private sitting room reading William's novel. It was doing an admirable job of blocking out the sound of the gunfire, the marching boots – my fear. Then came Simple Kitty's knock.

'Mr O'Neill wants to see you,' she said. 'He has blood over his shirt. And I think he's been crying.'

'*Crying*, Kitty?'

'He's making strange faces.' She shrugged. 'And there's the trouble at the Forbes camp ... Thirty or more dead, they're saying.'

I brushed past Kitty, still in my breakfast kimono, and headed downstairs to see the evidence for myself. Sure enough, there he stood, alone in our glittering hall, cocooned by our damask, our crystal, our velvet and gilt, his felt hat bloody in his hand, his tears flowing freely. 'Dora,' he said, 'something terrible ...' I was conscious of Simple Kitty lingering, but I did nothing about it. 'She is shot through the throat, Dora.'

'She is ... what?'

'I found her by the roadside – northward ... She is in the morgue.'

'In the morgue ...'

'Will you go?'

Something, because he hadn't said the words, made me cling to the idea that she was in the morgue for some other reason. In the morgue and yet alive: shot through the throat and waiting for me. I clung to the idea as I dressed, as I hurried through the horrible streets. Until the moment Mr Adamsson ushered me into that small room at the back, I had imagined her sitting up, legs swinging, eyes shining with the drama of it all, *waiting* for me, as she had the day I fetched her out of jail. My beautiful friend, Inez. But she lay very still.

Mr Adamsson, stout and grey, didn't much care who I was. He needed a name for the body, and a name of someone to take responsibility for it. So he stood close to me as I gazed down at her, unwilling to leave my side.

The bullet hole was neat: 'right through the jugular', he explained. The blackened marks around it, he said, were where the gunpowder had scorched her skin; and the thick crust of blood which coated everything – the bottom half of her face, the top half of her slim body – was only to be expected. He pointed to the wound, his finger scuffing it carelessly. 'She bled to death in just a minute or two,' he said. Her once-white shirtwaist, her coat, her skirt – the pantaloon skirt she was so proud of: all had been drenched, stained, ruined. 'Your friend found her lying out by the road to Forbes. I guess she was caught up in the gunfire ... But whatever was she doing out there?' he sounded plaintive. 'A young lady on her own. At a time like this. Why wasn't she home safe? You have to ask yourself.' —

'Are there many dead out there today?' I asked.

He shrugged. 'Forty or more, I heard ... I can't take them, anyways. They'll have to go on to Walsenburg. Maybe Pueblo.' He bent over the wound, his nose so close he seemed to sniff her. 'She would have had to be near to it, you know. Slammed up real close ... You can see.' He prodded. 'The bullet's gone right through ...'

He was slammed up too close to her blanched face. I longed to yank him back. 'Can I please have a moment with her, Mr Adamsson?'

He continued as if he hadn't heard me. 'Her shooter would have been right *there*, you understand. Right beside her, you see? Like ... Almost, she might've shot the thing off herself ...' He picked up her hand, caked in blood, frowned, gently laid it down again. 'I'm guessing they robbed her. She didn't come in with nothing.' He glanced up, seemed to remember my question. 'Well, Miss. *Ma'am.* I guess I can leave you for a second. But you mustn't run away. I need the papers done. I can't do nothing with the young lady until I got the papers done ... You kin?'

I shook my head.

He looked me up and down. 'Didn't think so.'

'But I can give you the names. Her uncle and aunt live nearby. And she has a brother. I only need a minute, sir. She was my friend.'

287

There was only one exit from the room, in any case. I couldn't have slipped away if I'd wanted to. 'Very well,' he said at last. 'You stay right here, mind. And I'll fetch the papers.' He held up a finger – the one that had scuffed at her wound. 'Don't go running away now.'

He left me, resting the door ajar, and Inez and I were alone together. Rather, I was alone. She was gone. I whispered my goodbye. But it was too late and I felt absurd. I looked at her still face. She was a stranger now, peaceful in a way that affronted me.

I tried to imagine the moment she was shot: the terror that would have run through her. They took her jewellery: the little gold bracelet she wore and the golden locket – both gone. She'd not died a martyr to any cause, as Lawrence wanted me to believe. She'd been robbed in the crossfire – nothing more. A victim of the chaos, who shouldn't have been there at all.

I wanted a memento of her. Something, before the McCullochs swooped, and our friendship was brushed into a corner. I scanned her body, arms, fingers, neck. The thieves had indeed taken every trinket. I remembered her pantaloon skirt had a hidden pocket inside the lining. 'For carrying the sorts of things that modern ladies aren't supposed to carry,' she had said to me once. And when I'd asked her *what* 'sorts of things', she didn't know or care. '*Heavens, you are boring, Dora!*' she'd said. 'What does it even matter? Cigarettes, perhaps? French letters?'

and then came that magical, happy laughter. 'I shall think of something! You can't have a secret pocket without putting *something* inside!'

At first I couldn't remember quite where the ludicrous pocket was located, and I hesitated to delve too deep. I patted the lower half of her, crusty with all the blood, and then, gingerly, half lifted the outer skirt. There it was, not so hidden after all, sewn between lining and outer fabric: a neat little pocket – with the bloodied corner of *something* peeping out.

I smiled to myself. A French letter? A cigarette pack?

It was a sealed envelope, smeared with blood, addressed to Max Eastman. I slipped it into my coat pocket, and waited for Mr Adamsson to return.

31

I am lunching with Max at the Ambassador today. He left a message to tell me he had reserved a table by the swimming pool. It is a beautiful day, and I suppose, in spite of everything, I am fond of him. I can't explain why – he was a lousy friend to Inez. But then again, maybe we all were. He is attractive and excellent company and, from the way he spoke about Inez at dinner last weekend, there is no doubt in my mind that he adored her, just as we all did.

Aside from which, if I'm honest, it's quite a thrill. Who knows what Hollywood star I may spot, roaming past the table in his bathing pants? I've been living in Hollywood long enough, by now I should have outgrown such cheap thrills. Well, too bad, because I have not. When a woman is tired of sitting poolside at the Ambassador, spotting Hollywood movie stars in their bathing trunks, she is tired of life. And I am *not* tired of life. I am looking forward to lunch – and to life – quite enormously.

I am wearing a yellow silk crepe two-piece for the occasion, made to measure, and a fedora tilt hat with matching silk brim and if I say so myself, the outfit suits me well. I look elegant and rather demure. Fit for the Ambassador.

When I arrive at the table, Max is already waiting for me. He is sitting, hunched and scowling, over something in the *Los Angeles Times* – a posture in which I imagine he has spent much of the past week. In front of him, beside a full glass of white wine, and an ashtray with smoking cigarette, he has a small book of poetry with several tabs sticking out of the pages. He too is looking elegant and respectable. Dressed in linen suit and panama, Max is as handsome as he ever was. As handsome as the devil himself.

As the devil himself, I find myself muttering, as I kiss his cheek, smell his cologne, and settle myself into the chair opposite.

'What's that about devils?' he asks, laughing. He has placed himself, gentleman that he is, with his back to the view, so that I can gaze out over the beautiful people of Hollywood, splashing in the giant pool, and he, poor man, can only gaze at me in my yellow suit, or at the vast pink building behind me.

'You look very well, Max,' I say. 'As ever.'

'You too.' He pauses. 'Really, it's hard to believe it's been almost twenty years.'

A waiter arrives, deferential and uniformed. We order a couple of martinis, and the wine menu.

'It's still such a thrill, isn't it,' I say to Max, 'to be allowed to order our hooch right here at the table. When do you suppose the novelty will wear off?'

'Never,' he says. And, for a moment, I fear he is going to launch into one of his political dissertations – about the importance of individual freedom and the American constitution, or some such – and I don't want that. It's not why we have met today. He can save all that for his speeches.

Fortunately, Max being Max, he seems to read the lack of interest in my face. He changes tack and, instead, says: 'I'm in no particular hurry. Are you? I do hope not. We have so much to talk about!'

I tell him we have the whole afternoon.

A silence between us. He fiddles with his wine glass, and I wait for my cocktail to arrive. He offers me a cigarette – I decline. He lights his own. He looks unhappy, boyish. Under the table, his foot jiggles; and I am torn. It's almost impossible to look at him without wanting to take care of him, ease his anxiety. But before I left this morning, I reread the letter Inez wrote him. Actually, I have reread it ten or fifteen times this week, having not looked at it for years. It's infuriatingly difficult to read. But I know it almost by heart. Opposite me, Max looks wistful and sad, here at the poolside, twenty years too late; but the words of her letter, brimming with her childish, hurt feelings, and stained with her blood, are still fresh in my mind. So I leave him to his anguish, his jiggling foot, his tobacco, and wait for him to speak.

Max had not even realized she was dead. When I told him at the dinner last Saturday, he was dumbstruck. He simply had no idea. He kept asking – it was all he could think to say – if I was 'absolutely certain' about it. For a clever man, it struck me as a slow response. For a clever man, it seemed to me to be extraordinary that he couldn't have known it already. After all, wasn't she supposed to have joined him in New York that same week? They were meant to be taking the same train out of Trinidad. But he swore on his ignorance again and again, and from the way he insisted, it was impossible not to believe him.

My cocktail arrives, and he looks up at the waiter with puppy-like gratitude, as if the waiter's presence might have let him off some imagined hook. But the waiter doesn't stay for long. He says he has forgotten the wine menu and will be back.

Beneath the table, Max's foot jiggles so hard it makes the linen cloth shake. I hold on to my glass, and wait. Finally he says:

'I don't know where to start. I feel dreadful.' Which, of course, are the only words I have come here to hear.

'I'm sorry,' I say. 'It must have been quite a shock.'

'It is a shock,' he says. 'It's been a shock all week. I've hardly thought of anything else. I don't quite know why. After all, it's twenty years since we saw each other – and she and I only knew each other a week.'

'Eight days,' I correct him – pointlessly. Only I don't feel inclined to let him off any hook. Not at all. Not if I can help it. 'The war lasted ten days. And if, as you claim, you left town two days after the massacre at Forbes—'

'You call that a massacre?' he says. It sounds irritable.

'It was nothing if not a massacre.'

'Well,' he says. 'It was in response to another massacre.'

'Of course it was. Both were massacres, Max. Don't tell me you're *still* playing goodies and baddies?' I don't wait for his reply. 'I brought the letter.'

He seems to pale a little, in the California sunlight. 'Oh good,' he says, without moving for it.

I place it on the table between us. The smears of blood on the envelope are a dark brown now, and the paper has yellowed. But there it lies between us. It is Inez's handwriting – whether Max recognizes it or not. There is no reason why he should. And there, on the yellowed envelope, in scrawled black ink, she has written:

Max Eastman, Corinado Hotel, By Hand

The words are as clear as they were twenty years ago.

He gazes at the envelope, as if the sight of it horrifies him. One arm is engaged in smoking, the other is crossed against his chest. Again, he doesn't move to take it. On the contrary, when I slide it gently across the table, closer towards him, he seems to recoil.

'Wait a moment,' he says, eyes still fixed on the envelope. 'Let's talk, for a bit ... Shall we? It seems ridiculous, I know ... but ...' He doesn't finish the sentence. 'It's her blood is it? I suppose? ... Yes. Of course it is. Oh Christ ... Poor, darling girl ...'

The waiter returns, bringing the wine menu, and leaves us alone again. Max takes a long time scrutinizing the list, debating which bottle to order. He asks me if I have any preference. I tell him, no. Red or white? I tell him, either. Which grape? I tell him I don't mind. Muscat, Semillon, Sauvignon, Pinot Blanc? I tell him I'll have whatever he is having.

He delays still further, summoning the sommelier and discussing the options – until finally I run out of patience. I lean towards him. 'Max,' I murmur. 'When I said I had plenty of time, I didn't mean ...' I smile. And, of course, Max responds at once.

He springs back from the wine menu as if the wretched thing is burning him, closes it and hands it to the man. 'Oh, bring us anything you like,' he says. 'Your house wine. Or, no. Champagne. Champagne, Dora?'

There isn't much to celebrate except, I suppose, that the sun is shining and we are both alive. I consider it. 'I would prefer a Martini,' I say.

He orders one for each of us and finally we are alone with the letter again.

He glances at it but doesn't pick it up. Instead, he asks me to tell him again how I tried and failed to deliver it to him. He is hoping that my answer will somehow exonerate him; though from what, he does not say. The fact is he had already checked out of the Corinado when I attempted to locate him there. I keep telling him so.

'Well then where *was* I?' he keeps asking.

And how in hell can I answer that? I haven't been accurate about the time I tried to deliver the letter. I left it a full day longer than I told him. But he never needs to know that.

'It doesn't make any sense,' he says. 'Why would they say I had checked out when I hadn't? And why would she even write me a letter?' He looks edgy, I think. Why does he look so damn edgy? 'Besides, we were friends. Anything she needed to tell me, she could have said it.'

Max wants to know why I didn't forward the letter to New York and I don't know what to answer. When I failed to find him at the Corinado, when they told me at the front desk that he and his colleagues had checked out, moved on to the next big story – what prevented me from simply sending it on to him at the magazine?

All I remember is the anger I felt: with Inez, for dying; with Xavier and myself for failing to protect her; with Trinidad, with everyone – and with Max, even before I had read the letter.

She was dead. Max had skipped town. Like Xavier, I was jealous of their friendship and I didn't want Max Eastman – this reporter, this smooth interloper – to be the last person she communicated with. Perhaps, because I had taken it from her dead body, and because it was splattered with her blood, and I was bereft without her, I simply couldn't bring myself to let the letter go.

There were plenty of reasons why I should have sent the letter to him in New York, and plenty of reasons why I didn't; none of which I feel inclined to offer up to him this sunny afternoon.

So I say: 'Well, why don't you read it, Max? Perhaps when you have read it, the answers may become clear.'

The waiter arrives with our grapefruit and avocado salads. They look unappetizing: too fresh and clean, with that grimy letter lying between us. Images of Inez, her clothes drenched in blood as she lay on the marble slab, and of the coffins stacked high on the open shelves in the room behind her, float to the surface of my mind. My throat closes. I push the plate away.

Max picks up his fork, as if to tuck in. But his face has turned a greenish yellow. It might be a reflection from the salad, but I think he feels as sick I do.

'Max, take the letter,' I snap at him. 'It's been waiting twenty years to be read. The least you can do is to read it before you eat the goddamn salad. Read it, or I will read it aloud to you while you eat.'

He lays down his fork. 'Why don't you read it to me, Dora? I remember she had difficult handwriting, even at the best of times. Read it me.'

I regret suggesting it at once. 'That's really what you want?'

He nods.

'But it's addressed to you.'

He snorts. 'A minor detail. And not one you were too terribly squeamish about before. You opened the damn thing. I know you've read it already. More than once, I assume. So read it. Please.' He takes a final, sickly look at his salad and gives up on it, sits back and lights a third – fourth – cigarette.

He offers me one. I refuse it. And then I pick up the envelope and open it, for the hundredth time that week. My hands are shaking slightly.

'It's dated – but the date doesn't match with the day of the week. I remember checking it at the time. And I verified it again this week. The day of the week is the day before she was killed, but the date – 29 April 1914 – is the day she was killed. I don't know if that's significant. Probably not. If she was shot in the afternoon, and I think she must have been. I don't know how long it takes for a body to go cold, do you? It was a warm day ...'

Max winces. I ignore it.

'But Lawrence said the ground was still damp with her blood ... The blood was still damp on her clothes when I found her.'

He nods. Inhales. He has pushed back his wicker chair, stretched out his long legs and crossed them at the ankle. He gazes at his knee, and the foot begins to jiggle.

'So it's my assumption,' I continue, remorseless, 'that she must have written it early, on the morning of the day she was killed. I think she simply got confused. Don't you?'

'Probably,' he says. It comes out like a small hiccup, as if he is holding back vomit.

But I don't care. I smile, remembering her affectionately. 'It would have been like Inez, wouldn't it? Always a bit dizzy about the details.'

He looks at me sharply. 'Not always so dizzy,' he says. 'Why don't you just read it?'

'It begins warmly, Max,' I say, playing for time. 'It begins warmly, but you have to brace yourself. Are you prepared for that? She was very angry with you. On second thoughts, I really think you should read it to yourself.'

299

'Oh, *c'mon*,' he says. 'It was a long time ago now. I can take it! And, by the way, Dora – I know what you're trying to do.'

'What?' I ask, confused. 'What am I trying to do?'

'April the twenty-ninth was the day they attacked Forbes,' he says. 'I left town May first.'

'So you say.'

'Well, you know that I did. You came to the Corinado on May first and they told you I was gone.'

'That's right.'

'So. Why didn't you come see me on the thirtieth? What stopped you?'

We gaze at each other. I don't have an answer.

I reply with a question of my own. 'Why didn't you wait for her, Max? She thought you were travelling back to New York together.'

He looks away. He doesn't seem to have an answer either.

'I'm only trying to warn you,' I tell him, after a pause, 'before I read it – Inez was very angry with you. That's all. So be prepared.'

I wait, but he doesn't respond. He gazes at his jiggling knee, nurses his cigarette. And so, at last, I begin:

Darling Max,
I loved you. I trusted you. I believed in you with all my heart.

Max issues a gentle snort and I pause. 'Oh, it's easy to scoff,' I say. 'Inez was not the fine writer that you are, Max. She was naive – and very foolish. Which is why this letter I am reading to you now is covered in her blood.'

'Give me a break, Dora,' Max says unhappily. 'I'm not scoffing. I guess I … just forgot the way young girls expressed themselves back then.'

'She was twenty-nine. Is that so young? How old were you in 1914?'

'Not much older,' he acknowledges. 'Thirty-one? But we were all young then.' He smiles at me, without warmth. 'Except for you, Dora. I don't think you were ever young, were you?'

'I was thirty-seven, Max.'

'Yes … I suppose I meant,' he says defensively, 'that you were always so worldly-wise.'

'I know just what you meant.'

I let the silence hang between us. I don't know why I am so hostile to him, after all these years. It's as if I want to lay everything at his feet: responsibility for everything that happened. And yet I know Inez was not a child. What she did, she chose to do. I ask myself why I have even come to this lunch. Why have I dressed myself in yellow silk crepe, tottered out here to this poolside table with this twenty-year-old, bloodstained letter in my purse? What did I think I would achieve by it? I consider leaving: simply folding the letter and walking away.

'Oh for heaven's sake,' he says. 'Read the damn thing, won't you? It can't change anything now, but at least you'll have the comfort of knowing I have read it at last.

He sounds softer again, as if he sees into my heart. 'After all these years, it might help a little bit. To know the letter finally reached its destination.'

'No more snorting,' I say. 'I can't read it if you are going to scoff. You wouldn't scoff, Max, if you had seen her there, with the letter so carefully hidden …'

Max leans across the table. 'Forgive me,' he says, touching the skin on my arm. 'Start from the beginning, won't you? There is nothing to scoff about.'

I hold it out to him. 'You read it. I think I know it by heart, so if there are any words you can't make out …' I shrug, embarrassed, and I wait until, at length, he takes it.

Darling Max,

I loved you. I trusted you. I believed in you with all my heart. I believed a new life was starting for me in New York – but you have betrayed me, Max. How could you?

You thought I wouldn't sneak a peek at your article while you were out? Did you really imagine that by tucking those pages under the papers on your desk I would not find them? You came here with your big city talk, and you lured me into

setting your trap only to make a mockery of us all!
No, Max, you make a mockery of your profession!
   Words cannot describe my feelings of hurt and
pain and disappointment. Of course I cannot come
to New York now. Please return my trunk to me as
soon as it arrives. Perhaps we were never friends
but I thought we were. We are not friends now.
Don't you think we are suffering enough in our
calamity-struck town? Murder and hatred at every
corner, and you have come to mock our honest
townsfolk. Shame on you, my treacherous friend.
I hope I never lay eyes on you again.
   Goodbye Max and may God forgive you.
   Inez

He lays it on the table with a sigh. Actually, he tosses
it onto the table. He is frowning and there is an expression, not of chagrin, as I was hoping, but of irritation
and confusion. He says nothing. He gazes at the pink
building behind my head, and then he takes the letter
back again. He reads it one more time, still scowling.

'Well?' I say. The silence is infuriating.

He doesn't look up, doesn't reply. He lays the letter
flat on the table, hunches over it, sucking on his cigarette,
blowing smoke over the paper.

'I read your article by the way,' I say to him. 'I still
have it somewhere. It was fairly loathsome, Max.'

'So were the women who came to the tea,' he mutters. 'You weren't there, Dora.' He looks up at last. 'You realize, don't you, that this letter makes no sense whatever?'

I take it back from the table, annoyed. 'It makes sense enough,' I say. 'We can't all be great writers and poets.'

'But she read the article. She read what I wrote.'

'So she says. You broke her heart, Max.'

'*Broke her heart?*' He laughs. 'I did nothing of the kind! And furthermore, I certainly did not hide the article from her. The last time we saw each other, she came round, and I read the wretched thing aloud to her. I hadn't finished it by then – it was a rough draft. I hadn't seen the wreckage out at Forbes by then – but the rest was all there. Ordinarily I would never do such a thing. A cardinal rule of journalism: *never* show an interested party what you are midway through writing. They will always want to meddle. But this was Inez. I couldn't resist ... And Dora, she loved it! She told me so.' He stops. There is a long pause. 'I am aware, by the way, that she told you we were lovers,' he says at last.

Behind him, a perfect bronze body dive-bombs into the water. Its head pops up, white teeth laughing, and I realize I recognize him. *Who is that?* I am thinking. What film have I seen him in before?

Max leans forward, distracting my attention. He puts a hand on mine. 'She told you we were lovers, didn't she?'

'She and I were close friends,' I reply. 'What do you expect?'

He says, 'Dora, you and Inez were close friends. And Inez and I were friends, too. But we weren't lovers. We never were, and we never intended to be. Inez already had a lover ...' He pauses. 'The Union man ... I told you, he turned up in Moscow. He was all she talked about. Lawrence O'Neill.'

'Nonsense,' I say. 'She was in love with you.'

He shakes his head. 'No, she wasn't.' He seems to be searching for the words. 'She encouraged you to *believe* that we were lovers ...'

'She didn't "encourage" me,' I correct him. 'She *told* me.'

But again he shakes his head. 'After the incident with the guns. At the cottage. You warned her off him – and quite rightly, I dare say. Inez wanted you and Xavier off her back. And it was a sort of ... well, I suppose it was an arrangement we came to. In exchange for all the help she gave me with the tea party, I agreed to keep her secret for her ... cover for her. I suppose I played along.'

What is he talking about?

'You must be confused,' I say.

'Inez and I were never lovers,' he says again. 'She was going to work at the magazine with me, but she was going to live with Lawrence O'Neill. They were besotted. He had a room in the Corinado, if you remember. Half the time she said she was helping me ...' He lets it hang.

305

'I don't believe you,' I say at last. And then: 'After all, it was twenty years ago. You may be confused. I have read that you are quite the lothario.'

'Ha!' It is dismissive.

'Well, it was only a few days, remember. And almost twenty years ago now. You have probably forgotten—'

'It was eight days. As you rightly reminded me. And thank you – I have certainly not forgotten. I remember very clearly the last time we saw each other ...'

32

'She came to my rooms. There was a sort of recklessness about her at the end, wasn't there? It was very attractive in the beginning, but the last time I saw her – it wasn't really attractive, it was alarming. The sense of decorum ... I'm not a stickler for these things – far from it. Even less so, back then. But it was only a small room. With a desk and a bed, and she used to ...' He pauses to choose the word. 'She used to seethe with this terrific sexual energy ... and I found it uncomfortable. Claustrophobic. She couldn't seem to stay still. She wouldn't settle. It was the day before the attack on Forbes – or was it the morning of Forbes? Yes. It must have been.'

'On the day she died?'

He nods. 'Because I went out much later that day, and then again the following day to see what carnage the strikers had wrought, and I couldn't wait to get back to my typewriter and set to work ... Which was – is – unusual, I assure you. Ordinarily I will do anything to avoid the moment of setting pen to paper. But the assault on Ludlow – and the way those ladies spoke during our tea—'

'Yes, yes,' I say impatiently.

'I had written three quarters of the article by the time she came by. She was wearing a black felt hat that flopped over her eyes and it made her look ... beautiful. Well, she was beautiful, I don't argue with that. Just deranged. She was on her way to see the mother of the poor boy she had befriended. He worked in the hardware store, and he had a connection with the Union. I don't remember his name. I never met him – he was already dead by the time I came to town.'

'Cody.'

'Cody. That's it. Bony Cody, she called him. She was on her way to meet with his mother. She had some cockeyed sense of *noblesse oblige*. She seemed to think her mere presence could alleviate the suffering of the lower classes. Hell, and perhaps it could. Who knows? She had such charm, such incredible warmth, didn't she? And of course, she was so beautiful.'

I smile. 'After Captain Lippiatt was murdered, she wanted to pay a visit to his widow. She asked me if I knew whether a widow existed. I laughed at her so hard! That was the first time we met ... Yes, she was very warm.

She said she was going to give cash to Cody's mother to help out. I don't know if she ever did.'

'That's right! She was carrying a bundle of dollars with her. A lot of cash. She came to my door. The desk clerk already knew her, of course, and I presumed she had come directly from Lawrence's room. I had no idea she was coming to see me until she was standing there, asking to come in. She said Lawrence had gone to Forbes to see what was happening out there and that I had missed the chance of a lift. 'It's all going crazy up at Forbes,' she said. 'The company guards have barricaded themselves inside the mine, and the strikers have got them hostage and they're threatening to blow it up. I'm surprised to find you sitting here.' She pushed her way into the room without asking, and I don't deny it, I was irritated. I had work to do. And yes – the tea party article was in my typewriter, and I wasn't terribly enthusiastic about letting her see it. Like any reporter, I wanted the article to appear, and I did not want to have to deal with her squeamishness before publication. She had done a great job setting the thing up.' He laughs. 'Inez knew just what I was after and, yes, I suppose by then – she had served her purpose. She couldn't help me any more by then. I just wanted to write the piece. And I suppose – *yes* – I was hoping that by the time the article was printed ... Oh, I don't know, that life would have moved on. She would have forgotten ...'

'She was coming to live with you in New York,' I insist. 'How *could* she have forgotten?'

'I already told you,' he says. 'She was never intending to live with me.' He waves at a passing waiter, and turns to me. 'Do you want another one?' He orders two more martinis. I wait. '... So, yes, she was coming to New York. Or she *said* she was coming to New York. But I never entirely believed it. Did you?'

'She sent her luggage on!'

'Which supports my point. I always assumed she sent the luggage on in an attempt to persuade herself she was truly going to follow. To make the move seem more real to her. I think she was terrified, Dora. I also think that whatever she did, ultimately, depended on what Lawrence O'Neill told her to do. Was he really coming to New York? It's what he told her, but I mean ...' Max stops. Looks up at the sun. 'It's getting rather hot, isn't it? I don't know how you Californians put up with this heat. When he returns with the drinks, I'm going to ask our friend to move us into the shade – if you're happy with that? Would it bother you?'

'Not at all. Tell me then ...' I am growing impatient. So much of what I thought I understood is beginning to unravel. Or is Max lying? But why would he? What is to be gained from it, after all this time? 'So Inez burst into the room and wouldn't sit down. Did you try to hide the article from her?'

'I did. At first. That is, I offered her a drink, and asked her – about ten times – to sit down. Her pacing was driving me crazy. I had the sense that she had something she wanted to tell me ... She'd start to say it and then look as if she might burst into tears, and stop – and then she'd leap off on another tangent entirely. Whatever it was she came to say, she never said it. Which is why that letter is so frustrating ... But she talked about you and her brother. She was unhappy because of your refusal to support her with the tea party. She called you "a pair of old bluenoses". She couldn't understand why you wouldn't support her. I could, of course ... I'm not sure that I tried very hard to explain it. She was terribly jealous of your friendship.'

'*Jealous?*' I am astonished and, I recognize, pathetically flattered. Inez? Jealous of us? I had always assumed that she pitied us. I laugh. 'I don't think so.'

Max sends me a queer look. He says, 'You and Xavier were her most loyal friends. Without you two to beat against, she would have been ...' he stops to think. 'She would have been rudderless. She needed you both, clucking and tutting around her. It gave her a kind of definition.'

'She had her aunt, as you put it, "clucking and tutting" for her. Tutting for all Colorado.'

'Yes. Her aunt was sweet, but she was dumb. She hardly counted. Inez was very fond of her, I remember.

311

She talked about how she would miss her when she came to live in New York. She worried about her aunt's health. Something about a bad heart. But, as I say, I'm not convinced that Inez ever really believed she would make the move. Even though I know a great part of her longed to do it. And, by the way, I think that was also what encouraged her to organize the wretched tea party. As if she was trying to make her own home uninhabitable. By alienating her friends and neighbours, she was attempting to drive herself out of town.'

'You've been reading too much Freud,' I say.

It seems to irritate him. He looks behind him, in search of distraction. 'Ah-ha!' he says. 'Our friend is here at last!' Actually our friend (the waiter) is several tables away. 'What I was absolutely longing for,' says Max, smiling into the eyes of his friend, 'was a *fruit ice*. Do you serve a fruit ice? Would you like a fruit ice, Dora?' he turns to me. 'I hear they are delicious here at the Ambassador. A speciality of the house!'

I shake my head. 'We have ordered fish, haven't we?'

'What? Why yes! How absurd. I had forgotten. Nevertheless ...' He laughs, that handsome, toothy laugh. But it doesn't ring true. Any more than his request for a fruit ice. I wonder why he is so uncomfortable.

The waiter takes the order and shimmies onward. I say to Max, 'Carry on. Don't stop. Nothing makes any sense yet.'

He nods. 'Our memories don't appear to match,' he agrees. 'The letter is a great mystery ... Well she was pacing my little room, making me seasick, and finally I persuaded her to sit on the chair by the bed. I was by the desk and, at first, I admit, I tried to extract the paper out of the cursed machine without her noticing.' He laughs. 'But she spotted it absolutely at once. That was the thing about Inez. One received the impression she was never *quite* concentrating, but she almost always *was*. She was never quite such the fool we all took her for.'

'Excepting that she wound up on a slab in the mortuary on Main Street, while the rest of us walked away,' I reply. It sounds far angrier than I intended. I suppose I am angry. I don't recognize the Inez that Max is describing.

'Indeed ...' he says. 'In any case, she spotted my ploy at once, Dora. She held out her little hand, like an empress – I can see her now! – and absolutely demanded to see what I had written.

'I shilly-shallied. As any reporter would, I hasten to add. But she insisted, and she wouldn't let it go – and finally she threatened tears and ...' He runs his hands through his thick, grey hair. Smoke curls from the cigarette between his fingers. I listen out for the sizzle of hair oil, but it doesn't come. 'I am hopeless when women weep. Putty in their hands.' He smiles. I feel irritated.

'So. What did you show her?'

'I had a fairly good draft of the first three quarters

or so. I handed her the sheet that was in the typewriter, but – of course – she wanted the rest. There was a heap of sheets on my desk. Of course Inez, not being a writer, had no comprehension of how loathsome it is when somebody reads something that is not quite ready to be read ...

'Anyway, she read it – actually, I read it to her. And, I swear to you Dora: she adored it! She laughed so much she wouldn't stop. Almost to the point where ...' He pauses. 'I think – well, I think we both know she was extremely excitable. The fact is,' he looks embarrassed, 'she wasn't terribly well, was she?'

'As far as I remember, your article wasn't terribly funny.'

'It certainly wasn't meant to be.'

'Ridiculous, maybe. But not funny.'

He tips his head, irritated again, and ignores the interruption. 'Anyway,' he says. 'She read it. It was lying on the desk when she came in. I certainly never left her alone in my room, and there was never any need for her to rifle through any drawers to find any papers ... Dora, I'll say it one more time. She and I were never lovers.'

'But you were!' I tell him.

He laughs, embarrassed.

I shake my head. I am embarrassed too ... But he *was* her lover! *Inez told me*. She went into the smallest detail: more detail than I wanted – how he undressed her this way and kissed her that way and how it had obliterated memories of all that had gone before. I asked her: Lawrence doesn't compare? And for a moment she looked blank, as if she couldn't even remember who I was talking about.

Max says, 'O'Neill took a room on the same floor at the Corinado. They were lovers, so far as I know, until the end. At least – that was the last time I saw her, and she certainly didn't mention it was over. The last time I saw her,' he says, gazing once again at the blue sky above my head, 'she said she was on her way to visit Bony Cody's uncle, or father ... Was it in Trinidad, or was it out of town? I don't remember. All I know is that she was on her way there, and she was carrying a lot of money. She and I squabbled – I told you that. But it wasn't about the article. It was about me, being rather petulant and asking her to leave me in peace so I could get on with my work, and Inez being – well, as I say, she was frantic, wasn't she? I couldn't get rid of her, so in the end I had to be rather blunt with her. But we left on good terms. Excellent terms, I might even be tempted to say ... At any rate, she gave me the most terrific hug before she left; wouldn't let go. She thanked me, though I wasn't sure what for; and I thanked her for all her help, and we agreed that we would see each other next at the train station. Although, I still contend that neither of us entirely believed it. And that was the last time I saw her.'

'So?'

He shrugs. 'So? Except for a trip out to Forbes the next morning, to examine the wreckage, I pretty much stayed in my room. At that point – after the Forbes battle – I was impatient to get back to New York again. If you had come to see me with Inez's letter that day, the day you *should* have delivered the letter, then perhaps all these questions might have been answered long ago. I left a note with the desk clerk at the Corinado, informing Inez what train I would be on. She never turned up. I wrote. I told you: a couple of times before the article was published, a couple of times after ... But I never heard from her again.'

We are silent. Nothing makes sense. And finally he leans forward. 'Why don't you tell me what happened Dora?' he says. 'I mean, after you identified her in the morgue ... I presume you never discovered who fired the shot?'

I shake my head. 'No, of course not. It might have been any one of them,' I say. 'From either side. You know how crazy it was. She was out on the prairie, on her own – on her way to deliver some message to Cody's uncle. Or something. Some money to Cody's mama ... Gosh – who knows? There was a heist. They took her motorcar, jewellery, the cash – if she was still carrying it. None of it was ever seen again. All she had was the letter.' I nod towards it, lying there, blood-spattered and inscrutable. 'There was nothing else.'

33

1914
Trinidad, Colorado

Mr Adamsson came shuffling into the room where Inez lay, and seemed to glower at my guilty hand as it tucked away the letter. But, if he noticed anything, he didn't say. He was more concerned with his paperwork. He carried a sheaf of papers with him and he pushed her small feet aside to clear a space on the marble slab so he could lean on it. Then he adjusted his eyeglass and set about his questions. Clearly he was worried that I might disappear before he had a chance to allocate responsibility for the body, and since Lawrence had already slipped away, I could hardly blame him.

So, with Inez lying between us, I offered up the necessary information. Name of Deceased? My name? Relationship to Deceased? Deceased Next of Kin? He recognised the McCulloch name, and as soon as I mentioned it, his manner lightened. After that, he could hardly wait to get rid of me.

I wandered out onto Main Street again. It was growing dark. The streets were almost empty, but the distant spatter of gunfire seemed to pound in my head, and echo from unknown corners.

I wandered aimlessly for a while, unable to make a decision. Mr Adamsson had suggested I inform the next of kin. I told him it would be better if he made the call himself. He didn't like that. But I could not return to the McCulloch porch yet again, this time to inform them that their beloved Inez was not lying sick in a brothel, but dead in the city morgue.

I don't know for how long I walked the streets. It must have been an hour at least. It was dark when my feet led me to the cottage. The drapes were pulled shut, but I could see the glow of electric light through the glass on the front door.

I knocked, and knocked again. Silence. Xavier wasn't there. Even so, I didn't want to leave. So I stood for a while and then, for the hell of it, I tried the door. Xavier rarely locked it. Sure enough there was a click, and the door opened wide – into the room I knew so well, and where I had spent all my happiest hours in Trinidad. With the drapes closed and the lamps lit, it was the only place in the world I could imagine being. The cottage beckoned me in.

At first I simply sat on the soft leather couch; and then, for a while, I lay on it, as I used to. I closed my eyes and tried to will back the evenings we had spent, Inez and I; and then Xavier, Inez and I, taking turns on the rocking chair, spilling liquor onto our stomachs as we squabbled or talked or laughed. There were moments when I felt she was there, back in the room with me. I wept, and I fell asleep, and I woke, my body cold as ice and with her warm laughter in my ear.

Xavier came back to the cottage some time after 2 a.m. He found me kneeling in the kitchen, hunched over the swordstick she had ordered from the spy shop in Philadelphia, and which she had given to her brother. I was struggling with the catch, trying to work out how the thing opened. I didn't hear him come in – not until I felt his hand on my shoulder, and I heard the crack of his knees as he crouched to join me. Without a word, he took the swordstick from me and slid it open. The slim silver blade glinted under the electric light.

'It's rather beautiful,' I said.

He slid it shut again. 'Keep it,' he said. 'I don't want it. And thank you, by the way.'

'What for?'

'The mortuary. I'm not good at that sort of thing.'

'*Sort of thing?*'

He shrugged. 'You know what I mean.'

He straightened up, so I followed suit. He had

discovered me in his cottage, uninvited, rifling though his belongings. It was understandable if he wanted me to leave. I cast around for my coat and an expression of panic crossed his face. 'You're not leaving?' he said. 'Dora, you can't leave!'

'I shouldn't be here. I'm so sorry.'

'Why? Where else should you be?'

'Nowhere else,' I said. 'But I'm not family. Your aunt and uncle probably need you.'

'They have each other,' he said. 'We don't.'

'They do ... I guess you're right.'

'I'll see them again in the morning. Right now, I was hoping we could sink a couple of bottles of whiskey together. That's all I want to do. Would you be in for that?'

We exchanged the ghosts of smiles. I didn't need to answer.

It was a warm night, but simultaneously we looked across at the ash-filled grate. 'I think we should light a fire,' he said. 'Don't you?'

'I think so, yes. You do it, Xavier. I'll fix us some drinks. There's something I want to show you.'

I waited until we were seated by the fire, each on our couch, the rocking chair empty in the corner between us. I pulled out the letter, and laid it on the ottoman. Xavier looked at it, spattered in her blood. He didn't take his eyes off it, but nor did he move to take it. After a moment, I took pity and took it back.

'It isn't properly sealed,' I said, holding it out towards him. 'Look, Xavier. We could open it now, perfectly easily, and close it up again. Max would be none the wiser. Do you think we could do that?' I longed for him to say 'open it', but even if he hadn't, I don't suppose I could have restrained myself for long. I had held back, waiting for Xavier's permission. But as I held the envelope, my fingers on the seal, it popped open as if it had a will of its own; as if Inez *wanted* it. It's what I told myself then. It's what Xavier told himself, too. We read the letter and we put it away. In the circumstances, though our objections to Max and his journalistic ambitions were vindicated, the letter seemed trivial to the point of irrelevance.

But it gave us a foe at least: a focus for our ire. Everything was Max's fault! And for a while – maybe an hour or two – it bolstered us through the grief.

We would help each other, so we said that night. Together, we would live through this. We talked about Inez, but never about her violent death. We drank two bottles of whiskey, and talked a lot and said nothing ... until the fire died and the room grew chilly again. Xavier offered me his bed to sleep in. I accepted the offer and when I woke he was lying fully dressed, on top of the covers, beside me. I was never more comforted by a sight.

We stayed indoors with the drapes drawn, while the sun beat down outside. Xavier shuffled off to make us coffee and he brought it through on a tray into his room, where I remained on his bed, and we lay side by side, like an old married couple, sipping coffee and staring at the wall.

It's how the day passed. We talked about my childhood in England, my father's return there and my decision not to follow him. My regrets. His regrets. We talked about his parents' death on the railroad, how he and Inez had travelled from Chicago together, and the kindness of his Aunt Philippa through it all. It troubled him that he couldn't be the man she wanted him to be. We told each other many things that day which I don't think either of us had told anyone before, but we didn't talk about Inez.

Hours passed as we lay on his bed. We had long since moved from coffee to whiskey again, and there was, for long stretches, a numb silence between us that I think we both found comforting. Our arms lay limp by our sides, close enough to feel the warmth from each other's skin, and I found that comforting too. He took my hand.

It was a trigger. It made me cry, which encouraged him, I think. He turned and kissed me.

The bed springs creaked as he twisted his body towards me and his lips touched mine. I waited. It wasn't what I wanted. It wasn't what he wanted. But people do the oddest things, in grief.

I felt his discomfort. He leaned closer towards me. I felt his shame. I felt my pity. I gave him a moment to extricate himself, but it seemed, having begun, that he lacked the nerve to pull back. So, finally, I pushed him gently away.

He rolled away from me at once. There was a long pause.

'Forgive me,' he said at length. 'That was the most ridiculous thing I think I have ever done. I am so sorry.'

I laughed. 'Forgive you? Whatever for?'

'I shouldn't have done it.'

'Trust me,' I told him. 'I've survived worse. And what's a kiss, between friends, after all?' I tried to take back his hand but he pulled it away.

'I've been meaning to do it for ages,' he said.

'Do what?' I asked, bemused now.

'*Kiss* you,' he said. He sounded angry. As if I were the stupid one.

'*Have* you?' I said. 'Why?'

There followed the longest silence yet. I watched the emotions churning in his handsome face and was struck more forcefully than ever by his similarity to his sister – and by the great differences. He was small and delicate, as she was. They had the same blond hair and grey eyes – and yet they could not have been more different. I thought all this, as the silence extended. He wanted to say something. He looked ready to burst with it, and I wanted to help him. On the other hand, he seemed angry. So I waited.

When he spoke, it sounded stilted and tight. 'You've become a good friend,' he said.

'I hope so. I consider you a friend.'

'Of course you do.'

It was an odd response. Again, I waited.

He said: 'It would make my Aunt Philippa so happy ...'

'What would make her happy?' I asked. 'Xavier, honey. You're not making sense.' Nor was he, but somewhere at the base of my neck, I could feel prickles of panic. In his clumsiness, his personal confusion, I hoped that he would not continue along the track I suspected he was laying out for us. I pulled myself up from the pillows and swung my legs to the ground. 'I'm hungry,' I announced. 'Aren't you? I don't even remember when I last ate. I could make us eggs. Do you have any eggs? I could make us eggs on toast ... Would you like that?'

But the track was laid – it was laid long ago, I suspect. From the moment we first met, and liked each other, and I took him to fetch Inez from my home at Plum Street. He tugged me back onto the bed. 'Wait! Dora. Please ... I don't know how to put this—'

'Then don't,' I said, sitting up again.

'If I could be a *normal* man ...'

'Oh, for crying out loud!'

'I've never even tried!'

'Well, darling – you're thirty-five years old. There's probably a reason you've not got around to it. Come on,' I nudged him and smiled. 'Don't do this. Please. You're a fairy. Always were and always will be. You are never going to be a normal man. Who cares?'

'A lot of people care. Actually. The Sheriff's Department at Long Beach. My Aunt Philippa – or she would if she knew. Uncle Richard. Inez ...'

A beat, while we remembered.

'Inez didn't know,' I said. 'I asked her once.'

'You didn't!' He was horrified.

'Not directly. Of course not. Indirectly, I asked her something about the possibility of you one day settling down and she was ...' He looked pained; I patted him on the leg. 'She hadn't the *faintest* idea, Xavier. Honestly, I got the sense it had simply never crossed her mind. I imagine it's the same with your Aunt Philippa.'

'That's the thing. Aunt Philippa was always so good to us, Dora. And now Inez is gone. And she has no children of her own. And she will be stuck with Uncle Richard and I swear he's no solace to anyone. I *owe* her ...'

'It's too bad for your Aunt Philippa,' I said.

He wasn't listening. 'I thought, with your experience, you might be able to help me ... Couldn't you? Teach me how ... And then I could find a nice girl, and we could settle down and have children together. And she and I could ... settle down and ...' He sighed. The despondency on his face as he envisaged it made me forget how much I disliked what he was suggesting and how hurtful I found it – and made me laugh instead.

'I can't help you, Xavier. You're going to have to find another hooker to work miracles for you ... Or maybe find another way to make your Aunt Philippa happy. Show her your movies. Invite her to California and show her the sunshine. Go visit her this afternoon. She needs you. And now – let me make some breakfast.'

We shuffled off the bed and wandered together into the parlour. Neither of us had undressed the previous night, and we were still wearing our clothes of the day before. Mine, I imagined, with some part of Inez still on them. I had worn them to the mortuary. I had brushed against her body as it lay on the slab, and I felt there was some physical remnant of her death that still clung to me.

'Xavier,' I said. 'I'm going to take a bath. Would you lend me a bathrobe?'

He lent me the paisley silk affair I had so admired when he opened the door to me last week. It smelled of his cologne and, as I wrapped it round me, there was something comforting about it. More than comforting. I held the fabric to my nose and inhaled – the smell of Xavier. It made me happy.

I had left him cooking the eggs. When I emerged from his bathroom, his robe around me, the cottage smelled like home: of wood smoke, from the fire last night, and buttered eggs, and grilling bread. I followed the smell into the kitchen, and watched while he worked. He looked older, grimmer, greyer, still in his clothes from yesterday.

'Gosh I'm going to miss you when you leave,' I said abruptly. 'Trinidad will be unbearable without you and Inez.'

He looked up from his cooking pan. 'One egg or two? Or three? I'm having three ... Pleasant bath?'

'Very pleasant,' I said. 'Two, please. Xavier. I suppose you *will* leave, won't you? Now that Inez is gone. When do you suppose you'll leave?'

'Soon,' he said, turning back to his hob. 'I have work to do in Hollywood. A bunch of projects. And I have debts.' He shivered – a comically expressive shiver: like a dancer. '*Horrible* debts. Thanks to my brilliant lawyers. I need to get back to work ... But you could come, Dora.'

'I would love to come with you. But I have debts too, and I have no money.'

'Ah!' He tossed the eggs, arranged the toasted bread, the slices of ham. 'I'd help you. I wish I could.'

'I'm sure you would,' I said.

'It seems kind of ridiculous, Dora. You charge – what do you charge? Thirty dollars a turn?'

'Fifty.'

He chuckled. 'It's a lot of money. Even if Phoebe takes sixty or seventy per cent, how is it possible that you're still broke?'

'Because Phoebe takes it all.' I sighed.

'That doesn't make sense.'

'No. It doesn't. But she does. She racks up imaginary debts.'

'Bring the whiskey,' he said. 'And a couple of glasses. And explain.' He picked up our plates and I followed him to the parlour. We took our places, each to our favourite couch, and rested our plates on our laps.

'Actually,' I said, 'she takes more than everything. She takes it all, and then she presents us with more receipts for things she says we owe her for – doctors' bills, cleaning bills, food, linen, drink, clothing, furniture ... It doesn't matter what. She thinks of something. And then we never have quite enough to pay. So she says: *never mind, darling. You can pay me next month* ... And so it goes on. Each month, she calls us into her parlour, and she has a great pile of papers before her; and she smiles as if ...' I laughed, and I know it sounded bitter. 'For a long time, Xavier, I used to believe her. She has the sweetest smile. I used to believe we were friends. And each month, when our little meetings came to an end, she would pat me on the back and thank me for my excellent work, as if Plum Street couldn't survive without me. She would say to me, "Don't you worry about the money. I'll take care of it. That's what I'm here for."'

'How long have you worked there?' he asked me.

'I don't like thinking about it. Too long.'

'I'll bet you don't,' he said. He laid down his knife and fork. 'But she's robbing you. Work it out! How many clients do you see in a week? How many weeks in a year? Let's say a hundred dollars a night, five nights a week? Six? Multiply that by fifty-two. And multiply that by – six years?' He came up with a figure without a beat. 'One hundred eighty-seven thousand, two hundred dollars.'

I laughed. 'Is that right? How did you do that? Actually it's seven years, coming along eight. And we're allowed a week off in the summer.'

'What if you simply refuse to play along? What if you say: Phoebe, this is absurd! I don't owe you this money. I never spent that kind of money in my life. If anything, you cocksucker, it's *you* who owes *me* money … Goddammit,' he broke off, 'why must *everyone* in life turn out to be a charlatan?'

Again, I laughed. 'Well she runs a brothel,' I said.

'They're charlatans in the movie business too,' he muttered. 'Every damned one of them.'

'Profanities won't help, Xavier.'

'Oh, don't be prim,' he said. 'It doesn't suit you. And you didn't answer the question. What could happen if you stood up to her?'

'She could throw me out of the house. For a start.'

'But you make her a lot of money. She won't want to do that.'

'She could send her heavies after me.' I had cleaned my plate, but I was still hungry. 'Trust me, Xavier, there are any number of things she could do, and none I would enjoy. Is there any more ham?'

'No more ham,' he said. 'So, Dora ... my friend.' He considered me. 'When you and Inez were plotting for you to set up as a singing instructress in town—?'

'I was living on cloud cuckoo. Shall we talk about something else?'

34

'Something else' presented itself at just that instant. Philippa McCulloch was at the door. And the next thing, before Xavier had time to collect himself, she had unlocked it herself, with her own set of keys, and walked right into the house. She stood at the threshold, unwelcome sunlight shining in behind her, a small, stout, wounded silhouette. She gazed at us. Poor, decent woman. It can't have been an uplifting sight. I lay sprawled on one couch, wrapped in her nephew's lilac paisley breakfast gown, an empty plate and a filled glass of whiskey on my belly; Xavier lay sprawled on the other, shirt undone and still crumpled from sleep, the bottle of whiskey nestled beside him; and between us the mess and remains of this morning's breakfast and last night's drinking.

We both struggled to pull ourselves together, but the impression was made, the damage done.

Xavier said: 'Aunt Philippa!' brushing toast crumbs off his bare chest. He stood to welcome her and his balance was just a little off. It occurred to me we were both probably quite drunk. 'I didn't realize you had keys. Maybe it's better if you knock?' He looked around him at the disarray, carefully avoiding my eye. 'I might have prepared things a little better.'

Mrs McCulloch moved into the room and the light from the door fell on her face. It was puffy with crying. Her hands were shaking. Her chest rose and fell, as if she were fighting for breath. She didn't speak.

'Although I agree,' he added, looking around him again, somewhat helplessly, 'it might have needed a little longer to get this place in order.'

She glanced across, but didn't acknowledge me. She perched herself at the end of the couch I had just vacated in her honour. 'You're drinking liquor,' she said. 'It's early to be drinking liquor. I wish you'd come home last night, Xavier. I sat up for you. I thought you were coming back but you didn't. I was worried about you, darling. But I see you were being looked after. *Looked after*,' she muttered the words again. 'So that's good.' It seemed hard to believe that she meant it. But at that point there was no disapproval, no bitterness in her voice.

'Would you like a drink?' he asked her.

'Yes,' she said. 'Very much. I have just come from the morgue. Mr Adamsson was very kind. Very helpful. Very kind and helpful. You should have gone to the morgue, Xavier. You're her brother.'

'I'm sorry,' he said.

We waited but he said nothing more.

'Is that it? You're sorry?'

'I should have gone to the morgue. I didn't think. At least I did. I thought …'

'You didn't think. You didn't think at all.'

I thought he was about to cry. I couldn't bear it for him. I said, 'Mrs McCulloch, I know he meant to go. I'm afraid I delayed him.'

She shot me a look: through the fog of grief, a spark of pure hostility. 'I'm sorry,' I said. 'I should leave.'

'Don't leave!' Xavier said. 'Stay.' He sounded desperate. 'We are all grieving. There is no reason why you should leave. You loved Incz too. I know you did. We all loved her. We should stay together.'

Mrs McCulloch, bolt upright on the couch, looked at the wall opposite and said nothing.

'I'll go get dressed,' I said.

'You do that,' she fired back. And then the strength left her; her shoulders hunched, she put her hands to her face and wept. She looked so pitiful I stopped, kneeled down and wrapped my arms around her. She rested her head on my shoulder, on the paisley silk that smelled of Xavier, and for a moment it was so simple. We helped each other.

Xavier loped off back to the kitchen to fetch his aunt a glass. He returned to the parlour, polishing it with his shirt-sleeve, and carefully filled it to the very brim before holding it out to her. She lifted her head from my shoulder, wiped her eyes and swallowed it in one – like an old cowboy.

'That's the spirit,' Xavier said, returning to his seat. I noticed he had fastened the buttons of his shirt. Somehow, in those few moments, he had managed to make himself look respectable. It rendered my own dishevelled and informal state even more uncomfortable.

'Really,' I said. 'I should go get dressed.'

Mrs McCulloch stared vacantly at the hearth. I padded across the parlour into Xavier's bedroom, and returned as soon as I could, hair tidied with the help of Xavier's combs, yesterday's clothes back in place. I could smell the morgue on them. At least – of course I couldn't. But I could feel it. And there was a speck of something on my cuff that looked like Inez's blood.

I intended to pick up my purse and slip away, but Mrs McCulloch said:

'Xavier tells me you have a letter. From Inez to that delightful gentleman, Mr Eastman. Are you going to deliver it to him?'

'Of course,' I said. I was surprised that Xavier had mentioned it to her. 'I had forgotten you met him.'

'Xavier brought him round, didn't you darling? I thought he was *exceptionally* charming.'

'Yes. Yes, he is, isn't he?'

'He talked of the deep affection and esteem he held for Inez ...' The tears began to roll again, but her voice didn't change. She continued to speak normally. 'He was going to take her to work for his little publication in New York. She was going to lodge in his sister's apartment, and –' she frowned uncertainly – 'in the fall, they were going to marry. It's what Inez said. But he was in mourning. Which is why there was no date set.' I could hear her doubts growing with each new word she uttered. 'He was a very handsome gentleman,' she said. 'Quite delightful. And the son of not *one* minister of the church but two! His mother is also a pastor! Imagine that!' She took another slug from her glass, found it empty, and held it towards Xavier to be topped up. 'I have tried to imagine it,' she added. 'But it's rather hard. Well. Nevertheless. What does it matter any more? Darlng Inez had finally found her love. I never saw her so happy as these past days, did you?' She glanced at us both but didn't seem to expect a reply. I didn't agree with her in any case. 'Mr Adamsson assures me he will provide the finest casket for her. Teak. Or ebony. Did he say ebony?'

'Ebony seems unlikely, Aunt. Mahogany perhaps?'

'That's right.' She glances at me, a fleeting look, sly and fearful. 'Well Miss – I don't even know *what* I am supposed to call you any longer. What name are you going by today?'

335

'My name is Dora Whitworth. I have told you before.'

'Yes indeed. Well, Miss Whitworth. I must admit I am not quite certain why the letter is still in your possession in any case. Or why it ever *was* in your possession. But it hardly matters any more. Are you going to show it to us?'

'Max's letter?'

'I don't know what other letter. Are you going to show it to us?'

I hesitated, looked at Xavier for guidance. But he was making a study of his fingernails. 'Well, Xavier has already seen it,' I said.

'So I understand.'

'Xavier?' But he wouldn't look at me. I wondered what had possessed him to tell her about the letter in the first place. 'I'm not sure I should ...' I said. It sounded feeble. 'Xavier, don't you agree? It was a private correspondence, after all. Between herself and her beloved. I probably shouldn't have read it myself.'

'But you *did* read it,' she said. 'And I would like to read it too. Very, very much. If you please, Miss Whitworth. I would be grateful.' Her chin was trembling. 'If it helps to explain what she was doing halfway to Forbes, in the middle of a battlefield ...'

'But that had nothing to do with Max,' I said. Again, I glanced at Xavier. He was lying back on the couch, dancer's body as limp as a ragdoll, looking from one to the other of us, an expression of immeasurable sadness on his face.

'Say what we will about Max,' I said to Xavier, 'but it was something to do with Cody – or maybe Cody's mother – that sent her out there. We can't blame it on Max.'

Mrs McCulloch began to cry again: this time, with every living part of her. Her face and shoulders crumpled. She held her head, whiskey glass in hand. 'I don't know anything about any Cody,' she said. 'Who is Cody?' Helplessly, I put a hand on her shoulder, but she shook it off, as I knew she would. She sobbed louder, until her body shook, and still, Xavier did nothing.

'Xavier!' I snapped at him. 'For heaven's sake don't just sit there! Help your aunt. Explain to her who Cody is. Won't you? I don't know what to tell her ...'

He said, as if it were obvious: 'Tell her the truth. I'm so sick of all the lies.'

I laughed. It occurred to me he wasn't talking about Inez. 'The truth? About what, Xavier? How can I tell her the truth? I don't even know what it is myself. You want me to show her Max's letter? Why?'

'She wants to know. We all do. Don't we? Aren't you sick of the lies?'

'*What* lies? Xavier, you're drunk. I don't know what you're talking about, but we are talking about the letter. You should shut your mouth if you can't keep a hold of what's coming out of it.'

'What was she *doing* all the way out there?' Mrs McCulloch cried. 'Yesterday, of all the days in the year?

337

Why?' She looked at me as if I not only knew all the answers but I was responsible for them, too. Responsible for everything that had happened.

'I honestly don't know,' I said.

I knew I should leave, and yet I couldn't do it. The thought of being any place where the world hadn't stopped for Inez was unbearable. So I sat still, not moving, knowing I should go, eyes lowered, drinking up the other woman's hostility: a price for being allowed to share in her grief.

Xavier's cold voice broke the silence. 'Don't look at her like that,' he said. At first I wasn't certain which of us he was addressing. I kept my eyes down, felt the itch of a tear rolling down the side of my nose but did nothing about it. 'Aunt Philippa,' Xavier said, 'I said: don't look at Dora like that. As if this were all her fault.'

'How can I not?' she began to sob again. 'Everything was all right until she came along. She thinks I don't know – but I do! I know everything!'

'What do you know?' I asked.

'I know that you have spent the night corrupting my nephew.'

'We were consoling each other, nothing more.'

'You were corrupting him.'

'No,' I said.

'I know that you are a whore.'

I said nothing.

'And that a woman like you has no business being a friend of my niece. Nor of my nephew. And –' her hysteria rising – 'most certainly not of me. How dare you remain in this room with me, while I am grieving my niece and you are a whore? Have you no sense of propriety?'

'Miss Whitworth is here because I have invited her here,' Xavier broke in. 'Which is more than I can say for you.'

'You!' she said to him. '*You!*' And in the tumult of her anger and grief, she seemed to lose her capacity for speech. In a moment her face seemed to lose its colour and then she began to cough and choke, as if on her own breath. It was time for me to leave. I picked up my purse.

But her choking grew frantic – too frantic to ignore. I hesitated, unsure what to do. 'Xavier?'

He was already on his feet. She had began to rasp and to clutch at her chest, and then, slowly, and yet so quickly that somehow neither of us prevented it – she rolled forwards, landing on her knees in front of the couch. Her head and neck, already white, turned from grey to deeper grey, and all the while her eyes were fixed on Xavier, an expression of helpless incomprehension on her face.

Xavier and I had both dropped to our knees, one on either side of her. Xavier held her shoulders. I scrabbled to loosen her corset. I don't know how many seconds or minutes passed. Her breath was still rasping when I ran to the kitchen to fetch her some water. It took a moment to locate a glass, and another moment to rinse it – and when I returned she was lying still, her eyes glazed, her head resting on Xavier's lap while he tenderly stroked her forehead.

'Oh dear God ...' I said.

'She's fine.' But he sounded terrified. 'She's breathing. She'll be fine. She'll be just fine ... You're going to be just fine, Aunt Philippa, you hear me? You stay exactly where you are. We're going to fetch you a doctor.'

There was no telephone at the cottage. I left the two of them on the floor by the hearth and ran to the nearest drugstore to call for a doctor.

I didn't go back again. I wanted to spend the rest of the day with Xavier and his whiskey, in his dirty house, beside his empty hearth. But it was impossible. Xavier knew where I was. I would wait until he came for me.

35

Two more days passed. The strikers had taken possession of the hospital. They helped themselves to whatever they liked from supply stores around town. Mrs Carravalho lost the side of her face when a stray bullet whistled through the glass window of the drugstore on North Commercial. The anarchy made front pages of newspapers across America and, in Trinidad, we stayed inside as much as we could.

Through all of it, Plum Street remained stubbornly open. But I never knew the place so quiet – nor Phoebe quite so bad tempered. She used to stand in the kitchen while the cook prepared our food, snarling at her to cut back on the ingredients, and in those bleak days, Phoebe's impotent, mean-spirited fury was the only thing that made me smile.

At the end of the third day I couldn't wait to hear from Xavier any longer. It was dusk and still too dangerous for ordinary folk to venture out. President Wilson had ordered up the troops and they were on their way at last, but they wouldn't arrive in Trinidad for a few days yet. Finally, after a glass of bourbon for Dutch courage, I made a telephone call to the McCulloch house.

It was the housekeeper who answered. She told me no one was available to talk. She told me Philippa McCulloch had died that morning.

'Of the shock,' the old woman reported, sniffing back tears. 'Her heart gave way. It was too much for her.'

'Well ... that's terrible news. I'm so very sorry ...'

'We all are.'

'And the funeral?' I asked.

'It's for family only. May I enquire who I am speaking with?'

'I meant – I'm so sorry. I meant for Inez.'

And then the line went dead. It was impossible to know if the housekeeper had ended the call, or if – as often happened back then – the connection had simply cut off by its own accord. I called again. It took a half-hour to get a line through. The same voice answered. I wanted to know if I could speak with Xavier.

'I just told you. It was you, wasn't it?'

'I think so.'

'The family doesn't want to speak with anyone for the moment.'

I asked if there was a date set for Inez's funeral. The housekeeper said the two women would now be buried together.

'When?' I asked desperately. 'Where?'

'I already told you,' she said. 'It's for family only … It's you, isn't it?'

'Who?'

'I know it's you so there's no good denying it anyways. You're the lady who's the cause of all the trouble. Aren't you? You came sniffing round here when Inez was sick.'

'I'm not the "cause" of any trouble,' I said. But it was a struggle for me to keep my voice even. 'This is Dora Whitworth.'

'That's right! I know who it is. The one who came round here dressed like a wop, pretending to be someone she wasn't. Next thing you came here dressed as … something else. But I know exactly what you are. And so did Mrs McCulloch.'

'Excuse me. You must have me confused.'

'You should be ashamed of yourself.'

'I've done nothing!'

'Leave this family alone. What's left of it. If you'd a grain of pride in you, which I doubt, you'd leave us in peace …'

I took a breath. 'I haven't rung to speak with you. I have rung to speak with Mr Dubois. Please go and fetch him at once.'

'They can't abide you and that's the fact of it. And nor can I. Mrs McCulloch spoke about you these past days. All the time, when the fever was with her.'

'I don't believe you ... Why would she?'

'The whore who dressed up as a wop, who came to this house pretending to be someone she wasn't, corrupting Miss Inez, then corrupting Mr Dubois ...'

'Nonsense!'

'They can't abide you.'

'No ... Xavier – Mr Dubois – is my good friend.'

'No, ma'am. He ain't your friend. No one in this house is your friend.'

'Is he there?' I asked her. 'Please! Won't you let me speak to him?'

But the line had gone down again and this time there could be no doubt that she had cut me off.

After that, I paced the house and gnawed at my finger ends, strummed at my harpsichord and stared blindly at my filthy French novel. The minutes crawled by. If I braved the streets (which for this, of course, I would) and went to call at the McCullochs', then the housekeeper would no doubt close the door in my face. She would refuse to take my letter from me. So I could either post it through the door without announcing myself, and scurry away, and only hope that the hateful woman didn't intercept it. Or I could deliver the letter to the cottage.

Strikers tended to congregate a few blocks north of it, and the route was more dangerous, but the cottage was perhaps the best way.

Finally, I wrote out the letter twice. Affectionate and brief, I expressed my regret for the death of his aunt. I told him how I longed to hear from him, and how much I hoped to be able to attend the funeral, if it was permitted. I waited until dark and set out to deliver them – one copy through the McCulloch front door and a second through the letterbox at the cottage.

The early spring warmth had abandoned us again, and there was a fresh dusting of snow on the ground. It was an hour-long round trip, the coldest and the most frightening I can remember taking. Every sound, every breeze made my heart stop; and, in the midst of it all, the odd gunshot, sometimes close by, sometimes from several blocks away. On Beech Street, two idling men pointed their rifles at me as I scurried past: I could feel the noses of their guns follow me, burning into my back, until the moment I turned the corner out of sight. On my return, I never felt so happy to walk through the doors at Plum Street.

It was a wasted effort. Xavier didn't reply to either letter. I discovered the date and location of the funeral only after Lawrence O'Neill dropped by to ask if I was attending. He hardly stayed a minute, but I cannot overstate what an extraordinary and welcome thing it was that he came at all. That week the Union was waging war, not on a single coal company but on American capitalism itself, or so we understood. Its call to arms – to union members nationwide – had brought men by the thousands into Trinidad. Every attack on every mine, on every scab and every company guard, needed to be planned and executed ... And yet, there stood Lawrence O'Neill in my crimson hallway once again, his hat in his hand, asking about Inez's funeral.

An announcement in the *Chronicle* had stated that the service was for close family only, but he had thought, considering our friendship, that I might have been made an exception.

I laughed. 'You seem to forget—'

He shook his head. Of course he hadn't forgotten. 'I just thought maybe – because you were friends with her brother, too. But I guess not. Have you seen him lately? How is he doing?'

'He's doing fine,' I replied. 'That is, so far as I know. He won't see me. I called the house – I think he has turned against me.'

'I'm sorry,' he shrugged.

'I thought we were friends.'

Lawrence nodded. 'Well – these are difficult times,' he said blandly. 'The man has lost his family. Maybe he'll soften.'

'They loved each other, you know. It was just the two of them ... orphans, really. And their aunt – and now she's gone too.'

There was no one else for me to talk to about them, and I longed for him to stay. But I was blethering, I knew it, and I knew there were many more pressing matters on his mind. Already he was backing towards the door. '*You* loved her, didn't you Lawrence?' I said.

'I sure miss her,' he said uncomfortably.

'I do too. God, I miss her ...'

'Dora, I just dropped by to check on you ... That's all ... Just wanted to see you were all right. I guess you're all right, are you?'

I am so very far from all right! I wanted to cry. *I am heartbroken and abandoned and ...* but I pulled myself up. I smiled. It was sweet of him to come. His desire to get back on the road shone like a sweat on his face. 'Thank you for calling by, Lawrence. I really appreciate it. I guess I can't attend the funeral. I mean – of course I can't. But I will walk by, I think, while it is happening. There can't be any harm in that, can there?'

'Don't see how,' he said, with another backward step. Simple Kitty – ever present – opened the front door behind him. He replaced his hat, glanced at one of the hundred mirrors around him and adjusted it an inch. 'Hang around some place they can't see you, maybe. Say your goodbyes,' he said. 'Say 'em for both of us, will you?'

'I'll do that,' I said. 'Thank you Lawrence.'

He nodded. 'You be careful now. Won't you. There's nowhere safe in Trinidad right now. You take care of yourself.' And with that, he marched through the snow, and out of sight.

Trinidad had seen enough funerals those past few days. Inez's and Philippa's were just two more. Only three days earlier, at the same handsome Catholic church, there had been the funeral service for the eleven children and three mothers who were trapped and burned alive out at Ludlow. After that service, the caskets had been carried by horse-drawn hearse to the cemetery on East Main, and the silent procession had brought everything in the city – including the gunfire – to a stop. Fifteen hundred mourners had lined the streets.

The funeral for Inez and Philippa McCulloch was a more subdued affair – and far quieter than a McCulloch funeral might have been on any other week. It was partly out of respect for the family's wishes, of course, as published in the *Chronicle*. They had requested a small and private service. But I wondered: had the family wanted a vast and public service, how many friends and neighbours might have found themselves indisposed that day?

Under other circumstances, the guest list of grievers might have read like a roll call of Union enemies. The McCullochs were at the heart of the Trinidad elite – much of which had grown wealthy off the mines, off the sweat of the miners, and was instinctively hostile towards the Union cause. The Northcutts owned the city newspaper which published hateful reports about the strikers' cause on a daily basis. The Johnsons owned a gun store which had only last week been ransacked by strikers, and robbed of every piece of ammunition on the shelves. This was not a week for the Trinidad wealthy to gather in public and make a show, unless it wanted to invite yet more funerals.

I found a place to stand behind an advertising board which lent me a view of the church door and which hid me from sight, and I waited for the hearse carrying Inez and her aunt to draw up.

They arrived together, through the damp snow: just two motorcars and one horse-drawn hearse. From the front car there stepped Richard McCulloch, followed by his nephew Xavier in sober, borrowed black; and, after them, two ladies of Mrs McCulloch's age, neither of whom I recognized. In colour and in build, both bore a heavy-jawed resemblance to Mr McCulloch, and so I concluded they were his sisters, come in from Denver. In the second car there came Mrs Johnson, whom I recognized from the music club, and whose loathsome views on the miners' situation had prompted Inez to invite her to Max Eastman's tea party. Mrs Johnson came with another woman, also present at the music club, but whose name I couldn't recollect.

Behind them, arriving on foot and dressed in black, came three more figures: two women, both holding handkerchiefs to their eyes. The stouter of the two I recognized as the McCulloch housekeeper. They were followed by an elderly gentleman, who walked very upright and wore a cap. I recognized him at once as the man who had come to fetch Inez from the Toltec the night she met Lawrence O'Neill. The night we befriended one another. The night all this began.

There were no friends present for Inez. None, except me, uninvited, hiding behind the hoarding in the bitter cold; and her brother, in formal black – wearing what looked like his uncle's mourning coat. It hung loose on him. He looked shattered in it: thin and white, and half dead himself.

I willed him to look up, but whether he felt my eyes on him or not, he didn't do it. He waited for his uncle to lead the way, and then the ladies, and then the servants, and then for the caskets to be carried in and, finally, with eyes still lowered, he scuttled into the church behind them.

It was snowing again and the wind was cruel. But I couldn't yet drag myself away. I imagined her, lying in her coffin, the blood from her neck wound wiped clean, her face still and hard and white – and no friend there to grieve for her but her brother. I couldn't abandon her mid-ceremony. To leave would have felt like desertion.

It is a large church and not one I had made a habit of entering. In fact, I had been inside it only twice; once, in a hailstorm when I was caught unprotected, and once, in the early days, I wandered in there in the way people are supposed to: looking for some peace, or some light – some love, I suppose, and forgiveness. I hadn't believed in God for many years and yet I do remember it was distinctly comforting.

Outside in the cold, I remembered that sense of comfort. And I imagined the small party huddled round the two coffins. They would be standing far away at the front of the church with their back to the door. If I could slide through the smallest crack, and creep to one side, and hide behind the great wooden font or perhaps behind one of the fat, stone pillars, would they notice me?

There was a slight creak as I pushed back the door. I waited a moment and then slowly, softly pushed it again. As I poked my head in, I saw Xavier twisting away from me, as if he had half spun round at the noise. Was he expecting me, I wondered? It seemed impossible that he could have forgotten me altogether.

I slipped through into the church and closed the door behind me. There it was, the great wooden font of my memory, only a handful of steps away but, sadly, not half as great as I remembered. I realized it wouldn't hide me. In fact, nothing about the church was as large as I remembered. The two coffins and the huddle of grievers were hardly any distance from me: close enough to have felt the cold breeze as I entered. There was a pillar that might have been wide enough to hide me, but it was at least ten or fifteen feet away. I couldn't risk it. So I stood frozen, uncertain which way to turn. I could have left, but the rich, sweet smell of the incense and the rhythmic clank of the burner, the chanting of the priest, the snuffling tears of the women, the warmth and the peace ... in truth I could not have left. They combined to lull and comfort and entrance me.

There was a bench behind me, beside the door I had just slipped through. I sat down on it.

The two caskets were identical, both of mahogany, richly carved, with large, curling silver handles. They rested, two caskets that were fit for kings, side by side, on two identical biers. Had *Cody* been buried in this sort of a box, I wondered? Of course he hadn't, and what did it matter anyway?

It was impossible to know who lay in which one, of course, and my gaze switched restlessly from one casket to the next. Was stout Mrs McCulloch resting inside this one, her kind face frozen in sadness and resentment, as it had been the last time I saw her? (I remembered how she rested her head on my shoulder, and felt a moment of sorrow for the strength of her suffering.)

Or was it Inez resting inside?

Was one casket a fraction wider than the other? No. One would assuredly be lighter – but I could hardly test that out. The two boxes were just the same, as short and wide as each other.

But how could I say my farewells without knowing where to look? I thought there might be a clue in the way the grievers had arranged themselves ... but no – at any rate, I could not be sure. And, for some reason, no matter which coffin I gazed on, I could only envisage the sad, stupid face of Mrs McCulloch inside.

I sat quietly, thinking I ought to leave. As long as I was uncertain which woman lay in which, there could be no comfort in gazing at the preposterous wooden boxes before me anyway. I was on the point of standing up when, for no reason whatsoever, Mr McCulloch slowly twisted round and stared at me.

The moment seemed to last forever. I stared back at him – it seemed the natural response. I nodded at him, not certain if he even knew who I was, but he didn't react. He turned back to the caskets, leaned towards Xavier, standing beside him, and whispered something in his ear.

If I'd possessed any presence of mind I might even then have slipped away, and yet ... some forlorn corner of my heart still clung to the idea that if only Xavier saw me, a cloud would lift and he would remember me, and welcome me back again.

He looked at me at last, but no cloud lifted. His expression didn't change. He looked at me as if I were no one, nothing – not even there: and then he looked away again.

A most pathetic cry escaped me, and I left at once.

36

At last the president's troops arrived and, with the troops, came order. Soon after that, the newspaper reporters packed up and left, and then, finally, so did the Union ... It had run out of funds, and after a long winter under snow and canvas, the strikers had run out of fight. They trickled back to the mines that had previously employed them and, slowly, the town returned to a sullen and unhappy version of its older self.

In December 1914, fifteen months after Mother Jones had stood on the stage and shouted to that defiant, packed-out theatre hall: 'It is slavery or strike!', the miners opted for a return to slavery again. They had suffered enough. The strike was over. Nothing had changed, the world's attention had moved on, and the mood in Trinidad could not have been more wretched.

Death and dishonour hung in the air. It clung to every one of us.

After Inez died, there was nothing much to keep Xavier in Trinidad. I had resisted the temptation to approach him after the incident at the church. He had made it very clear that our friendship counted more to me than to him. He made it clearer still, about a week after the funeral. I came home from a solitary amble through town, hoping as ever that I might bump into him, and instead found a letter awaiting me. He had come to call, and I had not been there.

He could not have lingered for long. I was only walking a short while. I wondered whether he had waited until I was out before presenting himself, because the letter he left, bidding me farewell and apologizing for having missed me, was written on his aunt's stationery, indicating he had written it before he even set out.

Words could never express the sense of loss I felt when I read the note and realized he was gone. He wrote that he was taking the train to Hollywood and, in my desperation, I set out to catch him at the station.

Spring had returned and the weather was warm again. I didn't bother with a coat. Instead, I ran. I ran as far as the ticket booth and was about to burst onto the platform when I caught myself. *Was I mad or stupid?* If Xavier had wanted to find me, he would have done so.

He didn't want to find me. He didn't want me to rush to the train station and bid him farewell. He wanted to leave. Without me. So I turned away. And, once again, made the long trudge home to Plum Street.

His letter had offered no forwarding address.

37

The town was subdued and so was Plum Street, but it had been ten months since the troops had been and gone, and at least we were still in business. Several of the better brothels in town had recently gone under, so we girls hardly dared to complain. But we were bored, and we spent our empty days and evenings squabbling. Phoebe was the worst. As her income dwindled, she lost any inclination to be remotely civil to us. She looked on us with a sort of calculating resentfulness, so much so that we used to laugh about it, if only to relieve the tension.

'Watch out,' we whispered to each other. 'She's comparing how many clients you entertained last week with how many slices of ham you ate for breakfast this morning. Better put a slice back!'

We laughed about it together, yes, but in secret we did a fair amount of client-to-ham-slice calculating ourselves.

We were frightened. With business this quiet, sooner or later one of us would have to go, and with Phoebe as capricious as she was, there could be no knowing which of us she might choose.

Although I suppose, of the eight of us, I was most likely at the front of the line. I'd been in the house too long. My habits had grown expensive and – there was no denying it – I had grown lazy. Yes, I brought in my regulars. But if I left the house, my regulars would settle for someone else soon enough. And it had been a while since I had done much in the way of attracting new clients. At thirty-eight, I wasn't old. There were plenty of working girls in Trinidad far older than I was, and plenty of johns who preferred us. Then again, neither was I young. And, frankly, there were plenty of other johns who preferred the younger girls.

Anyone as business-minded as Phoebe would have seen all that; anyone as vicious as Phoebe would have rejoiced in it, too. In retrospect, I realize that Phoebe's mind was probably unbalanced, and had grown steadily more so as the years rolled on. Necessary toughness had curdled into a kind of brutality that tipped, at times, into pure sadism.

I would feel her eyes on me constantly. It was only a matter of time before she drew me aside: time in which, I tried to reassure myself, I could surely make her think again. Perhaps I could direct her attention towards

Jasmine, who would never take more than two clients in a day. Or to Poppy, who took so much laudanum that her hair had started to fall out. Or to Nora, who ate and drank with the appetite of three men. Or to Primrose, who could often turn tiresome and violent when she drank.

We were all of us imperfect. But I was old and tired out. And Phoebe sensed it. She sensed my sadness and despair. She sensed my neediness. Since the strike – or before that, since the death of Lippiatt and my friendship with Inez, I had been absent from Plum Street on too many evenings. Add to that, her cruelty. Phoebe liked to go after us girls when we were down.

As the weeks and months rolled by, the tension became fairly unbearable. I suppose it was a relief when she finally called me in.

She had her own parlour at the front of the house, on the second floor. It was where she attended to her business correspondence. It was also where she kept the overnight safe, and the room was locked, always. Either from the inside (if she was *in situ*) or from the outside, if she was elsewhere. Apart from our monthly accounting meetings, when each girl would file through, one after the other, it was a rare and alarming thing to be invited inside: the mark of one of two things – either you were about to be thrown out of the house altogether, or you were, for whatever reason, her current favourite, in which case you were expected to sit and play cards with her, and surrender as much unpleasant gossip as you could about the other girls or the punters. It didn't matter which. Phoebe lapped it all up. In exchange, you received the warm glow of her approval, a fleeting sense of friendship and sisterliness and security and, above all, an overwhelming sense of relief to have survived the summons with roof and livelihood intact.

I hadn't been called in for one of her gossip and canasta sessions in a year or more. She had summoned me when she heard the rumours about the music school and sent a warning. Most girls weren't given warnings. But the salon had been so busy then, she had been unwilling to lose me.

When she summoned me now, there seemed to be no doubt that my time had come. The girls and I were in the ballroom. It was early evening and we were dressed for work. Up on the stage, Mr Truman hammered out the ragtime. Behind the bar, Jeremiah polished the glasses. Above us, our crystal chandeliers sparkled with the promise of laughter and joy, but the place was as quiet as death. Not a man in sight, if you didn't count the staff – and we didn't. We were idling the hour away, reminiscing about the busy times, wondering if Plum Street would ever again be returned to its former glory, when Simple Kitty tripped across the carpet towards us, looking sorrowfully at me.

'Excuse me for troubling you, Miss Dora. Mrs Phoebe says you're to come and see her at once.' She bobbed me a curtsy, which was something she never did.

'Oh Lord,' drawled Poppy. 'Kitty's curtsying. Not a good sign. What do you suppose she wants, Kitty?'

Kitty shook her head. 'She just said she wants to see you right away.'

'You think you're out?' asked Jasmine with unconcealed relish. 'What are you going to do, Dora? Oh dear Lord, where are you going to go?'

I picked up my full whiskey glass and swallowed it back.

'That's the way!' Nora said, edging her bulk towards me, leaning over to offer my arm a reassuring pat. She didn't move close enough, though, so she patted the air next to me instead. 'Have another one before you go.'

'Might as well,' said Jasmine. 'You've probably got nothing to lose.' I knew it wasn't meant unkindly – she was only saying what everyone else was thinking. I stood up too quickly, swayed a little and set out.

'Good luck!' they called after me, and there was kindness in their voices. I know it, because on other occasions my own voice had been among them. I have sat and watched, while Kitty led other girls upstairs. So I know about the kindness, and how mixed it was with relief.

Kitty was the only person in Plum Street allowed a key to Phoebe's parlour door. I stood behind her while she first knocked and then unlocked it. Shyly, she poked her head into the room. 'Miss Phoebe? I have brought Miss Dora to see you if you please. Shall I tell her to come in?'

I waited, imagined the scene: a fire in the grate, Phoebe straight backed at her desk, scribbling away, counting her money, writing her cheques. Or perhaps she was stretched out on the couch? Except Phoebe never stretched out. Her back never bent or curved or sloped, nor her neck and shoulders. She was regal – nowadays. Once upon a time, she had been a working girl herself. But I could never imagine it. Phoebe, naked, was an absurd and impossible prospect.

There came no reply from her. Finally, Kitty cleared her throat, glanced back at me apologetically, and prepared to say it again. 'Pardon me, Mrs Phoebe ...'

'Yes, I heard you, Kitty. Send her in.'

She was by the fire, pretending (I assume) to read a novel. She closed it, and placed the book on the table beside her. As always I was struck by the extreme sumptuousness of the room, and of the matching sumptuousness of the woman who presided over it. The two together always brought on a faint queasiness. Phoebe, magnificent in pale green silk – with diamonds sparkling at her throat and a curl of ostrich feathers framing her black-dyed hair – was as bolt upright as ever, seated in the corner of a vast couch, which was upholstered in some sort of silver-embroidered, blue velvet damask. The walls were of paler blue satin, complementing the couch, the dress, the diamonds ... The room was busy with objects: silver and ivory carved animals littered every surface: on the walls there were small paintings, mostly of naked women; on windowsills and mantelpiece, ornaments were scattered in crystal and gold, and on chairs and couches lay count-less glass-tasselled velvet cushions. It was an Aladdin's cave, a fairy queen's throne room. And, in the midst of this opulence, Phoebe herself seemed to glow: *my name is Phoebe, Queen of Queens. Look on my preposterous trinkets, ye mighty, and despair ...*

Under the circumstances, it was rather hard not to despair.

She told me to sit down, which I did, in the armchair opposite her.

'Drink? Whiskey, isn't it? Kitty, before you go, give Dora a glass of whiskey, would you? And on the desktop there ... Bring me – do you see it, Kitty? There is an envelope. An open envelope. It has writing on the front. Big black writing. There is only one open envelope. Bring it to me. And then leave. If you please. Thank you Kitty.'

I sucked on the whiskey and tried to see what was written on the envelope, but her hand obstructed my view. She said nothing, so to break the silence, I said:

'It's quiet downstairs tonight.'

'It's quiet downstairs every night. This place is like a ghost town.'

'It won't last.'

'We must hope not.'

Silence. The sound of Truman's ragtime seeped softly from the empty ballroom below, and there was the hiss of burning coal in the grate. It was too hot in there. She fondled the letter with her short, fat, jewelled fingers and seemed to consider what to say.

'It never does last,' I said. 'Don't you remember what a lull there was after the Summer Fair, year before last? We worried the entire male population of Colorado had been struck down with a—'

'I have good news for you,' she interrupted. There was a glint in her eye. For a moment she looked quite merry.

'Good news?' I repeated. 'Well! ... *Good news*, you say?'

I laughed, and she laughed with me.

'I have to say,' I said, 'that's not quite what I was expecting.'

'No, I don't suppose.' She beamed at me. 'The way you've been acting lately, Dora, you're lucky I don't throw you out on your ass this minute.'

I laughed, too loudly. It died among all the velvet cushions, but Phoebe continued to grin, silently.

She had tiny teeth. Lots of tiny teeth, like in the pictures of piranha fish, I thought. I shook my head to free it of the image. It wasn't a time to be thinking about piranhas.

I said: 'I admit, I have been a little distracted. You probably remember my friend – the sick girl in my room;

you were kind enough to allow her to stay a while back. We had to hide her in the maid's room.'

'I certainly remember that,' she said. She nodded, and her cheeks looked quite rosy with amusement. 'Yes. That gave me quite a shock.'

'Yes. I'm so sorry. You were so kind. Well, she ...' Why was I telling her this? 'She died. In the troubles. Someone shot her out on the road to Forbes.'

'*Really?*' Phoebe said. 'Why yes, of course they did! Now I recollect someone mentioning it. There was a double funeral, wasn't there? I hear old Mr McCulloch sold up and went to Williamsburg straight after.'

'Yes ... I heard that too,' I said, unable to hide my surprise. Was there nothing that escaped this woman's notice? 'That's right, he did,' I muttered.

She tilted her head, amused by my surprise. 'You think I walk around this town with eyes closed?'

'No! Certainly not. I guess I just didn't think—'

'Your little friend Inez was shot in the throat and delivered to Adamsson's funeral home by our friend Mr O'Neill ... Your friend, I should say. Didn't you spend a night with him at the Toltec last fall?'

'Last fall? No—'

She waved it aside. 'Those dreadful Union men. Penny-pinchers, they were. Lousy customers. I couldn't stand them.'

'You couldn't? I never guessed.'

'Why would you?' She eyed me, as if the question required an answer.

'I don't know,' I muttered. She had thrown me with the mention of my night at the Toltec. Did she know, then, that I had taken payment for it? But how could she know it? If she knew I had taken payment, and had left her out of the commission, there would be hell to pay. In Phoebe's mind it was the ultimate – the only – sin.

'You don't know what?' she asked, with a little frown of confusion.

'Well, I don't know,' I answered hopelessly. 'I'm just sorry ... about not being so on top of things lately. But I'm back now, full of vim! And no friends to distract me!'

'No johns to distract you neither ...' She released a heavy sigh. 'I simply don't know what we're going to do.'

'Things will improve!' I said again. 'Mark my words. We've both been in this game long enough ... it goes in cylces, don't you think so? Sometimes it's so darned busy, I just *long* for some peace and quiet. And sometimes it's so darned quiet ...' She had stopped listening. She turned away from me, and looked at the fire. I took it as a signal to hush up.

Silence.

What did she want from me? When would she come to the point? Finally I said, 'Maybe ... shall I find us some playing cards?'

'Heavens, no,' she said, gazing at the fire. She gave a little laugh, showy and hollow. 'I was going to tell you the good news!'

Abruptly, she tossed me the envelope. The black writing, it transpired, spelled my name.

Miss Dora Whitworth

And I recognized the writing at once. It was the same as on the parcels of erotic French novels sent to me so regularly, for so long. My heart leapt: a mix of fear and confusion, jubilation and hope.

'From William Paxton?' I said.

'That's right, Dora.'

'But the envelope is empty ...'

'Oh! Is it? I do apologize, Dora. I thought I had left the contents inside. There was an accompanying letter from Paxton to his lawyer. I think I have that on my desk. Would you be kind enough?'

'Of course!' I jumped to my feet.

'It's just a single sheet ... I think it's the only sheet of paper on the desk. Is it? Can you see it?'

Find enclosed $2,500, to be delivered into the hand of my friend and comfort, to whom I am forever indebted, Miss Dora Whitworth, resident of 27 Plum Street, Trinidad, Colorado, either on the event of

367

my death, or by the last day of December 1914,
which ever should first occur.

'We are in February,' I said.

'What's that? Bring the letter to me, please.'

'William died way back in April, Phoebe. And the last
day of December was some time ago … Even so … Gosh,
I'm certainly not complaining! This is wonderful news!'

'I told you there was good news,' she said. 'Please.
Bring the letter to me now. I would like to read it again.'

Two thousand five hundred dollars! Could anyone
imagine the rate my head was spinning as I tripped back
across the carpet and handed the letter to her? There were,
of course, a million questions. Why had the letter taken
so long to reach me? And why was it ever in Phoebe's
possession? Above all of course: *where was the money?*

But they were not uppermost in my mind just then.
Actually, I was caught in a wave of happy emotions –
warmth and gratitude and affection for William. He
had not forgotten me! And of relief and excitement … I
would move to Denver – no, Los Angeles – no, Chicago!
I would open a music school. I would buy myself a little
house, and a good piano and, in the evenings, if I was
lonesome, I would sing to myself … And I would find
a companion and a handful of friends, and we would
grow old together, and I would never need to remember

368

these past few years in Trinidad. It was all possible. I could start my life over again …

'Sit down, won't you?' Phoebe said. 'It's making me jumpy, you hovering over me like a cat on heat.' I did as I was told.

She watched me, and then took a moment, squeezing cigarette into tortoiseshell holder, and puffing on it until the tobacco caught. I waited until I thought I would burst with impatience.

'How did the letter come to reach you first?' I asked.

She threw me a glance as if I was stupid. Because everything reached Phoebe first, especially if money was involved. She didn't bother to reply. Instead, she exhaled a lungful of tobacco and watched the smoke float into the room.

'You want a smoke?' she asked me.

'No. Thank you … I must say this is quite a turn of events. I can hardly quite believe it! When did you receive the letter, Phoebe? May I ask that?' I smiled what I hoped was a playful, teasing smile – it was not a smile I would have attempted ten minutes earlier. 'How long have you been keeping this wonderful secret of mine to yourself? When did you—'

'Oh, shut up.'

I did. She smoked. I flushed, uncertain how to proceed. Where was the money? And when would she hand it over to me? It was all that mattered. Nothing else. She could insult me if she liked – and, no doubt, insist on a cut ... a hefty cut, knowing her. It didn't matter. None of it mattered. If I could get out of that room with half the money, and on civilized terms, I would consider myself the luckiest woman alive. The money would be mine; and so long as we kept our negotiations reasonable, and I sounded suitably grateful to her, I would be safe. I would be free. Moments passed. A pause in the music from downstairs. Perhaps some guests had arrived at last? Perhaps I would never again have to dance around that ballroom.

When would she speak?

'This glass is empty,' I said. 'Mind if I fetch myself another one? And you?'

But her glass was still half full. She ignored me, so I trekked across the room and filled the glass in silence, liquor bottle clanging against the glass because my hands had started to shake. I could feel her eyes on the back of my neck.

'I didn't know you and William had formed such a close connection,' she said at last.

'Well – and neither did I,' I lied. 'It's quite a surprise. I'm overwhelmed.'

'It's against the house rules. As you know.'

I laughed. Couldn't help myself. 'What is against the rules, Phoebe? To be left money in a man's will?' Her expression didn't change, but the moment I said it I knew it was a mistake. 'I didn't form a close tie with William. I guess he just became attached to me without my realizing it. Because I did my work so well. It can hardly be against house rules to be good at my work?'

She waved it aside. 'I'm gonna overlook it.'

'Well, thank you, Phoebe.'

I tried and failed to keep the sarcasm out of my voice. She shot me an untroubled look and heaved herself delicately to her feet. Phoebe wore corsets, unfashionably tight even then. It made all her movements slow and cumbersome – and no doubt contributed in large part to her perennial ill humour. I was still on my feet, returning from the drinks table. She brushed past me and sat down at her desk. It was a gilt chair, upholstered in the same silver damask as the drapes, and it looked suitably like a throne.

There followed more painstaking bending and twisting from inside her inflexible corset. I stayed where I was, holding my breath. She unhooked a small oil painting from the wall beside her chair (it was of a couple of women, both naked, one of them grotesquely fat with a parrot perched on her nipple), and revealed a safe. She affixed a pince-nez from a long golden chain around her neck, and began to fiddle with the dial.

'Come!' she said, beckoning me to sit. She had pulled a thick sheaf of papers from within, and an even thicker wad of dollar bills.

My dollar bills.

'Bless him,' I burst out, eyes fixed on the money: my ticket out of here. 'He was a good man, wasn't he? ... I miss him. I do.'

'Sit down,' she said. 'There are some formalities we must see to.'

'Yes! Yes of course.'

As I sat, she lifted her beady eyes from the cash, looked up at me over her pince-nez: 'By the way, I have a new girl arriving at the end of the week.'

'A new girl! Well, well!' I laughed, giddy, in a way I never was. 'And there we were downstairs, worrying you might be about to send one of us packing.'

'Mary-Lou's Parlour House went out of business last week. You probably heard. I figure once the men in this state finally wake up out of their goddamn stupor – finally pull their cocks out of their crapholes – the business has got to go somewhere, hasn't it? I've taken one of her girls. Nice little thing. Rosette. French. So I'm going to need your rooms.'

'Oh!' It was more sudden than I'd expected. I had envisaged taking my time, making plans. To my surprise, I felt a wave of sadness. Plum Street had been home for so many years. 'Well – all right then. I guess. What day do you want me out?' I laughed. 'I'm going to miss you all!'

'Friday,' she said.

'Friday.' It was only three days away.

'Please. I'm going to lend you Carlos. He'll help you move your things out. But you'll need to find some place for him to take them. All right. And now, to business. We can settle our accounts here and now, and after that –' she offered me a wide, piranha grin – 'you, Miss Dora Whitworth, are free to go!'

I should have known. I should have guessed. That bitch sat me down beside her, and from the sheaf of papers she produced bills and more bills – for hats and ribbons and shoes and medical supplies, for bed linen and soap and bags of coal, for champagne and chocolate cakes and every single cup of breakfast coffee delivered to my bedroom since the day I'd joined the household.

'I thought …' I said at one point, as she scribbled figures in margins, and added this one to that one and the other to the next, and my eyesight blurred with the vision of them all. 'I had always understood that the bulk of my living costs were to be met by the house. That is, I thought, why you always charged such a hefty commission.'

She said, 'I don't know where you got that idea, Dora.' And she paused, pen in hand, dollar signs whirring behind the eyeballs. 'What did you think? I'm running some kind of vacation resort? I'm not in this business for my health.'

'No, of course. But … neither am I.'

I had no recourse. I knew it and so did she. There was no legal contract between us. And, in the mean-time, William's dollar bills rested on her desk. Short of making a grab for them and running like hell (except I was locked inside, and it was well known she kept a loaded pistol in her desk), there was nothing I could do. Phoebe held this town in the palm of her fat, jewelled hand. So I waited quietly, with my whiskey glass, as she presented me with another ancient bill, and then another, and then another ...

'But I don't recall ever owning a purple chiffon dinner dress. I dislike purple. I dislike chiffon. Are you certain that wasn't for another girl? Perhaps one of the girls who left already. Or Larenne. Remember Larenne?' Larenne had only lasted a couple of years. She died of an overdose of laudanum. Suicide.

Phoebe looked blank.

'Larenne! *You must remember Larenne!* She used to adore purple. It was the only colour she would ever wear.'

Phoebe shook her head. Apparently she didn't remember Larenne. I was wasting my breath. Whether the bill once belonged to Larenne, or whether Phoebe had written out the damn bill herself, it was immaterial anyway. She intended to subtract the cost of it from my inheritance. And the cost of everything else, too. Whatever she felt like subtracting.

'Well then,' she said at last, sitting back in her gilt throne, removing her pince-nez, *smiling*. 'I think that's just about it. You can check my calculations if you like. By all means ...' She pushed a piece of paper across the desk towards me: there was a scrawl of tiny black figures, and at the bottom of the longest column, a final number.

I looked down at it. Couldn't bring my mind to bear. Was that it? The final number. Was it what she intended to give to me, or what she intended to take?

'And if you're agreeable with that ...' she said. She picked up the dollar bills, *my* dollar bills, the dollar bills William Paxton had left for me, and she began to count them out.

'Ten ... Twenty ... Thirty ... Forty ... Fifty ... Fifty-five ...' She stopped.

She waited. I waited. She waited.

'*Fifty-five dollars?*' I said at last.

'That's right,' she said. She indicated the paper sheet with a slight tilt of the chin. 'That's what it says. Fifty-three dollars and forty cents. I rounded it up.'

'Out of two thousand five hundred? What are you, crazy? I'm not accepting that.'

She feigned gentle confusion. Then she smiled. 'You'll accept it,' she said softly. 'You'll accept whatever I give you.' She surveyed me and then she sat back with a small sigh of surrender. 'However, because I'm fond of you, Dora ... Ha! Yes. You may well raise your eyebrows at that, but it's true. Over the years, I've come to like the way you ...' Nothing seemed to come to mind. She shrugged. 'In any case, I want to be good to you. I'm going to be generous.' She opened a drawer beneath the desk and pulled out yet another sheet of paper. She slid it across the table top towards me.

It was a document from William's lawyer.

'You need to sign it,' she said. 'To confirm you have received the funds.'

'But I haven't received the funds! You are keeping them from me.'

'Because of debts outstanding, Dora. How many times must I explain it?' She sighed. '*However*, as I say, I am willing to be generous. I am going to cancel a further two hundred and fifty dollars of the debt, allowing you to leave this room with ... Let me think: three hundred and five dollars. Hell, I'll throw in another fifty! The liquor must be fuzzing my old noddlebox! That leaves you with three hundred and fifty-five ... And your freedom, Dora. Imagine that. I know how long you've hankered for it. But you need to sign the document.' She flashed me another grin. (How I detested the sight of her little teeth!) 'What do you say?'

'What if I refuse to sign it?'

She shrugged. 'Of course. It's up to you.'

38

April 1933
Ambassador Hotel, Los Angeles, California

Max has his fruit ice. He took some time choosing the flavour and finally settled on coconut and pineapple. And I can't be certain if he has any idea how infuriating it is, to watch him nibbling on his fruit ice, when we still have so many questions unanswered. He swears he was not her lover – and I do not believe him. I wonder why he ever arranged for us to meet, since he can only tell me lies, and nibble on ices. I am thinking that perhaps it is time for me to leave. In fact, I regret very much having agreed to see him. His lack of concern for Inez can hardly come as a surprise, but still, I see her lying in the morgue; I see him savouring his fruit ice. I see the letter, in all its girlish pain; I see him savouring his fruit ice. How can a man reach his age and still have such a healthy head of hair? It's a mark of *something*, I decide. Something callous. Shallow. Max Eastman has words for everything, but feelings for nothing. I reach for my purse.

'I have to leave,' I say. 'I have an appointment.'

He looks surprised. Hurt, even. 'What?' he says. 'Why? What kind of an appointment? We haven't even started to reach the bottom of this. I thought you said you had all afternoon.'

Did I say that? I don't remember. 'I have a client,' I say vaguely. 'Out in Santa Monica. They are expecting me at five.'

'A *client*?' Max Eastman blushes. 'I'm so sorry ...'

'Please, don't apologize.'

'I thought you said ... Of course you didn't actually tell me what you were doing nowadays. I thought you'd given all that up.'

'Oh. No. A different kind of client,' I say.

'Yes?'

'I work for the studios now. I coach new actors to sing.'

'Oh!'

'We have sound. The people want to hear their idols sing.'

'Ha! Yes, of course they do. You bet!'

'Musicals are all the rage.'

'Oh well. Gosh. That sounds—'

'It is. It's wonderful. I'm very fortunate.' I take up the letter. He watches me folding it, tucking it into my purse;

and, as I do so – God knows why – I feel my eyes stinging with tears. It's the disappointment. No, it's the fruit ice. Max and his bloody fruit ice. All these years I have imagined how he would react were he ever to read her letter. I imagined his dismay, his guilt, his grief. I had imagined that my failure to deliver the damn thing to him might in some way have been a mercy. I had spared him from it; the dying wrath of his beloved – and I had nursed that. But here he sits by the pool of the Ambassador, basking in the California sun, telling me lies and slurping like a puppy on the speciality of the house. I want to pick up the bowl and throw its contents into his lap.

There is a pause. He lays down his spoon. Swallows. 'Dora, is my fruit ice repelling you?'

'No,' I reply. I laugh. I can't help it. All those years of hiding my distastes – had I made it so obvious? 'No, of course it's not ...'

'Indeed it *is*!' he says. 'I shall send it away. Waiter! Ah, hello. Thank you. Could you kindly relieve me ...' He hands the waiter his bowl. 'You're very kind. It was delicious but I have had enough.' He turns back to me, raises an eyebrow. Smiles. 'You misconstrued my enjoyment, Dora. I was thinking. That's all. Sometimes a small *amuse-gueule* can help one to concentrate. I am sorry if it seemed callous. I was trying to understand ... And, by the way. It didn't help. Not on this occasion. I have nothing. I am as bewildered as you are.'

'What might help,' I say, 'is if you started telling the truth. You were in love with each other. Anyone could see it. I don't know why you would want to deny it after all these years. What does it even matter any more?'

He shakes his head. 'What can I say to persuade you?'

'Nothing,' I say. 'And really, I have to leave. Please, don't get up.' In fact he has made no sign that he might. I am pushing back the chair. My eyes are blurred with tears now. It's important that I leave before giving way to them. 'It was good to see you, after all these years. I only wish it could have been more illuminating ...' I feel a hand on my shoulder, and in an instant, Max's expression alters: from frustration, to astonishment, to alarm – to delight.

39

'Good God!' he says. 'For a moment I thought you were – but you look so alike! I had forgotten how alike you always were. Although I declare I think you have grown *even more* alike.' Now Max is on his feet. He has leapt to his feet, and his face is alight with pleasure. 'Xavier Dubois! It *is* you, isn't it? Tell me it's you! – Well, I know it is. How could it be anyone else?' He wraps his long arms around Xavier's shoulders and hugs him.

When Max pulls back they both laugh, as surprised as each other by his warmth.

'Hello there Max,' Xavier says. 'Well, well! ... Here you are!'

'Yes indeed!' grins Max.

'Dora mentioned she was meeting with you and I must admit I rather insisted on being allowed to barge in. Sidled out of a godawful meeting this afternoon ...

381

You don't mind me joining you, I hope?'

'My friend, I couldn't be more delighted!' cries Max.
Xavier nods and smiles. '... I see you still have all
your hair.' He lifts his boater, reveals a forehead several
inches higher than it used to be.

Max examines the hairline. 'Oh, you just need to brush
it forward a bit, old chap. Plus you're tall enough. Most
people don't even get a chance to see the top of your head.'

I laugh. Poor Xavier! I tell him he still looks good – and
he does, too. But this is Hollywood. He minds about his
hairline more than he ought, perhaps. 'Is that really all
you have to say to each other,' I ask, 'after all these years?'

'Far from it,' Xavier says. 'It's just the *first* thing we
have to say to each other. After all these years. We have
plenty more to talk about now we've settled that.'

'Nineteen years,' Max says. 'Nineteen years almost
to the day – do you realize? Dora – you didn't tell me
Xavier would be joining us. I had no idea.'

'I wasn't sure myself if he would make it,' I reply.
'Hello darling,' I say to him.

He swoops to kiss me. It lands half on my head, half
on the edge of my hat. He takes my hand and squeezes
it. 'Am I too late?' he asks us. 'I'm sorry. I couldn't
get away before. Dora, darling – you looked as if you
were leaving?'

'Well, I thought I had an appointment,' I mutter.

'But you said you'd kept the afternoon free! Can't you

stay for a drink? Now that I've made it all the way out here? Please, darling?'

The pleading is a formality. He knows I will stay for a drink now. Because he is impossible to refuse, just as his sister was. So I put my purse down again, and he nods at a passing waiter. 'What are we all having?' he asks.

'Max is having the fruit ice,' I say.

Max chuckles. 'I am decidedly *not* having the fruit ice. Another martini, I think. What about you?'

'Three martinis,' Xavier says. 'However my friends took them. I'll have the same. Thank you.'

He sits down. I notice for the first time what he is carrying. Actually, he produced it – Inez's swordstick – from the back of a cupboard, the evening I returned from the restaurant and told him about my encounter with Max. It was covered in dust, and the silver blade had turned black, having been so long neglected in its casing. Now the silver catch glistens in the sunlight. He has polished it up for the occasion.

We exchange glances. He is not sure, I think, if I approve of his bringing it out with him today. But who am I to approve or disapprove? What difference does it make? When he talks to Max, and discovers the extent of his callousness, as I have in the past hour or so, he will no doubt wish he had left it in the dark cupboard where it belongs.

Max leans back in his wicker seat, the better to examine his new guest. 'God, you look well! Is there something in the water here in California? The pair of you don't look a day older! Are you living here too, Xavier? Of course you are! You were making films even back then. Are you still? And have you at any point had the good fortune to encounter my great friend Charles Chaplin? We've fallen out rather, lately, sadly. Politics. But I am awfully fond of him, you know.'

Xavier takes a cigarette from the silver box that Max holds out to him, attaches it to his cigarette holder. 'I've met him often,' Xavier says. 'He's not an easy man to work with.' He produces his lighter – gold. I gave it to him last birthday, engraved with his name. 'And yes, to answer your question. Absolutely, I live in California. Here in Hollywood. Dora and I live together.'

'Oh!' Max looks embarrassed and slightly confused. 'I'm not sure I understand.'

Xavier looks politely surprised. 'Which bit?'

I smother a laugh. I want to redirect us back to the letter. I want to hear Max telling Xavier what he has just told me – and to see how Xavier reacts to it. I am pulling the letter back out of my purse when the golden-limbed, dive-bombing Adonis – whose face I had recognized previously – approaches the table. We wait, while he and Xavier exchange pleasantries, and then Xavier introduces us all. We have met before, he reminds me. I had forgotten. He is not a famous movie star – though Xavier assures him and us that he soon will be. He is a friend of Xavier's. Ah – too bad! He is a sight for sore eyes, no matter what.

I indicate the ebony swordstick; say to Max: 'Look familiar?'

He picks it up. 'I can't say that it does …' He fiddles with the catch, and the blade slides out. 'Oh indeed! Dora, it's not what I think, is it? *Is it?*' He looks, for once, quite misty eyed. 'I never saw it before, but she told me about it. She was terribly proud of it. Isn't it part of the notorious "spy equipment" she ordered down from Chicago or somewhere? It's actually rather beautiful …' He continues to fiddle with it, sliding out the blade. 'Do you remember that wonderful little pistol-in-a-purse she was so pleased with? I wonder what became of it.'

'We never found it,' Xavier says, turning back to us, his handsome friend having been sent on his way. 'Presumably it was in the auto. We never saw her car again either. Vanished without a trace … I often think,' he adds, after a pause, 'how lucky we were that they left us a body. If it's not too macabre to say so. At least now we know what became of her.'

'Well,' says Max. 'But I'm not so sure that we *do* know, do we? That is to say …' He looks to me to pick up.

'Max has read the letter,' I tell Xavier. 'He says it doesn't make sense.'

'Sure it makes sense,' Xavier chips in. 'You have to take into account the situation when she was writing it. Maybe it's a little hysterical. But it makes perfect sense.' He stops, as the waiter delivers our martinis.

'Max isn't talking about the tone, Xavier. He's saying the letter doesn't make any sense because he *says* ...' I shoot Max a look, as hostile as I feel. Max opens his mouth to defend himself, but I talk through him. 'Max *claims* that he showed his article to Inez before she died, and that she adored it.'

'Oh really?' says Xavier, excessively polite.

'I tell you she adored it!' cries Max.

'He also claims that he and Inez were never lovers.'

'Nor were we,' Max nods.

Xavier looks from one of us to the other, swallows half his drink in a single gulp. 'Well that's absurd,' he says at last. But I can hear a note of something in his voice. There is hesitation. Not the astonishment and outrage I had been expecting. As if this isn't the first time the idea has crossed his mind.

'You bet it's absurd!' I say. 'Inez told us. Don't you remember?'

Slowly, he says, 'No, Dora darling. She told you. And quite rightly assumed that you would tell me. Remember?'

'The letter doesn't make any sense,' Max says irritably, yet again. He picks it up, opens it, starts to read it one more time. 'This is her blood. Is it?' he asks, looking at the smears with delicate horror.

'Of course it is,' I reply.

'Not that it's any of our business,' Xavier says, 'but perhaps you could explain to us, Max – why in hell Inez would have told Dora that you and she were lovers if you weren't?'

Max lays the letter back down on the table. 'Well, I would have thought that was obvious.'

'Far from it,' Xavier says. 'Is it obvious to you, Dora?'

'Not at all. She was moving to New York to be with you.'

'She was moving to New York,' Max says impatiently, as if *we* were the fools, 'to be with Lawrence O'Neill.'

'No,' I say. 'That's not possible. He didn't live in New York. You did. She was in love with you.'

'She was not in love with me.' Max is sounding quite irritable now. 'She was in love with O'Neill. And, so far as I knew, he was moving to New York. And, by the way, on the few occasions I saw them together—'

'When did you see them together?' Xavier asks him. 'When could you possibly have seen them together?'

'Well – of course I saw them together. I already told Dora – O'Neill took a room at the Corinado. She was with him constantly. They couldn't be seen in public. But they used to come to my rooms often, ask me how my story was going, and so on. O'Neill used to give me leads. He arranged one or two introductions – although there were reasons I never did take them up. In any case, Inez was smitten with O'Neill – there was no doubt about that. And I would have said that the feeling was mutual. O'Neill adored her.' Max pauses. 'What man didn't adore her, of course? We all adored her. But O'Neill was smitten too. Absolutely. You must at least have realized that?' Max looks at me.

I picture Lawrence's face in the hallway at Plum Street, the day he came to tell me she was dead. I picture him at the Toltec, when he came over to introduce himself to Max, his hand brushing on the back of her neck, and Inez seeming not to notice it; his standing so close to the back of her chair. I picture him in the tearoom, asking me over and again if she was all right. 'Yes ... I guess so,' I said. 'Yes, I knew *he* was smitten. But Inez had moved on. She said so. Why would she bother to lie?'

Max shrugs. He opens his mouth to say something and then seems to think better of it.

'For heaven's sake Max,' Xavier says. 'If there's something you know, that might shed some light – just spit it out, won't you? We've waited long enough.'

'Very well,' Max says carefully. 'It may shed no light whatsoever, of course. After all this time I'm not certain anything will. But I remember Inez mentioned she had been terribly ill shortly before we all arrived in Trinidad. There had been a riot involving Mother Jones, and Inez was put in the cells for a night.'

'Not quite a night,' I nod. 'But yes. For a few hours.'

'Fair enough,' Max says. 'Inez told me it was a whole night but Inez was prone to exaggeration. It doesn't matter, in any case. It was long enough for the munitions – the stash of Colt-Brownings in her basement to have been stolen. And, after that, from what I understood, everything became nigh on impossible for them both. It was imperative, for both their sakes, that no one should see them together. You two – and the young lad, Cody, of course – were the only people in Trinidad who had any idea there had ever been any friendship between them. Except for me. But I hardly counted. I was only passing through. And, in any case, as you can see, they needed a cover. Inez couldn't write poetry.' He glances at the bloodstained letter lying open on the table between them. 'Or prose, for that matter. But she was a lot smarter than I think any of us took her for.'

'But you misunderstand. The weaponry,' says Xavier quietly, 'the Colt-Brownings – they weren't stolen from her cellar. They were simply moved to another safe house.'

'That's the reason—' He stops, stares at Xavier, and then at me. He's looking at us with a mixture of embarrassment, astonishment – and pity. 'Well *of course* the stuff was stolen! It was *stolen* while Inez was in the cells. When you went by the cottage and she was lying sick in the maid's room at Plum Street, the cellar was empty, correct? Everything had been removed, yes?'

'Yes,' I say. '*Removed*. Nobody said anything about being stolen.'

Max takes a moment to absorb this – the depth of our ignorance. And so do we. Xavier reaches for the letter again. He clutches at it. *The blood is real. The paper is real. The handwriting is hers.*

'The same Colt-Brownings that were in her cellar,' Max says carefully, 'they weren't simply any old rifles, that's the thing. They turned up at Ludlow.'

'Of course they turned up at Ludlow!' I say. I have to stop myself from shouting. 'Where else would they have gone?'

'But not in the Union's hands. Don't you see? The company guards had them! The general's men! When Inez and I went out to Ludlow – you remember? The day we arrived in Trinidad? It was the *company guards* who were holding them ... Colt-Browning, automatic rifles. "Potato diggers", she used to call them. I forget why ... Inez could have told you. Something about the mechanism made them unusual. But the rifles were unusual. That's the point. Inez had made a study of them. She knew them. And *she identified them that afternoon.* We were in the middle of negotiating with one of the guards. She was trying to get a bunch of us reporters into the ruined camp. She was being her delightful self, and I reckoned, the way the guard was melting, we were as good as in. Suddenly, she stopped dead. He was *holding* one of the rifles ... And she knew it. It was as if she had seen a ghost. She simply *stopped talking*. She couldn't take her eyes off the damn gun.'

'How do you know that was what stopped her?' I ask him. 'She might have suddenly simply found the horror of the camp too unbearable, the smell and the smoke and the bodies being brought out ... What makes you so sure it was—'

'Because she told me.'

'That the guns had been stolen?'

'What? No! Not right then. A couple of days later. She told me the gun he was holding had been taken from her cellar, and it was why she had fallen silent. That she recognized it.'

'And you believed her?' I ask. I turn to Xavier but he is buried in the letter again, scowling over the words as if they might yet offer up an answer. 'Xavier, are you listening to this?'

'Of course,' he mutters. 'And it's a good question. Given my sister's somewhat fanciful approach to life ... Why did you believe her?'

'Because of the way she stopped mid-sentence. As I say, she looked as if she had seen a ghost. If you had seen the change in her, you wouldn't have been in any doubt either.'

'And did you get the impression – when she saw the guard holding the gun, was she already aware that the arsenal had been *stolen* from her cellar? Or had she been under the impression, as we have been, all this time, that it had simply been removed by the Union to a safer hiding place?'

'She said she had no idea it had been stolen,' says Max. He is silent for a long time. Finally, he says, 'But I didn't believe her. I think she knew very well that the weaponry had been stolen, and I think she knew by whom. And I think that those same guns were then almost certainly turned on the very people she thought she was fighting for ... It's not something any of us would much want to confront, is it? ... I suspect that she couldn't allow herself to confront it either. She couldn't accept it. She couldn't bear it. So she raced around like a dervish, keeping herself busy, righting wrongs, fighting the cause, burying her head in the sand. I think she—'

Xavier gasps. He's not listening.

'No, I think it makes sense,' Max glances at Xavier, and continues more emphatically. 'She was in love with O'Neill. He was going to New York. He had some kind of job, he said. I don't remember what, but maybe he was leaving the Union, maybe he wasn't. From what I understood, he was never anything more than a brute-for-hire, who just happened to have been hired by the Union side. But Inez was in love with O'Neill. She wanted to believe the best of him. Added to which – leaving aside her own stubbornly unacknowledged fears about him, she knew that *no one* would have allowed her to leave town with him. It would have been out of the question. Her aunt and uncle – *your* aunt and uncle of course,' he says, nodding to Xavier, 'would have cut off her money supply. They would never have forgiven her.' He stops, shrugs. 'At any rate, that's what she told me.'

But Xavier still isn't listening. He is hunched over the damn letter, pulling on his eyeglasses, holding Inez's bloodstained letter up to the sunlight. And then slowly, softly, he begins to laugh. '... *Dora!*' he whispers. 'Darling Dora, how long have we carried this ludicrous letter around with us? How many times, between us, have we gazed at this darned thing? *How could we not have seen?* It's so damnably ... so utterly, wonderfully, gloriously *like Inez ...*'

'What?' I ask him. 'For heaven's sake – what is so gloriously like Inez that we haven't seen these twenty years?'

'Oh my sister,' he says. And he is half laughing, half crying. 'God, how I miss that girl. *Look!*'

He is still holding the letter up to the light. His finger is pointing to the top right-hand corner of the sheet. There is a dark smudge of old, brown blood. And behind it, what looks like a faint ink mark. A scribble of some sort. Max and I crane forward to see it more closely.

'Is it an F?' asks Max doubtfully.

'It *is* an F!' cries Xavier. 'A single, solitary F at the top of the page ... Come on, Dora! Don't you remember?

You *must* remember! For a while, it was almost the only thing she would talk about. The swordstick ... And the little gun purse ... and that idiotic device for listening to people in the room next door, which never worked. Don't you remember she tested it on us?'

'And the invisible ink!' I shout. 'An F! It's an F! Xavier – we are fools! How can we have been so stupid?' I throw my arms around him, and we hold each other, both of us half laughing and half crying, unwilling to let each other go.

'When you've quite finished,' Max says, sounding put out, 'you might be kind enough to remember that I too am sitting here ...'

We giggle like a pair of children, and apologize.

Max continues, 'Perhaps you'll be kind enough to explain what in hell you are talking about? An F? An F stands for what?'

40

'F stands for *FIRE*!' Xavier and I cry at once.

'Listen,' I say to Max. 'There are two types of invisible ink.'

'There is "Organic",' Xavier says, 'And—'

'Sympathetic,' I continue. 'Did Inez not tell you this? She must have told you! How could you have spent more than an hour in her company without the subject coming up? Well, I suppose by the time you arrived, everything had become so much more serious. Cody was already dead. And Ludlow ... In any case the invisible ink came with the rest of the junk she ordered from the detective store. There was the invisible ink hidden in a bottle of hair tonic, but that was the chemical type. "Sympathetic", as Xavier calls it ... Are you sure that's right, Xavie? Not synthetic? I always thought it was synthetic.'

'Definitely sympathetic,' Xavier says.

Max waves it aside.

'The point is,' I continue, 'we are lucky there isn't an "S" up there in the blood ... It's *not* an S, is it? It's definitely an F.'

The men look again. We agree that yes, the mark we have missed for all these years, is indeed an F.

'If it were an S, we would need to locate the "re-agent", which would have been made specifically for this particular invisible ink. And, honestly, after so many years, Gosh only knows where we would find it ...'

'*Organic* invisible ink, on the other hand,' Xavier continues, 'alters the fibres of the paper it is written on, making the fibres burn at a lower temperature than the rest of the paper.'

'I see ...' Max says, though for such a clever man, he seems to be taking a while to catch on.

'Which means we only have to hold this paper to a source of heat – a lighter, for example, for the message written beneath it to become clear.' Xavier giggles, a nervous giggle, because God only knows what we are about to uncover. 'You will see,' he says to Max, 'that Inez taught her students well. I could remember all that nonsense as if she had told us yesterday.'

We all laugh. It's not terribly funny. But we are nervous suddenly. And we have drunk too much.

'First,' says Xavier, 'I think we should order some more martinis. To steady the nerves. Are we agreed?'

'Absolutely,' Max and I say together.

'And perhaps we could ask for a lamp or something … A source of heat. Ah, waiter!'

The waiter is happy to oblige with the martinis, but he can't provide a lamp. There is a problem with electric leads, he says. They don't extend as far as the poolside.

Never mind. Max has a lighter in his pocket. We discuss whether it's a sensible option to use a naked flame, and decide that it is. There is no breeze to speak of. And the lighter gives a steady flame. But the truth is, our curiosity overwhelms us. Her message has been hidden for twenty years, and now we cannot wait another moment to uncover it.

It is decided that Xavier, having arrived later and therefore having drunk less than either of us, has the steadiest hand. He takes the letter from the table, the lighter from Max, and as he sets the flame beneath the paper, we fall silent.

Nothing happens.

'You need to put the flame a little closer,' Max says. 'A bit higher …'

'Be careful,' I say. 'Not too close.'

Xavier ignores us. We are standing behind him, craning over it.

'It's not working,' says Max. 'There's nothing there …'

… But there *is* something there. In the gaps between the lines of the original letter, a script appears, and it is as clear as if it had been written yesterday. The handwriting is cramped, smaller and much neater than on the letter above.

The three of us wait, hardly daring to breath, as the first few words appear.

Darling Max,
I suppose that if you are reading this ...

I breathe in. Feel a chill crawl over my skin. Time retracts. It is her voice, her hand. She is alive again. Max and I squeeze closer to the paper, jostle one another for a better view, and Max accidentally knocks Xavier's shoulder. I suggest we stand back and let him get on with it, block by block, paragraph by paragraph. As each paragraph reveals itself, Xavier can lay the paper down, and we will read it together.

It's not feasible, of course. We don't have a fraction of the patience. We need to see the words as they appear. And the writing is minuscule. So we crouch towards the paper, as close as we can without falling over. Xavier reads each line as the heat from his lighter reveals it:

I will either be standing right beside you ... laughing
at what a silly ... dramatic fool I have been ... and
feeling thoroughly ashamed of myself (although
terribly proud of this fabulous ink ... Has it really

worked?) or, well, I don't suppose you ever will see this letter—

'She manages to be verbose, even from beyond the grave,' Xavier mutters. But the letter sounds so like her. It's as if she is right there with us by the sunny poolside, chattering away from a place and time the rest of us left behind long ago.

... since I don't think you listen to a word I ever tell you – although I have told you about the F and the invisible ink ...

'She never told me,' Max says.

'I'll bet she did tell you,' says Xavier. 'But she talked nineteen to the dozen, Max. Lest we forget. You can hardly be blamed for not listening to every word.'

'It doesn't matter,' I say. 'Please, Xavier, carry on.'

Max, if some harm should come to me this afternoon, as I fear it might, and if you happen to remember all the nonsense I talk ... and if you or someone else should come upon this letter, as I intend, in the pocket of my skirt ... If you do ever find this message and I am gone from – Max, if I am dead, it is because I have fallen in love with a villain, and I deserve it.

*

Xavier stops. He places the letter on the table and kills the lighter flame.

'What are you doing?' I cry. 'Xavier, don't stop!'

He says, 'My arm is aching.' He means his heart, of course. 'I need a break. Wait a moment will you? Just a minute.'

Max fidgets. 'Want me to take over?' he asks.

'No ... thank you,' Xavier adds.

'I should've said something,' Max says. 'I always suspected. But you can't help who you fall in love with, can you? None of us can.'

'What are you saying?' I ask him. It's not really a question. Once again, I picture Lawrence's face as he stood in the hall at Plum Street, the tears running down his cheeks. '*This is all nonsense!* Inez told me she was in love with you!'

'So you keep saying,' Max says. 'And as I keep explaining, she was not. Xavier, shall you keep at the task? Or would you rather Dora or I continue? This midway pause is rather hard to bear.'

Xavier shakes his head. 'Why don't you both sit down,' he says. 'Perhaps if I can finish off quietly – would it be all right with you? And then once it's done and we have it all, then we can read it together. The whole thing. Can we do it that way? It might be easier on us.'

I think Max and I both want to argue, but Xavier looks ashen under his handsome, sun-kissed skin; and out of all of us – of course – he has the greater claim on grief. She was his sister, his only living relative. The same thoughts occur to Max, I assume. We are being tactless. Too demanding. We both pull back at once.

'I am so sorry,' Max says.

'No, no, not at all,' Xavier replies. 'I'm being feeble. It's so long ago, after all. Dora, forgive me. I know how much you loved her. The last thing I want is ...' He leaves the sentence unfinished. He gulps back the remainder of his martini in a single swallow, beckons the waiter for another, and picks up the lighter again.

Max and I return to our places and wait. Xavier's fingers are shaking, and I rest a hand on his leg, beneath the table. It seems to help a little. After a while, Max looks up at the blue sky and says:

'It's hot.'

'So it is,' I say.

Another long silence. Max taps and fiddles, says rather irritably: 'I'd like to light a cigarette but I suppose I can't. While you are doing that with the lighter. How are you getting along?'

Xavier doesn't reply.

'Lawrence loved her, you know,' I say. 'You said it yourself, Max. If you had seen him that day, after he had taken her to the mortuary ... He was weeping.'

'Yes, I believe he loved her,' says Max. 'No matter what else happened.'

'And I suppose he wept after Cody died, too – did he?' Xavier mumbles.

'I'm sure he did,' I reply, and I turn, the better to send him my cold air, but he is bent over the paper, not looking at me. He is about three-quarters of the way down now, and from what I can see the writing is getting smaller. He hunches closer to his work.

'The print is getting fainter down here,' he says. 'It's harder to read.'

'Maybe it needs more heat,' says Max. 'Are you certain I can't help?'

'I'm doing fine,' Xavier assures him, but as he speaks the flame dances; it's just a second – a half-second – the flame pulls at the bottom corner of the sheet and the smoke darkens.

'*Watch out!*' Max and I shout at once. We both leap to our feet, Max knocking both our chairs to the floor. 'Xavier!' I yell at him. 'Pull the lighter away!' He has already done it, but the flame has taken. He throws the paper onto the table top, and the three of us fumble for something to put it out. Max picks up his martini glass.

'No! The ink!' I cry. 'Watch out for the ink. Don't ...'

Xavier has bent his body over the table; he has laid both hands onto the flame and he keeps them

402

there. I can see the pain in his face and I can't bear it. Without thinking, I push at him, away from its source, and unbalance him. He staggers backwards, leaving the smouldering letter where it is.

The flame has died now, but it has taken something with it. We gaze down in silence. From the place where the lighter burned through, to the bottom corner of the sheet, nothing of the letter remains.

'... What do you suppose?' Max says at last. 'How much have we lost?'

'Not so much,' Xavier replies hopefully. 'The last quarter, maybe? But the writing was getting so small.'

'Well. What does it say?' I ask. 'For heaven's sake, read it to us. At least read what we have.'

He shakes his head. 'Why don't you read it yourself? I think it might be better.' And then, in a burst of anguish, 'The son of a bitch killed her. *He killed her.* How about that?'

I don't say anything, and he doesn't wait for my response. 'I'm going to take a walk,' he announces.

'But you're coming back?' I don't want him to leave. I need him to be with me.

'Sure. I'm coming back.' But then he doesn't move. 'Well go on!' he says. 'Read the damn thing!'

Max picks it up. Little pieces of ash leave a floating trail behind it. He hands what remains of the burned sheet to me. And so we sit, the three of us, side by side in the sunshine, and – twenty years too late – we read from the beginning.

Darling Max,

I suppose that if you are reading this I will either be standing right beside you, laughing at what a silly, dramatic fool I have been and feeling thoroughly ashamed of myself (although terribly proud of this fabulous ink. Has it really worked?) or, well, I don't suppose you ever will see this letter, since I don't believe you listen to a word I ever tell you – although I have told you about the F and the invisible ink.

Max, if some harm should come to me this afternoon, as I fear it might, and if you happen to remember all the nonsense I talk, and if you or someone else should come upon this letter, as I intend, in the pocket of my skirt ... If you do ever find this message and I am gone from – Max, if I am dead, it is because I have fallen in love with a villain, and I deserve it.

Cody tried to warn me. He told me Lawrence was passing information to the other side but I wouldn't listen. And – of course – there was the potato digger at Ludlow and then, after Cody was shot, his poor Mama said to me the very thing I most dreaded. I won't believe it. I mustn't believe it. But Max, I watched him last night when he thought I was sleeping, and he was counting out great fistfuls of dollars. He is not the man he pretends to be. And yet, god knows why, I still love him!

He says he will marry me when we get to New York. How can I marry him now? I am going to confront him. This afternoon, Max. I am going to tell him what I know, and if he loves me, as I believe he does, he will listen to me. I know he will. He will repent. We will start afresh. And if not –

'And if not?' I say to Max and Xavier. 'And if not, what?'

But the answer is obvious. The answer is Inez with her throat shot through, lying on a slab at the mortuary; and Lawrence O'Neill with blood on his shirt, sobbing in the hallway at Plum Street.

A long silence. Nobody answers. Xavier moves near us and we read the letter again. And then, I suppose, again.

'So now what?' Xavier says.

41

1914
Trinidad, Colorado

Phoebe gave me a week to clear out. I think she believed she was being generous. Certainly when other girls were ejected, the process had always been brutal. They rarely stayed longer than a couple of nights in the house, no matter what wretched state they were in. Phoebe didn't like advertising their departure to the johns – for obvious reasons. The johns belonged to Plum Street, not to the girls.

She allowed me to stay for a week, but she didn't allow me into the ballroom, nor any of the common parts, and I was forbidden from talking to any visitors – not that there were any that week. Kitty brought my meals to my room, and I was left to pack and arrange my future in peace.

At least I could throw out the trinkets that had cluttered my rooms for so long: the French novels, the crystal ornaments, the glass jewellery; the mass of valueless gifts, offered to me as sentimental mementos by men I never wanted to remember. Anything I couldn't offload on the other girls (and they had enough junk of their own), I threw out joyfully.

By the time Carlos came to transport my belongings, aside from the harpsichord, I had only a single trunk's-worth left to take and, in fact, as I followed Carlos down the back stairs and slipped away from Plum Street for the last time, it seemed to me that even a single trunk was too much. I was thirty-eight years old, and I had never felt such tiredness.

I needed time to think, of course; an inexpensive place to perch while I calculated how and where I would dispense with the remaining years of my life. I would sell the harpsichord as soon as possible – it might fetch $50 if I was lucky. Add that to the $350 I was taking from Phoebe, and in truth it was not *nothing*. I could leave town, rent a room, set myself up someplace else, do something else … But all of that involved an investment of energy and hope, and I didn't possess either.

Carlos carried my belongings to a small crib a few blocks away, which I had taken on a week-by-week arrangement. Still in our red-light district, where I felt most comfortable, it was one in a row of identical clapboard structures, single-storey, single-roomed and windowless. (For natural light, I had to open the door.) It hardly mattered. I didn't need light. I needed sleep. Oblivion.

There was a single cot at the front of the room, with a throw of some sort, which could be converted into a couch during the day. There was a small table with two chairs, and at the back of the room, behind a worn curtain, a stove and a small basin. At the end of the row there was a toilet, shared between fifteen of us.

Every crib in the row belonged to a working girl, and consequently the smell of antiseptic was forever lingering in the air. Somehow, at Plum Street, there were other smells to cover it: fresh flowers and burning essences and expensive soaps and perfumes. Here, the smell hung unadorned. It was the smell of hookers' fear; and even today I can't smell it without feeling a wave of misery.

The room cost only $17 a week. I could have afforded something better, but I only ever intended to stay there for a fortnight or so, to give myself time to collect myself and form a plan.

I lacked the will to collect myself. The idea of 'forming a plan' was repellent. I was thirty-eight, and alone: truly alone. My family was dead. My husband could have been dead for all I cared; my darling friend Inez was dead, and William Paxton too. I had left no friends behind at Plum Street. In all the world there was only one person I wanted to see, and he had left town and returned to Hollywood without me, without even saying goodbye. I was tired. So very tired. I only wanted somewhere to lie where I would not have to speak, or look, or think.

One day the money ran out. I looked into my tin box, and there was nothing left inside. And yet there I was – somehow still alive. My $17-a-week crib needed to be paid for somehow. As long as I lived, I needed to eat – or, preferably, drink. So I opened my trunk, pulled out a yellow silk tea dress, rather crumpled after all the months lying in an unpacked heap. I poured myself a drink, burned a little incense, sprayed a little scent – and opened the door. And that's how I survived.

It's not a period of my life I like to dwell on too much. And in retrospect I can only think what a miracle it was I survived at all. Many a time I considered ending it. In the time I stayed there (it was longer than a year, and less than two), three girls in the row did just that. They poisoned themselves. It was the cheapest method. The rest of us, who lacked the courage to take that, more efficient exit, slowly poisoned ourselves with liquor instead.

I hardly ventured into town. The months passed; the summer came and went, and then another long winter. Slowly, as the miners returned to the camps, so the work returned to my district, too. In some ways, crib work was easier than at Plum Street. There was never any need for conversation. Barely any need to undress. And though the rest of the week was quiet, on a Saturday night, if the weather was mild, we could turn three – maybe four – tricks in a night. It kept the roof over my head, and it kept me in drink. When a person has made such a hash of her life, and she wakes each day with the smell of disinfectant deep beneath her skin, liquor is of course the important thing.

One early dusk in September, 1916, eighteen months after peace had returned to our miserable streets, as I lay sleeping off the gin of the long night before, I was awoken by the sound of music. Somewhere in the town, not far from my crib, a band was playing. There were trumpets and tubas and drums and violins; and, even more unusually, rippling through the air to my bedside, the sound of laughter! In any case, I was sufficiently curious that, instead of lying there limp, soaking afresh in my despair (as was my normal method of re-entering the world each day), I clambered out of my cot and pulled open the door. Girls looking similarly sleepy and dishevelled peered out from the doors on either side.

'Is that laughter?' we asked.

'Do you hear it too?'

Of course we did. We all heard it! The sounds were growing louder. The music and laughter, and the cheering and the marching of feet, and even a motorcar honking its horn to the music – it was coming our way.

We listened in silence. It had been a long, long time since such a happy sound had been heard in unhappy Trinidad, and I think it struck us all just then, quite how much we had missed it.

'It's magic,' the girl beside me murmured. And it was, too: the sweetest, freshest breath of magic to have touched our street all year long; and I swear, just then, something wonderful happened: a tiny spark of the magic found its way to me and it punctured my long hibernation.

'I'm going to find out what it is,' I announced. 'Who wants to come?'

My two neighbours looked at me curiously. They were more words than cither had heard me speak since I arrived on the street.

The music grew louder.

'Come on!' I said to them. 'Can you hear it? *People are dancing!*'

I dressed – not in the first dress that came to hand, but another one, a blue serge morning dress that still lay folded at the bottom of my chest. It was loose now – so loose I considered taking it off and putting on something else instead. But the girl from the neighbouring crib – she never told me her name – was standing at my door, urging me to hurry.

'It's Rockefeller. That's who it is. They said he was coming, didn't they?'

I had heard nothing about it. Then again, I had heard nothing about anything for a long time.

'No, I didn't believe them neither,' she said, when I didn't reply. 'Matter of fact, no one prob'ly did. But he's here all right. He was in Cokedale last night, Pru says.' She nodded to a crib further up. 'He spent the night in one of the miners' houses. With all his millions and millions of dollars. The wife cooked him his dinner and everything.'

'Surely,' I said, 'the miners would shoot him first!'

She shrugged. 'That's what all the noise is about. He's doing a make-peace tour of all his mines and all his precious company towns. Due to being the most hated man in Colorado … He's talking to the men and he's dancing with the wives and apologizing and making promises about how it's all going to change – and they love him!'

I laughed, and she laughed too.

'It makes no sense,' I protested.

'Of course not,' she said. 'But there's no explaining folks, is there? Except, I guess, we've all got damn short memories. And thank the devil for it.' The sound of music and laughter seemed to have turned away from us now. It was heading uptown. 'Well, are you coming or ain't you?' she said. 'Better hurry or we may miss everything. It'll be quite a sight, I'll bet. So hurry up now. *Let's go!*'

We ran through the warm streets. I felt weak. It occurred to me as I tried to keep abreast of my companion that I had not run for many years. Not since I was a child, not since I'd left England, perhaps. Well, I ran that day. And I still have no idea quite why, or what possessed me to do it.

On Main Street, we collided with the crowd. Not so long ago, the same crowd had marched the same route to follow the coffins of slaughtered men, women and children. But perhaps there is a rhythm to these things, after all. No matter who or what or how or why, there comes a time when we cannot grieve any longer. Now the time had come to celebrate – something, anything. And here was Mr Rockefeller, who owned most of the mines in Colorado, who was the source of all our misery. He had come to apologize and make peace.

Our route had taken us close to the front of the parade. Mr Rockefeller himself passed only a few yards before us. A giant, heavy-jawed man, solemnly dressed, he was grinning and waving, and everything about him was joyful and incongruous. And behind him, grinning and laughing, joyful and incongruous, was the crowd. He looked grateful – happy. Everyone did. Everywhere, there was happiness in the air.

'But this is madness!' I shouted to the girl – my neighbour who never told me her name. 'How can our memories be so short?' She glanced at me without curiosity. I don't think she heard what I said. In any case, she was younger and fitter than I was. The next time I turned to her, she was lost in the crowd. I didn't see her again that day. In fact, I'm not certain I ever laid eyes on her again.

The car and the band and the dancing crowd spilled on past, and Main Street was quiet again. I needed to sit down with some urgency, I realized. I felt faint, and my blue dress was sticky with sweat. What I needed was a drink. I looked about me – the spark of joy extinguished. Here I stood, on the corner of Main and Commercial. It was the very spot where Inez and I had stood that first time we met, and Inez had grasped hold of my shoulder, white as a ghost: *What do you say we sit down?*

I'd not been back to the Toltec since Inez was alive. But I needed a drink. I needed to sit … And it probably sounds silly, but I like to imagine there was something more to it than that. Something seemed to tug at me. I stumbled to the Toltec, one foot in front of the other, without quite thinking about why. I had been avoiding it for too long, perhaps.

One quick drink, then I would head home to the crib, get ready to work. The drinks in town were more expensive than I could afford, in any case. Just one quick drink, for old times' sake, to see out that short-lived spark of whatever it was that almost felt like joy.

The smell of polished wood, and spittle and tobacco, the hard sound of men's voices bouncing off the hard wooden floor – the smell and the noise of the place echoed bittersweet familiarity. The tin roof had dimmed, I noticed. A year and a half's worth of tobacco smoke had turned it dull and black in patches.

And there he stood at the bar. My fairweather friend. Xavier.

He was as dapper as ever, in a linen suit, straw boater resting on the counter beside him. He held his head in his hands and in front of him (I could never picture him without) stood a half-empty glass of bourbon.

I hesitated. Was it really him, or was I only imagining him there? It crossed my mind. The smells and sounds of the place were so familiar, and so entangled in shared memories – perhaps he was a ghost?

The saloon wasn't terribly full. When I called out his name, he dropped the hands from his face and turned and looked at me.

'There you are!' he said, as if I'd only returned from a trip to the bathroom.

He looked bruised. His face looked bruised, and his lip was cut. Why was his face bruised? *Was I dreaming?* I couldn't be sure. It wouldn't be the first time I had dreamed of him. I had dreamed of him as a cadaver before this. Lying on a slab in Adamsson's morgue. *So – was I dreaming?* There was half a room between us and I wasn't sure that I would make it across to him. If it was him. I saw a chair and empty table just beside me and I went to that instead. I needed to sit down. If he was real, perhaps he would come and join me.

'*Dora?*' The room was darkening. There was a noise. Feet moving. And then a crash. My head, knocking against the table, and a glass dropping. And the smell of Xavier's cologne. I came round to the sound of his voice. He was kneeling beside me, calling me softly, and when I opened my eyes he was crouched beside me, wearing an expression of such tenderness ... I cannot explain. They say a vision of your entire existence passes before your eyes at the moment of death, and maybe it does. Maybe it will. But there is only one moment, one vision I know I will remember. Xavier, as he looked at me then, his face bruised, his lip cut, was the happiest sight, the happiest moment of my life.

I said: 'Is this a dream?'

He laughed. 'I was going to ask you the same question. They've been telling me you were dead.'

'Who said I was dead?' I sat up slowly.

'Phoebe said so,' Xavier told me, a hand on each of my shoulders. He gazed into my face. '... I didn't believe her, Dora. I've been here five days, searching for you. I asked for you at Plum Street – nobody had seen you. Nobody knew. Nobody's seen you, Dora! They thought maybe you'd left town. Maybe you were dead ...' He smiled. 'And then Phoebe got wind I was in town and she sent a guy to beat the hell out of me ...'

'Ah.' It explained the bruises. 'Well, she does that.'

'But you're *here*, Dora. And you're alive! Just as I was about to start searching the cemeteries ... You're looking terrible, by the way.' He let go of me, sat back on his haunches and inspected me more carefully. 'What the hell happened to you?'

'I've been keeping a low profile,' I said. It was meant to be funny. I'm not certain how. It was the truth, in any case: a profile so low, indeed, that the people at Plum Street dared to pretend they thought I was dead. 'It's a long story.' I reconsidered. 'Matter of fact, no it's not. Get me a drink, Xavier. And something to eat. I think I need something to eat. And I'll tell you. You look well, by the way – aside from being black and blue ...'

'I *am* rather well,' he said, as if the fact surprised him. 'That is, everything is going well back in Hollywood. And now, at last, I have found you.' He smiled at me: a glorious beam of purest, sweetest affection – and all for me.

I was too wan to return it. Besides, there were questions. A second later he spun away from me – that dancer's precision – and shouted at the barman to bring me food and drink. 'And perhaps a bottle of bourbon for the both of us.'

We didn't say much until the food came. He watched me, and I gazed at the table, worried that if I spoke a word, I might just fall apart altogether. The sense of being cared for, of being watched with love – the words to describe it don't come to me. Like stumbling across a grassy knoll, a trickling stream, a soft, sweet breeze and a long ice-cool drink, after being lost in the burning desert all your life long.

'You still a fairy?' I asked him at last. I smiled. I knew the answer anyway.

'What do you think?' he replied.

I sighed. 'Shame.'

'Not really. You still a hooker?'

'Ha!'

The food arrived. Beef and potatoes. He watched me eating it, took some off my plate in his fingers and put it into his own mouth. I couldn't eat much, but Xavier finished what I left. Afterwards, I pushed the empty plate away and sat back. I'd eaten very little, but I'd not eaten so much in a long time.

'You got scrawny,' he said.

'You disappeared altogether,' I replied.

He nodded.

'Well? You have anything to say about it?'

Slowly, he shook his head. 'I wish I could undo it, Dora. I wish I could. That's all. I can tell you I'm sorry. But I think – maybe it would infuriate you. I am sorry. So very sorry. I wrote to you a hundred times and then to Phoebe – god knows, so many times. Finally she wrote back, said you'd left the house. And then I wrote again asking for an address, and she said you were dead. So I got on the next train and I came back to find you, and apologize. And explain. I just prayed it wasn't true. I wanted to tell you ...' He looked uncertain. 'Maybe it should wait. I should let you talk first. Throw something at me. Beat the hell out of me. I deserve it. But I came to find you, Dora, because ...' He leaned towards me. 'Do you remember we talked about it? We talked about it often. You said you might come to Hollywood with me, start afresh ...'

'I do remember. I explained there were a few obstacles. And then, well – everything changed, didn't it?' I couldn't quite hide the bitterness.

'Yes, it did.'

My glass was empty. (When wasn't it?) I reached for the bourbon bottle in the middle of the table, but Xavier pre-empted me. He slid the bottle beyond my reach.

'Pass it to me,' I said.

'No.'

I swore at him. It was all I could do. It was all I had. And then I sat, with my hands in my lap. And I imagined what a picture I made. But there was no fight in me left. So I continued to sit, and let the tears roll down my cheeks.

He continued, conversationally: 'So I understand Phoebe threw you out.'

'Who told you?'

'I heard she took a whole lot of money off you in the process. Which is presumably why she didn't want you found. I finally spoke with the maid ... I hid outside until she came out. Simple something – what did you call her?'

'Simple Kitty.' I almost smiled. 'Poor darling. She wasn't simple at all. No more simple than the rest of us, anyway. How was she?'

'She was fine. At least until Phoebe sent one of her flunkeys to drag the poor girl back in the house ... She told me about the john who remembered you in his will.'

'William Paxton.' I nodded. 'Remember him? Two thousand five hundred dollars, Xavier.' Finally, I looked at him and laughed. Just for a moment, the absurdity of it all: Phoebe's greed, my disappointment, William putting all that money into an envelope for me, and the lawyer handing it all to Phoebe, the pair of us locked inside her airless little parlour, squabbling over who owed what – it all seemed so silly, so absurd, just so incredibly *funny*. 'It was only money, Xavier,' I muttered.

'Only money,' agreed Xavier. 'I'm glad you say that. I have an awful lot of it now.'

'You do? I'm happy for you.'

'More money than I know what to do with. You remember *The Adventures of Agatha*? Well, now I have so much work and so much money I don't know what to do with myself.'

'That's nice.' I shrugged. 'Want to see where I'm living now? Want to know what I've been up to?'

'Yes!' he said. 'Of course I do! It's why I've come back to this godforsaken hellhole. I told you. I came back to find you, Dora. My friend, my *dearest* friend ... My only friend.'

'Fairweather friend.'

'No! Yes – *then*. But not now. Never again. It was for Aunt Philippa. I don't expect you to understand. I just – I believed I had to. Because we broke her heart, Inez and I. And when she was dying, it was all she raved about. Her hatred of you, Dora. As if everything that had happened to Inez was your fault. I knew it wasn't true. Of course I knew it. But abandoning you, my closest friend, my *only* friend ... it was my penance – can you understand that? No, and why the hell should you? I'm not sure I understand it myself. But then – back then – in the thick of grief, it seemed the only way to redress her suffering, and the death of Inez. I thought I – *we* – you and I, had to pay.'

Grief, I reflected, can send us all a little mad.

'... Never again,' he was saying. '*Never* again your fairweather friend. I swear to it, if you will ever forgive me. And I have money, Dora! More than I can spend. And I miss you. I've missed you every day. So I am begging you to come back to Hollywood with me. I can set you up with singing classes, if you want. Dora, it's a city

421

full of actors. There are theatres and musicals – the city is populated with exhibitionists and everybody likes to sing! I have a house that's so large I don't know what to do with it. And I'm lonely, Dora. *I miss you.* Please. Please, darling? Won't you come back with me?'

A moment passed.

'What about your boyfriends?' I asked him.

He said, 'What about yours? What does it even matter?'

I said, 'Well. It's rather unconventional.'

And he laughed – a great bellow of laughter. The sound bounced off the tin ceiling and filled the room. 'Is that an objection, Dora?'

'We might get awfully jealous …'

'We might,' he said. 'And if it's miserable, or we want to set up with someone else, then we can always change it. You could stay with me until you are on your feet. Or you could stay with me forever. We might – very likely – get desperately, horribly jealous of one another. Of course we will. But we might just make each other happy.'

42

April 1933
Ambassador Hotel, Los Angeles, California

We did both. We still do. There have been times, over the years, when we've considered going our own ways, and yet we never have. Today it's not Xavier who brings in the bulk of our income, it's me. Tomorrow, next month, next year – who knows? People go in and out of vogue in this crazy film business. Maybe it will be his turn again soon. In the meantime, here we find ourselves, poolside at the Ambassador – Max Eastman, Xavier and me, with a heap of cinders between us and the remains of a letter from the woman who brought us all together. A letter that poses as many questions as it answers.

Xavier gazes at the cinders. '... So now what?' he is saying.

423

'I still have the luggage she sent on to New York,' Max reminds us. 'It's in a store-room somewhere. I could send for it. We could examine the contents for clues.'

'I suppose we could do that,' murmurs Xavier, but he shudders.

I feel the same. Clues to what, after all? And to what end? Even so, I am compelled to add: 'What about O'Neill? If he's still alive we should try to find him. Track him down. *Do something ...*'

'I told you,' says Max. 'If he's still alive, he's rotting away in a Russian labour camp, and has been these past ten years. If he's still alive, he probably wishes he wasn't.'

'Did you really see him there, Max?' I ask. 'How do you know?'

He says Upton Sinclair told him.

'So Upton saw him?' Xavier asks.

'No. Gertrude Singer saw him. She—'

'Well shouldn't we check it out?' I interrupt. 'Shouldn't we *do* something?'

Xavier gazes at me. 'What kind of something, Dora?'

'Well, I don't know. If he killed her, and if we could prove it—'

'Unlikely,' Max says.

'Highly unlikely,' I acknowledge. 'I realise that.'

'And even if we could prove it,' Xavier says. 'And even if he's somehow escaped his godforsaken Gulag and is a free man, back home in America. Then what? We go after him and punish him? Inez is already dead. And O'Neill has already suffered. What would anyone gain from it?'

There is nothing to be gained of course, nothing whatsoever.

Max breaks the silence. 'You know what though,' he bursts out. He sounds suddenly, ludicrously cheerful, and gosh, it jars. 'You know what?' he says, 'There *was* something good that came out of Old Snatchville! Something quite wonderful.'

Xavier and I look at him, waiting to hear what.

'Why, *you two*! ...' he cries. 'You guys met in Trinidad, did you not? What were the chances of that?'

'Why yes, we did,' Xavier and I both agree.

'*Yes, you did,*' repeats Max. He laughs: a fat, joyful laugh. 'So *something* lasted! You see?' He grins at us. 'Something wonderful.'

Something wonderful has lasted. Yes. We grin back at him.

And it's not such a bad moment, as moments go.

'My friends,' he says, waving a wrist and conjuring a waiter to his side, 'I think we should celebrate! We should order more martinis. Don't you? I think we should drink.'

To Inez.

And old Snatchville.

425

And short memories.
And survival.

And that's what we're doing right now.

ACKNOWLEDGEMENTS

The old frontier town of Trinidad, Colorado (pop. 8,771), where this novel is set, has seen better days. Once grand and bustling, much of it stands grand and empty today. The basement morgue below Jamieson's Department Store, the Westfield of the nineteenth-century Middle West, is now a junk room (quite eerie, with its unused coffin-shaped shelves). Upstairs, the old emporium is home to a dusty museum, mostly filled with paintings of cowboys, and staffed by volunteers. The theatre where Mother Jones roused a packed house of miners to 'starve and strike' stands on the edge of the old red-light district: massive, empty and crumbling. But it's all still there! The Toltec, with its magnificent pressed-tin ceiling (now a gym) ... the Corinado Hotel where Max Eastman held his disgraceful tea party ... the Columbia Hotel (empty) ... the Opera House (empty, crumbling, boarded off) ... and ten or so miles out of town, in the middle of open prairie, there is Ludlow. A monument stands on the

427

spot where the women and children burned, and at the bottom of the field, trains still run along the track that, a hundred years ago, brought in America's finest, most outraged reporters. I imagine handsome Max Eastman gazing out of his window as the train chugged through the wreckage, the stench of burnt flesh shocking him to silence (for once). There is a plaque on Commercial Street, where a well-known cowboy was shot dead, and on Main Street, carved into the wall of a building, there is a bust of Trinidad's most powerful madam. But the spot where Detectives Belcher and Belk shot dead the Unionist, Captain Lippiatt, remains unmarked. Time has stood still in Trinidad for the most part. It's beautiful, romantic, compact. And there's free wifi in McDonald's.

Above all, I want to thank the local writer and historian Cosette Henritze. What happened out at Ludlow is still a sore subject in Trinidad. Cosette introduced me to people with strong views and anecdotes from both sides of the fight. She is wisdom and warmth personified, and I cannot thank her enough. I have taken numerous liberties with facts. Cosette Henritze has nothing to do with any of them.

I would also like to thank Mike Haddad for opening up the old theatre for me; Shirley Donachy, for showing me round Ludlow; Joe Tarabino; David Barrack – and everyone in Trinidad for their knowledge and the generosity of their welcome. Please forgive my inaccuracies.

Thanks too – as always – to Clare Alexander: probably the best agent in the world. Thank you, Kimberley Young, Louise Swannell, and all at HarperCollins. Thank you Peter, Bashie, Zebedee – and especially, Panda, thank you. xxx

Read on for more from

DAISY WAUGH

Max Eastman's article about his visit
to Trinidad in the aftermath of the
Ludlow Massacre, which appeared
in The Masses in July 1914
(and which inspired this novel).

THE NICE PEOPLE OF TRINIDAD

MAX EASTMAN

PUBLISHED IN THE MASSES, JULY 1914

With a crowd of children, out of bullet-shot, in the cellar of Baye's ranch, a mile away. The next morning she crept up to the telephone to listen for news. And this is what she heard:

Mrs. Curry, the wife of the company's physician at the Hastings mine, was talking with Mrs. Cameron, the wife of the mine superintendent.

'Well, what do you think of yesterday's work?' she said.

'Wasn't that fine!'

'They got Fyler and Tikas.'

'Wasn't that fine!'

'The dirty old tent-colony is burnt down, and we know of twenty-eight of the dirty brutes we've roasted alive down there.'

Later she heard two men discussing the same subject.

'We have all the important ones we wanted now,' they agreed, 'except John Lawson and the Weinburg boys.'

Pearl Jolly is a cool, clever and happy-hearted American girl, the wife of a miner. She stood in her tent making egg sandwiches for the people in the holes, while bullets clattered the glassware to the floor on all sides of her.

'Tikas asked me if I was afraid to stay,' she said. 'I was, but I stayed.'

When Pearl Jolly tells you exactly what she heard over the telephone, correcting you if you misplace a monosyllable, it is difficult to retain the incredulity proper to an impartial investigator. But still it is possible, for the thing she heard is a shade too barbarous to believe. The quality of cruelty is a little strained. And so I shook hands with Pearl Jolly and hastened away from her honest face, in order to do my duty of disbelieving.

Subsequently I heard with my own ears, not from professional gunmen or plug-uglies, but from the nicest ladies of Trinidad, sentiments quite equal in Christian delicacy to those she plucked out of the telephone. And I quote these sentiments verbatim here because they prove, as no legal narrative ever can prove, where lay the cause of the massacre of Ludlow, in whose hearts the deliberate plan of that Indian orgy was hatched.

NOT AN ARMED MAN WAS IN SIGHT AS WE DROVE INTO THE CAMP

A visit to the general manager of the Victor American Company, an introduction from him to his superintendents, Snodgrass at Delagua and Cameron at Hastings, a charming and judicial lecture from these gentlemen, had netted us nothing more than a smile at the smoothness with which a murder business can be conducted. Not an armed man was in sight as we drove into the camp, not a question asked at the gate, everything wide open and free as the prairie. Did we wish to see the superintendent? Oh, yes — his name was Snodgrass. We had mislaid our letter of introduction? Well, it would hardly matter at all, because in fact the general manager happened to be telephoning this morning and he mentioned our coming.

So began a most genial conversation as to the humane efforts of the companies to conduct the strike fairly and without aggression upon their side, whatever indiscretions might be committed by the miners. I had just come up from the black acre at Ludlow, where I had counted twenty-one bullet holes in one wash-tub, and yet when that Snodgrass assured me that there had been no firing on the tent-colony at all I was within a breath of believing him. There are such men in the world, mixing cruelty and lies with a magnetic smile, and most of them out of politics are superintendents of labor camps.

So we learned nothing to corroborate Mrs. Jolly from the company's men — except, perhaps, an accidental remark of Mr. Cameron's 'town marshal,' A. W. Brown, that the strikers got so obstreperous last fall that he 'really had to plant a few of 'em' — a remark we may set down to the vanity of one grown old as a gunman in the company's service. Excepting that, the men behaved as men of the world have learned to behave under the eyes of the press.

SO WE LEARNED NOTHING TO CORROBORATE MRS. JOLLY FROM THE COMPANY'S MEN

And for this reason we turned to the women.

We secured from the librarian

at Trinidad a sort of social register of the town's elite. We selected —and 'we' at this point means Elsa Euland, who was representing the *Independent* — selected and invited to a cup of afternoon coffee at the Hotel Corinado a dozen of the most representative ladies of the elegance of the town. And as the town's elegance rests exclusively upon a foundation of mining stock, these ladies were also representative of the sentiment of the mine-owners in general.

There was Mrs. McLoughlin, who is Governor Ammon's sister and the wife of an independent mine-owner — an active worker also in the uplift or moral betterment of the miners' wives.

There was Mrs. Howell, whose husband is manager of the Colorado Supply Company, operating the 'Company Stores,' of which we have heard so much.

Mrs. Stratton, whose husband heads a commercial college in Trinidad.

Mrs. Rose, whose husband is superintendent of the coal railroad that runs up from Ludlow field into the Hastings mine.

Mrs. Chandler, the Presbyterian minister's wife.

Mrs. Northcutt, the wife of the chief attorney for the coal companies, the owner also of the bitterest anti-labor newspaper of those counties, the *Chronicle-News*.

THERE WAS MRS. HOWELL, WHOSE HUSBAND IS MANAGER OF THE COLORADO SUPPLY COMPANY

One or two others were there, but these furnished the evidence. And they furnished it with such happy volubility to our sympathetic ears, and note-books, that I feel no hesitation in reproducing their words exactly as I copied them there.

'You have been having a regular civil war here, haven't you?' we asked.

'It was no war at all,' said Mrs. McLoughlin. 'It was as if I had my home and my children, and somebody came in from the outside and said, "Here, you have no right to your children — we intend to get them out of your control" — And I tell you I'd take a gun, if I could get one, and I'd fight to defend my children!'

A mild statement, by what was to follow, but to my thinking a significant one. For what exists in those mining camps — incorporated towns of Colorado, with a United States postoffice and a public highway, all located within a gate called 'Private Property' — what exists there, is a state of feudal serfdom. The miners *belong* to the mine-owners in

the first place, and what follows from that.

'Then you attribute the fighting,' I said, 'solely to these agitators who come in here where they don't belong and start trouble?'

YOU HAVE BEEN HAVING A REGULAR CIVIL WAR HERE, HAVEN'T YOU?' WE ASKED.

'Just these men who came in here and raised a row. There was nothing the matter. We had a pretty good brotherly feeling in the mines before they came.'

'Yes,' said Mrs. Northcutt, 'I've had a hired girl from the mining camps tell me how much money the miners get — but *they never save a cent.* "I tell you we live high," she would say, "we buy the very best canned goods we can get."'

'Yes — the men who are *willing* to work make five and six

dollars a day. Of course the lazy ones don't. But the majority of them in the Delagua camp just simply *cried* when the strike was called! They didn't want to go out.'

'Isn't that strange,' I said. 'How do you account for 80 or 90 per cent of them going out when they didn't want to?'

'Well, the union compelled them — that's all. You know all the good miners have left here now. That is always the way in a strike. The better class go on to other fields.'

THESE PEOPLE ARE IGNORANT, YOU SEE, AND THAT'S WHY THEY WILL DO THE MENIAL WORK.

'Then you feel that the low character of the strikers themselves is what made it possible for these trouble-makers to succeed here?'

'That's it exactly — they are ignorant and lawless foreigners, every one of them that caused the trouble. I've thought if only we could have a tag, and tag all the foreigners so you could recognize them at a glance — I believe if Roosevelt were here he'd deport them.'

This subject of the native iniquity of every person not born on American soil was then tossed from chair to chair for the space of about an hour. It is the common opinion in Trinidad society. We even heard it voiced by a Swedish lady of wealth, who had herself been less than ten years in America.

'Americans, you know, won't work in the mines at all.'

'I wonder why that is.'

'Well, I don't know. They don't want to go under ground, I suppose,' was one answer. Another was:

'These people are ignorant,

you see, and that's why they will do the menial work.'

'I see,' I said.

'And you must understand that our town was absolutely turned over to these people for a week. They were armed with guns and singing their war songs in the streets. The policemen knew they could do nothing and stayed home. I kept my children in the basement.'

'Was the larger part of the town sympathetic to the strikers?'

'Well, those of us who weren't sympathetic thought best either to keep still or pretend we were!'

'I understand. And what did they do?'

'Had control of the town, that's all! And don't hesitate to say that we didn't have any mayor.'

'What became of your mayor?'

THEY WERE ARMED WITH GUNS AND SINGING THEIR WAR SONGS IN THE STREETS.

'The mayor received some letters and he was called suddenly away, that's what became of him! And the sheriff — they say he went to Albuquerque for his wife's health — but his wife stayed at home.'

'You know our church is right next door to the union headquarters, and on Sunday morning there was such a crowd of these people around there that we couldn't get to church. I wasn't going to pick my way through these people to get to church' — this is the minister's wife speaking — 'so I called up the chief of police and asked him to clear the street. He said he had no authority, it was a county matter. So I called up the sheriff's office, and they said they couldn't do it. Finally we had to call up the labor union secretary himself!'

'Has the church done anything to try to help these people, or bring about peace?' we asked.

'I think it's the most useless thing in the world to attempt it,' she answered. And there followed the story, which I had also from a priest himself, of how a Catholic father was reported as a scab and compelled to stop preaching because he taught that 'idleness is the root of evil,' and tried to advise the men to return to work.

'Christianity could prevail, of course,' was her conclusion, 'but we haven't enough of it.'

HAS THE CHURCH DONE ANYTHING TO TRY TO HELP THESE PEOPLE

'You haven't a spiritual leader in the community, have you?' said the least tactful of us.

'We haven't a spiritual *community!*' said the minister's wife.

'And how do you feel about the disaster at Ludlow?' we asked. It was Mrs. Northcutt who answered.

'I think there has been a lot of maudlin sentiment in the newspapers about those women and children. There were only two women, and they make such a fuss about those two! It was their own fault, anyway.'

'You mean that the papers are to blame for all the trouble they have caused?'

'The sensational papers,' she added. 'They're looking for something to sell their papers, that's all.'

'I guess that's true,' I said, and thanked God they were.

'The worst that has come out of this strike,' Mrs. Northcutt continued, 'is the way those poor militia boys have been treated. They've just had abuse heaped upon them. Yes, my heart has felt very sore for those boys who came down here full of patriotic feelings!'

THEY'RE NOTHING BUT CATTLE, AND THE ONLY WAY IS TO KILL THEM OFF.

'And General Chase certainly was a fine man,' said another, 'one of the Lord's own! Do you know that at the time they broke up the Mother Jones parade a woman stuck her hatpin in the general's horse, and the horse threw him off?'

'That was just it — the low things they would do!' came the refrain. 'And he hasn't a bit of cowardice in him. He rode around all day just the same! I tell you the soldiers behaved themselves nobly down here.'

'And yet people object,' said Mrs. Stratton, 'because they occasionally got drunk — didn't General Grant get drunk? Did they expect a lot of angels to come down here and fight a lot of *cattle*?'

Mrs. Stratton had touched the key-word — *cattle* — and from that word ensued a conversational debauch of murder-wishing class-hatred of which I can only give a suggestion.

'That's it,' said Mrs. Rose, 'they're nothing but cattle, and the only way is to kill them off.'

I think one of us winced a little at this, and the speaker rested a sympathetic hand on her shoulder. 'Nothing but cattle, honey!' she said.

'They ought to have shot Tikas to *start with*,' added the minister's wife, a woman of more definite mind than the others. 'That's the whole trouble. It's a pity they didn't get him first instead of last.'

'You know, there's a general belief around here,' she continued, 'that those women and children were put in that hole and sealed up on purpose because they mere a drain on the union.'

'Yes, those low people, they'll stoop to anything,' agreed Mrs. Northcutt.

'They're brutal, you know,' continued the minister's wife. 'They simply don't regard human life. And they're ignorant. They can't read or write. They don't know anything. They don't even know the Christmas story!'

'Is that possible!' I gasped.

'Yes, sir; there was a little girl, one of the daughters of a miner, and she was asked on Christmas day what day it was, and she said, "Well, it's somebody's birthday, but I've forgotten whose!"'

THEY SIMPLY DON'T REGARD HUMAN LIFE. AND THEY'RE IGNORANT.

'All you ladies, I suppose, are members of the church?' we asked in conclusion.

'Oh, yes; all of us.'

'Well — we are glad to have met you all and found out the true cause of the trouble,' we said.

And here I turned to Mrs. Rose — whose word comes, remember, straight from the mine above Ludlow. 'What do you seriously think,' I said, 'is the final solution of this problem?'

'Kill 'em off — that's all,' she answered with equal seriousness.

So that is how I returned to my original faith in Pearl Jolly's story of what she heard over the telephone. And when she tells me that while she was assisting in lifting twelve corpses out of that black pit, the soldiers of the National Guard stood by insulting her in a manner that she will not repeat, and one of them said, 'Sorry we didn't have more in there for you to take out,' I believe that, too.

When a train despatcher at Ludlow and his assistant both assure me that at 9:20 A. M. on Monday, the 23d of April, from their office, square in front of the two military camps, they saw and heard the militia fire the first shot, and that the machine guns were trained directly on the tent-colony from the start, although never a shot was fired from the colony all day, I believe that.

This 'Battle of Ludlow' has been portrayed in the best of the press as a 'shooting-up' of the tent-colony by soldiers from a distance, while armed miners 'shot-up' the soldiers to some extent, also, from another distance.

The final burning and murder of women and children has been described as a semi-accidental consequence, due perhaps to irresponsible individuals.

THEY SAW AND HEARD THE MILITIA FIRE THE FIRST SHOT

I want to record my opinion, and that of my companions in the investigation, that this battle was from the first a deliberate effort of the soldiers to assault the tent-colony, with purpose to burn, pillage and kill, and that the fire of the miners with their forty rises from a railroad cut and an arroyo on two sides of the colony was the one and only thing that held off that assault and massacre until after dark. It was those forty rises that enabled as many of the women and children to escape as did escape.

Every person in and in the vicinity of the colony reports the training of machine guns on women and children as targets in the open field. Mrs. Low, whose husband kept a pump-house for the railroad near the tent-colony, tells me that she had gone to Trinidad the day of the massacre. She came back at 12.45, alighted at a station a mile away, and started running across the prairie to save her little girl whom she had left alone in a tiny white house exactly in the line of fire. They trained a machine gun on her as she ran there.

'I had bought six new handkerchiefs in Trinidad,' she said, 'and I held them up and waved them for truce flags, but the bullets kep' coming. They come so thick my mind wasn't even on the bullets, but I remember they struck the dust and sent it up in my face. Finally some of the strikers saw I was going right on into the bullets — I was bound to save my little girl — and they risked their lives to run out from the arroyo and drag me down after them. I didn't know where my baby was, or whether she was alive, till four-thirty that afternoon.'

I HELD THEM UP AND WAVED THEM FOR TRUCE FLAGS

Her baby, as I learned, had run to her father in the pump-house at the first fire, and had been followed in there by a rain of .48-calibre bullets, one of which knocked a pipe out of her father's hand while she was trying to persuade him to be alarmed. He carried her down into the well and they stayed there until nightfall, when a freight train stopped in the line of fire and gave them a chance to run up the arroyo where the mother was hiding.

This has all grown very easy for me to believe since that bloody conversation over the coffee cups. And when citizens of Trinidad testify that they saw troops of armed soldiers marching through on their way to Ludlow at midnight of the night before the massacre, that too, and all that it implies, is easy to believe. It prepares one's mind for the testimony of Mrs. Toner, a French woman with five children, who lay all day in a pit under her tent, until the tent was 'just like lace from the bullets.' At dark she heard a noise 'something like paper was blowing around.'

'I looked out then, and the whole back of my tent was blazing, with me under it, and my children. I run to a Mexican tent next door, screaming like a woman that had gone insane. I was fainting, and Tikas caught me and threw water in my face. I was so thrubled up, I says, "My God, I forgot one, I forgot one!" and I was going back. And Mrs. Jolly told me, "It's all right. They're all here." And I heard the children crying in that other hole, the ones that died, and Mrs. Costa crying, "Santa Maria, have mercy!" and I heard the soldier say, "We've got orders to kill you and we're going to do it!'

'"We've got plenty of ammunition, just turn her loose, boys," they said.

THAT WAS ONE OF THE SADDEST THINGS WAS EVER WENT THROUGH!

'Oh, I tell you, that was one of the saddest things was ever went through! When I was lying in my tent there, Mr. Snyder come running in to me with his two hands out just like this. "Oh, my God, Mis' Toner," he said, "my boy's head's blown off. My God, if your children won't lay down, just knock'em down rather'n see 'em die." He was just like wild.

HE DIDN'T HAVE HARDLY A SHIRT TO HIS NAME.

'I didn't like to say it before the children — but I was going to have this baby in a day or two, and when I got to that tent I was having awful pains and everything. And there I had to run a mile across the prairie with my five children in that condition. You talk about the Virgin Mary, she had a time to save her baby from all the trouble, and I thought to myself I was havin' a time, too.

'He was born in a stable, I says, but mine come pretty near bein' born in a prairie. Look at him — I had everything nice for him, and here he's come,

and he didn't have hardly a shirt to his name.'

Mrs. Toner sat up languidly from a dark and aching bed in a tiny rented room in Trinidad.

'I lost everything,' she said. 'All my jewelry. A $35 watch and $8 chain my father gave me when he died. A $3 charm I'd bought for my husband. My fountain pen, spectacles, two hats that cost $10 and $7, my furs, a brown suit, a black one, a blue shirt-waist, a white one — well, just everything we had left. I don't believe the Turks would have been half so mean to us.'

'Whom do you blame for it?'

'Do you know who I blame? Linderfelt, Chase and Governor Ammons — I think one of 'em as bad as the other. If Linderfelt had got any of my children I bet I'd have got him by and by. But then it's the coal companies, too, for that matter — if they wouldn't hire such people.

'They searched my tent eight different times, tore up the floor, went through all my trunks, and drawers. One of the dirty men asked me for a kiss. I picked up my iron handle, and I says, "If you ask me that again I'll hit you between the teeth."

'If they hadn't brought those bloodhounds in here there'd have been no trouble. They started it on us every time. They'd often threatened to burn it up, you know, but we said, "Oh, that's just talk."

I BROUGHT MY CHILDREN OUT ALIVE AND I'M GOING TO KEEP 'EM ALIVE

'Look at him! I tell you it's a wonder he was born at all!

'Just the same I'd go through the same performance again before I'd scab. I'd see the rope first. I was the first woman in that colony and I was the last one out — alive. They took my husband up to the mine, and offered him $300 a month to run a machine. He'd been getting $2.95 a day before, and they offered to pay up his back debts at the store, too.

'"You'll need a wash-tub to come after your pay," they said.

'"Yes," he said, "why didn't you offer me that before the strike?"

'Oh, we ain't bluffed out at all — only I'll never go back and live in a tent. I brought my children out alive and I'm going to keep 'em alive.

'You know the children run cryin' when they see a yellow suit — even the Federals. All yellow suits look alike to them!'

I have trusted Mrs. Toner's own words to convey, better than I could, the spirit of the women on strike. But I wish I could add to that a portrait of the young Italian mother,

Mrs. Petrucci, who survived her babies in that death-hole at Ludlow — sweet, strong, slender-fingered, exquisite Italian Mother-of-God! If there is more fineness or more tenderness in the world than dwells in those now pitifully vague and wandering eyes, I have lived without finding it.

It would be both futile and foolish, I suppose, to pretend that there is hatred, ignorant hatred of dwarfed and silly minds, only upon the 'capital' side of this struggle. Yet I must record my true conviction, that the purpose to shoot, slaughter, and burn at Ludlow was absolutely deliberate and avowed in the mines and the camps of the militia; that it was an inevitable outcome of the temper of contemptuous race and class-hatred, the righteous indignation of the slave-driver, with which these mine-owners met the struggle of their men for freedom; and that upon

the strikers' side is to be found both more of the gentleness and more of the understanding that are supposed to be fruits of civilization, than upon the mine-owners'. It will be granted, perhaps, even by those who love it, that our system of business competition tends to select for success characters with a fair admixture of cruel complaisance, and that those excessively weighted with human love or humility gravitate toward the bottom? At least, if this *is* granted to begin with, it will be heartily confirmed by the facts for anyone who visits the people of Las Animas County.

BUT IT WOULD NEVER GET US BACK WHAT WE LOST

'Revenge?' said Mrs. Fyler to me — and Mrs. Fyler's

husband was caught that night in the tent-colony unarmed, led to the track and murdered in cold blood by the soldiers — 'Revenge? We might go out there and stay five years to get revenge, but it would never get us back what we lost. It would only be that much on our own heads.'

Q&A with

DAISY WAUGH

The Ludlow Massacre is a little-known chapter of American history. How did you come across it, and what inspired you to write this novel?

I came across it while I was researching my last novel, *Melting the Snow on Hester Street.* In that novel, my fictional characters were caught up in a devastating factory fire which occurred in Manhattan a few months before Ludlow. Over a hundred workers were burned to death, and like the massacre of women and children at Ludlow, the incident shocked the fat capitalists of America. Briefly, at least.

1913-4 was a time of tremendous worker unrest in America, and around the world. I was moved to write a novel about Ludlow after reading Max Eastman's article, which is printed at the end of this book. For such a clever man, it struck me as a ludicrously one-sided, unhelpful, and ultimately rather silly piece. It reminded me of Michael Moore's journalistic efforts today, and its drum-beating and shallowness infuriated me.

It reduced human beings to one-dimensional "goodies" and "baddies", which we all know is absurd. So I wanted to write a novel about the tragic winter at Ludlow in which there are no sides, and where politics is almost incidental.

Where did the inspiration for Dora and Inez's characters come from?

There's quite a lot of me in both of them, I think. Or I hope there is – in Dora, especially. She's pretty cool.

How big an impact did the union strikers have on modern American labour laws?

The Union lost the fight in Southern Colorado and the workers returned to the mines as before. What happened at Ludlow helped no one, and changed nothing. It was, simply, a tragedy – one in which many people suffered and almost no one behaved well.

What was different about how Max Eastman and his colleagues reported on the Ludlow tragedy, compared with how it might be written about now, in the era of 24/7 news?

Not much, in my opinion. The media swooped: it came, it saw, it drew hurried conclusions. It took sides, and ground political axes. It lurched for the nearest piece of safe, moral high ground, filed stories – and moved on. The only obvious difference between then and now, so far as I can see, is that it took days, rather than minutes, for the tragic news to reach consumers. I'm not sure, ultimately, how that changes much.

Are there any particular books or films about this period that you would recommend?

I would recommend a trip to Trinidad in Colorado! Failing that, I recommend a film called Reds, directed by Warren Beatty. It's about John Reed and the Greenwich Village intellectuals – and the October

Revolution in Russia which obviously took place a few years later. Many of the characters who tipped up in Trinidad after Ludlow appear in the film, including Max Eastman (although he doesn't have a particularly interesting part). It's a fantastic film.

ONE NIGHT. ONE DANCE.
ONE LOVE TO LAST A LIFETIME.

'A gripping,
bittersweet love story'
SUNDAY TIMES

LAST DANCE
With
VALENTINO

DAISY WAUGH

1916. Leaving war-ravaged London, Jenny Doyle sets sail for
New York where she is to work for the de Saulles family.
Their home, Gatsby-like in elegance, is rife with intrigue and
madness. Only Jenny's friendship with dancer Rodolfo offers
escape... until, one tragic day, the household is changed forever.

1926. America booms, prohibition rules and Rodolfo has taken
his place on the silver screen as Rudolph Valentino. Will
the world's most desired film star and his lost love have their
Hollywood happy ending, or will the tragic echoes from their time
with the de Saulles thwart them one last time?

'Impeccably researched and beautifully-written'
DAILY MAIL

RICH. BEAUTIFUL. DAMNED.

October 1929: As America helterskelters through the last days before the great crash the cream of Hollywood parties heedlessly on.

Beneath the sophistication and elegance, Hollywood society couple Max and Eleanor Beecham are on the brink of divorce, their finances teetering on a knife's edge after a series of failed films. As the stock market tumbles it seems they have nowhere to turn but to the arms of their waiting lovers.

Hope is delivered in an invitation to one of the legendary weekend parties at Hearst Castle, where the prohibition champagne will be flowing and the room filled with every Hollywood big-shot around. They cannot resist one last chance of making it.

Scandalous, absurdly glamorous, the Hearst party is the epitome of Golden Era decadence, but for Max and Eleanor the time has come to make a decision that will change their future. Will they sacrifice everything for fame and fortune or plunge into their hidden past and grasp one last chance to love each other again?

Sumptuously evoking the Golden Age of Hollywood, a time when money is built on greed and love can be a trick of the light, Daisy Waugh's stunning novel is a compelling portrait of love, fame, and survival.

Keep up to date with all the latest news on
Daisy Waugh and her books at:

 facebook.com/daisywaughauthor

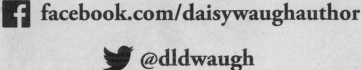 @dldwaugh

www.daisywaugh.co.uk